BAD BLOOD

Eric Hodgson

First published by E Hodgson

Copyright © 2015 E Hodgson

The right of Eric Hodgson to be identified as the author of this work has been asserted by him in accordance with the Copyright, Designs and Patents Act 1988.

All rights reserved. No part of this publication may be reproduced, stored in a retrieval system, or transmitted, in any form or by any means, electronic mechanical, photocopying, recording or otherwise, without the prior permission of the copyright owner.

All the characters in this book are fictitious, and any resemblance to actual persons, living or dead, is purely coincidental.

Eric Hodgson Books

Bad Blood

2010

All eyes were on the man with the laptop. They waited, in silence. He waited.

A quiet pop. At last, the email had arrived.

A long intake of breath, "The money is in the Lebanese account." As he read on, the thinnest smile formed. "And the money is also in the Swiss account."

His heart soared, and he wished Amy was still alive to see this day. He raised his eyes and turned towards the head of the table.

The others followed his gaze. Amy's protégé had displayed a stroke of pure brilliance... she had proved herself in the most spectacular of ways. She had arrived! No one said a word, but in their minds they were as one...

The Queen is dead... Long live the Queen.

In The Beginning

The memories of the day had withstood the tests of a life time because of what had happened after the sun had set. In 1920, Amy Bary had loved Berlin. The cruel post war fingers that locked firmly onto the German poor, imprisoning them within struggle and hunger, did not touch children of the elite.

What Amy remembered was the playful protestations of Frederick, her thirteen year-old twin, as the family shopped for outfits for Uncle Johann's grand birthday ball. She remembered Mother's gentle teasing of little Thomas while supping sparkling champagne in the tea rooms of the sparkling German boulevards. She remembered Father's rich laugh...

And then, the Christmas sun had set on their day... and on their lives.

As darkness descended it was accompanied by sub zero temperature and terror. The coldness, a consequence of a cloudless sky. The terror, of vicious assassins.

Her heart pounded... she struggled to suppress the rising scream... even in the throes of terror she was thinking clearly enough to know that any sound would have meant certain death. Thomas clung to her, petrified. She held her hand over his mouth, just in case, he had buried his head into her woollen top in an attempt to lock out the noises of the men, the shouting and the clattering.

She couldn't help herself, the noises compelled her. She peered through the gap in the wooden wall and could see a man sitting on the bench on the other side of the scullery, looking in her direction... instinctively she pulled back. But the need to see was too strong. Tentatively she returned her eyes, the man hadn't moved... this time she held her nerve.

The width of the crack allowed her to see, because he sat, everything above his knees, which were apart because he was too fat to sit with his legs together. Below those knees and out of sight lay her father and mother... dead.

He shouted his orders. Find the children, look in the garden, in the bedrooms, under the beds. People, men, dashed backwards and forwards through her line of vision, hiding the fat man as they passed, looking for the children. *Bring me the children*.

Then somebody pushed a boy forward into view, it was Frederick, her twin brother. *Hello*, said the fat man. *Hello sir*. The boy struggled to speak, peering downwards. *Don't look at them, look at me. Come here.* Frederick stumbled towards the man, crying as he did so.

"What's your name?"

"F... Frederick Bary, Sir."

"Well Frederick Bary, don't be afraid. How old are you?"

"Thirteen, and a half."

The fat man stood and placed a friendly arm around the boy's shoulder. "Thirteen and a half, that's quite old, old enough for you to deliver a message. Now, your father and your mother lay here, dead, not my doing you understand, I am just a simple soldier carrying out orders. So, I need you, when you enter the Kingdom of Heaven, to tell your father and your mother that I, Carl Froebel, am just a poor soldier carrying out these deeds for Johann Heinrich Huth, for Willie von Seeckt, for Hans Hasenclever and for Peter Emmerich. Do you understand? Who are these people?"

"My uncles," sobbed Frederick.

"Yes. Now, where are your sister and your little brother?"

The girl held her breath.

"I don't know. I have just returned from a Wandervogel brigade meeting."

A voice from an unseen source confirmed this.

"Ah yes," continued Froebel, "your youth movement, you look like a good scout; a fine and fit young German. Alright Frederick, repeat the message."

"I must tell my mother and father that the uncles had them killed."

"That's very good. This is so they can haunt the correct people in revenge for this hideous crime. We wouldn't want them disturbing Carl Froebel and his brothers, mistakenly, I must add." There was laughter all around. Frederick smiled nervously, because he thought he should, and as he smiled a fat hand smothered his face... he struggled to breathe and his body wriggled for freedom, but his young undeveloped muscles were no match for those of the older man. His bulging eyes looked directly at the gap into the secret room, pleading. Help me please... *Help me please*. It was not long before the struggling and wriggling ceased. The hand relaxed and the boy slowly slid to the floor, slid from his sister's view.

She trembled violently, uncontrollably. Her little brother sensed her terror and gasped. The fat man stood and walked towards them. Please God, please, she prayed.

He stood directly in front of them, studying the wall which separated them from the monster. Eventually, he turned around and resumed giving his orders. "Right, load this lot onto the truck and throw them into the Havel. As far as Huth and his family are concerned the other two children have also been fed to the fishes. I will go and tell them this and sort out our fee." The men worked quickly and the place soon fell into silence.

Thirteen-year-old Amy Bary and her little brother, both paralysed by fear, could do nothing but wait to find out what fate had in store.

The old woman awoke feeling a little strange; for a moment forgetting where she was. Her head was swimming with distant memories… so many memories, so many recollections… Ah yes. She managed to hook some out; recollections of what fate had eventually bestowed upon Carl Froebel and his brothers… and for all those uncles and *their* families. Those memories brought a wry smile to her face.

Then she remembered the girl.

She shuffled across the room to the couch on which Jennifer Emmerich had been laid. It was hard, painful work, and it took a while, but somehow she managed to lower herself onto her knees. From this position she gently caressed the young girl's soft blond hair and for a long while studied her. The old eyes moistened and a tear wormed its way down the wrinkled face. "Mama," Amy whispered, and leaned forward and kissed the girl on the lips.

Book One

Bad Blood

Jennifer Emmerich Must Die

Chapter 1

Santander to Portsmouth Ferry
Tuesday 20th October 1991

The bed dropped away and left her stranded in mid air. Oh God! She felt awful… "Gerald… I think I'm going to die."

Gerald was already beside her, the bunk above her, empty. "Andrea," he whispered, trying to soothe her. He brushed his fingers across her forehead.

She pushed his hand aside. "Make it stop… oh God. Please."

"Perhaps if you sat up," he suggested. She was a deathly pale and he wondered if he should call the medical centre, or whatever they had on a ferry.

She tried to raise herself but the effort was too much and she slumped back onto the bed.

He held her head against his chest and tried to counter the rocking of the ship, and she began to drift off to sleep. The crashing of unsecured items reverberated through the creaking mass of the ship's hull with every lurch. It sounded as though the boat would be ripped apart at any moment. God! What a nightmare. He'd been on these crossings a few times, and it was often choppy; but never like this. This sea was not what the doctor ordered.

In fact the whole trip had been hard work; three weeks of travelling around Southern Spain. It had been his sister-in law's idea; a break after the deaths of their two oldest daughters… Tabby and Max… to help get over the tragedy. But you don't get over something like that. Ever.

He turned to check on Jennifer. The little girl was awake, watching her father look after his wife. "Is Mummy going to die?"

Gerald choked. He couldn't bear the thought of his tiny daughter thinking about death… about her sisters. "No darling, of course she isn't. She's just feeling sea sick. She'll be better soon."

Jennifer nodded, pretending she understood. *But Mummy said she was going to die.*

Suddenly the boat lurched violently and Andrea was awake again. Each outward breath was accompanied by a low groan; the sound of illness.

Gerald decided he needed to go for help. "Can you wait here; I'll get something to stop you feeling ill."

"Oh, don't leave me. Stay here, I'll go. Perhaps the walk will make me feel better." She tried to raise her body.

"You can't go alone." He turned to Jennifer, "Jennifer, can you be a big girl and wait here in your bed."

Jennifer nodded. She didn't like the idea, but Mummy was ill.

"Daddy is going to take Mummy to get something to make her better." He explained.

"Where are you going?"

To the medical centre, or the information desk. It was easier to say, the shop. "We'll buy something in the shop, we'll be back soon, try to sleep."

"Can you turn the telly on?"

He leant over and kissed her, then turned on the TV. "Here's the remote, don't have it too loud," he whispered. Andrea was sitting up, wrapped in her blanket and waiting to go.

Television had become very special to Jennifer, she needed to watch it as much as possible. Her friend, Al Tucker, had let her into a secret; so long as she didn't tell any grown up about it, one day her sisters would fly down from heaven and appear on the screen, to say hello.

Mrs Benton studied the little girl; she couldn't have been more than five years old, perhaps even younger! The lady wasn't normally the type to interfere and had hoped that somebody would walk up and claim the child... a boat this big and this busy was not the sort of place for any youngster to be alone. However, nobody had claimed her.

The little girl was angry... how could they have left her? She didn't like the way the old lady kept looking at her, either.

For the second time the announcement rained over the heads of the passengers; "*Would Mr and Mrs Emmerich please return to their cabin.*"

"Excuse me dear."

Jennifer glanced upwards without moving her head.

The old lady bent forward and tilted hers. "Are you alone?"

Of course I'm alone, stupid. She nodded.

"No Mummy or Daddy?"

Jennifer shrugged. She was sulking.

Passengers were getting ready to disembark, congregating and waiting for the announcement which would instruct them to make their way to the lower decks and to their cars. The area around the information desk, crowded with people and luggage, was becoming noisier in anticipation as the journey neared its end; this Santander to Portsmouth crossing had been a long, rough ride.

Mrs Benton beckoned to her husband, and with her hand shielding her mouth she spoke softly in his ear, "I knew there was something amiss, neither of those other couples were the girl's parents, go and fetch somebody who works for the ferry."

He wanted to mind his own business, "Should we be getting involved?" The look gave him the answer...

As the husband weaved his way towards the desk, Mrs Benton turned her attention back to the girl, smiled kindly and asked, "What's your name dear?"

"Jennifer." She whispered.

The old lady had to ask her to repeat it. Jennifer was angry with her parents for leaving her for such a long time, alone in the cabin. She wanted to show them just how angry she was... when they finally returned. She didn't want to waste time talking to anybody else.

However, this old lady was not going to give up... Jennifer let out a long fed up sigh, and not wanting to have to say everything twice, or maybe even three times, decided to cooperate. "Jennifer," she shouted.

The woman flinched, and recovered. "Where are Mummy and Daddy?"

A younger woman wearing an official dark suit and light blue silk scarf stepped up beside the old lady as the question was being asked; the husband peered over their shoulders.

Again, for the third time; "*Would Mr and Mrs Emmerich please return to their cabin.*"

Jennifer pointed into the air behind their heads. All three turned, expecting the arrival of the girl's parents.

"That's my mum and dad!"

"Sorry…"

"Mr and Mrs Emmerich… Mummy and Daddy."

At that moment, another announcement; travellers with vehicles on decks three and four were to make their way to the garage areas. The couple apologised to Jennifer, explaining that they had to leave, but that she was in good hands (with the suited lady) and with smiles and waves, said their goodbyes.

Jennifer was still angry, but not as angry as before. Passengers shuffled towards the stairways and lifts and it was not long before she and the suited lady were alone. Now she was becoming anxious. *What if Mummy and Daddy had forgotten her?* "How will I get home if they leave me behind?"

The suited lady sat down beside Jennifer, smiled and took the child's hand. "Don't worry. They've probably got lost looking for you."

"They can't have been lost since last night."

"Last night?"

"Yes. They left me in the cabin and went to the shop. When they didn't come back I went to sleep."

"They left you alone in your cabin?"

"Not alone… I was with the television."

"And they didn't return this morning?"

"No. So I decided to make them sorry. I packed my case and came here." She moved her feet apart to reveal a small pink leather case under her seat. She forced a smile… and then burst into tears.

"Oh, you poor dear." The stewardess waved to an officer who was standing by the information desk, "Call security."

Chapter 2

**Henly's Wine Bar, London.
Early 1992**

"I do not want to adopt this child!" Susan Emmerich realized that she was speaking too loudly, and blushed slightly with embarrassment.

Monica Davies pretended not to notice. "It really is your decision as much as it's Michael's," she pointed out whilst replenishing the glasses with white wine. "Have you spoken to him... about how you feel?"

Susan sighed. It was mid afternoon and the wine bar was sparsely occupied and quite quiet. She didn't want strangers eavesdropping on her tale of woes. However, it was good to have the ear of her friend. Monica Davies was also the family's lawyer. "How can I discuss this with him? Jennifer is his dead brother's daughter. He's also her God Parent. The girl has nobody else, not since Gerald and Andrea disappeared from the ferry. The thing is, Monica, I feel trapped... I feel mean and uncharitable. I have nothing against the child, but I know that I could never accept her as a daughter, never as an equal of Rachel."

Monica sipped her wine. "I think I understand." The lawyer was both single and childless. "Never-the-less, you know that you must speak to Michael... I appreciate that your marriage is not going so well, but..."

Susan objected, "The marriage is okay, really. I've been giving that situation a lot of thought. It's become a little stale, that's all. But, all in all, it's okay."

"That's not what you were saying the last time you came into town."

"We've been under a lot of pressure, you know, with Gerald and Andrea... and *that* coming so soon after the girls..."

"What you need, my dear, is cheering up."

"I know what your sort of cheering up is. I'm a married woman."

"You didn't protest last time."

Susan turned bright red. "Shhh... I didn't know *that* was on the menu."

Monica laughed. *That* was on the menu again. She'd discovered Susan's weakness.

Susan Emmerich felt a rush of excitement... Weekends in town were now much more interesting when there was forbidden fruit to be picked. Her lawyer friend was young and single and enjoyed an interesting life style... and seemed keen to involve this older woman. Susan suddenly felt impatient for the evening to come... however... "Monica, what am I to do, about Jennifer?"

"What are you frightened of?"

"I know where my bread is buttered, financially. I've married a wealthy man, but I know that he'll treat Jennifer and Rachel as equals, regarding inheritance, but Rachel is my daughter. She deserves everything."

"My God, you're still in your thirties."

"So when am I supposed to think about this?"

Monica shrugged. "Leave everything to Rachel in your will."

"I've considered that. If I died first and left all I have to Rachel, I know Michael, he'd compensate for Jennifer in his estate. And he'll make sure that both girls equally benefit should he die first. Rachel is my daughter. She, and she alone, is the one who has to inherit everything."

"If that's all you are worried about, don't. For a start, Michael is at least ten years older than you…"

"Twelve."

"Well then, I'm sure that you'll outlive him anyway. Michael has put a significant amount of capital into the hands of the firm's financial arm; tax avoidance. A lot of complicated investing takes place, manipulation of funds. I'll have a word, and make sure that, in the case of his death, the complete account moves on to Rachel. Your signature will be enough."

"You can do that?"

Monica nodded and continued. "In your will, leave a reasonable amount to each girl, so not to arouse suspicion, and I promise you I'll then make sure that Rachel is the sole beneficiary of your husband's estate."

"You can really do that?"

"Absolutely. The thing is, you have a great deal to lose if your marriage breaks down. And think of what Rachel could miss out on, should he then remarry. I've met Jennifer, she's a sweet child. She is very much like Rachel was at her age… they could easily be sisters… and she appears to be healthy and intelligent. Why don't you adopt? It'll make your husband very happy. I understand though, that you'll always be closer to Rachel."

Susan shrugged. She'd think about it… as long as Rachel was to be taken care of. She could tolerate married life and two kids while she had a friend like Monica Davis. She couldn't hide the grin which appeared as she contemplated their evening ahead.

Monica knew exactly what Susan Emmerich was thinking. "Tonight, first we are dining at The Savoy…" She turned and waved to a male who sat alone on the other side of the wine bar. "Our driver. Let's get you to your hotel so that you can prepare yourself for an evening like you've not had for a long time."

The man looked slightly older than Monica, and had similar colouring. He was very good looking. Susan thought that he and the lawyer might be related. She wondered… and bit her bottom lip in anticipation… and she tingled throughout like a young girl on her first date… her juices were flowing.

He pushed aside his soft drink, patted his wet lips with a serviette, and stood. His name was Hans.

The Plough Inn, Belfont-st-Mary, England.
Tuesday 23rd February 1999

The door of the pub flew open and Michael Emmerich hurled himself into the road, almost stumbling… damn it, too late, the woman had gone. He stood, hands on hips, looking in both directions up and down the dark and empty street. Two kids were leaning against the wall, smoking between drinks. "Which way did she go?"

They nodded in unison, that way. "Black car, with a bloke driving."

"What sort of car?"

Shrugs. "A black one."

He sighed. Two of his friends stepped through the door and joined him at the edge of the road. "What the hell was that about?" they wanted to know.

Michael looked down at the crumpled note in his hand. "This."

Jake the landlord, wearing a look of genuine concern, stood behind his bar waiting for his three regulars to come back into the pub. "Are you alright Michael?"

Michael wasn't sure how to respond. He gave a weak nod and sighed, "Yeah, thanks." He didn't believe his own words though.

The woman had placed the sealed envelope in front of him, on the table, and by the time he had opened it she had disappeared. Now, around the same table, his friends stared open mouthed as the words appeared from beneath his trembling fingers... *Michael Emmerich - kill yourself or your family will suffer.*

An uneasy sense of foreboding spread throughout Michael's body and he shuddered as he pushed the note away. Please God... Thoughts of violence crossed his mind, violence that had, over the years, taken his two brothers and their families...

The police were called and, after taking statements, they took the note away for forensic examination. "It was probably just a vicious and nasty prank," they said. But Michael knew better. The bad luck, unexplained occurrences, nasty accidents; call them what you like, they were no different from some incurable hereditary disease... they always ended the same way; death... a slow, tormenting death. Now... was it his turn? And if it was, why... and why now?

The headquarters of the Guardia Urbana, Barcelona.
Saturday 17ᵗʰ July 1999

Rory Mitchell looked totally at ease. He sat, not quite upright, with his legs stretched under the table and crossed at the ankles. He wore an expensive beige pin-striped suit with a soft white silk shirt. The top two buttons of the shirt were undone and it was worn loose, not tucked into his trousers. His hair would be walnut in colour if it was not cropped so short and his skin had a perfect tan. He looked very good.

He wasn't relaxed though. His heart raced like a train, he felt sick and he was terrified. He had a big problem. He was on his way back to England, to prison, and in all probability, death. Once in prison the family would find him, and kaput; no more Rory. One stupid bloody mistake! Now his boiler-room scam had been closed down and he was in big trouble. He listened to Wentworth's little speech; *no more of the high life, no more sunning it in Barcelona.* Well, that's life, the man had concluded. Well, actually, thought Rory, that's more like *no life*.

DI Wentworth, sitting opposite, was pleased with the way the interview had gone, but something was niggling at him. Although he was sure he'd never met this guy before today, there was something about him that seemed familiar, he reminded him of somebody. A sudden thought! "One last thing Mitch, have you ever heard the term *boiled alive*, perhaps used to describe a criminal activity?"

Rory took a long look at his questioner while he considered his response. Maybe there *was* a way out of his predicament. Just maybe…

"Boiled alive? Actually, yes…"

Chapter 3

Belfont-St-Mary

The village of Belfont-St-Mary straddles the River Stour, half in Essex and half in Suffolk. The river flows from west to east, passing the gardens and moorings of the two thousand or so residents. It flows alongside the recreation ground, by the old mill and, after a sharp bend, on into open farmland.

In the dry summer months when the flow is slow a stony beach appears just beyond the bend, and was the place where the village teenagers hung out.

A gang of nine boys and girls and mountain bikes jostled for position on the footpath overlooking the beach. They were focussed on Billy Saunders, who stood at the water's edge beside an idle fishing rod, and Jennifer Emmerich; his bait maker for the day. "Come on you two, football's better than fishing."

Billy was adamant, "No, how many times do I have to say? We're staying here. Can't be bothered with all that running around, it's way too hot."

"You haven't caught anything, it must be really boring." The boys didn't understand – Billy would play football in a furnace if that was the only option. He was brilliant, representing Essex schoolboys in the under-thirteen's team and was Belfont-St-Mary's very own sporting child prodigy. The kids hero-worshipped him. The girls did understand though. "Don't do anything we wouldn't, Jen!" and they convinced the boys to give up their quest. They began to move off and after a few steps and some serious whispering they all began to giggle. Then a chorus of, "We know what you're doing – we know what you're doing," rang out, and continued as the group moved on towards the playing field.

Both Billy and Jennifer were more than a little embarrassed at their friends' childish behaviour. Billy raised his eyebrows, grinned a *'they need to grow up'* grin and reeled in the line. Jennifer re-baited the hook with a small ball of doughy bread and then he expertly recast. "Are you sure you don't want to play football?" she asked.

"Nah. It's way too hot."

"Let's sit under the tree then."

The shadow of the old willow covered more than a quarter of the beach and was a welcome retreat from the hot early afternoon sun. Billy carefully set his rod on its rest and allowed himself to be led into the shade. They sat on the big log and quietly watched the float as it bobbed and weaved in the slow, lazy flow of the river.

He was desperately trying to think of something to say and pointed out that it was probably even too hot for the fish to bite.

"You know so much about things." She was so pleased that he preferred to be with her than to play football – she understood just how important the game was to him. "The others, do you think they know how we feel about each other?"

A tough question for a thirteen year-old boy!

She leant against him and he wrapped his left arm around her shoulder and stroked the soft, cool skin of her upper arm. He had butterflies in his tummy and his normally slow and even pulse raced. Not knowing quite what to say, he lowered his head to look at her and the next moment they were kissing. How did that happen? The kiss was long. Neither knew how long a kiss should last so they kissed and they kissed. He felt a great beautiful heat spread throughout his body. She felt strangely light-headed, faint, and wanted to float away. She was in heaven. She couldn't get enough of the kiss and pulled him closer. She felt his strong hand on the back of her head and his lips push tightly onto hers. She felt their bodies press against each other. She felt his hand move down her back, down her tingling spine, and the skin on her thighs gorgeously tickled as the hand gently stroked her bare leg, and she felt his fingers press against… There! She pushed his hand away. No! No Billy. She pulled herself away from the panting, hot and blushing Billy.

He wasn't quite sure what had happened and it took him a few moments to calm down and compose himself. Then, without saying anything, he stood, walked over to the fishing rod, picked it up, tweaked the line and placed it back on the rest. He stood with his back to her, pretending to study the opposite bank as he tried to plan his next move. Then he felt her beside him. She stood on tiptoe and kissed him on the cheek. She was in control.

"See that old can over there," she pointed at a discarded carbonated drink tin stuck in a scraggly bunch of reeds on the other bank. She picked up a small pebble and threw it, missing the target by a yard.

"Crap!" He picked up a stone and hit the can. "How's that?"

"That's because you're older than me."

"Only by a couple of months. It's because you're a girl, and girls can't throw for toffee."

"Right, this is war." She picked up a stone about the size of her fist and threw it 'shot' fashion – it almost reached the other bank.

It wasn't long before they were both at it, the stones getting progressively bigger. Then she selected a really large one, picked it up with both hands and dropped it; almost onto her foot. "Careful!"

After that she chose a smaller and more manageable one, it was flat, and decided to throw it 'discus' fashion – she twirled once, twice and launched the rock. It skimmed Billy on the side of the head as it whizzed past. "Ouch!" and he collapsed to the ground, his hand clasped against the point of impact.

Shocked and shaking she rushed over and knelt beside him, "I'm sorry. I'm sorry Billy, I'm so sorry." She began to cry and reached out to touch the hand holding his head. He slowly moved it away and exposed a nasty gash; oozing blood. She took off her T-shirt and held it against the wound. "I'm really, really sorry Billy, I didn't mean it."

"It's all right," he said bravely, "it doesn't hurt." She was wearing a little white bra and he felt special because she had been willing to strip down to her underwear for him in his moment of need, even though she *had* nearly killed him. He studied her silky white skin. They stayed like this for a while, her, the nurse, he, the patient. He was happy and she was sorry, and suddenly, both were in love.

She was brought out of her dreamy state with a start – she heard something; a twig snap? She definitely heard something. She slipped on her white windcheater but left Billy with the bloody shirt. She checked his wound. The flow of blood had slowed. "I think we should leave."

Billy suddenly turned defiant, "No, I'm not going anywhere, I want to stay and fish."

Jennifer pleaded with him to leave with her, the cut definitely needed stitches, she said, he might even bleed to death. But he had decided that he had had enough of this 'love' lark for one day – it was much too dangerous, out of his control. He was staying put.

She was still unsure about leaving him. "Please Billy, you need to get it looked at, at least get it cleaned. Come on, let's go."

"No, honest, I'm okay. Look, it's stopped bleeding. You go. And I'll see you later."

"Sure?"

"Sure."

She gave up. "Ok then, you can keep my shirt."

"Thanks."

As she made her way across the meadow, towards the cluster of houses which was the village, something didn't feel right. She didn't feel right; her legs were weak, struggling to bear her weight. She should turn around and force Billy to return with her to the village. But how was she to do that? Jennifer could feel his exploring hands on her again and she felt the skin on her face warm... she knew she was blushing. At that moment, the feeling which rose from deep within, she mistook as the excitement of forbidden sexual pleasure, not the warning of menace that it predicted.

Jennifer reached the village, and by this time was bursting to tell somebody just how much she was in love. The other kids were nowhere to be seen so she decided to drop in on Susan Jones. Susan was not her best friend, that was Katy Wellington, but Katy was away at her grandparents in Norwich. So Susan would have to do. They both shared the same birthday, thirteen years old in two weeks. That was a lot in common, enough to share even the biggest secrets. She passed David Thompson's mum and another lady in the High Street. "Are you alright Jennifer?"

"Yes." Jennifer was a little bewildered by the question.

"You have blood all down the side of your top," Mrs Thompson said, pointing.

Jennifer looked down. "Oh. It's okay, it's not mine," and decided that maybe she should go home and change first.

Chapter 4

Rory was silent for a while. How much, if anything, should he tell Wentworth? And what could he tell this policeman that would delay his return to England? He could answer his *boiled alive* question and at the same time tell him about Christopher Huth, that would definitely give the copper something to sink his teeth into. Though that might also result in him returning home even faster, so he needed to be very careful, string it out. At the moment he was probably facing a couple of years in an open prison. If he went back on a murder charge it would be life in a high security one. However, that was probably a bonus, he would be in a secure prison, making it much harder for them to get to him; he might be banged up but at least he would be alive.

He thought as he spoke. "You must have heard it said that if you drop a frog into a pan of hot water it will jump right out again, but if you place him in tepid water and turn the heat on low he'll quite happily sit there while he boils to death."

Wentworth stroked his soft new beard as he listened without emotion, waiting... for what?

"Why did you ask?" said Rory.

"Because I may have come across you before, although not as Rory Mitchell, I'm especially good at remembering names. Anyway, you seem familiar, I was fishing."

"And."

Wentworth shrugged, still stroking his beard.

"But why *boiled alive*?" asked Rory. "There must have been a reason for you to ask that particular question."

"Well, you tell me. As yet you haven't explained anything." Wentworth waited but Rory was silent, so he continued, "An instinct prompted me. It happens sometimes. Something stirred, a vague memory perhaps, and something from deep within prompted me to ask that question, I really don't know why though."

Wentworth was actually telling the truth, however, Rory didn't believe him. Rory could read people and it was becoming blatantly obvious to him that Wentworth remembered him... but from when, or where? It must have been a brief encounter, before he called himself Rory Mitchell. He tried, but couldn't recall the occasion. Still, on reflection and under the circumstances it didn't really matter, it wasn't an issue. But then... to ask that question; boiled alive. It was the term the family used when they were doing a long job on another family. Rory had a revelation. Somebody else must be talking to the law, somebody from the family. All the same, that didn't alter the fact that he was in trouble... he had to plough on. Whether-or-not he was the first to ever double-cross the family was irrelevant; he knew their laws, their rules. He knew because he was one of them, and he knew that when they caught up with him... he would die. Vague memory had prompted Wentworth. Fear suddenly prompted Rory. "My name is not Rory Mitchell, I am not Rory Mitchell."

"Who are you then?"

Rory took a deep breath, paused, then, "My name is Terence."

Wentworth looked at the man, waiting for him to continue. He encouraged him, made a gesture by raising a hand slightly, willing him to say more. When he didn't he asked, "Terence who?"

"Just Terence. No-one in our family has a surname. Our family has no surname."

"That's ridiculous, everybody has a surname."

"No. We've no need. We're on no government record, or if we are, it's when we're using a false name or a stolen identity. We have no birth certificates or…"

"I don't believe you."

"Maybe you don't, but it's true. Not only is that true but this family is one of the largest crime organisations around. If I return to England I'm a dead man, I've double-crossed them and they'll kill me. If they find me, wherever I am, they'll kill me. So I've decided to help you. Maybe, just maybe, you can get them before they get me, and as slim a possibility as that is, it's the only choice I have." He shrugged. "With my help you might uncover and destroy a massive crime family. The crimes include murder, kidnap, people trafficking, drug running and money laundering on a scale you cannot imagine." Rory leaned forward, "This is an incredibly close-knit group of people. They own no property, have no bank accounts and pay no taxes. But they control millions, probably billions of pounds, dollars, marks, you name it. They work for big crime, big business and big government, yet on record they don't exist. They'll steal millions from a government or they'll murder an old lady for a tenner.

They don't care. I'll tell you what boiled alive means, from a criminal perspective. It was done to the Huth family… remember Jamie and Christopher Huth?

Wentworth didn't know what to think. "Look Rory, you're a petty criminal. I've been asked to process the paperwork and take you back to England because I happened to be in Barcelona. You've been investigated and your dirty deeds uncovered by a joint UK, Spanish operation of, well, not to be too unkind, low ranking plod. I'm part of the flying squad, you know, serious crime, and quite frankly I've been around a bit and I've never heard so much crap." This all sounded like bullshit and he didn't intend to fall for it and be made to look an idiot.

But Rory Mitchell, or whatever his name was, had, up until a few minutes ago, come across as a pretty level headed individual. And the Huth case! Wentworth was never part of the Huth investigation but his interest in it had been as keen as that of any detective. Both the Huth sons had been abducted in the summer of 1990. The eldest, fourteen year old Jamie's body had been found brutally murdered just days after he was seized. Christopher was twelve when he disappeared and had never been seen since. He would be nineteen now. Wentworth considered what Rory had just told him. "Ok. What can you tell me about Christopher Huth?"

"I killed Christopher Huth."

Wentworth wasn't expecting this. "You killed…"

"Yes. And I'll tell you all about it. But first, you wanted to know what *boiled alive* means. When the two brothers were taken, the Huths were worth about fifteen million pounds. Then the mother died, killed in a road accident, and the last Huth, the father, committed suicide. He died penniless, in fact he was in debt. This all happened over the course of a number of years. Even before the boys were kidnapped Huth's advisory team had been well and truly infiltrated by the family. Now, Joseph Huth had been a very intelligent chap and not prone to accepting bad advice. However, this contaminated team of advisers had consistently given him very good and profitable council, over time building invaluable trust and becoming the dominant element of Huth's business investments and legal affairs. What the Huths didn't know was, their bank accounts had become Huth bank accounts in name only; the real account holders were the family. When Jamie turned up dead, and with no word of Christopher, the advisers were able to make themselves totally indispensable and over time took control of all affairs. Joseph, distraught and distracted, was grateful for the help. The Huth fortune was slowly plundered, without Huth or his wife ever knowing it was happening. They were boiled alive, just as the frog was boiled alive."

"So a wealthy family is targeted, tragedies and distractions introduced, and with their attentions elsewhere they are taken advantage of. Was Mrs Huth, the mother, murdered?"

"Yes. She was made of stronger stuff than her husband, more difficult to deceive. It made sense to get rid of her because she was becoming hard work. As a bonus, her death made her old man even more vulnerable."

"Tell me about Christopher. If he's dead, where are his remains?"

* * *

What Rory was about to tell Wentworth was painful. He took a deep breath and began his story. "I'll tell you about Christopher, about how he died. The whereabouts of the remains… I'll tell you that later."

"Why not now?"

"Later. I'll tell you though, that his final hideout was near Leeds, north of the city, about fifteen miles north."

"So he was moved around. When did he die?"

"November 27th 1993."

"Pretty precise."

"I remember it exactly. I killed him. My first murder. And before you ask, my last. His death was why I left the family. I was not the organiser of the project, just a young member of a vicious family, but I knew the plan. The Huths were to be relieved of all their wealth in the manner of which I have just explained, so, after a couple of years of entwining ourselves into their everyday affairs, the two sons were kidnapped. The plan was to murder the eldest and to keep the other one alive, to give Joseph Huth and his wife some hope; something to cling to. After Jamie was killed Christopher was moved from pillar to post for about three years. Photographs, letters and recordings were sent via Huth's lawyers, our people of course. Bogus private investigators hired by the lawyers almost found him on a couple of occasions, much, much more success than the police had ever had. It gave the parents false hope."

Wentworth recalled the fervour the case aroused. "I remember how long the story ran... all the tv and newspaper coverage."

"I became involved about a year before he died, as a guard. There were always at least two of us looking after him. Mostly I worked with Peter, an older guy, older than me, anyway, and a real sadist. Hans was our boss. He came and went and gave the orders. On that night, *the* night, after we had finished eating, Hans pulled a piece of rope from a bag. He tied a knot and formed a noose.

"We were at a farmhouse in Yorkshire and Christopher was in a windowless room at the back of the house. I'd formed quite a good relationship with him, good under the circumstances anyway. He was about fifteen by then and I was just nineteen. I had lots of conversations with him, news and events of the day, football, girls, *you know*. All from the other side of the locked door; he'd never actually seen our faces. We knew, at the end, he would die by our hands but Hans said it would be better for all of us if he thought he would eventually be let free, *to go home*, as Christopher often put it.

"We went to the room and Hans informed the boy that we were about to enter and he was to stand with his back to the door. We always entered the room in this fashion, and he did just as he was told.

"The three of us wore hoods. Christopher might have been alarmed if we hadn't. *We were about to murder him but we didn't want to alarm him.* Peter and me followed Hans into the room. I remember the boy looked very feeble. As our hostage, he had only ever been outside when we changed location, maybe six or seven times in three years, and had never seen the sun during that period. He was so thin… and weak."

Rory faltered for a moment. He was evoking memories which had supposed to have been locked away for good. He cleared his throat, "As I was saying, Christopher had his back to us, and Hans held the noose ready while Peter seized him by his upper arms and shoulders.

"Hans slipped the noose over the boy's head and around his neck. He pulled it hard and Christopher fell over, onto his back. Peter sat on his legs and Hans climbed onto his chest. He passed me the end of the rope and nodded.

"I sat on the floor astride Christopher's head, placed my feet against his shoulders and pulled. He was so weak it was hardly necessary to hold him down. He didn't resist at all. The big knot on the noose was in the wrong position, under his chin rather than at the back of his neck, and sort of pulling his head back, so he was looking at me as I did what I did… He looked at me. He stared at me before a single, slow spasm shook his body. My legs were shaking so much that one of my feet slipped off the boy's shoulder. I couldn't breathe properly so I swapped places with Hans and he finished the job. I couldn't stop looking at Christopher's face and I remember how a single tear snaked down his cheek as he died. It had taken so long for him to die." Rory wiped *his* eyes with trembling hands. "I'll never forget that day. I need to tell you everything I know about these people. I owe it to the boy."

Chapter 5

Sunday 18ᵗʰ July 1999

Jennifer was almost awake, in that drowsy state when you're really still asleep but vaguely aware of what's going on around you. She heard the mumbling of strangers' voices from downstairs and her mother calling her father in from his Sunday morning garden chores. Then she slid back into unconsciousness and was back with Billy at the bend, not talking, just sitting together, warm under the afternoon sun. *At first she's relaxed. Then something begins to trouble her. She shivers as the sun disappears; gone, as if turned off by a switch. The recollection of something, maybe a previous dream, maybe real, begins to emerge slowly from her subconscious. She remembers somebody hurting her. She remembered Billy hurting her, but she cannot remember how. "No Billy, please no." Then Billy speaks her name but it's not Billy's voice she hears. Jennifer. Jennifer. It's her mother's voice. She's confused. Suddenly she's rocking, gently at first, then more fiercely. Jennifer.* "Jennifer."

"Jennifer, you need to come downstairs, there are some people who want to talk to you, Jennifer, are you awake?" It was her mother beside the bed.

Jennifer's eyelids fluttered. "Ok, yes. People, what people?"

"Just some people, hurry up, they are waiting. Just quickly make yourself decent and come downstairs."

Her mother left her to pull on some jeans and a top. She quickly visited the bathroom and freshened up, checked herself in the mirror and wondered why people wanted to see her. She found it a little odd that her mother had not mentioned who they were. She went back to her bedroom and collected her watch. Nine-forty-five. Her sister's bedroom door was closed. By now Jennifer was wide awake and skipped down the stairs and into the lounge – it was empty. Her mother called out from the office, which Jennifer thought strange; she was generally only summoned to Dad's office when she was in some kind of trouble.

"Jennifer, these people are police officers and need to ask you some questions about Billy Saunders."

There were two officers, neither in uniform, one male and one female. The female butted in before Jennifer's mother could add to what she was saying and introduced herself to Jennifer as Detective Sergeant Sally Whitnell. Then she asked, "Can you tell us where you were yesterday afternoon?"

"Why?"

"Jennifer, answer the question." It was her mother.

D.S. Whitnell gently raised a finger in front of Mrs Emmerich's face. "It's alright Mrs Emmerich, we're not in any hurry." Then she continued to speak to Jennifer. "We want to know how Billy Saunders spent his afternoon. We understand you were with him, so if you tell us what you did and where you went during that time it would help us hugely with our inquiries."

"What's Billy done?"

The detective ignored her question. "Jennifer, please. Can you tell us how you spent yesterday afternoon?"

Jennifer glanced at her parents. Both looked pensive, they were pale faced and silent. *What had Billy done?* She needed to take care with what she said, in case he was in trouble; she didn't want to make it worse for him. "We had a light lunch…"

"We?"

"Me, Mum and Rachel. That's my sister. We ate here, at home. After that I went to the bend to see Billy, he was fishing."

"The bend, where is that?" DS Whitnell interrupted.

"A local meeting place on the river," her mother answered for Jennifer.

Jennifer continued, "He'd been there all morning. I spent the rest of the day with him, and then came home."

"What time did you get home?"

Her first lie; she could get away with this because both her parents and Rachel had been clothes shopping in Chelmsford and had not returned home until after six pm. "Six o'clock."

"Were you with Billy all this time?"

The second lie. "Yes, we walked back into the village together."

The two officers glanced at each other and the man scribbled in his notebook. DI Whitnell turned to Jennifer's parents. "Mr and Mrs Emmerich, we need to continue this interview with Jennifer at the police station."

"Michael, Mr Emmerich, is a lawyer, he works for the Government." Mrs Emmerich just about managed to say, shocked at the development.

"Susan!" Michael Emmerich was annoyed with his wife for continually interrupting proceedings, which he put down to nerves. "Susan," he said, "I'll take care of this." He turned to the detectives. "Jennifer's mother will accompany our daughter to the police station but there will be no interview until I've arranged representation and that representation is present."

"I think we'll decide that," said the male detective.

"You will not decide anything of the sort. Jennifer is a minor and if you so much as pass the time of day with her without her being represented I'll make sure that you are both in a lot of trouble. Is that clear?"

Jennifer was very frightened now. "Dad, what's happening?"

"Listen carefully to me Jennifer." Michael gently pulled her in front of him. "Now, I want you to be a brave girl." He paused, allowing his daughter time to compose herself. "Jennifer... Billy was found dead at the bend yesterday afternoon."

"No! That can't be. He was alive when I left him. No. No."

"Jennifer, Jennifer. Please listen to what I have to say. Think very carefully about what happened yesterday afternoon. Do not lie. A lady called Monica Davies will be with you to help you, but please tell the truth at all times. Your mother will go with you to the police station and I'll join you as soon as I can." Michael Emmerich stroked his daughter's hair and he pulled her to him. As they embraced he felt her tremble.

Jennifer started to cry. "Please Dad, please. I didn't mean to do it; he said he was alright when I left."

For Michael Emmerich, alarm bells were ringing. Something deep within raged… guilt perhaps!

Chapter 6

Wednesday 21ˢᵗ July 1999

In the Barcelona interview room Wentworth lowered himself into the chair across the table from Rory and turned on the recorder. Feelings towards the criminal had changed for the police officer. He'd originally been instructed to apprehend a fraudster, and while he didn't have a lot of time for these lawbreakers, (he had met many a poor victim), fraudsters were *not* murderers. Before speaking he placed the folder he carried onto the desk and pulled out some sheets of paper; forms. He studied them for a moment and then raised his eyes. After the official opening he spoke slowly. "This is how it is Mr Mitchell, we have discovered the remains of four bodies at the farm. None have yet been identified nor the manner of deaths established, but I have been instructed to charge you with the murder of Christopher Huth." He then charged him.

Rory had known this was coming but it had still been difficult to prepare for. He shrugged nervously, "What now?" He felt his bottom lip tremble as he spoke.

"Well, we have a little time before you return to the United Kingdom. The officer spoke very slowly and his head very slightly bobbled from side to side, "Possibly your age at the time of the murder might make a difference... and depending on the quality of information you give us about this organisation..." he shrugged, "it could count in your favour with regards a sentence." He stroked his forefinger across his lips, and paused, indicating that this consideration was borderline, at best. He then picked up a sheet of paper from the pile in front of him. "It does appear that there are one or two legal agencies around the world aware of, in fact very interested in your *family,* as you call it. As it stands at the moment I am to stay with you here in Barcelona. It seems a special consideration has already been made in return for your cooperation." Wentworth waited a moment as he observed some colour return to Rory's cheeks. "How do I address you?" he asked Rory.

"What?"

"Your name, do you prefer to be addressed as Rory Mitchell or Terence?" Wentworth chuckled to himself at the ridiculousness of the question.

"Rory Mitchell. I think it's a good name. Mitch if you like."

Wentworth looked at him long and hard. Sitting across from him was a child killer. He felt disgusted and sick in the stomach for having to pass any time at all with the smarmy, yuppie sleaze-bag. He had the looks, the talk... Wentworth would have taken great pleasure in smashing him to a pulp against this interview room wall. He *was* capable. His training stopped him. Finally he said, "Rory will do." That was difficult!

Rory had recovered from the initial shock of being formally charged. "It surprises me that there are agencies, or whatever you call them, aware of the family."

"The US Drugs Enforcement Agency is one. And FATF."

This name was new to Rory. "FATF. I've never heard of them."

"They're an organisation set up by the Group of Seven Nations Summit of 1989. It stands for Financial Action Task Force on Money Laundering. They seem very interested in you."

"As far as I know we, can I say *we*? You know I'm not part of the family anymore but it just seems easier to say *we*."

Wentworth didn't care a fig. He shrugged.

"We don't actually get directly involved with drugs, or prostitution or human trafficking. The closest we get to the mucky stuff is providing finance for deals and projects. But our main involvement is the movement of money and the conversion of illegal cash, so I can see why these money laundering people would be interested. I just find it a surprise that they actually know anything about us."

"You get involved with murder, that's pretty mucky. What about thugs like Hans and Peter?"

"This family has been operating since the middle of the nineteenth century, one hundred and fifty years. Just to stay in business, let alone be successful, you need to have the ability to take care of problems. This is what the Hans and Peters are there for, to take care of problems."

"And to kill little boys?"

"You would have to know our history, the family history, to understand."

"You can tell me about your family history until the cows come home, I would still not understand, I can assure you of that." Because of the way he felt about Mitchell, the relationship between the two men was fragile. He was to no longer question the man, just charge him, mind him until investigators from other agencies arrived, allow them time with him… and then bring him *home*. He had things to get on with back in London, his own cases; he was a DI, not a bloody wet-nurse. Anyway, he felt sure they could just as easily find out about Mitchell's family, the Huths or any-bloody-thing-else, if they were in the UK.

Rory tried to read Wentworth's mind, the vibes being given out were not what he expected. He studied the officer. What did he want to know? Was he interested in the family, or not? Having recovered from the emotion of three days ago, the confession of the murder, Rory no longer had the urge to destroy the family, just to stop them from destroying him. If they sent him back to England now, all he would have achieved was to be going as a murderer, as opposed to a thief. He needed to stay in Spain, that was his priority. He made an attempt to get the interview back on course. "What about these agents, what do you think they want to know?"

"You'll find that out when you return to England." Wentworth almost burst out laughing as he witnessed Rory's reaction.

"As soon as I set foot on English soil, I stop talking."

"You'll not stop talking until you're six feet under. You can't help yourself."

"As soon as I get to England I fucking will be six feet under you fucking idiot."

"Now, now, Mr Mitchell. Let's calm down a little, shall we."

"We had a deal. As long as I tell you stuff, good stuff, we can stay here."

"I don't do deals with baby killers."

"Fuck you."

"It's a good job we don't have a swear box."

"We fucking haven't, so fuck you."

Wentworth was amused at the way Rory Mitchell squirmed, but he wasn't supposed to agitate the guy… he gave himself a ticking off. "Let's have a cuppa. Look, I was pulling your leg. A United States investigator is in the air as we speak, coming here to Barcelona, all the way from Washington, just to interview *you*. So, let's be friends again. Tell me about your family history."

Rory remained silent. He was no longer in the mood.

Shit! Wentworth so wanted to hit him. He took a long slow and deep breath while he looked at the papers spread in front of him and wondered how many steps up the chain of command the order had been made to play along with this scum-bag. His immediate superiors would want them both back at the yard as soon as possible, so he had to assume that the order came from way up, and whoever made it was probably not interested in the opinion of a shitty little detective inspector, so he slid the papers back into the folder, concluded the interview, and stood. But before leaving he lent over towards his prisoner and added. "To tell you the truth *Rory*, I don't care if you are refusing to talk. I'll actually talk to my bosses and let them know that you are refusing to cooperate and recommend that we get you home as quickly as possible. Just think, if it's true what you are saying, you could be dead in a couple of days." He pressed the call button on the wall next to the door and a few seconds later there was a buzz and the door opened. He left without looking back.

Chapter 7

Later that day, Wentworth sat in the busy reception area of the Barcelona police headquarters awaiting the arrival of special investigator, Pamela Lewinski. It was early afternoon and he felt tired, bored. He thought about Rory. He'd sent instruction about forty-five minutes ago, that Rory Mitchell should be taken back to the interview room. *He* must be really bored. That thought made the policeman feel a little better.

"Sir." Suddenly there appeared, from nowhere, a middle aged woman dressed in a dark blue suit, standing directly in front of him. He realised with some embarrassment that he had nodded off.

He jumped up, a little too quickly. "Sorry," he spluttered and held out his hand. "Umm I…"

She laughed. "The desk pointed you out. DI Wentworth. I'm Federal Agent Pamela Lewinski." They shook hands.

He felt himself redden up. "I, I'm sorry. I must have dozed off… yes, I'm David Wentworth." He took back his hand. "Um, can I help you with your stuff?" He looked around. She had no stuff.

She laughed again. "Should I go outside and then come back in again, give you time to compose yourself. I've booked in to the hotel across the square. My *stuff* is there. Maybe we should stroll. You can show me around, I've been told that Barcelona's a nice city. You can also tell me about your prisoner, and I'll tell you about our interest in him."

He was about to agree to a walk but the subject of Rory halted him. He checked his watch. "Mitchell has been waiting in the interview room for over an hour."

"Do you care?"

He smiled. "No." He walked over to the desk and told them in fluent Spanish that, providing the room was not required by anybody else, they should not move his prisoner.

"So, you're FBI then?"

"Yes. I'm seconded to the Financial Action Task Force, do you know what it is?"

"Yeah, I know, the Sub-superintendent filled me in with the details."

"I assume he's the second in command here. I noticed your Spanish is excellent."

"My mum was Spanish. This organisation, it's predominantly made up of lawyers. Are you a lawyer?"

Most of our people are lawyers and accountants. However, although I *am* a lawyer, I'm also a federal investigator with lots of hands-on experience, so I'm part of *the law enforcement expertise,* as they call it. I flit back and forth between this lot and the FBI."

As she sipped her ice-cold beer she noted Wentworth's glance at the ring-less fingers of her left hand. "We got word of your Rory Mitchell and his talk of the family," she said. "Well, we felt *we* should talk to him, so here I am."

"So how would somebody in Washington hear about a conversation between a middle ranking police officer and a small-time criminal?"

"Somebody in London is on the ball. It was the mention of a criminal organisation whose members have no surnames. There has been a long running world-wide investigation into a large organisation which is, frankly, getting nowhere fast. They've even managed to fleece us out of a couple of million dollars. They've taken it and there is no trace of it. Heads have rolled I can assure you but, more to the point, we've been embarrassed and we don't like that. So here I am, probably clutching straws, but hey?"

"Tell me more." Wentworth ordered two Americana coffees.

She protested. "I might have liked another beer."

Wentworth ignored her. "Tell me, how did they get this *couple of million?*"

"Well, we know they have a very clever set-up but we don't know how they do it. Let's say cocaine originating from Columbia is sold in the US. The dollars need to be transferred back into pesos in Columbia. Normally this is quite a process, dangerous for the traffickers because of the amount of stages and people involved. When they use this organisation a courier collects the suitcase, or whatever, stuffed full of cash in America, and within a couple of days an equivalent amount of local currency, less commission, is delivered to the head of the gang in Columbia. The money comes with legal history, clean as a whistle."

"Wow, sounds impressive."

"You're not kidding. Anyway, to get to know more we set up a sting operation and arranged to have around one million US dollars collected in New York to be changed into Columbian currency and delivered straight into a bank account, which they opened by the way, in Bogotá. They assured us that the money by that time would be totally clean. The funds were duly collected and that was it. Nothing. The delivery was never made and our contacts disappeared from the face of the earth."

"You never got anywhere with it at all?"

"No. And what's more, we tried it again, this time the country involved was Thailand, absolutely no connection with the first deal. This deal was to launder just under a million bucks. Wham, bam, gone. People and money." She shook her head in amazement, even though she was the one telling the story.

"So, Rory Mitchell may be a lead?"

"At the moment we are chasing anything that may remotely get us somewhere. I've simplified the stories about how we lost that money, but the point is, the laundering of the proceeds is an essential part of any crime cycle and needs to be broken. This stage of the cycle has also historically been a major stumbling block for the perpetrators of crimes, you know, follow the money etcetera, and because of this *family* we are losing that advantage. Criminals are getting their hands on clean money, risk free. We know it's not just drugs we're dealing with, it includes human trafficking, the sex trade, arms, extortion and blackmail. You can see why we have to break this organisation. They are making life too easy for the criminals. We have to chase any lead… however unlikely it looks."

"I've been listening to Mitchell for a few days, and you know, I think you might have struck lucky."

Wentworth checked his watch. "The poor bastard has been waiting for us for nearly three hours, I think we should be making our way back."

They finished their drinks and returned to the police station, sorted a visitor badge for Pamela Lewinski, and then went directly to the interview room. It was empty! "Damn, I told them not to move him."

But they hadn't! Somehow or other Rory had managed to disappear from a locked and guarded room deep in the belly of the headquarters of the Guardia Urbana, Barcelona.

Chapter 8

Courtroom Number One - Ipswich Crown Court
Thursday 27th January 2000

Silence fell upon the courtroom as the sentence was announced. The judge then instructed that the prisoner be taken down to the cells, but nobody moved, and still nobody uttered a sound. Never before had a thirteen-year-old girl felt so alone. Her eyes frantically searched the room for her father or her sister. Neither one was there. She wanted them and their support so badly. Her mother *was* there. She felt her cold stare bore right into her but she couldn't fight it – not then. One day she *would* though… and then her mother would be so sorry.

Set upon and beaten by the state, abandoned by her father and sister and betrayed by her mother. She caught the judge's eye as he discreetly nodded, and Jennifer Emmerich was led away.

Chapter 9

**The Pyrenees Mountains
A Sunny Day**

Hans hauled the trussed up body from the jeep as though it were a sack of potatoes, and threw it to the ground as such. Rory whimpered. He'd screamed and cried and begged... now all he could manage was a whimper. He wished he had a mother to plead for him, to care for him... to save him. His body hurt so much and in so many places that the pain which jarred through his side on impact with the hard rocky earth hardly registered.

He lay sobbing on the ground, hands bound behind his back and his legs tied together. He watched his captor return to the jeep and close the back doors. If he was going to kill Rory, he was taking his time.

Hans returned and picked the body up, face down, by the collar and the belt, and swung it onto a low wide wall. Rory gasped for air as his stomach and chest smashed onto the rim of a well, and he found himself looking down a deep, dark pit. Suddenly he remembered, in the old days, he'd mentioned to Hans that his most dreaded way to die would be stuck in a shaft, too narrow to go forward and unable to reverse. "No-please-Hans-no!" he gasped. He had dropped begging for the option to live and now pleaded for a kinder way to die.

Hans never said a word. He waited, cruelly, holding the body in position on the wall; giving Rory plenty of time to work out what was about to happen to him. He then slowly inched the body forward until gravity took over. The shouting and writhing mass gathered pace and slid head-forward into the shaft. And then, for Hans, it was all over. He stood, looked around, breathed the cool mountain air and returned to the vehicle.

Rory's face itched and his eyes stung. Urine, his, trickled from his neck, over his chin and lips, into his nostrils and over his forehead. That was how he determined that he was upside down; there was no other way he would have known. He could open and close his eyes but he couldn't see anything. Not one ray of light was able to get past the body and clothing that blocked the shaft. He felt strange though. No pain. In fact he felt nothing, not cold, nor wet, absolutely nothing from his neck down, or up? He couldn't move his head... it just hung, like the head of a dead turkey in the butcher's window. He tried to feel afraid, to feel his stomach churn, but there was nothing. What could he do? He could think. But what was the point of that. He was going to die. Here. He could count. He began to count. He tried to speak but it didn't come out right, just a gurgle. But he could hear. He could hear his mind counting anyway. So in his mind he counted, trying to forget the itch. One two three four...

... Two thousand and forty two, two... Something was happening. He couldn't feel anything but something was happening - he sensed it. His head was jogging and then some light sneaked past his body. He could see. He could see the walls of the well moving down, away from him. No, he was going up, but still he didn't feel anything. He was travelling in a slow motion reverse of his descent into the well, except this time there was no pain… and no fear. He travelled up and over the wall. The well disappeared from view and bright light forced him to close his eyes. When he reopened them he was floating in the air. He could see the bright blue sky, upside-down treetops and mountains. He floated down until he felt the back of his head touch something soft. A face, then a second, came into view. A soft tissue wiped away the itch that he'd almost forgotten about. "Terence," one of them said. "Terence, you're safe now. We'll take care of you. Hans went too far, but now you're safe."

Chapter 10

Berlin, December, 1920

It was cold. The wind had switched and now gusted from the north, keeping the temperature well below zero, and after the recent warm weather the change had come as a shock. Large quayside buildings on the far side of the waterfront served as a huge wind break and partially sheltered the gang, making the night almost bearable. The grossly overweight Carl Froebel stamped his feet and violently flapped his arms around himself in an effort to keep warm.

A dirty brick built wall dropped seven feet from the road, vertically, like a huge step from the uneven harbour front onto the hard craggy bank of the river. Froebel, standing at the bottom of it, leant into the brickwork as close as he could without muddying his long dark overcoat and waited for the two rowing boats to return to the river bank. He could see neither of them, nor could he hear them, but he knew they were out there, close.

It was late, close to mid-night, and dark low clouds filled the sky, threatening snow. There was no moon or starlight to help this murderous gang conduct their ungodly work. With Carl Froebel, and feeling the cold much more so, were two other, less fat, less wrapped up, gang members. They were up on the road on lookout, just in case somebody should stumble across them, but who the hell would be out on a night like this?

After about fifteen minutes both boats silently glided over the water and thudded into the muddy bank, first one, and then the other. Froebel was pleased with his boys; they had actually appeared without him hearing them. He stepped forward, "Well done lads," he whispered, "no problems?" Nobody answered. A wet rope was thrown from the first boat, which he caught and kept taut while the three occupants scrambled ashore. Two of those assisted the landing of the second boat. "How did it go?" he quietly asked the third, a brother, Gerard.

"Fine, nobody will ever see those bodies again. I don't think I could ever find them if you asked me to."

Froebel moved in as close as he could get to his kin, for warmth as much as privacy. "Good. I've collected the cash... but the three kids, the ones we've supposed to have done away with along with the others, well they're going to show up sooner or later, which will be one hell of a shock for Johann Huth, as he now believes they are out there at the bottom of the river with their mummies and daddies. I've sent two boys to each house to wait for them to hopefully show their faces."

"And if they don't?" Gerard put his mouth within an inch of his brother's ear. Carl could feel the warmth of the breath against the side of his face as the words were repeated. "And if they don't show?" Then he added: "We'll be fucked. We can't mess with Huth, you know that. We have to get out of Berlin... tonight."

"We can't move that fast; the women will want some time, and these boys…" Carl trailed off as it dawned on him just what his brother was implying.

"Leave the women and leave the boys," hissed Gerard. "We've got the money, let's just grab Victor and slip away."

"You mean…"

"Yeah. You know what I mean, just the three of us. Now! We'll take the money and disappear."

The brothers halted their little conference and stamped their feet and blew warm breath into cupped hands as they waited for the third Froebel. As soon as the second boat was tied, Victor and the other four boatmen clambered up the bank and gathered around the two men. They were joined by the two lookouts.

Carl looked Gerard in the eye before speaking. "I'm going back to the hut. Victor, you and Gerard have to go to and see Johann Huth to get the money."

Victor interrupted him. "What's going on? I thought you had been to collect it… is there a problem?"

Gerard intervened, to help Carl, "There's no problem Victor, I'll explain as we go."

Carl then addressed the rest of the gang. "Three of you go back to Karl Richard's place and the rest of you to Albert Bary's. Wait there! It's fucking important that we find those other kids. When you do, don't wait for us, just finish the bastards off and dump them in there," he pointed to the murky water, "with the rest of their families."

Chapter 11

**Belfont-St-Mary.
Saturday 26th January 2008**

Adam Saunders had been training, had prepared himself for the arrival of this very moment. How to think! How to react! Now, with luck, they would lead him straight to the bitch; Jennifer Emmerich.

The story doing the rounds was that she'd been released a few weeks ago, after just eight years inside. Adam's viewpoint was that Emmerich deserved to die in prison, not freed to get on with her life. But it was obvious that she would, one day, be out; that's how it worked, and that was why he had been secretly coaching himself – for the day when he would have to kill her. A violent death, just like the violent death which ended his brother's life. Hardly a day passed without him thinking about Billy.

His friend Tony was droning on and on and on about last Saturday. *For fuck sake!* Adam manoeuvred himself further back into the shadow of the doorway. He had just glimpsed the distinctive blond hair of Jennifer's sister, Rachel Emmerich, going into the baker's shop across the street, and right at this moment he could do without this moron... A quick glance down the narrow street revealed her unmistakeable flashy bright yellow Audi parked outside the church. Somebody, possibly her father, sat in the passenger seat. Rachel Emmerich hardly ever visited the village these days and intuition told Adam this was an opportunity he couldn't afford to miss.

He looked at his watch and interrupted his friend. "Sorry Tony, I've got things to do. Look, we'll catch up later, how about a pint at Jake's tonight." Jake was the landlord of the Plough Inn.

Tony had been on a roll and being stopped in mid sentence put him off his stroke, "Oh yeah, right, okay then. That'll be good. See you, say, seven o'clock," he spluttered.

"Seven. That's ideal. Sorry to cut you short like that. See ya in the pub, must fly."

Adam walked briskly, hands in pockets, towards Rachel Emmerich's parked vehicle, keeping his head turned away from the bakery. Before he reached the car he could see it *was* the old man sitting inside. Yes! This really could be his lucky day. The car was facing away from him so he was able to pass it without Michael Emmerich recognising him. Not such a feat these days; he'd heard recently that the old man had suffered *another* stroke. Good, the more he had, the better. Adam's car was parked about fifty yards further on and fortunately positioned so that once he sat in his driver's seat he could see Emmerich's car perfectly through the rear view mirror.

He waited, but not for long. He caught sight of her in his mirror walking towards her car. A dark blue shoulder bag hung on her right side and she carried a shopping bag in her left hand. It didn't look very full; maybe she'd just picked up a loaf to take back to the house. But, he reasoned with himself, if she had just popped out for a few groceries, why would she have brought her father along? Or perhaps they were returning home after an outing? She opened the door of her car, put the bag on the rear seat, climbed in and started it. They pulled away and drove past him, not in the direction of their house.

Adam was able to follow easily from a reasonable distance, the Emmerich car being such a distinctive colour. As they drove through built up areas he closed the gap; to reduce the possibility of being left at traffic lights or a junction, and then he would let the gap grow again on long stretches of road. He was feeling pleased with himself, the professional way he went about his *tail*. He would make a good policeman. Maybe that could be a career option. He was thinking about this as they arrived at Ongar, in Essex. Straight away he could see they were driving differently, slower, as if they were looking for somewhere. They were!

They turned off the High Road and pulled up and parked in a residential parking zone, outside a row of apartment blocks. Adam drove by, it was his only option. He needed to stop, but there were no empty parking spaces, so, after about fifty yards he just halted the car and turned on the hazard lights. Cursing drivers slowly manoeuvred around him. He released the bonnet catch, got out of the car and lifted the bonnet. It had begun to rain. The drivers of the inconvenienced vehicles stopped cursing and thanked their lucky stars it was somebody else who had broken down in such an awkward spot.

From his position behind the bonnet Adam spied Rachel and the old man couple cross the road and stop at the entrance of one of the apartment blocks. After pressing the call button and speaking into the intercom, the door opened and they disappeared inside. Adam was able to see that Rachel had pressed the bottom button. He lowered the bonnet, got back into the car and drove until he found a parking spot. He could park here legally for up to two hours. The notice reminded him to check for surveillance cameras… he couldn't see any – phew, lucky! Nobody must know he was here.

It was lightly raining. He was able to pull his jacket up over his head without feeling or looking conspicuous. He walked to the apartment block and discreetly checked the label next to the call button, it read S. Mannion. If he had to put money on it though, he would bet that they were visiting Jennifer Emmerich.

Chapter 12

Manfred was the son of Karl Richard Huth, and Karl Richard was the youngest of the six Maximilian Huth Children. Karl Richard, his wife and their daughter had been murdered that night on the orders of the oldest Huth and his three brothers-in-law. Manfred should have also been dead.

Karl Richard's sister Ilse, and brother-in law Albert Bary, had also been assassinated. Those killings had been witnessed by Amy and Thomas.

Manfred didn't know he was on that deadly hit-list... yet. He had no idea of any murders, let alone those of his parents and sister. The house where they had met their end was in Lichterfelde-Ost. It was a very large art deco town house with a forty foot frontage. Richly decorated rooms spread over five floors. The home had a huge front door, made from imported English oak, which was only usually used for the arrival and departure of important guests. The real entrance was through a pair of large wrought iron gates at the rear of the property.

Manfred had just paid for his cab ride and stood under a street lamp on the opposite side of the road, looking through the gates towards the house... something wasn't right. The gates were open and there was no gate keeper present. Additionally, there were two strangers waiting at the open back door to the house, one leaning against the wall and the other sitting on the step.

He stood and stared, which he soon realised was a mistake. The two men stared back, watching him intently, until they concluded that the boy must be Huth's son. What else would the kid be doing, standing, open mouthed like an idiot, and on a freezing night like tonight... unless he lived here! "Albert!" one shouted as both leaped forward.

Manfred turned and fled, dropping his overcoat so he could run faster. It didn't take him long to outrun and lose the two men, and as a soon as he had he paused for breath and to wonder what was going on? They were after *him*; there was no mistaking that, but why? They didn't look like policemen. As soon as he stopped he felt the cold and decided to go to his closest relation, Uncle Albert... But wait, didn't one of the men shout "Albert" as they jumped up to chase him.

Now he was even more confused... it had to be a different Albert, surely? It had to be, if his uncle had been there he would have called out to Manfred to join him, which Manfred would have done and there would have been no need to chase him down the street. But what if it *was* him?

He needed to get out of the cold though. He jogged, which kept him warm, towards Volkspark Friedrichshain where his uncle lived. When he arrived he was on his guard and again sensed all was not well. His uncle was as security conscious as his father and would never have left any of the entrances to the grounds open and unattended. And... there were strangers guarding the front door!

He crept around the back of the house, managed to get into the gardens without being seen and made his way to the large shabby building where the gardening tools were stored. He quietly pushed open the door and eased himself inside. Even inside he still felt very cold and was beginning to lose the feeling in his hands. Shivering, he felt down behind a work bench and managed to dislodge a loose brick from the wall, behind it should have been the key to the basement… it wasn't there. When he tried the door he found it unlocked… he slipped inside.

The lanterns were still hanging in place, unused. He listened out and allowed time for his eyes to adjust to the darkness. The only sound was of his own shivering breath. He left the lanterns. He didn't need light; he knew the layout of the rooms and passageways backwards. Anyway, if there were others down here they would be using lanterns, and he would have the advantage of seeing them before they saw him.

He crept forward, towards the scullery area, where, not only would it be a little warmer, he would also be able to see into the house through holes in the wall. As he entered the chamber he halted as he heard a sharp intake of air, a gasp. He saw what looked like a bundle of something in the corner, and as he was trying to make out what it was, a quiet voice muttered, "Manfred?"

It was his cousin, Amy! And with her, clinging to her, was little Thomas.

Chapter 13

Tuesday 29th January 2008

Jennifer was bored and depressed; release from her detention had turned out to be such an anticlimax. She'd been looking forward to meeting ordinary people, shopping, going out on the town, dancing... but she hadn't reckoned on a complete loss of confidence. Despite the regular visits of her probation officer and the obligatory rehabilitation course with social services, she still felt terrified of venturing out. She hadn't mentioned her fears; after all, those fears were her problem.

And she didn't want to be seen as needy. That's why she hadn't spoken to her sister about the problem. After so long apart, she didn't really know her sister anyway, not as a sister.

She'd learnt to drive while inside and Rachel had organised a new Ford Focus for her when she moved into the flat but, so far, she hadn't even built up enough courage to go down to the garage and start the damn thing, let alone drive it.

She would laugh if it wasn't so tragic; since being freed, her only friend had been a fucking canary...

She hadn't noticed him at first. The bird must have been twittering away for ages, maybe days, before she became conscious of his existence; the tweets came from next door's balcony. To see onto the neighbour's balcony meant she had to lean out precariously over the wall of her own. Not only dangerous, but potentially embarrassing; if the person living there discovered her peeking into his or her property that way… She overcame the problem by taping a small mirror onto the end of a broom handle, and she could see around the corner with ease.

And there he was. A small yellow creature perched in a cage, sitting, happily chattering away, its little beak going nine to the dozen. Jennifer whistled. The bird stopped chirping. She watched his reflection in the mirror, head cocked to one side. Jennifer whistled again. The bird cheeped. Again she whistled; again the bird cheeped. This time he also ruffled his feathers. And Jennifer laughed. It had been the first nice experience she'd encountered since her release.

Two weeks went by… the two buddies secretly passing time together before Jennifer began to worry. Her little friend was distressed. She could tell, there was less and less chattering, and when she whistled the reply was in a sad and drawn out lower tone. Birdie produced a very poor reflection in the mirror. Jennifer wanted to release him, to free him… but.

Before she realised it another two weeks had passed by, and for a few days now there had been no chattering, and in the mirror, just an empty cage.

She was feeling pretty low. It was time for bed, unhappiness physically drained her. Her anxiety needed to be overcome; it had resulted in her faltering when she should have acted quickly. Because of her lack of action a friend had suffered.

* * *

They were sitting on the floor. Although the light was poor Manfred could see they were both very distressed, especially Thomas. He knelt down and reached out to comfort them. "What has happened?" he asked quietly.

Thomas looked at him blankly and didn't answer, and Amy took a while before she spoke. "Manfred... they killed Mama and Papa... and Freddy. We watched... I watched them do it and there was nothing I could do... and they're after us."

Manfred felt himself tense up. A peculiar sensation spread throughout his body as he realised that his parents... and his sister Anita... No... that wasn't possible. He tried to put the thought to one side, ignore it. The idea was preposterous. But he was suddenly frightened and stumbled over his own words. "What... what do you mean?"

Manfred could only just make out what Amy was telling him, she spoke so quietly and wasn't very coherent; he had to work out and rearrange the words before they meant anything. "Those men, the ones in the house, they killed Papa, then Mama and then Freddy. They strangled them. Uncle Johann had them killed." Manfred allowed the words to sink in and then prompted her to continue, to explain more clearly. "The man who killed them was called Carl Froebel, and he told Freddy that he and his brothers were hired to kill our family for Johann Heinrich Huth, for Willie von Seeckt, for Hans Hasenclever and for Peter Emmerich. He asked Freddy, who are these people? My uncles, he replied, and then Froebel asked, now, where are your sister and your little brother?" Freddy knew we were here, I could tell, but he didn't tell them." She sneered, "He didn't tell them, Manfred. Then the fat man, this Carl Froebel, strangled Freddy; the same way as I watched him strangle Mama and Papa."

Manfred whispered, "There are men still here, there are men at my house as well and they chased me"

Amy considered this; her breathing slowed as she regained some control. She didn't say anything, she didn't have to.

"Maybe my family are not dead. Perhaps they were out, like I was. When they return… I need to go back to the house, to warn them of the danger that awaits them… when they return." He stood and held out a hand, "Come on, come with me, you can't stay here. It's only a matter of time before they find you."

Amy knew this was true, she had already heard them try the doors from inside the house to the basement area. Sooner or later they would be here. She stood and pulled Thomas up. He remained silent and followed along the passageway, out of the basement and into the garden store room. When there, Amy quietly searched the building and found some leather coats and fur hats, much too big for her and Thomas, but fitted Manfred fairly well. It didn't matter, at least they wouldn't freeze. They found gloves and thick socks as well.

The journey to Manfred's house was slow and foreboding. In his heart he knew that his parents and sister were dead.

Chapter 14

Adam had had the block of flats under surveillance for the last three days and although he had seen neither head nor hair of Jennifer Emmerich, he was convinced she was there. He'd seen nothing to deter him from going through with his plan. He was also confident that she was alone. He had managed to obtain the entry code into the foyer by watching the postman and another guy, who he assumed to be a maintenance engineer of some sort. Residents had their own key. The street lighting was poor, but it was a clear night, so not to arouse the suspicions of anybody who might be watching, he pretended to use a key as he quickly tapped the numbers on the key pad. He heard the electric catch release - so far so good. He glanced at the name plate as he slid into the lobby and wondered who S Mannion was. A new identity? Or a boyfriend? Or perhaps it was just the name of a previous tenant. He was taking a chance by not checking this out but he had become impatient, and he could think of no better way of finding out… other than to do what he was doing.

He was nervous. He held his trembling hands out in front of him and concentrated hard to steady them. He then felt for the flick knife in his pocket; it was still there, why shouldn't it be, and this gave him the tiny boost of courage he needed. He reached the second floor and the door to the apartment. It had a Yale lock, which pleased him, and a high security deadlock, which did not. He had been practicing picking Yales for a long time, practicing for this very moment and had become quite expert. But deadlocks; those were something else.

He silently worked his needles until there was a click, turned the barrel and gently pushed open the door. The other lock had not been used. No squeaks. He waited. Patience was the name of this game. He checked his watch, just after one am; everything was very dark and, thankfully, very quiet. He slipped silently into the hallway, controlling his breathing as he did so, his heart was thumping and he paused… waited for it to settle down. His body urged him forward, faster, in anticipation of what lay ahead, but he had coached himself well enough not to make *that* mistake. He continued slowly, eyes adjusting to the darkness as he did so. He edged his way along the wall, each foot forward, lowered gently, careful of hazards which may have been left on the floor, or of low tables, or anything waiting to crash and wake up the world, and to destroy his! He had to be so careful not to brush against hanging pictures or mirrors.

He drew the knife from his pocket and flicked out the blade, producing a slight click. He waited to see if the noise had disturbed anybody. Everything seemed good. His mouth was dry. The first door he came to was on the opposite side of the hall and was wide open, through it an empty lounge. The hall was L shaped and he turned right. The next two doors were opposite each other - the kitchen and the bathroom, both unoccupied.

Peering through the darkness, he made out the last two doors, which clearly led to the bedrooms; the one on the left *had* to be the largest; that would be the one he would have chosen to sleep in had he lived here.

Both doors were closed. He quietly twisted the knob of the one on the right, the smaller, and held his breath as he oh, so slowly, pushed it open, making a gap just wide enough to be able to peer around and into the room. An empty bed! Brilliant! He was right again - now for the final door.

Again he slowly, even more slowly, turned the knob and pushed open the door. He heard the gentle, consistent breathing of a lone body and a rush of nervous tension engulfed him, so much so that he almost passed out. He took deep, silent breaths. When he felt better he continued to push open the door, then crept to the side of the bed and peered down. In the darkness he could just make out the figure of a body sleeping in the foetal position, its head facing his knees. He felt its warm breath on his left hand as he reached over with his right, and readied himself. Then, in a single move he jumped on top of the body and pinned it down, clasped one hand over the mouth and raised the knife to its throat with his other.

Chapter 15

She was instantly awake and managed to straighten her body, but the weight on top of her and the tightness of the sheets restrained any major movement. Her arms were trapped. She felt the sharpness of the blade against her throat. The hand without the knife was over her mouth and his face was only inches from hers; his breath was clammy and hot. They were both motionless for, what seemed to her, an age. The hand across her face made breathing difficult, panic set in and she began to struggle.

"Make a sound and I'll kill you," he whispered, and slowly removed the hand from her mouth; she gulped air. She felt the weight of his body shift as he leant to his left, to turn on a bedside lamp. The light momentarily blinded her and then he was back, his face right up against hers, she tried, but couldn't make out if she knew him, his face was too close. He backed away and she was able to study him; he looked familiar but, no, she had no idea who he was.

He was startled by what he saw. He had expected to find thirteen year old Jennifer Emmerich, not a twenty-one year old woman. Was this Jennifer? In this confused state he dropped his guard slightly and she managed to slip her arms up from under his weight. Before he realised what had happened she'd pushed the knife away from her neck and a bucking body had thrown him from the bed.

To escape from the room she needed to jump over him, which she tried. He grabbed a foot and grappled her to the floor. He had lost the knife though. He pulled her to her feet and attempted to throw her back onto the bed; she was stronger than he had anticipated and it was a struggle. Eventually he overcame her, and was back on top... on the bed and in control, but he still didn't have the knife. He couldn't see it. He twisted his body to look over his shoulder, to check the bed and the floor behind. He spied it on the carpet and simultaneously noticed her night shirt had ridden up around her waist. She was naked beneath it and he felt embarrassed. This was a woman, not the little killer he had come to kill. And then he was conscious of her breasts pressed against his thighs.

He jumped up, flipped her over onto her stomach and pulled her left arm up between her shoulder blades. This was painful and she struggled in vain to get free as he retrieved the knife from the floor. Back on top of her he paused to think. He felt her body breathing heavily beneath him. Stupid; of course she's a woman. He should have imagined her as a grown woman in his many deadly fantasies, not as the kid who had killed his brother – that way he wouldn't have been confused by her looks, her size. Again he brought the knife to her throat and she gasped as she felt the sharp blade against her flesh. This was it. She closed her eyes, held her breath and waited for the moment, then, nothing.

Adam relaxed his grip. The knife slid from his fingers and landed on the floor with a thud. He slowly rolled over the side of the bed, dropped to his knees and began to sob. Now it was Jennifer's turn to be confused. She slowly turned over and sat up, pulling her night-shirt down over herself at the same time - and stared at her attacker.

She uttered a name, which was just audible. "Adam Saunders?" With streams of tears down his face he stood and started for the door. "Oh no you don't," she shouted, and jumped up to bar his way. She pushed him back onto the bed. "What the fuck are you doing?"

"I couldn't," he blubbered.

"You couldn't what?"

He buried his face in his hands, blood, snot and tears running through his fingers; his nose was bleeding. She fetched a towel from the bathroom and handed it to him. As she did so she thought of that moment with Billy, when she had handed him her top.

"You wanted to kill me, revenge for Billy. Adam, I swear to you, I didn't do it. And I will kill whoever did, I promise you that. It's my life's mission. I loved Billy, he was my best friend. I did not kill him."

"You were found guilty." He sniffed and wiped his face, the anger was subsiding and in its place, embarrassment.

"Yeah, maybe I was, but I'm telling you now that I *am* innocent."

His mind was foggy. Now what? Should he just get up and go? Will she call the police? Should he still kill her? That thought was ridiculous. That was the one thing that was no longer going to happen. "Now what?" he asked, more to himself than to her.

She knew what he meant. Adam was still sobbing like a child. In fact he *was* still a child. She recalled that he was a good three, maybe four years younger than her. "It's okay Adam. I don't blame you for what you just tried to do, but," she shrugged, "you couldn't do it.

Not because you couldn't. It's because, deep down, you know I didn't kill Billy. Children who kill come from deprived and depraved backgrounds, or they have something wrong in their head. They are animals, scum. I met their kind in detention, maybe not killers, but still scum. I was forced to mix with them and somebody is going to pay for sending me there." Jennifer knelt at his knees. "Adam, I was never deprived of anything. I was loved. My family was normal. How could somebody like me do such a thing, especially to Billy?"

Adam was not listening. The little speech was wasted on him, he just wanted to leave. "I have to go. I'm sorry."

"No way, you'll go when I tell you to. If you try to leave I'll call the police, tell them that you broke in and..." She left *that* thought floating.

He was taken aback by this, the last thing he expected. Maybe she was joking. His brain was issuing instruction to leave but she didn't give him the time to physically move.

"No, I'm sorry, you can't go." She stressed, very assertively.

He couldn't come to terms with what he was hearing. Surely she had to kick him out; for what he'd just tried to do. She started to frighten him and it showed on his snotty face, a frightened little animal, cornered and confused. The state he was reduced to revived a forgotten strength of hers. Control! This felt like control and she was enjoying the feeling. A plan was evolving, slowly emerging and taking shape. She jumped up. "I've got some cider, come on, let's sit in the lounge. I'll put some music on. You need to relax"

"I... I can't drink, I need to drive home." It was the only thing he could think of saying, but he knew he was trapped, how was he going to get out of this? This was not right. Only minutes before she was his brother's murderer... Now she wasn't? Well, she had planted that seed in his mind and now it was growing fast, so fast that his hatred and his anger had completely dissipated and left him floundering like a fish out of water. The situation had completely overwhelmed him, and the harder he tried to think of ways to get out of it, the less he came up with. All he wanted was to leave. He never wanted to see this *woman* again. What does she want? She turned and left him sitting on the bed.

Jennifer was ecstatic. She wanted to whoop and skip and found it almost impossible not to laugh aloud. She locked the front door using the deadlock and slid the key under the sofa... it was lucky that she hadn't been too security conscious before; he would never have been able to break in! She then went to the fridge and selected two bottles of medium dry cider. She had stocked up with various ciders, beers and alcho-pops with the idea of learning how to drink, to be ready for when she began to socialise. Well, she thought, now she was about to socialise and learn to drink at the same time. She selected some music, *The Verve*. Not too loud... and dimmed the lights, no, too dim, and adjusted them up again. Perfect. Now, where was that boy?

Adam soon found himself sitting on a large, expensive and very comfortable easy chair listening to familiar music, his dad had played this particular CD a lot before he upped and moved to Spain with Mum. He noticed his hand trembling as he tentatively sipped his drink. He waited for Jennifer to say something.

He didn't wait long.

"Tell me about Belfont, what's happened?" she asked.

Belfont? Nothing much happened there worth talking about. He looked at her sitting on the large sofa, still wearing just the shirt; if the circumstances were different? She looked terrific and sexy and he was still finding it difficult to come to terms with the obvious fact that she was older now than she was eight years ago. "Don't you think you should get dressed?"

"Listen pal, this is my home. You broke in here, in the middle of the night. Why should I get dressed? You didn't seem to mind earlier."

"That was different."

"Different, in what way? Because you were trying to kill me! Well, get used to it, I'm staying dressed just as I am."

To be honest he didn't really mind, in fact he couldn't believe he'd complained. She looked fantastic in the shirt, though he worried that she looked too fantastic... was she setting out to trap him? He might not be able to control himself. *Where did that thought come from?* There was no way he had the guts to do anything of the sort, not now anyway. He had destroyed any manly, aggressive cell that previously existed in his previously manly, aggressive body. He felt both a failure and a fool.

They both sat silent for a while. When she leant forward to pick up a packet of cigarettes and a lighter from the floor he caught a glimpse of her breasts under the flimsy top. He couldn't help it, his eyes lingered slightly too long and she caught his act of voyeurism. He felt himself redden. She was toying with him.

She offered him a cigarette. "No thanks." He tried but failed to stare her out as she sat back; holding the cigarette to one side and allowing the smoke to escape through her parted lips.

"I was sorry to hear about your mum," said Adam.

This took the wind out of her sails. She shrugged. "She believed, you know, that I did it, killed Billy. And now she has died before I can prove I didn't. I'll never forgive her for thinking *that*, or for dying."

"It was a shock. After Billy died we never saw your family. Your dad had his strokes, Rachel went to Cambridge and, well, we never saw any of them. But, because they still lived at the farmhouse, it was still a quite a shock when we heard about the crash."

Jennifer wanted to talk. She also wanted to flirt, flirting was new to her and she was having a good time. She also wanted to make him suffer. Who did he think he was, the little shit-face, breaking into her house. However, she wanted to talk. "She wasn't my real mum."

Adam didn't answer.

"My parents fell from a ferry and drowned when I was five years old. Michael Emmerich was my dad's brother and he and Susan adopted me, became my parents. I think that's why she was prepared to believe that I did it; a real mum would never think that."

"I didn't know that… that you were adopted."

"It was never a secret, but I was only young, and I almost forgot my real parents. I consider Michael as my dad. In fact it had been a long, long time since I thought about my birth parents; until I was locked away."

"Considering she's not your real sister, you and Rachel look so alike."

"Well, we *are* cousins."

Adam was silent as he digested the news.

"What do people think, believe?" she asked.

"Think about what?"

"Well, about my mum's death, people must have had an opinion."

"Most people think it strange, how it happened, going off the road like that, nobody else involved. The police left an open verdict you know."

"Yes, of course I know." This bloke was a fucking idiot. She might have been locked up in a young offenders detention centre, but they would obviously have told her everything. "What about Billy, don't you want to find out who killed him?" she asked.

"I haven't had time to think about that. Up until tonight I thought it was you. But yes, of course I do. Do you know, or have any idea?"

Jennifer took a long draw on her cigarette and then flicked ash into the ash tray. "No. Rachel says she will help, investigate. She says that her firm will help as well."

"Her firm?"

"Yes, didn't you know? Dad helped her get a job with the legal firm who defended me. She did really brilliantly at Uni. She got a Doctorate of Philosophy in Law. One of the best graduates in law to come out of Cambridge that year, so they say."

"She's a lawyer? No, I didn't know that. I don't suppose anybody from the village does. In many ways your family may as well have moved away."

"My sister refused to have anything to do with me until Mum died, said that I had ruined her life."

"What made her change her mind?"

"I don't know, not really. She says she doesn't know either, she just said that she sat down one day and thought about it and realised that I couldn't have done it. Suddenly she stopped hating me, just like that! After four years."

Adam himself thought he may be having the same experience as Rachel, a sudden realisation. He pondered on that for a while, and then asked, "How come you didn't scream or shout when I was, you know…?"

Jennifer let out a short laugh and pulled her feet up under her body. She noticed his involuntary glance before turning away.

"When I was locked up, any disagreements or fights were carried out without a fuss, no shouting or swearing, you just had to quietly get on with it. If you made a noise it was when you'd had enough, when you were beaten. That's when they would come and break it up. I never ever made a sound - never!" She stubbed out the cigarette and fetched two more drinks from the kitchen, lagers this time.

Adam protested. "No thanks, I'd better not."

She carried on pouring as though he hadn't said anything. She walked around the room and stopped in front of him, conscious all the time of his eyes following her. She placed the full glass next to the half full glass on the small coffee table beside him. This was the first time in her life that she'd ever flirted so openly... she wondered how she was doing. "You've got some catching up to do," she said, meaning the drink.

Adam couldn't take any more of this. He stood up and announced that he was going to leave, walked to the main door; only to find it locked. "Where's the key?"

"I told you, you're not leaving."

"I'll break down the door."

"Go ahead, that'll wake up everybody in the block. Then the police will turn up. What will you tell them? Oh, I just broke into the flat to kill her but changed my mind, and then she wouldn't let me leave. If I was a policeman I would really believe that."

"Why do you want me to stay?"

"Because I do. And because you broke into my flat and tried to kill me, I think you owe me, to do just as I want you to."

"I still don't understand why. Why do you want me to stay?

Jennifer disapproved of his pointless questioning and refused to say anymore on the topic.

"I want to leave" He demanded.

"No."

"Give me the key. I don't care about the police. I'll break down the fucking door."

"What about your knife?"

"Wha..." This stopped him in mid sentence. The knife! "The knife."

"Yeah you moron, the knife. You'll not stand a chance. Just being in possession of a flick knife is one thing. Trying to kill somebody with it, well..." She knew she had him. They stood opposite one another like wild-west gunslingers, each waiting for the other to make the first move. Then she undid the top buttons of her shirt and it slid down her body; she was completely naked and Adam, stunned, stared, rooted to the spot. She walked over to the music system and changed the CD; she put on some Bob Marley, then walked to the couch, sat and sipped her drink. "What's the matter? Never seen a naked woman before?"

"You're a whore, get some clothes on."

"I'm actually still a virgin, and I'm staying just like this. Sit down and drink." But he didn't. He remained exactly where he was.

Jennifer stood up, walked across the room and grabbed the front of his jeans. "You're hard. That can't lie."

He lashed out with a fist and caught the side of her face. Shocked, she raised her hand to her mouth and touched her lip. There was blood on her fingers, and then she could taste it. She punched him straight on the nose, which had been damaged earlier, and blood spattered easily. Then she couldn't stop herself, she attacked him with all her strength, pounding, punch after punch; the naked woman pummelling the cowering man. He fell to the floor, as much trying to escape the punches as actually being floored, but this didn't stop her. She followed him down with more punches. Then she straightened up and took a wild kick. Pain shot through her foot and up her leg as the kick connected with his head.

Adam jumped up and wrapped his arms around her, pinning her arms beside her body and hung on until she ceased struggling. When she finally did, he waited for a moment longer, and then released her. He gently pushed her away, but couldn't take his eyes off her.

Jennifer walked from the room, slamming the door behind her, and climbed into her bed. Her heart was pounding. She closed her eyes but the pounding didn't stop. Bastard! Bastard! Bastard! Completely tense and unable to think straight, she felt him climb into the bed beside her. He was naked.

Chapter 16

Berlin

After leaving the cellar, Manfred, Amy and Thomas went to Manfred's family home. However, Froebel's men were still hanging around. They passed unseen and trudged south through the city in silence, the cold wind sapping their strength, until they reached an abandoned industrial area. Unable to walk any further, they huddled together for warmth inside a building littered with unused machinery and racks of rusting metal. Machines and metal radiated coldness, but at least they were out of the wind.

Whoever awoke first disturbed the other two. All were stiff and drained of emotion. Their words floated away as clouds of mist.

"I have some money," said Manfred, "We'll find a tea room, it will be warm."

"I don't want to eat," said Amy.

"I want to be warm."

"I want to see Frederick."

Manfred shrugged, not sure how to reply. "First, we need to drink, and then to find somewhere better than this, to stay."

"We could check your house again. Maybe those men have left."

"And maybe they'll come back. The next time I see them I want to kill *them*, not the other way around. We need to be prepared, to make plans. No. First we have to get warm, then I'll go back, to warn Papa."

"If…" Amy stopped herself, and then nodded. She knew Manfred needed to do this.

They found a tea room. It was dirty, as were the staff and the noisy clientele. The tin mugs were hot though, and the pleasure of wrapping their hands around them was a joy they savoured in silence.

Manfred bent forward and tentatively sipped the hot fluid… it was thick and strong and it burned his lips, but he didn't care. He closed his eyes and enjoyed the sensation of the liquid descending towards his stomach. He was concentrating on the warmth but hadn't missed the interest they had aroused in the establishment. They were unkempt and grubby after their bitter night and the outer garments they were wearing were ill fitting. But they were still a different class to these people. However bad their night had been, the three still stood out as kids with money.

Amy hadn't missed the curiosity they'd sparked either, and looked Manfred in the eyes… *you brought us here, you sort it.*

Manfred continued to sip his tea, fully aware of the change of atmosphere, but he wanted to savour the warm liquid, however foul it tasted. Amy and Thomas studied him, wondering how he was going to deal with the situation.

He slipped a hand inside his coat and pulled out a crumpled bank note and slowly and deliberately placed it onto the table in front of them, ironing it flat with a forefinger, then pinned it there with his now empty mug; it was a 500 mark note. The clatter and babble reduced to just a murmur. Amy and Thomas continued to drink, intrigued. Manfred sat back in his chair… and waited, daring somebody to come forward. As he waited, he slid his right hand inside his coat, unseen fingers crossed. As far as any of these strangers knew, those fingers could have been stroking the trigger of a loaded pistol.

But 500 marks was a lot of money, and one man, broad shouldered and mean looking, stood, and approached the three. "I'm going to take that," he growled, his eyes fixed on the bank note. "What are you going to do about it?"

Manfred nonchalantly studied the man; he was a brut, big. "What could I do?" he replied. "If you want to take it, I could never stop you. But, if you do, that's all you'll get." He puffed himself up slightly. "However, if I was to give it to you, that would be a different matter. And if you then had it in your heart to assist us, there would be more where that came from, much more."

The man thought about this, gave an approving nod, and then a thin smile crossed his face. "How could somebody like me help three little rich kids like you?"

"Well, for a start, we need a place to stay, somewhere very private. And warm."

"And I get 500, just for that?"

"This 500 is yours. You will get more when you help us."

After a short consideration, the man pulled a chair and joined them at the table, held out his right hand and introduced himself. "Willie Wirth, decommissioned captain of the Marine Brigade Erhardt."

Manfred pulled out his hand and clasped the captain's. "Thank you sir. Take the money; I'm sure you've made the right decision." However, he didn't introduce himself, nor Amy or Thomas.

Amy was impressed by the quick thinking of her cousin, but hoped he had more cash on him; this giant of a man looked a tough ruffian and she wouldn't want to cross him. She studied him closer, and her stomach churned; his looks, his build, his mannerism… he could easily have been any one of Carl Froebel's gang. An urge to kill him began to grow from within…

Willie Wirth looked around the tea room, scowled, and the place reverted to its original noisy establishment as everybody returned to minding their own business. Obviously, Amy wasn't alone in not wanting to cross this man. Manfred ordered four teas and, as they drank, explained to Willie Wirth what was required of him.

An hour later the three found themselves in a room on the top floor of a run down tenement block. Many of the upper apartments remained vacant because of the distance to the latrines and, because of that, they had fallen into poor condition. There was one damp and smelly bed; more a wide bench than what they were used to. The disused factory where they had slept the previous night would have been just as good, apart from, in one corner, there was a stove. "What do we burn in it?"

"Wood."

"Can you get some for us?"

"Collecting wood is a job for women and children." Wirth assured Manfred though, that he would keep them free from harm or interference. He also told them that he lived on the ground floor. It turned out that he was the self appointed caretaker of the block; he selected the tenants and collected the rents. He would give Manfred and his cousins a couple of days to settle in before discussing their account.

When he left, he took Thomas with him down the three flights of stairs, who returned a few minutes later with half a box of matches and a bundle of kindling. Manfred showed him how to light the fire, and soon the stove began to radiate some heat.

"I need to go back to my house and check on Papa," said Manfred. "Both of you should stay here and get settled. Perhaps you could find more wood."

"If the men have gone, what will you do? If Karl Richard and your Mama are not there don't wait for them, it'll be too dangerous."

"Papa has a hidden place where he keeps personal things. I'll leave a message, a note. He also keeps cash there. I'll also collect my identity papers…" Manfred was trying hard to convince himself that his parents and sister were safe, but negative thoughts continually pounded at his fragile confidence.

"Remember, Mama and Papa and Freddie were murdered on the orders of our uncles. Whatever you do, don't trust them. Don't trust any family member other than me or Thomas."

"Or my family."

Amy was tempted to say that she and Thomas was his family, for his safety.

Manfred continued. "I still can't believe that they would do this. We were all in Berlin for Uncle Johann's sixtieth birthday. Why would he invite us all if he hated us that much?"

"I've been thinking about that," said Amy. The three of us, and Freddie and Anita, would normally be away at school. The only reason we were all in Berlin was for the party. It was a rue to get us all here, together with our parents. It was a perfect moment. What I don't understand is, why?"

"Papa and Uncle Albert were having a big dispute with the other four. I don't know much about it, but Papa and your papa had backed Doctor Kapp and the anti-government movement in March, against the wishes of Uncle Johann and the others. Doctor Kapp had visited our house and held meetings with our fathers, I met him twice. Grandpa Huth, when he was alive, insisted that the family kept politicians at arm's length, use them, but don't get involved. Our fathers broke that rule… and it now seems that we've all had to pay the price."

Amy was quiet for a while. "I know that you have to go back… please be careful."

Manfred looked around the room. "I'll also bring back a sack of bedding."

Back at Lichterfelde-Ost, the men had gone. To be doubly sure, Manfred waited for as long as his patience allowed and then slipped into the house through the iron gates at the back. He had an urge to shout for his sister and run through the rooms but, if his family was here, he'd soon find them without being quite so careless. The house was empty.

He'd expected the place to have been ransacked, but everything seemed in order; as if the occupants had just slipped out for a short while. He thoroughly searched each room in turn, hoping to find a clue or an indication of the state of things. He filled one sack with some of his clothes and another with the bed linen he'd promised Amy. He collected his own valuables; watches, a wallet containing a few hundred marks and the ring his father had given him when he had returned to school at the end of the last holiday. He also took his mother's costume jewellery. He then went to his father's study and to the hidden drawer; it was empty.

He checked the safe. All the real family valuables, identity papers and passports had gone and, again, no cash.

He heard footsteps!

From behind a heavy curtain he listened to the unmistakeable voices of his uncles, Johann Heinrich Huth and Peter Emmerich.

"Don't get all righteous now Peter. It had to be done."

"I know. We had no choice regarding Karl-Richard or Albert. But it seems so un-Godly that the wives and children should also have had to perish."

"The assets of the family must stay intact. It was the only way. Anyway, it's done now. What about Froebel and his brothers?"

"They really do seem to have fled. The others in the gang have been taken care of. From that end, it all went according to plan, and there is nothing linking our involvement, here or with *those* killings, but the Froebel brothers could become a problem."

"Froebel has turned out to be more intelligent than I gave him credit for. Still, as you say, everything else has gone to plan, we'll take care of the loose ends over time. The most important thing is, the family and all its wealth are united again. Chin up; we now have more than a birthday to celebrate."

Manfred was still shaking with rage as he relayed what he'd heard to Amy and Thomas when he got back to the tenement block.

"We have to become strong," said Amy. "I promise you that every one of those uncles and their families will all die a terrible death and that all the wealth of the Huth Family will belong to us. I shall plan to do this, even if it takes a whole life-time. In fact I shall prepare my children to continue my promise if it hasn't been completely fulfilled by the time of my own death."

Thomas didn't speak. He hadn't spoken since *the cellar*. He produced a small knife and slid it across the palm of his left hand; as young blood eased from the wound, he held it high, in front of him. Manfred took the knife and followed suit, as did Amy. The three hands met and clasped and their blood became one.

They were not comfortable, but they were warm. As night fell they huddled together as best they could on the narrow bed, still talking about their murderous plans. Amy snuggled into Thomas's back, and Manfred into hers. She felt Manfred's hand beneath her skirt; she'd been expecting it.

Before, when they used to watch the staff through the gap in the scullery wall, she and Manfred experimented in these things, and she'd laughed and enjoyed it. The fact that it was so clandestine and potentially dangerous, made their coming together so exciting. Now it felt good, but that was all. She felt him, warm inside her, and then she slept.

The following day, she and Manfred returned to Volkspark Friedrichshain, to her home. She felt just a twinge of remorse; other things now consumed her thoughts. As at Manfred's home, most valuables and forms of identity had been removed. She collected warm clothing for herself and Thomas, some items that she thought might be useful and a box of family photographs. She also collected her father's cut throat razor and sharpening belt.

* * *

Willie Wirth stopped at the open door and looked in. Eyes darted around the small room before settling on Amy. "Tell your cousin to come and see me," he instructed. "We need to talk about the rent."

Amy was wearing unlaced black boots and a large shirt covered by a heavy trench coat. "You can talk to me," she said.

Wirth hungrily eyed up the young figure beneath the bulky clothing. Too many buttons of the shirt had been left undone for the girl to be totally innocent, and this observation gave him rights! "Of course, we could maybe factor in a discount."

She stepped back as he entered the room, the door gently closing behind him.

"Could we?" she said. "Money is so hard to come by."

Frau Hestler waited with fingers crossed for Wirth at the door to his apartment, praying that her husband didn't come home early, for she already had an arrangement with the caretaker similar to the one that was being negotiated with Amy on the top floor... and the rent was due.

Most Fridays she didn't give much thought about what she did, after all, Wirth was normally in his apartment, waiting, and when he was, the encounter was generally over almost before it began, and the speed of it suppressed feelings of guilt.

Occasionally though, it wasn't over so quickly. After such occasions she felt dirty and deceitful, and despised whoring herself. After those occasions she hated him; the things he made her do.

And sometimes it was even worse, when she had to wait. As she waited now. Waiting made her nervous. Fear of exposure made her nervous. Jingling nerves induced emotions, sensations. The erupting sensations from deep within revealed a truth about herself... that she craved for the fieriness and violence of the forbidden act, so unlike the lazy and infrequent sexual activities with her husband. She whored herself to pay the rent, but when she allowed herself to analyse it, she knew that she'd do it for free! Where was he?

She was frantic by the time the new girl from the top floor walked down the stairs and opened Wirth's door.

"Come in." Amy stepped back, holding the door open, a welcoming gesture.

Frau Hestler hesitated. "Who are you? I need to see Herr Wirth."

Amy smiled. "Reason?" It was asked with kindness.

"What's it to you?"

Amy ignored the terseness of the words as Frau Hestler entered. "Because I am the caretaker of the block. What do you want?"

"Caretaker?"

"New caretaker. Herr Wirth has retired. Now, how can I help you?"

Frau Hestler's body screamed for attention and demanded answers. "What do you mean, retired? Herr Wirth said nothing of retiring. He would have told me! Where is he?"

"Retired. Do you owe rent?"

The woman didn't reply.

Amy took a punt. "So you had an arrangement with Herr Wirth. It was mentioned in conversation. However, now it's over and you'll have to pay, like others have to pay. If you want him to, I'll arrange for my cousin Manfred to speak with your husband about it, we might even allow a slight reduction, after all, *we* are not the greedy Willie Wirth."

Frau Hestler was speechless. She shook her head. "No!"

Amy raised her brow. "No? No what?"

The woman shoved her hands into her overcoat pocket and pulled out what notes she had. Not enough! "Please, you cannot talk to my husband about this." She trembled violently. "Please."

"Put your money away." Amy held out a steadying hand and laid it on Frau Hestler's. "Put the money back in your pocket and tell me about your arrangement with Herr Wirth."

"Please don't talk to my husband."

Amy didn't respond, just waited.

Frau Hestler pushed the cash back into her pocket. "It was Herr Wirth's idea. He said that I could keep the rent money, if I…"

"If you let him have you?"

Frau Hestler nodded.

"It's alright, you were just working for him," Amy shrugged, "and being paid. I fully understand. He tried to *recruit* me."

Frau Hestler's body was beginning to calm, allowing her brain to function properly. This woman was no more than a girl… but there was an aura about her, how she held herself, how she spoke, and what she said. "Where is he?"

"Dead!" The reply was so matter-of-fact.

"Dead?"

Amy nodded. "Now *I'm* the caretaker. And you are out of a job."

Frau Hestler would never have put it that way. "I'll survive." *As long as you don't talk to my husband.*

"I think that your business with Herr Wirth was *your* business. However, to keep it *your* business, you should consider working for me." Hestler understood the veiled threat. "In fact, working for me would be much more profitable, safer and, if you want, just as much fun. Can you read and write?"

Hestler feigned offence. "Of course."

"In that case, you can start right away. Write me a list of the names of all the tenants. We'll work out a new rent for them. You do this while I start to prepare this apartment, we're moving in."

"We?"

"The family." Amy liked the words.

"Where is Herr Wirth?" asked Frau Hestler again.

"Not here. He's waiting for the removal men, so don't concern yourself, it's not your business."

Frau Hestler slowly sat herself down at the table and Amy handed her a sheet of paper and a pen and some ink. She began to write: TENANTS - DECEMBER 24th 1920...

Chapter 17

**Mansion House, Hertfordshire.
Thursday 14th February 2008**

Nearly eighty-eight years later the vultures were circling. Who would be chosen to step into Amy's shoes? Who was soon to become head of the wealthiest crime family on the planet? Soon, surely, Amy must make her choice.

Except for one, the entire family was present at the mansion house to celebrate the old lady's birthday. The missing person was Terrence. He occupied an iron lung in a private London hospital. The event, as always, was very formal, and was one of the few annual occasions when the wealth of the family was openly flaunted, although the get-together was so private that only the family could appreciate it.

The Great Hall took up nearly half of the ground floor. Old masters, magnificent statues and gold leaf adorned surfaces that weren't solid oaks or marble, sumptuously textured or deep carpeted. Ben studied the family milling around him. A small handful of them regarded the surroundings with a familiarity that spoke volumes for their standing within the family; they were the elite. However, most, including himself, gazed in wonder at the riches.

Ben was fourth generation, just into his thirties. He had done the rounds, so to speak, and was standing by himself, with his hands tucked into his pockets; he fancied a cigarette and was toying with the notion of a walk in the gardens. He spied Marylyn sitting alone in a corner of the Great Hall, and thought about her and about Terrence. She was probably the only family member celebrating the occasion who didn't want to be here, preferring to be at Terrence's bedside.

Ben's mind drifted back to when he had helped her save him, pulling him from that well in the Pyrenees Mountains. Ironically, so the poor sod could spend the next eight years of his life in a bedridden hell; paralysed from the neck down and, other than gurgle or move his eyes, unable to communicate. And thinking about the saving of Terrence led to him thinking about Hans. He and Marylyn had both defied Hans! Christ, they must have been mad. He decided to give Marylyn a wide birth, in case being seen together reminded the killer about the episode.

He wondered about Hans. Who would he support? Although everybody was here because of Amy's birthday, their real interest was finding out who was to step into her shoes when she eventually dies. She was old, really old, and soon she *must* make *that* decision; who would she choose to be her successor?

There were two front runners; Edith and Dieter, and an outsider, Franz. They called Franz 'the policeman' because he oversaw the violent arm of the family and maintained order. He was the *Caporegime* at the head of his *soldati*. He was totally loyal to Amy and to the rules and the ways of the family, and if he wasn't chosen he would support whoever was… with his life.

His dominance of the clan and the absolute devotion to its customs made him a strong possibility for the promotion. However, he was eighty-four. Would his age go against him? And really, did he want the position?

That question was not an issue when it came to either Edith or Dieter. Both would probably kill to be *the one*, especially Edith. And... what about Hans? Would he kill for Edith? They were very, very close... but his loyalty to Franz was also indisputable.

Ben's and Marylyn's defiance of Hans probably meant that they had also crossed Edith, and, if she were chosen, Hans would certainly be her right hand man. Ben concluded that it would be a very dangerous time for him. The thought made him shudder.

Where Edith was ruthless and ambitious, Dieter was intelligent and ambitious. He controlled the business. As far as Ben knew, Dieter had never used an assumed name; he had absolutely no direct contact with anybody from outside the family. He ran the show; pulled the strings, and made the money. The rest did the legwork. This is what made him such a strong contender. Edith lived most of her life as the lawyer, Monica Davies. Amy existed in the real world as Hilda Von Seeckt. Ben himself went by any number of aliases. Even the killers, such as Hans and Peter, often used different identities. But never Dieter; he was entirely unknown by the outside world, and yet his tentacles spread to every continent and into the highest echelons of many great administrations. If Franz was the policeman of the family, Dieter was the puppet master of the world.

For Ben, Dieter would be the *almost* perfect choice, at least while Franz was around. Or even Franz, he would be acceptable. But in no way could he risk the possibility of Edith being chosen. Really, as far as Ben was concerned, the only good choice would be Ben himself. Then he was back to his same old line of thinking. He needed to be cleverer than Dieter, more ruthless than Edith and tougher than Franz. The trouble was; he was the only one who recognised those strengths in himself… at the moment.

It wasn't just for self-preservation that he yearned for the position. As head of this family he would have so much power. He found it deliciously difficult to comprehend the enormous wealth which would be at his disposal.

If Franz was chosen, Ben would have time to develop and display the attributes he possessed. However, if it went to Dieter, whilst it would solve one problem, the wait, for Ben and his dream, would be intolerable; Dieter wasn't even fifty.

The sight of Teresa interrupted his thoughts. Ben had not seen her for years. He caught her eye as she crossed the hall and she changed direction and headed for him.

"Hello Ben," she kissed him. "Long time no see." Ben thought she was beautiful, a twenty year old beauty.

"Hello Tess, wow, you've turned into a stunner. How was prison?" Teresa had spent time in detention as Holly Andrews; for the sole purpose of befriending Jennifer Emmerich.

She laughed. "Young person's detention centre if you don't mind. It went perfectly. It was a long time though."

"You gave up a lot for the family. I hope they recognise that. How is the Emmerich project going?"

"As well as can be expected, although I never realised that *boiling* a family would take so long."

"What's the situation, at the moment?"

"Jennifer Emmerich has just been released. Edith thinks that her sister and father are almost ripe for the picking; then it will be just a case of putting pressure on Jennifer. So, any time soon it will be the end of a lot of years of hard work."

"It will be worth it though. They're worth a lot of money."

"I think that Jennifer is going to be a hard nut to crack."

Ben detected a slight wobble in her voice as she said that. "How do you feel about that, becoming somebody's best friend just to get at her money, plus she'll be killed as soon as we have it."

Teresa shrugged. "It had to be done. And it's not just the money is it? You know what they did to Amy's family, to our family, in front of her very eyes."

"That wasn't Jennifer Emmerich, Tess; it was a long time ago, she doesn't even know it happened."

Teresa looked at him, a little lost for words, none of the others talked to her this way, and she had done her duty by befriending the girl, guiding her. Just as Edith manipulated them by pretending to be their lawyer, and just as the rest of the team carried out their tasks on the project.

Sensing her confusion, Ben changed tact, "Just teasing you, look, I think you're doing very well. It doesn't matter how close you become to somebody from outside the family, you have to always remember that he or she is exactly that, an outsider; what name did you use?"

"Holly Andrews." She was feeling a little uncomfortable and Ben sensed that she wanted to move on.

"Nice name. Do you fancy a walk in the gardens, or a cup of tea? I need a smoke." There was never any alcohol at these get-togethers. Nobody attended for fun.

"Later, I've been summoned to see Dieter," she said this with a certain degree of pride.

Ben hid his annoyance. "Good on ya, you had better not keep him waiting." *He could be number one soon*, he wanted to add, but didn't.

Ben watched the girl walk away and then returned his thoughts to Marylyn. She still sat alone. Most of the family indulged her, looking after Terrence the way she did. In fact, some of his generation openly admired her spunk. But what will happen to her after Terrence dies? And that can't be long now. However, he guessed that if Hans dared to lay a finger on her, there would be anarchy from within the younger generations…

It's strange how an idea suddenly hits a person.

Chapter 18

Northampton, England
Monday 18th February 2008

Councillor Denning was astounded when the policeman told him the news – somebody had deposited two hundred thousand pounds into his current account. It was the first he knew of the transaction – nevertheless, he was struggling to convince Detective Sergeant Maxwell that his ignorance of the matter was in fact the truth.

The policeman slammed the *Evening News* down onto the councillor's desk; the story was spread right across the front page - 'Councillor in Bribery Scandal'. "You're probably the only person who doesn't know." He leant forward over the newspaper as he spoke.

"Well, maybe, but it is the truth, I can assure you," pleaded Denning. "Who would put it there?" The councillor read the first couple of paragraphs of the article, which alleged that Leeston Associates had made the transaction. "And why would they do it?" As much to himself as to the policeman. He nervously swivelled his chair to face his computer, "Do you mind if I look at my account?" Without waiting for a reply he opened up his bank's site and typed in his details.

Maxwell laughed to himself, "No, go ahead." Then added, "You're on the committee which will decide who wins the Wenring shopping complex contract aren't you?"

"Yes. We finally make *the* decision next month."

"And Leeston Associates, are they bidding for that contract?"

"They are on the shortlist with three other companies."

"Are you going to award it to Leeston Associates?"

"I'm afraid I cannot tell you that!"

"What *can* you tell me?"

Denning opened up his current account, and there it was. The sight of his balance had distracted him a little and he had to ask Maxwell to repeat the question.

Maxwell leant forward and studied the screen along with the councillor, he also thought the statement looked good, and imagined how he would feel if his looked this healthy. He pulled up a chair and sat down. "If you can't tell me who the successful bidder is, perhaps you can tell me who you, personally, are backing."

The councillor looked around his office, double-checking for listening ears. "Surely you must know I cannot divulge that sort of information, even to you."

"Look Mr. Denning... Councillor, I need you to tell me. At the moment I believe you, if you were going to get a backhander, especially one this big, it would never have been placed in your bank account in such a brazen manner. Additionally... what makes me *really* suspicious is that the press got hold of the story so quickly. If I had to hazard a guess, I would say that somebody was trying to tarnish your good name, and queer Leeston Associate's pitch at the same time, you know, shit sticks, even if it's not your own." Maxwell looked the man directly in the eye. "Now, please, Councillor, between you and me, how close was Leeston Associates to winning that contract."

Denning really had no choice other than tell Maxwell, in confidence. He sighed. "The tenders submitted for the project are all so close that it has come down to a point scoring process based on previous work for this and other authorities, on other things, such as how much of the work will not be contracted out to third parties and by personal endorsements made by members of the committee. Additionally each company has to forward further information regarding their financial status. But it is still up for discussion and the contract could go any way. After these points are awarded there will be a further round of voting. However, if there is still no clear winner, it rests on my shoulders, I decide." He sucked his upper lip. "I have already recommended that the project is awarded to Leeston Associates, and I see no reason why, in three weeks time, I would change my decision."

"You do realise that this news," Maxwell pointed at the newspaper article, "has really put a spanner in the works, as far as Leeston winning the contract is concerned. If you read the article it clearly implies that Leeston Associates is trying to influence you using illegal methods. I would think that now, both you and Leeston are out of the equation."

Denning wanted to disagree, but could see where the detective was coming from. "I think I should call my lawyer."

"I think you should, and the council's lawyers." He then asked, "Is there anybody at Leeston Associates who you don't get on with, or somebody you think could do this?"

Denning considered the question carefully. "Honestly, no. I know their project team and all of the local directors very well, especially the contracts director. There is no reason for doing anything like this. I have met the Managing Director and the Chairman of the PLC which owns the company, however, I don't know them, and anyway, what would they have to gain from it?"

Maxwell stood. "Well, if you think of anybody or anything which could be important, let me know." He handed the councillor his card.

As soon as the policeman had left Denning went back to his bank account and dreamed. *If only it were mine.*

* * *

Maxwell found Detective Constable Theo Tester waiting for him in the reception of the council offices. Tester held up a memory stick and smiled, "Got it sir." While the senior policeman was interviewing the recipient of the two hundred thousand pounds, the constable had visited Denning's bank, which was just along the High Street, and had, without a warrant, managed to collect copies of statements of the Councillor's current and savings accounts held there. "Where are we off to now?" he asked his superior.

It took real effort for Maxwell to resist from asking how Tester had persuaded the bank to hand over the information. "We're going to visit the accounts department of Leeston Associates," he grunted.

"Is that around here?"

"Coventry Road commercial estate."

Theo followed his superior as they made their way to the car. "Coventry Road?" he asked.

"You should know where that is Tester, how long is it since you transferred here?"

"Nearly three months sir, it's just that I get the trading estates mixed up."

"It's the estate which is off the road which goes to Coventry." Theo didn't detect much humour in the reply.

"Okay." He didn't know Maxwell well enough to determine whether or not the man was reprimanding him. Just in case, he remained silent during the fifteen minute car ride and listened attentively to his superior's opinion of Denning and the bank transfer. They arrived at the company unannounced but the financial director immediately dropped whatever he was doing and hurried to reception to speak to the pair. After his initial display of disbelief and outrage at the newspaper allegations, he took them along to the accounts department and to the office of the accounts manager.

The manager's office was a room within a fairly large open plan area containing twelve work stations. Most of the desks were occupied; the one or two which were not belonged to staff conferring close by with a colleague. One such standing employee caught the eye of the young detective constable as the group crossed the room to the smaller office. The man looked to be in his late twenties, perhaps early thirties, medium build and walnut brown hair, and was attentively studying the screen of a colleague's computer, so much so that he didn't notice Tester's passing interest in him.

The policeman turned away, scuttled into the manager's office and spoke quietly to his boss. "Sir, do you mind if I pay a visit to Human Recourses, we passed the offices on the way here." Maxwell considered the request and determined that Tester must have a good reason for asking, *or he better had*. He sanctioned it.

Tester introduced himself to the HR manager, then, "Would it be possible for you to send me the records of all the personnel who work in your accounts department?" he asked. When she didn't answer straight away, Tester added, "You can get clearance for the action from your finance director, Mr Stonehouse."

"What do you mean by records?" she asked.

"Just names, dates when their employment with Leeston Associates began, and photographs, nothing else."

"I can probably give you those now, if that's all you want."

"That's all I want at the moment. Can you do it yourself? The fewer staff who know about it, the better." Just ten minutes later Tester had a second memory-stick in his pocket. He called Maxwell on his mobile and told him that he wanted to be picked up at the bus stop outside on the main road. He would explain his actions then.

* * *

"I recognised one of the workers in the accounts office sir. About four years ago, when I was doing my training in Birmingham I spent a period with the serious crime squad. While I was with them I tagged along with two officers working on the investigation into the murder of a villain known locally as Genghis Khan, real name Mohammed Khan. His nickname was Genghis because he always strutted around acting like a big-time gangster. He was actually the top man of a fairly large narcotics empire, but that only came out after his death. I'm pretty certain that the chap I clocked in the office was a friend of one of Genghis Khan's sons; I helped haul him in to be interviewed. The son was a right obvious crook, I remember that, although at the time this guy checked out clean, apart from the company he kept; however…"

Maxwell nodded. "Good work son, you did the right thing. Did he see you?"

"No. He was preoccupied with his work and I managed to slip out before he looked in our direction. I've got names, pictures and starting dates of everybody working in accounts." He held up the memory-stick.

Maxwell suddenly felt upbeat about the investigation. "Well, let's get back to the station and see what we have."

* * *

Maxwell fingered the two pictures, the one from Leeston Associates HR records and the one they had asked to be mailed from the M Khan Murder file; they were of the same man. "The fact that he goes by two different names make it all the more suspicious. Look, he's Graham Morris at Leeston Associates and Jonathon Wade in the Khan file." He swivelled and asked Theo, "What was the outcome of this murder investigation?"

"As far as I can remember, nothing sir." Tester stood behind Maxwell, looking over his sergeant's shoulder at the photographs.

"Um… Sit down." Tester sat. "What might connect a drug baron with a bribery scandal?" He was thinking aloud.

"It might be nothing, he may just be an innocent coincidence."

"If that's what you think why did you bother mentioning him?"

"That's not what I think, but it's a possibility. I would say the obvious connection is money."

Maxwell was nodding like a model dog in the rear window of a car. "Yes, I'm inclined to agree. I'm going to take what we have to the Chief."

Tester was disappointed.

The sergeant sensed his subordinate's frustration, "I have to Theo, it's what we call *procedure*." He said it with a little sarcasm, "Although I'm sure we'll both still be on the case. But all of this is beginning to look much, much bigger than our original bribery investigation, and it's likely to involve more than just our constabulary. I wouldn't be too disappointed though, whatever the outcome; you'll be getting lots of Brownie points with the way you acted." Maxwell patted the younger man's shoulder as he stood, "I'll let you know how I get on, but in the meantime, well done."

* * *

Twenty minutes later Theo Tester, DS Ivan Maxwell and their boss, DI Danny Hanson sat around a large table.

With them was DCI Brian Cook. "Good work Tester, you'll make a detective yet." He paused and pulled the two photographs in front of him. "I've spoken to Warwickshire's serious crime squad and they're in agreement with me, and that's *not* to pick up this person, but to have him placed under surveillance. Apparently, the only thing that was established with regard to the Khan murder was that it was an organised crime affair and Warwickshire are hoping Graham Morris, or whatever his name is, will lead us all to bigger fish. They have offered to share the costs and have given us the go-ahead for an around the clock watch. Danny, you'll lead the investigation."

DI Hanson nodded.

Cook continued. "While he's not at work I want Morris followed. I want details of everywhere he goes and everybody he comes in contact with. Find out where he lives *without* going through Leeston Associates… keep away from him at work, we don't want to spook him."

Chapter 19

Berlin 1925

By 1925 the German economy was recovering from the hardships brought about by their defeat in the Great War. The whole of Europe was being hauled out of the doldrums by the tremendous economic growth of the United States. A mixture of German creative government and the help of American loans produced a country which was, at last, beginning to flourish. Additionally, the relaxation of the censorship laws meant that not only was Berlin *the* place to find work, it was also the place to have fun. But, with its political extremes, it was also a place fraught with danger.

Manfred, Amy and Thomas had set up home on the top floor of a tenement block in Simeonstrasse, a very poor district and a place where being crafty, streetwise and having a predisposition for violence were all necessary requirements for economic advancement. A flagrant disregard of the law was also an asset. The three prospered greatly.

After the killing of Willie Wirth, Amy and Manfred spent a year trying, without success, to start a family, and Manfred became extremely violent because of the question of his manliness arose. Things came to a head when Amy was on the receiving end of one of his nasty attacks, which left her face slightly disfigured... when she smiled she looked quite hideous. But the attack delivered results, Amy had seemed forever with child since the beating, and Manfred was able to attach the label 'proud and successful father' to his reputation.

By 1925 Amy had had three children and was heavily pregnant with a fourth. She had also been busy economically, and, among other things, ran a string of girls who worked the streets of the centre of the city. The migrant workers in particular were a good source of income. At only eighteen years old she had developed a reputation as a hard but fair handler within the sex industry, and if anybody messed with Amy or her girls, they had to contend with Manfred. Not many did, and times were good. However, Amy was becoming successful enough for bigger fish to notice.

Things had also turned out well for the assassins, Carl Froebel and his two brothers. They had taken the Huth blood money but had fled Berlin having only completed part of their job; Amy, Manfred and Thomas survived.

After time, and with the lack of any news of those children, they had slipped back into the city and to their old way of life. They had built up a string of dubious business establishments: brothels, bars, casinos and drug dens. Operating in an era where anything went, without interference from the law, and where the violent and the unscrupulous thrived, they soon became top dogs.

Their pride and joy was the Glücklicher Mensch at Alexanderplatz, an opulent and noisy cabaret bar. It was in a grand office at the rear of the establishment that the three were interrogating a pretty Lithuanian girl. She was unsure what was happening after being picked up by Victor for, she had assumed, a bout of financially rewarding sex. These men, especially the fat one, were now asking some strange questions. "How long have you been working Alexanderplatz?"

She shrugged, "I don't know, a year maybe."

"And who is your boss?"

"That's not your business. If you want me, you pay. Nothing else is for sale," and she added indignantly, "we start, or I go."

"Now don't get upset," said Carl. "You'll have your fun and you'll be well paid. Neither me or my brothers are homosexuals." He looked around at the others, trying to muster a laugh.

The girl studied the fat man, momentarily visualising him naked with another man, and had to stifle a laugh. "But why the questions? Let's get on with it, I have to earn money."

Victor spoke. "We've been watching you. You're very good at your job and we would like you to work for us. However, for you to do that would mean we would have to pay compensation to your boss."

The girl puffed out a short laugh, "I would not want to tell her I was changing bosses. I think I would be in big trouble."

Her! "There's no need to tell her. We'll go to see her and make her an offer. Then you'll no longer have to work on the street, you'll also be under our protection."

She thought about this… and licked her lips at the idea of not having to get her arse cold, up against a backstreet wall. "Ok, her name is Amy."

"Amy who?"

The girl shrugged. She didn't know.

The Froebels didn't know of any Amy. "How can we get in touch with her?"

"I work from an office by the S-Bahn railway, opposite Maxine's department store. I hand my takings over to Amy's man."

"What's his name?"

The girl shrugged again.

"I think I know the offices, a row of five ramshackle huts," said Gerard.

"Yes. Our office is at the far end, with a rusty red door. It's the only one with curtains."

"Good," said Carl Froebel. "Now don't you say a word about this to anybody, you hear. Soon you'll be earning much, much more, and with good bosses." He smiled. "Now come over here."

She sidled over to him and he slipped his hand inside her clothing. He had nice fat fingers.

He was already breathing heavily, "Now I think it's time you earned some real money," he said. "Come on boys, let's see how good our new recruit actually is."

Wednesday 20th February 2008

Hanson, Maxwell, Tester and six other detectives sat around the conference table. Hanson had just finished summarising the investigation so far, and he turned to Maxwell. "Ivan, what would have been your next move with the Denning case if Theo hadn't recognised Morris?"

Ivan Maxwell was digging something from between his teeth with a plastic toothpick. He made the others wait for an answer; most of them knew it was one of his peculiar ways of giving himself time to think before speaking. When he'd finished he said, "Inspect the procedures used by Leeston Associates in their accounts department, to see how easy it would be for somebody to make this transaction."

"You need to go through with that," said Hanson, "as if we are following up that case, otherwise Morris/Wade might work out that we're on to him. Take somebody from IT to help. It might be a good idea to pull in Councillor Denning for questioning as well."

Addressing Tester. "Regarding the surveillance, you and Wilson can take up the first shift."

DC Wilson glanced at Theo; they had not worked together before.

Hanson continued, "Tail him from the moment he leaves work and stay as close as possible. Take cameras and long distance listening equipment and, if he meets, or passes the time of day with anybody, however brief, that person will also become a suspect and another target. Don't lose our man… or any of his contacts, until we can eliminate them in the investigation. Keep the team in the loop at all times. Let us know the instant there are any developments so we can add support." He opened up and addressed the whole team. "I don't have to tell you how important it is not to spook him. You're all on twenty four hour call so lay off the booze."

Friday 29th February 2008

By Friday the following week, Morris/Wade had been under constant 'around the clock' surveillance while not at work and, as yet, had not spoken to a soul, not even a good morning to a neighbour or a passing nod to a street vendor. "This has to be the most boring stakeout I've ever been on," said Wilson for the hundredth time. It was nine-thirty pm.

"What would you be doing if you were off duty?" asked Tester.

"Having a night out, especially as it's Friday. By now I'd be loosening up down the pub, getting warmed up for the club."

"Which club?" Tester was eying the front of Morris's apartment through the lens of his camera as he spoke.

"The Hip' mostly. It's alright there on Fridays and Saturdays."

"I've tried it," said Tester. "Not my scene really."

"What's your scene then?" asked Wilson. "Let me have a look through the camera."

Tester handed it to him. "I prefer to go into the city, or West Bromwich, to my old stamping ground; I stay over."

"Sounds okay, where do you go?"

"There are so many places. You'll have to come along next time I go."

Wilson gave his partner a long cynical look. "Yeah, I'll think about it, thanks for asking though... Hey look, he's off."

"I'll take him on foot," said Tester, "you follow in the car." He jumped out of the vehicle.

* * *

Ben, known as Graham Morris and Jonathon Wade by the police, cursed. It had begun to rain, so he hailed a passing cab. It wasn't far to the centre and he arrived early, so he nipped into a late shopping mart and bought a copy of the *Evening News*. The Denning-Leeston story was still making the front pages; he would read it in the Red Lion, where he was due to meet Marylyn at ten. He had fifteen minutes to kill, assuming she was on time. The Lion had a mezzanine floor with small round tables, and sitting at any of the ones next to the wooden balustrade gave a good view of the entrance and the bar. It was fairly quiet for a Friday night. He bought a beer and took it upstairs.

Marylyn was also early and they spied each other the moment she walked onto the premises. He watched as the guy behind the bar made her coffee. It always takes an age for a barman to serve coffee, giving Ben time to study the rest of the bar. When she finally made it he stood to welcome her, although the greeting was hardly cordial, a small peck on the cheek. "Hello Marylyn, I hope you didn't get too wet, it's real crap out there."

"Ben," she smiled. "No, I made sure I was dropped off right outside. How did you find Amy's birthday party, we didn't get to talk, it seems much longer than two weeks ago."

Ben wondered if *she* ever thought about the consequences of pulling Terrence from that well in the Pyrenees. If she did, she'd understand exactly why they didn't mix while in the presence of Hans.

As she removed her jacket and placed it over the back of the neighbouring chair she cocked her head and looked at the newspaper. She nodded, "Well done. Things look to be going to plan. Any trouble?"

"None at all." He ignored the reference to Amy's birthday and rubbed his hands across the paper to flatten it out "I've just read it. Poor old Councillor Denning is fighting a losing battle, and I think Leeston Associates are really struggling to clear up the mess."

"No problems from the police?"

"They have no idea. I think they're just going through the motions, for the sake of keeping the media happy, but that's all."

"Have they spoken to you?" She sipped her coffee.

"No, they haven't interviewed any of the staff, other than management. The company's system is deemed foolproof, the transaction could never be made without a manager processing it, or that's what they think. And so that's how the police investigation is panning out. I'll hang around until after the final council meeting and then, as long as the contract is awarded to the right firm, I'll be gone."

"That might arouse suspicion, have you thought of that?"

Ben couldn't believe she had asked that. "Of course I've thought about that. I've got it under control." He looked at her, she was different. She looked drawn. "Are you alright?" And he thought of Terrence. "How is Terrence?"

"Not good Ben, I don't think he'll last much longer… it's his birthday today." She didn't cry, but her eyes moistened up.

Ben did his best to look deflated, and pretended that he was angry with himself for not thinking of him earlier. The truth was though, he thought of little else. "Where is he, at your place or…"

"Hospital. I'm going straight to him after this."

"You shouldn't have come tonight, they could have sent somebody else."

"That's not how it's done, you know that."

Yes, he knew that. He also knew it would be for the best, all round, when Terrence had gone, poor bloke. All those years living in an 'iron lung', it must have been hell, for him and for Marylyn, caring for him. He couldn't bring himself to say those words though. All he could say was, "Are you going to be alright?"

Marylyn shrugged. "I'll have to be." And then she said, as an amendment. "Yes, of course I'm going to be alright." She shifted and sat more upright, as though she were pulling herself together. "All being well then, what are your plans after the meeting?"

Ben was impressed by her resolve; he wouldn't want to be in her shoes right now. "I'll give it long enough, probably a couple of weeks, and then I'll shoot over to Paris. I think I need to operate in another country for a while. Pass that on, okay."

"Fine." She handed him the package of instructions from Dieter. "Do we need to meet again?"

"Probably not, but you never know. I'll pop down to London next Saturday, normal time, usual place. I'll give you a progress report and you can tell me about Terrence. You know, if anything happens to him, I'm afraid I can't come to the funeral."

Marylyn let out a short sarcastic laugh. "Ben. Nobody comes to our funerals."

Chapter 20

Manfred was thinking about the future. He and Amy had done well during the years of high inflation, buying up bankrupt businesses and selling off the assets at a premium, and for dollars. It was easy money. But now that time was over. They'd become involved with the political gangs, with some control of where and when demonstrations took place, and which business establishments were to be attacked. This had led to offering protection to the potential victims... also good, easy money.

There was a charity which helped to rehabilitate ex-convicts and Amy was keen to become involved; on the basis that they would be able to get their hands on a ready supply of quality labour. It was this he mostly had his mind on as he approached his wooden office.

There was very little furniture in the place; a desk with a phone and two chairs. Everything else was stored in his head. He unlocked the door and entered. Before he realised anything untoward he was punched hard in the kidneys from behind. He collapsed onto the floor and was immediately kicked in the head.

But then the attack stopped. When he looked up, a well dressed fat man sat on one of the chairs. A thug sat on the table and there was at least one more standing behind them. The next sentence was a gift from the gods.

"My name is Carl Froebel and these are my brothers," said the seated man. He paused as Manfred licked his lips… Froebel thought it was to taste the blood that now covered them. He continued. "You run girls on our patch and we are here to explain to you why you can't do that. From today, these girls work for the Froebel brothers. We're closing you down." Again he paused. "Ok boys, pay the man some compensation for his losses." With that, Carl Froebel stood and walked outside, closing the door behind him. With his back to the building, he expertly struck a match and lit a huge habanos. He rocked on his feet, savouring the tastes of the Cuban cigar and the position of power.

Manfred felt a boot smash into the side of his head from behind and used his arms to soften the blows of those from the front. He managed to cling to the flailing boot of that kicker and twisted his body. His swinging foot smashed into the back of the thigh of the other attacker; he wasn't going to just lay there and take a beating.

Outside, Carl Froebel sucked his cigar as the noise of his brothers paying out *his* style of compensation emanated through the walls. He waited… the din continued for a few minutes, before eventually dying down to nothing… they had really given the bastard something to remember; beatings didn't usually take this long. The hiding will send out the required message to anybody else who might fancy taking on the Froebels. He turned to greet his brothers as the door opened.

Manfred stepped forward with one of the chairs in his left hand.

Confused, Froebel looked over the man's shoulders, he expected his brothers to follow him out.

Manfred plucked the cigar from Froebel's mouth and threw it to the ground. "Sit," growled Manfred. Froebel sat, open mouthed, still confused. Manfred placed a hand on a fat shoulder and slowly walked around him. "Your brothers are not dead, not yet. Tomorrow, at exactly this time, I will meet you back here. Bring your lawyer if you have one, and we'll discuss business... your business. Let yourself into the office, you obviously have a key. It really has been nice to meet you. You have no idea the pleasure you have afforded me." With that he left the man looking stupid, sitting beside the street on an upright chair.

East London Wednesday 5th March, 2008

At last Jennifer was beginning to enjoy her freedom, the friendship which developed with Adam had worked wonders for her confidence and self esteem: shopping and visiting bars with him, dancing with him, driving with him, and then venturing out alone to rendezvous with him at some pre-arranged destination. Now she seldom stayed in, the flimsiest excuse found her walking along a high street or driving around the M25. As far as Adam knew though, she had never been anything else other than the confident and outgoing being she had turned into. The sociophobia she had suffered from was no more. Her new self was that of a domineering control freak – as far as Adam was concerned anyway; she was enjoying it and it made her feel good.

She'd become fed up of living in Ongar and had been house hunting. She was being pulled by the life that London offered, but knowing she couldn't afford the city prices, she'd come up with a plan. She had done some homework and found that similar properties to the family home, the old farm house in Belfont-St-Mary, were up for sale at around one and a half million pounds. That figure had made her giggle. So much money! When she found the perfect property they could sell Belfont, Dad would move in with her and she could look after him, easy. It would leave the family with a nice pile of money and she was sure that her sister Rachel would think it a good idea.

She was in a property in Leytonstone. It had three bedrooms, a garage, a nice kitchen and two reception rooms. The owner was an old man and who had lived here, with his wife, for ever. She had died and he had gone into a home. The old couple had extended the ground floor to make the kitchen larger and added a downstairs bathroom. It was ideal. The front room could be Dad's bedroom... he wouldn't have to climb the stairs if his illness got worse. There was quite a large garden, which he would like. She would be able to drive out into the country or get the underground into the city. It was for sale for five hundred and seventy five thousand pounds... she needed to talk with Rachel.

* * *

If Amy's young lawyer was affected by the dead Victor Froebel, he hadn't shown it. They were in the office of the Glücklicher Mensch at Alexanderplatz, the jewel of the Froebel Empire. Of course, the three Froebel brothers had ignored Manfred's invitation and had not turned up at the ramshackle office. So he, Amy and Thomas decided to pay them a visit at their flagship cabaret bar instead, along with the lawyer, Herman Vogel.

So, just over a week after Manfred had had his first meet with the brothers, the four sauntered into the cabaret bar. The clientele at the Glücklicher Mensch were particularly noisy that night, enjoying a raunchy little act on stage, loudly cheering every thrust, and bawdily singing along. The noise had conveniently drowned the screams of the dying Victor.

The unfortunate man lay spread-eagled on the blood soaked carpet, and the heavily pregnant Amy stood over him with a very short bladed knife, breathing heavily. Carl and Gerard stood, handcuffed, up against a wall. Up until that moment, no words had been spoken by the intruders, and the two had watched in bewildered horror as the woman sliced off parts of their dying brother and threw them onto the open fire. After the gruesome performance was over, she asked, "What do you think of my little act?" She smiled and the two shrank back. "Which one of you would like to be next?"

Gerard didn't say anything but Carl screamed, "Him..." pointing his handcuffed hands towards his brother. "Please don't hurt me!"

"How about we play a little game," said Amy. "Whoever first works out who we are can walk free."

Fat Carl fell to his knees. "Please, take our business, our clubs, our money..."

"Stand," ordered Manfred. "Speak only when the lady asks you a question." He grabbed a handful of greasy hair and pulled the blubbering man to his feet.

"What are our names?" she asked, slowly pacing forward and backward in front of them, like a school mistress might in front of two naughty pupils.

They both looked at her blankly, and then Gerard said, "Amy, you are Amy."

"Correct! And this is?" She pointed at Manfred.

Gerard shrugged.

"Come on gentlemen, your lives are at stake. Think!" When no reply was forthcoming she suddenly thrust the short blade into Carl's testicles, and his scream put the screams of his dead brother to shame. Manfred and Thomas looked at each other, worried that the world would hear, even over the roars of the noisy mass outside. Again, Carl was hauled to his feet, only this time he immediately collapsed back to the floor. "Fuck. You piece of shit!" She yelled down into his face. "My name is Amy Bary. *His* name is Thomas Bary. And *his* name is Manfred Huth. Now do you fucking remember who we are?"

The two finally realised they were in big trouble! Gerard's reaction was to kick out at Amy and caught her hard on the knee. "Bastard!" and she swung her hand and stabbed him in the eye.

Now both the brothers were screeching and the blood was flowing. Thomas smashed holes into the ceiling and fastened two ropes, each with a noose. The two men were gagged and then stood with the nooses around their necks. As long as they stayed standing, they were okay, but if they collapsed... Neither was sure if the game was still in play... would the last one standing survive?

Amy, Manfred and Thomas, with the lawyer, rifled through the drawers and filing cabinets and sorted all the interesting paperwork. After a long night's work, during which both the Froebels finally succumbed and left this world, the three had become owners of a nice little empire.

Chapter 21

Friday 7ᵗʰ March 2008.

"The DNA matches your Rory Mitchell."

The name was an unexpected blast from the past for Detective Chief Inspector David Wentworth. "Rory Mitchell, well I never!" He'd given up on that name years ago.

DI Hanson dived into his briefcase and pulled out the file. "He's in a private hospital under the name of Kevin Shiften; he's been in an iron lung for years."

"What, at the hospital?"

"No. He's being cared for by a woman going by the name of Patricia Fairport. She's under surveillance." Hanson told Wentworth the sequence of events which had begun in the accounts department of Leeston Associates. "After meeting with Morris/Wade on Friday evening she returned to London and made her way straight to the hospital. She stayed at his side until Monday night." She calls and sees him every day. It was Friday now.

Wentworth was almost not listening, and he repeated, "Well I never… Rory Mitchell. Obviously you're still tailing the woman?" He asked.

"We're keeping an eye on Mitchell at the hospital, and we're continuing our interest in Morris/Wade, Patricia Fairport and anybody else they come into contact with, although so far, that's nobody."

"And you think there may be a link between this bribery attempt and the murder of Mohamed Khan."

Hanson nodded. "There's still no connection, other than the involvement of Morris/Wade himself. But now your Rory Mitchell has turned up... it all adds to the intrigue. I understand that he's wanted for murder, and that you collared him for running a boiler room scam from Barcelona."

Wentworth nodded and took a deep breath. "Well, it wasn't actually my collar, all I was supposed to do was collect him and bring him back to London; it was convenient because I happened to be in Barcelona. However, the case was nothing to do with me. He was arrested at the end of a joint Spanish, UK investigation. All I was supposed to do was conduct an interview to formalise the paperwork before bringing him back. But, as it turned out, there was more to him than we first thought. In the interview he claimed to have belonged to a massive crime family, and he was scared shitless that they were out to kill him, for stealing money from them. Initially I was sceptical. It was then that he confessed to the murder of Christopher Huth. That interview turned into a series of interviews, and along the line an investigator from the FBI turned up and told me the little they knew about this family. Well..." he paused and shrugged his shoulders, "There's a damn good chance he was telling the truth. And then, after all that, he bloody disappeared! To this day I have no idea how he did it. There was an investigation, but..." He thought he was getting a little carried away and stopped himself. "Anyway, why have you come to see *me*?"

"We're really not sure what we have. At the moment we're following two people around and spying on a hospital patient, all on a hunch." Hanson leant forward, he looked apprehensive. "We're beginning to feel a little uneasy about not hauling them in, especially now that another unsolved murder has turned up."

"And, perhaps, treading on the toes of another Police Force?"

"Precisely. We could be wasting our time and taking the risk of allowing them to slip away. So, I'm looking for a little input, or at least an opinion."

Wentworth wanted to support the officer. "I can tell you that we're obviously still interested in Mitchell. In fact his connection with an international criminal organisation interests a lot of people. Added to that there is an unsolved murder case gathering dust in Yorkshire. Look, this is *your* case and you are at liberty to tell us all to back off, but the fact is, you don't have to. I'm totally behind you and I will not make waves, whatever the outcome. Under the circumstances I would do exactly the same as you are proposing."

Hanson was suddenly a little confused. "An international criminal organisation?"

"Yes. I'm not kidding. There are even suspicions that there have been unlawful connections with American law enforcement groups."

Hanson whistled.

"I know. It does seem a little far fetched, that your little bribery incident could be turning into… well," he raised both hands, as if he were preaching, "A massive international criminal investigation."

Hanson gave a small nervous laugh. Was this all a dream?

Suddenly Wentworth asked, "The suspects, what about their premises, their homes?"

"It's awkward, I don't want them spooked. I was holding back about getting a warrant."

"Get your Super' to contact the secret service; after all, that's what they're there for. They'll get you all the information you want without having to 'spook' anybody."

"I was hoping to keep the people in the loop to a minimum."

"I feel the same about most of my cases, but sometimes you just have to bite the bullet and take your chances. I'll tell you now, if Rory Mitchell was telling the truth, back in Barcelona, this could all become bigger than you could ever imagine, and the sooner you ramp up the investigation to a higher level, the better off you'll be." Wentworth nodded as he spoke. Self glorification was a mistake made by most of his colleagues, and contrary to popular thinking, it placed a definite upper limit on promotion. Being a team player was the way to go. The fact that Hanson had come to him, and not tried to go it alone, meant that Wentworth could trust the man.

The thought of the growing size of his case made Hanson tingle with excitement. "Can I tell my boss that you said that?"

"Quote me. Do you mind if I contact an American FBI officer I know, she was, is, interested in this mob; she works with an organisation called the Financial Action Task Force on Money Laundering, it was…"

"F.A.T.F., I know of it."

Wentworth raised his brow in admiration, "So, do you mind?"

"If you think it's the correct thing to do, go ahead. Another thing, is there any chance of some help, perhaps a co-ordinated effort?"

"Bloody right there is. I think you'll need it anyway. I think I should come up and see your operation, and I'll bring along a couple of my team, to get up to speed. After that, we, the Met, will be at your disposal; we'll be happy to look after any surveillances taking place in the London area."

"Excellent, thank you sir" Hanson stood, "Sir, I don't think I could have hoped for a better response."

Wentworth held out his hand "David, call me David."

Chapter 22

Chelsea. Saturday 8th March 2008

Rachel lived in London. Her apartment was above a trendy boutique in The King's Road, Chelsea, and had two bedrooms, and all the rooms were large, with high ceilings, fancy carved coving and roses. The doors were solid and heavy, and all the wood was oak. She loved living here and loved showing the place off, and was therefore overjoyed when Jennifer turned up. "You've arrived just at the right time. You can help me lift this basket onto the hook?"

Jennifer was a little bewildered. "Why?"

"I've had the hook put there to hang a wicker chair from, but I haven't seen one I like yet, so in the meantime I'm hanging this basket from it."

Jennifer rolled her eyes. *Was this the real world?* They were in the bigger of the two bedrooms, the one Rachel slept in. She had a large potted spider plant sitting in a huge rope basket and wanted to hang it from the hook in the ceiling in one corner. Rachel had borrowed a step ladder from the boutique, the ceiling being too high to reach by using just a chair, but, even together, the sisters struggled, however, they eventually managed to slip the rope over the hook and hang the basket.

"What do you think?" asked Rachel.

Jennifer really couldn't see the point of it, it took up too much room, but at the same time didn't want to hurt her sister's feelings. "It's lovely, are you sure the hook is strong enough?"

"Jack's friend, Ian, said you could hang an elephant from it."

"How does *he* know?"

Rachel shrugged. "He's in the building trade…"

"When am I going to meet Jack? What's he like?"

Rachel smiled. "He'll be here in a couple of hours. He really wants to meet you and get to know you, and he *is* very nice. He wants to take us both out for an expensive dinner tonight. Do you fancy that?"

"That'll be nice," she answered. "Is he classy?"

"Very. He certainly knows his way around a wine list."

Jennifer thought about that. "Does he know where I've been?" she asked.

Rachel stepped forward and took her sister's hands "Oh Jennifer. Yes, he does. But he knows you are innocent."

"That's not really the problem; it's just that it's been a long time since I've been to a really posh restaurant. I…" She hadn't had much use for etiquette recently.

"Don't worry yourself. Jack will take care of both of us. Jen, I'm so glad you're alright, and here."

Jennifer still felt anxious, but very happy. "Rachel, can we talk about the house in Leytonstone before he gets here?" Jennifer and Rachel had spoken briefly on the phone earlier.

"Yeah, of course we can. I think it's a good idea for you to move into London, but why Leytonstone. And why on earth would you want Dad with you?"

"Dad *does* need looking after."

"Yes, I agree, absolutely. He has full time care at Belfont, around the clock nursing and domestic care."

"But that's not the same as being with family."

"Having to be at his beck and call twenty-four hours a day would not be something I would want to be saddled with. Look Jen, I think I know why you're suggesting this. You don't need to."

"What do you mean?"

"You think that looking after Dad will help your move into London."

"I thought it was a good plan. You live in London, why can't I?"

"But you can." Rachel sensed that she was upsetting her sister. "Tell me about this house, and your plan."

Jennifer had lost a little of her enthusiasm, she was annoyed with Rachel for bursting her little bubble. She continued, although not in the up-beat manner with which she had begun the subject. "I've found an ideal place, in Leytonstone. It's a nice three bedroom semi with off-road parking, up for five hundred and seventy five thousand. We could sell the farmhouse, and me and Dad could move in together. By caring for Dad I would be making a contribution, you know, financially. All those staff at the farm must cost quite a bit."

Rachel looked at her sister before replying, then, "There is no need to sell Belfont. We can afford to keep it, with all the staff... *and* buy your house. Dad can continue to live where he is."

"Are you sure? Did you hear me, the house is five hundred and seventy five thousand pounds, and then there are all the other costs."

"Absolutely, I heard you, you can actually afford more, much more if you'd rather."

"No. The place is fine." *It was a few minutes ago, anyway.* "What do you mean, much more? How much more?"

"Dad is worth about sixteen million pounds," Rachel shrugged, "probably more."

Jennifer was flabbergasted. "Fuck. Sixteen million!"

"And what belongs to Dad, belongs to us. However, you are worth about three million pounds in your own right."

"Fuck! Fuck-fuck. How?" Jennifer was stunned.

"We, the family I mean, have always been rich. Mum left us both some when she died, and now, with dad's help, yours is worth about three million. At thirteen you didn't know about money, the value of it, and neither Mum nor I could see the point of telling you about our financial situation until the time was right. I hope you are okay with that. I sought advice on the subject and that advice was always the same; await your release and let you settle down before telling you. If you had got into trouble of any sort, both inside or now, I would have obviously told you earlier. But I always made sure that you had enough. Because of Dad's illness, I have power of attorney and look after the estate - and that includes your inheritance, but your money *is* yours, to take and do what you want with."

Jennifer was astounded, and could only make a wild guess at what it was going to be like, being so wealthy – though she knew that the figures were enormous. She was attempting to recall how she felt *before Billy*, had she felt part of a wealthy family? She was also wondering how life might pan out for her now, her whole future changed in a sentence. Her sister continued.

"Anyway Jen, there is no need for you to make any sort of financial contribution, other than to help me look after the estate. Officially, I'm the one who makes the decisions, but it's your money as well. It is only right that you have as much a say in our financial affairs as I do. Dad helps, half of the time he is still quite capable."

"Wow. I'm trying to get my head around what you're saying. There are so many questions. Where did the money come from? How did he, or they, become that wealthy?"

"Well, although he did really well at the Foreign Office he inherited a lot from Grandpa Emmerich. Dad has invested cleverly as well. I think Mum was also very good. We can go through all of this later. Jack will be here soon and he doesn't know how much we are worth. Before you ask, there's no reason for not telling him, other than it is nobody else's business."

"Yeah. I'll go with that."

"Anyway, I know I said Dad puts in his two penny worth, but really it's down to you and me, to take care of the family fortune, and buying another London property will not be a bad move."

"Another?"

"Yes… this one, stupid."

"Oh yeah. I can't believe it though, sixteen fucking million. So I don't have to get a job."

"Never, that is, of course, if you don't want to. What about taking care of Dad? Do you still want to, even though you don't have to?"

Jennifer let out a half laugh. "I don't know. Give me some time to think about it." The idea didn't seem quite so desirable now. She thought about her new status. "I wonder how Grandpa Emmerich became so wealthy."

"All I know is that it was his father, great-Grandpa Emmerich, who made the fortune in Germany. They came to England in 1934, already rich. But that's as much as I've ever been able to find out."

"What about Dad, doesn't he know?"

"I don't think so; it was him who told me what I have just told you."

"Mmmm..." Jennifer tried to think about her ancestors and was quiet for a while. They both moved into the kitchen so that Rachel could make tea. Jennifer sat on a chair at the breakfast bar and looked on. She decided to contemplate the family fortune later, when she was alone, and surprised her sister by changing the subject. "So how long have you been going out with Jack?"

"For about a year. His sister is a secretary in our office and I met him at one of her parties."

Jennifer felt a wave of jealousy sweep over her. "A party! The last party I went to was Katy Wellington's thirteenth."

"Oh Jen... You'll get to go to loads of parties. You're so lovely. You wait and see, you'll soon have your own circle of friends, just give it time."

"They'll all run for cover as soon as they find out about me." Jennifer laughed. "On that subject though, I have decided that I'm not going to hide any more; I'm going to use my own name when I can."

"I don't blame you." Rachel turned up her nose. "Sandra Mannion, who on earth came up with that? But are you sure you want to revert back to calling yourself Jennifer Emmerich? You know what the media are like. At the moment they are not allowed to report anything about you, but if you go back to using your real name the injunction won't mean a thing, and they could have a field day. I think you need to think about it a little."

"I have thought about it. I am innocent and I would like to shout about that, maybe to make a fuss, and having the press on hand may help."

"They might also crucify you."

"They can all go to hell." Both girls quietly reflected on that future before Jennifer continued, "I suppose I'll have to use *Sandra Mannion* for bank accounts and other official stuff. It might actually come in handy to have two identities. But mostly I'll be Jennifer Emmerich. Who does Jack know me as?"

"Jennifer of course, that's a stupid question. I couldn't bring myself to call you anything else. What will your probation officer say?"

"I don't know, but I'll worry about that when I have to. As long as they don't pack me off back inside for it. Anyway, back to Jack. Is he romantic?"

"Jack? Yes, he's lovely." The kettle boiled and Rachel carried on talking as she poured. "What about Adam Saunders?"

"Adam, how do you know about Adam?"

"You've mentioned him once. So are you seeing him?"

Jennifer couldn't recall mentioning him, why would she? "He came to see me about Billy, and…"

"*About Billy*, what do you mean? And how did he find you?"

"He just wanted to talk. He wanted to ask me, to my face, if I killed Billy. It doesn't matter how he found me. But he's been a really fantastic help, I needed somebody to hold my hand in this big new world. He has helped with my driving, my drinking, shopping," she shrugged, "and generally with my socialising. He's the first friend I've made since getting out."

"I never thought about you socialising, I should have. Sorry. You know how we all get so wrapped up in our own little worlds. Were you lonely? If you were, you hid it very well. Why didn't you tell me at the time? What about sex?"

"What, now? I don't think it's allowed between sisters. If my probation officer finds out, well…"

"Funny. I mean with Adam."

"I don't know if I should tell you."

"Tell me about Adam and I'll tell you about Jack."

Jennifer sipped her tea and thought for a moment, "Okay, the first time I did it was with Adam… I lost my virginity with Adam." There… that wasn't difficult. "The time it happened I had flirted and teased him like mad, and it all turned *me* on so much that now I can't stop, flirting I mean. Sometimes I actually worry about myself. When I flirt I feel this fantastic sense of power, power over men. Any man, as long as I fancy them. And I also treat Adam like shit, and the buzz I get when I do that, well it's like being high. Sometimes we have sex until we drop and other times I tease, and then refuse him when he is totally worked up, and as soon as he's gone, usually by that time in a terrible tantrum, I'm off and out flirting with the first man I fancy."

"Bloody hell, Jen. Do you sleep around?"

"No. I've only ever done it with Adam, but I do get the urge, all of the time. Perhaps it's because I'm a late starter."

"You need to be careful. If you flirt too much you might get more than you bargained for, especially with strangers."

"I can take care of myself. Being locked up at her majesty's pleasure certainly taught me how to do that."

"Maybe, but just be careful."

They both sat sipping their tea and collected their thoughts. Then Jennifer asked about the security of the apartment. "I noticed that you have two locks on the main door."

"That's right. One Yale and one lever lock." Rachel drank down the remainder of her tea and stood. "Come on, I'll show you around." She then led her sister around the flat, pointing as she talked. "All of the windows have locks and the glass is high impact double glazed, unbreakable. And I *always* use both locks on the door; it's even locked that way now. A spare set of keys, for the door and the windows, always hang up here..." she returned to the kitchen and pointed to the keys on a hook beside the oven extractor hood, "just in case you need them one day."

"Why?"

"Why what? Why might you need them?"

"No, why all the security?"

"It was something Jack said. I was telling him about the way Mum died. You know; the reasons why the police left it as an open case. He said that maybe somebody has something against our family."

Jennifer sat back down on her breakfast bar chair and Rachel followed suit. "He said *that*. You know, I've wondered much the same, but carry on, let's hear what you have to say first. By the way, did you have the locks fitted at Ongar?"

"Yes. Anyhow – He figured that if Billy's murder was made to look as though you did it, then it's highly possible, actually he thinks very likely, that Mum was murdered. Anyway, it freaked me out enough to get me a bit paranoid."

"Have you ever told him that I'm adopted? And about what happened to my real parents."

Rachel nervously rubbed her hands over the bar. "I couldn't help it. He knows, though, that you're my sister, in every way. He would never think otherwise."

"It doesn't matter. Growing up, I'd forgotten about where I came from, and what had happened... But during the last few years I've had plenty of time to think, and although there've been too many unanswered tragedies for them not to be connected, I still can't see the link." Jennifer was silent for a moment, before adding, "I don't think your paranoia is unfounded."

"I can't stop thinking about it," said Rachel. "This is the only place in the whole world where I feel totally safe. I very seldom go out alone, especially after dark. If I did, it would need to be for a bloody good reason."

"Do you think I should make the Leytonstone house secure then, when we eventually buy it?"

"Absolutely. In fact, while you're still living there, you should make the Ongar place more secure. I thought that, with your new identity, you would be safe, but as you are thinking of continuing life under your real name I think it may be wise to introduce a little paranoia into *your* life."

Jennifer allowed her mind to wander for a moment and, as always, that question which bugged her for years was her top thought; if there is somebody out there after her - why? The strongest theory was that it had to do with one of her birth parent's past life, but now there was another possible reason – money. And she didn't just want to discover the reasons behind what was happening; she fantasised turning the tables, becoming the hunter rather than the hunted. If only she could.

Rachel misunderstood Jennifer's silence and stood and wrapped her arms around her sister. "Oh Jen, I didn't mean to frighten you. I just wanted to tell you how I'm feeling, and to warn you, just in case." Tears welled in her eyes, and for the first time she felt very close to Jennifer.

To lighten the mood Jennifer decided she wanted to experience the whole apartment and led her sister by the hand through to the lounge. They each chose a couch and sat opposite each other. Both sniffed and laughed nervous laughs. "Let's pull ourselves together, we have to be strong sis," said Jennifer. Then she asked Rachel that question. "I wonder why somebody might be picking on us. Have you ever spoken to Dad about it?"

Rachel sub-consciously rubbed her hands on her legs as she answered, "I've tried, but he seems unable to come up with anything constructive. In fact he tries to change the subject, as if he's afraid to talk about it."

Jennifer said, "But, if we have been, or are being persecuted, I've always thought it must be something to do with my real mum or dad, or perhaps Mum; the way she died, until now anyway. Maybe it's about the money. Both of us were too young to have made any enemies at the time Billy died. In prison, after she was killed, I wondered if Mum had an affair and the jilted man is a maniac, but that doesn't make sense if her death and my parent's deaths are linked. Do you know if they had money?"

Rachel shrugged; she didn't think so. "I seem to recall Dad saying that they had died owing money. I also think that Mum would have said something to the police if there had been a jilted ex-lover lurking about. It would have surfaced during the *Billy investigation*."

"Maybe, maybe not. She had a lot to lose if the marriage went tits-up. You just mentioned sixteen million reasons. But then, when I analyse it, if it *was* anything to do with her, why did she seem so convinced that I did it. I could tell she thought that, by the way she looked at me as I was led from the dock, after the verdict. So coldly I'll never, ever, forget it."

Rachel thought back to that day when she had childishly and selfishly refused to accompany her mother to the last day of the trial, demanding that she had her own life to get on with, wanting to disassociate herself from her killer step sister. The thought made her feel very guilty.

Jennifer was about to carry on with the subject of her mother's hypothetical relationship when there was a loud buzz. "It's Jack," shrieked Rachel. A few moments later Jennifer and Jack met for the first time.

Jack was bigger than Jennifer had expected, much bigger, and good looking to boot. The introductions were pleasant and upbeat, and then he went to the bathroom to freshen up; "Wow Rachel, he's gorgeous." She excitedly jumped and skipped around the apartment as Rachel looked on, amusingly entertained.

"Just keep your hands off. He's spoken for." Rachel laughed as she playfully warned off her sister.

"What's that?" asked Jack, as he rejoined them.

"I'm just telling my little sister that she could be in grave danger if she doesn't change her ways."

Jack simulated confusion (he was not stupid) and Jennifer stuck out her tongue in the direction of her sister.

Small talk followed and Jack and Jennifer got to know each other, and then it was time for dinner. They walked along The King's Road to a small bistro. Once seated, the conversation returned to the family security.

Jack brought it up. "You know, Jen, you'll be much safer in this place in Leytonstone, assuming you go ahead with it. We can fit the latest security devices and the best locks. Belfont would be very difficult, and very expensive, to sort out. If you don't mind I can arrange it for Leytonstone."

"Yes Jen, Jack has lots of connections and he'll not let us get ripped off."

"That's fine by me," replied Jennifer. "One thing less for me to worry about. I think I'll make an offer and Dad can visit a lot. But you're right Rachel, I don't think I could care for him constantly. One thing I would especially like though, is to set up a web cam, so that I can check in on him via my lap top if he does stay, and I go out."

Rachel was surprised, "He will not like that," she pointed out.

"That's not a problem," said Jack. "We can have the camera installed and he'll never know it's there. You said earlier that you want to convert the front reception room into his bedroom. We can easily place covert stuff in there."

"It's too intrusive," replied Rachel. "It could turn out to be very embarrassing for everybody."

Jennifer answered. "Not everybody. I'll be the only person to see anything, and whatever happens; nobody else other than us will ever know about it. I just want to be able to pop out at any time knowing that I can check on him, especially if he's having a bad day."

Rachel still had her reservations, but decided that it was not too much of an issue; she would bring up the subject at a later date. "Well, make an offer for the place, and when we know it's yours, we can discuss this and any building and decorating work that's needed."

"Rachel," Jennifer asked. "Can I sleep at your place tonight?"

"Of course you can. I'm so sorry Jen, I was going to offer earlier, but we've been having such a good time I forgot, just leave my big man alone, that's all I ask." They all laughed.

Later, when Rachel visited the 'ladies room' Jennifer took advantage of the opportunity to talk privately to Jack. "I want the camera in case he breaks in."

"Who?"

"Don't be stupid Jack, we haven't got time. If I can, I'm going to set cameras up at the farmhouse for the same reason. At the moment I don't know what else to do, but I'm not going to hang around doing nothing."

"And you don't want Rachel to know."

"Not yet. I've only just decided to do it. Look, she'll be back soon so we'll talk about it another time, not tonight. I just wanted to let you know that I intend to fight back. For now though, let's enjoy ourselves."

After dinner they returned to the apartment. Rachel left Jack and Jennifer giggling and larking around in the lounge while she freshened up. In the bedroom she sensed something odd. She didn't notice anything immediately, but had a feeling that things were not as they should be. She inspected the room carefully and noticed that somebody had been at her desk; the pile of legal papers, copies of the *'Earl v Lorane'* documents, had been tampered with. The top two copies, almost identical, had been moved and put back in the wrong order, something she would not have done. She didn't think she would have, anyway. "Jack."

Jack pounded into the room, still laughing at some outrageously funny remark made by one of them. "Yeah, what?"

It suddenly seemed trivial. "Um, oh nothing, it doesn't matter. I was thinking of something, but it's not important."

He shrugged and returned to the room of fun.

Rachel decided not to make a fuss. It would spoil a good evening. She ruled out Jack and decided it must have been Jennifer, after all, although they were sisters, she didn't really know her. They can't have spent much more than twenty-four hours together during the last eight or nine years, and that included nearly twelve hours today. And, she thought, before Jennifer was convicted, Rachel recollected that she was a troublesome and annoying irritation. Though, to be fair, most teenage girls would consider their 'four years younger sister' in a similar light. She thought about the pile of papers and then looked around the bedroom, searching for more evidence of any intrusion. But why? Why would she have been snooping around like this? Then she decided to let it go; I'll keep an eye on her.

Chapter 23

Friday 20th March 2008.

Ben wasn't stupid. He realised he was being followed soon after his meet with Marylyn. He came to the conclusion that they must have latched on to him while tailing her. Sitting opposite him was Spider, not his real name, Ben had no idea what that was, and it wasn't important. What did matter was that they looked alike. So alike in fact that if Ben knew who his mother was, he was sure she wouldn't be able to tell them apart.

Spider had the Graham Morris passport in his left hand; he'd used it before, but that didn't stop him leafing through it to make sure all was in order. In his left hand was £2000 in cash.

"The ferry is booked," said Ben. "Take the car, you'll find the driving licence and the rest of the documentation under the dash." He held out a debit card. "Use this. You'll be able to draw a grand a week with it."

Spider nodded and smiled. "Is there anything I can't do?"

"You can't leave Paris and you can't get into any trouble. There's also a mobile and charger with the documents; the slightest problem, get in touch. The apartment has a PC and is connected to the net... Don't use any email, not even a new account. Only use your laptop at other locations, and switch those locations as much as possible… Look, you know the drill, just relax, have a good time, and be me for a while." As spider stood, Ben added, "By the way, you're going to be followed around a bit. Don't let it bother you; it'll be the French authorities, probably 36 quai des Orfèvres. Make sure that you don't let them know that you know they're there."

Wednesday 26th March 2008.

Theo Tester entered the small operations room. "Graham Morris has moved into an apartment in Paris."

DI Hanson had been alone in the room. Frustrated by the lack of progress being made in the case, and with nothing better to do, he'd been scrolling through reports which had been sent to him from London's Met, hopefully trying to find something that others may have missed. He liked Tester, and greeted him accordingly. Both were at least relieved that their man hadn't completely disappeared; a small token of good news, at best. "Who's keeping an eye on him?"

"The DRPJ Paris."

Hanson shook his head and sighed. "The case has gone bloody international and we still only have three suspects. Plus we're not sure which crime we are investigating."

"I can't see how you can say that," replied Tester, "we're poking around two big cases. Just think, if we can get somewhere with the Christopher Huth and the Genghis Khan investigations, or even just one of them, we'll be heroes… it'll be well worth the effort."

"We're not here to be heroes Theo." He was trying to be comical but Hanson felt stupid as soon as the words came out. He wanted Tester to admire him, not to put him in the same category as those daft old coppers who used to say such things to him when he was a young detective. He laughed to emphasise he wasn't being serious, "I was thinking though, we're not making much progress here. Now, with Morris gone, I feel completely cut off from the whole investigation. How do you fancy working in London? The Met will supply us with an office, I'll feel much happier running this from there."

Tester beamed. "Hey boss, no kidding. I'm up for that. Do you really think you can swing it?"

Hanson was really pleased with the boy's reaction and, as for 'swinging it', at the moment it was still his investigation and he could do just about as he thought fit. "There was nothing in Morris's flat, no phone, not a television, he didn't even use a computer... just a few basic things; clothes, food, and a bed. I've just received the information from Cook. They went in there prior to Morris legging it."

"Maybe they frightened him off."

"No, I don't think so. Cook said the search was undertaken by the secret service."

"Secret service?"

"MI5."

Tester was impressed, MI5 on *their* case.

"Keep that information to yourself Theo. I'm not supposed to know."

"What about Patricia Fairport's place?" Tester asked.

"They did hers last night. She was at the hospital visiting Rory Mitchell. Again, no TV or computer. But she does have a nice sound system and a phone which she apparently uses a lot. She seems to be ringing just about everybody in London, on the pretext of seeking the permission of home owners to record a scene for a film outside their front door. She also asks them to call back in a couple of weeks for more information, whether or not it's going to take place; money will change hands if it does, so you can imagine, there are hundreds of calls being made in both directions."

"Are the calls kosher?"

"We don't know, not yet, but it doesn't look like it. She doesn't keep any record of any calls, or at least there was none in the house, and when an inquiry is made the answer is always the same – not this time, sorry – so it all looks pretty strange."

"I bet somewhere amongst all those calls is some sort of message."

"That's what both me and DCI Cook think. Every call is being monitored, in case one leads somewhere. We've also bugged the property."

"What are we going to do in London?"

"To start with you can help out with the surveillance of Patricia Fairport's property, until something else crops up. But I need you there with me, to bounce ideas off."

That suited Theo; this meant he would remain at the heart of the investigation.

Chapter 24

**Leytonstone.
Tuesday 29th April 2008**

Jennifer watched herself on the screen of her laptop; she held up her right arm and waved. Good. She'd had a dongle fitted to her laptop, so, providing she could get a mobile signal, she should be able to watch live video of the room from anywhere. She selected the option which recorded while she watched and then played it back, and was pleased with the result. She decided to phone Jack later, to thank him for sorting it all out. She looked up. Even though she knew exactly where the camera was situated, and as hard as she tried, she couldn't see it. She would find out as well, over the next few weeks, if her builders discover it.

Then she turned her attention to the mysterious A4 size envelope which lay on the table next to the laptop. Across the front was scribbled, in black ink, just one word, 'Jennifer'. She inspected and prodded it; there was no stamp, so it was delivered by hand - before gently opening it to reveal a Sunday broadsheet newspaper article about a Midlands family, the Huths, who had been murdered in the nineties. There was a short scrawled message in the top margin by the date – *take care, this could be you*. Jennifer studied the hand writing… she didn't recognise it, and wondered if Holly had sent it? She speculated about how her old friend had found out about her new home so quickly. She'd only owned the Leytonstone house for a few days and last night was the first night she'd stayed, having slept rough in the bedroom. This so that she could meet the builders before they began their work. Speak of the devils; just at that moment she heard them arrive. She slipped the article back inside the envelope, logged off and closed the lid of her computer.

Wednesday 30th April 2008.

Theo was no stranger to city life, and his first month in London had been taken in his stride. He had a few mates potted about the city and, socially, he was enjoying himself. However, life within the Met was not quite so rosy. He sensed a strong undercurrent of racism, which had resulted in him keeping a lower profile than he naturally would have. Danny Hanson came and went. Theo got to know David Wentworth quite well and learnt all that was known about the elusive family, which wasn't a lot, and the Huth incident.

He had compartmentalised the three crimes which touched the investigation; the Leeston Associates bribery, the Mohamed Khan murder and the Huth affair, and looked for links. *The Huth affair!* If the motive had been fraud, then the way it had rolled out seemed clinical and well rehearsed; could it have been done to other families, on other occasions? He trawled the files and the internet day after day in search of families suffering similar fates, spoke to banks and newspapers, looking for forgotten incidents. He logged every situation where a complete family died after losing all their money... there were hundreds recorded. How many more, unknown, unrecorded?

Patricia Fairport lived in the end terrace of a block of six houses. Theo was working his shift, watching and listening to the activities of number eleven, Fairport's house. The acoustics of a hammer drill had caught his attention... The sound was coming from an adjoining property, not from number eleven, and whoever was using the tool was obviously a football supporter...

Da da dadada dadadada da da (Da da dadada dadadada *Chelsea*).

Theo had laughed to himself the first time he had heard it... Three days ago! Today he was listening to a recording.

* * *

He met up with Hanson outside Forensics. "I should have seen it earlier," he confessed.

"Don't beat yourself up Theo, just tell me what you have."

"She's obviously known about the bugs for the last month, almost as soon as they were installed. We've been sitting in that damn place for over four weeks listening to recordings while she's gallivanting about and getting on with her business."

"How do you think she's been leaving the house without being detected?"

"The technical boys have listed all the dates and times of when we've been listening to pre-recorded material."

"As opposed to live stuff?"

"Yeah. Anyway, I've checked our logs and the woman who lives at number three always left her property just after the recordings start and returns just prior to them finishing. Her name is Jasmine Hussein, or at least that's the name registered for that property on the electoral roll. She's a Muslim, and always wears a full Burka. They," he pointed over his shoulder towards the lab, "They've detected variations of sounds caused by changes of air pressures, which indicates a hatch being opened and closed, probably the loft hatch. The events always coincide with the Muslim leaving or returning."

"So Fairport's been using the roof space to make her way back and forth." Hanson pondered for a moment. "Whatever you think, Theo, your discovery is a breakthrough, and the fact that she's been able to hoodwink us for a while could actually work in our favour. Perhaps, after a month of successes she'll not be quite so vigilant."

Chapter 25

Thursday 1st May 2008

Theo had just settled down at the beginning of another shift and was listening to the sounds of a single woman getting herself ready for her day. He noticed the curtains twitch at number three; the Muslim's house. She was on the move. Again he was listening to a recording, only this time he knew it! He phoned control and reported the development.

He followed the darkly dressed woman as she travelled by taxi to Clifton Hill in Wimbledon, where she alighted outside the entrance of a medium size apartment block. There, in one of those apartments, she changed into another set of clothing; expensive looking stretch corduroy jeans, blouse and padded jacket. She had a shoulder bag to match and had also slipped on a pair of Bvlgari sunglasses. It wasn't particularly sunny, and a cool breeze whipped leaves and small pieces of litter around the street, but she still looked perfectly in tune with Wimbledon. Patricia Fairport didn't look like Patricia Fairport, or like the Muslim. However, Tester had been following her long enough to instantly recognise her gait as she re-emerged through the front door. Tester's cabby was a diamond. As soon as Theo had explained that he was on police business the man had stopped talking nonsense and enthusiastically followed orders.

She waited for a short while, until another cab turned up, and then Tester's man duly followed them in the direction of the West End. By this time Danny Hanson had made his way to control and informed Theo that the taxi they were following was a fake, it wasn't registered. Theo was getting excited. The vehicle pulled up outside Harrods and Fairport climbed out. Tellingly, the cab then pulled into a side street and parked up, with the driver at the ready.

Tester put his cabby on standby, who was also happy to keep an eye on the fake while staying out of sight. The policeman and the taxi driver quickly exchanged mobile numbers and then Tester continued his tail of Patricia Fairport.

Initially he lost her. Then, a couple of minutes later, he spied her in the food hall. She had already made a purchase, a fairly large Harrods bag hung from her right arm. She spent a short time looking at the celebration cakes and then made her way back towards the street and her taxi.

Theo and his cabby were on her tail. They followed her across the city and into Docklands, where she left her vehicle and made her way on foot. Theo noticed that she didn't pay her fair. He thanked his cabby for the support and was about to pay his fare and follow the woman, when a well dressed and familiar looking man climbed into the back of the fake taxi. Shit! Who was that guy?

"Well blow me… that's Malcolm Henderson." Cabby pointed out.

Of course, Defence Secretary, Sir Malcolm Henderson MP. Bloody hell! There was no way he could assign his cabby to continue the tail, could he? Theo needed to follow Fairport, he knew something was going down and he didn't want to miss it, but...

A stroke of luck! The passing special constable had Theo's ID thrust in front of his face, was bundled into the back of the taxi and handed Theo's mobile all in one quick movement. The man was listening to Danny Hanson via the mobile in one ear and being brought up to speed by the cabby in the other.

Patricia Fairport made her way by foot, tube and bus across the south of London, back to the apartment in Wimbledon, and then, as the Muslim, back to number three, this time in a cab which she had hailed down in the street. All without incident. Theo had managed to stay with her. She had carried the Harrods bag for the complete journey, both as the rich woman and as the Muslim, and Theo deduced that she was either confident she wasn't being followed or taking the piss. He had a niggling feeling that he had missed something. Why would she go to all that trouble just to shop at Harrods? However, as soon as he was able to contact Hanson again, things began to get a little clearer. Malcolm Henderson, MP, had been dropped off by his ride at his London residence. When he stepped from the cab he had a Harrods bag, which, Theo and the cab driver could both testify, he didn't have when he had climbed into the fake taxi.

Theo also concluded that he had missed something during the period when he had lost the woman while in

Harrods. It wasn't something that had been purchased in the store that was passed to the MP... she had liaised with somebody.

* * *

One of the team had dropped off a mobile for Theo at the stakeout, and he was just settling down again when he heard Patricia Fairport's telephone ring. She answered, there followed a short period of silence. She phoned for a cab. This time she travelled without disguise; and this time she was in a hurry... She was heading for the hospital; Rory Mitchell had taken a turn for the worse.

* * *

When Theo arrived at the hospital he was instructed to remain outside, DCI Wentworth was inside.

* * *

Patricia Fairport was well aware that she had been followed, but she didn't care; all she wanted was to get to Terrence before...

She sat down by his side. Most of the tubes and breathing aids had been removed and, although at death's door, he looked more alive now than he had for a long time. His breathing was very shallow and his eyes were closed, he looked relaxed; serene, she thought.

She held his hand. Her eyes became moist, but she didn't want him to hear her cry, and, with an effort, choked back a sob. "Terrence, my darling. It's *your* darling, Marylyn. I'm with you now." She brushed his hair with her fingers. Suddenly she didn't know what to say, other than goodbye. But she couldn't say it. She just held his hand and looked into his face.

She sat at his side for a long time after his breathing had stopped. A nurse had entered the room and looked over Marylyn's shoulder, and had then left the couple in peace.

* * *

Wentworth was sitting in the reception area of the hospital when the girl finally emerged. He knew that Rory Mitchell was dead.

An inner sense warned *her* that the seated man was the enemy, but she was spent... she didn't want to fight any more. She stalled long enough for him to rise and approach.

"Miss Fairport. I am DCI David Wentworth." He held out some ID. "I'm sorry for your loss, I knew Terrence from time spent in Barcelona." He held out a hand, tentatively she took it, confused.

She was very upset. But how did this man know Terrence? This man wasn't family. If he had called him Rory... But he hadn't. "Thank you..."

"Do you mind sitting," he gently held her upper arm and directed her towards where he'd been waiting. "We should talk."

Dazed, she allowed herself to be manoeuvred towards the seating.

"Please don't think I'm being insensitive, but it's very important we have this discussion." He paused, he was taking a risk. "Your family did this to Terrence."

The policeman had reasoned this, and he prayed he was right. "You have to help us, you cannot let them get away with what they've done."

Marylyn sat for a while. She knew he was right; they shouldn't get away with it. But, much more than her anguish, she was scared. "I'm sorry, I don't know what you're talking about. Terrence was hurt in an accident, a long time ago. Please, I would like to leave." She made a move to stand.

"Please. Miss Fairport. I know this is difficult for you. But you can *really* help yourself by helping us."

Wentworth had hit a chord. Marylyn hated this family… this life… but they would win, whatever this man said, they would win and she would lose. But she was a good person, not like the others; she was just trapped, born into a life of crime. She considered telling him… Suddenly she had an idea. She would go and see Amy. With Terrence gone she now had nothing to lose. She would see Amy and ask her to release her from this life.

Wentworth sensed that she was about to loosen up and his hopes rose.

But it was too late, the moment had passed. The girl didn't say any more, she just stood and quickly walked away.

* * *

Ben witnessed the short discussion Marylyn had with the stranger. He also spied Theo Tester as he moved in behind her; following at a safe distance.

* * *

Theo followed her, and Ben followed them both. She wasn't in the same state of urgency as before... she walked as though she was deliberating. And she walked, and walked. No cabs, no buses, no underground. She walked for almost two hours, until she reached Liverpool Street Station. She made her way down to the Circle Line and waited for the westbound train. It was the rush hour and the station was extremely busy and, surrounded by hordes of people, Theo had a problem keeping her in view.

Ben was in the throng. He slid a long thick needle from inside his jacket.

A huge burden had suddenly lifted from Marylyn. The thought of leaving the family, never having to think about every move, never having to worry about every small detail of everything she did. She would be normal, mourn Terrence as a normal human being. Amy would understand... surely?

Theo lost sight of her as a couple of taller guys moved behind her. He manoeuvred himself to keep her in his sight. He was so busy keeping sight of Marylyn that he didn't see Ben slip behind him. As the train approached everybody began to move, to get ready to board, and he lost her again. He decided to get closer but it wasn't easy. As the doors of the train folded open there was a scuffle and some screams from the direction of the girl. A hole in the crowd formed as people moved back. He couldn't see her. He pushed forward into the opening... she was on the ground.

Theo knelt beside her, telling onlookers he was a policeman; the crowd fell silent as they followed events. He heard the doors of the train shut. Shit! But then they reopened. Somebody had pulled the emergency cord. He called for backup and medical assistance as he tried to find a pulse which wasn't there. A woman stepped out from the mass and offered help; she was a doctor. Two transport policemen turned up. As the doctor administered what aid she could, Theo simultaneously scanned the crowd and tried to replay the images of the last few minutes over in his mind.

As the doctor tried to resuscitate the girl a murmur began to rise from the crowd. Blood had emerged from beneath Marylyn's body. On closer inspection there appeared to be a puncture wound of some kind to the back. Somebody said loudly that the girl had been stabbed and many of the travellers decided it was time to leave. The word spread, and a frantic exodus from the station ensued. More Underground security arrived, but there was not a lot they could have done to prevent the evacuation. None of this helped Theo put together the events of the last moments of Patricia Fairport's life.

* * *

CCTV covered every inch of the station and the carriages of the Circle Line train, but there was nothing which led to the discovery of who had murdered Patricia. There was a moment when something obscured the camera in the carriage, but whether or not this concealed anything of importance was impossible to tell. Likewise, video footage of in and around the hospital and the route to Liverpool Street was studied. Again this revealed nothing.

Chapter 26

Berlin 1934

Anna Semper was experienced and skilled enough to be able to type *and* follow the movements of the grey suited man who moved through the typing pool. Not only follow his movements, but to study him in detail. He was around thirty, handsome and upright, and walked amongst the desks with a confidence that frightened her. He inspected the work of every woman as he slowly passed, studying the paperwork and diaries piled in front of them. He didn't ask questions though, he didn't say anything. But, she thought, he didn't look happy!

Each step was slow and deliberate, like a funeral march. He moved from one work station to the next, however, his eyes darted back and forth as a hawk's would as he scanned every inch of the office. He spent many minutes looking down at each worker as he passed, but he lingered longer at the desk of Anna's best friend, Franziska. He watched as she typed. Anna wondered what he was looking for. His hands were held behind his back as he leaned forward to read the words as they emerged line by line from the type writer, but, as the page was completed, it was *his* hand, and not Franziska's, which plucked it from the machine.

He held it close to his face as he reread it, and then an upward glance, a coded command, had one of the black uniformed officers scurry over to him. The suited man moved half a step back and placed his free hand on the typist's arm, just below her elbow. Involuntarily, Franziska stood. Anna could feel the fear of her friend. The suited man handed the officer the sheet of paper, manoeuvred the girl away from her chair, nodded, and Franziska was led from the office.

Anna quickly studied her own typing. She usually worked mechanically, almost not knowing what she was typing. But now she read, frantically. What was she typing? Would she be led away? But reading it made no difference because she had no idea what the Secret Service man was looking for. He had disappeared from her view. He was, by this time, behind her. A few desks behind her… walking down her row! He wasn't with her yet, but that didn't stop her imagining his hot breath on the back of her neck as he looked over her shoulder, studying her work… her skin tingled and her heart rate increased. She pressed an *h* instead of a *g*.

Since 1925, Manfred, Thomas and Amy had continued to build their business empire, using intimidation and violence to take control of legitimate and dubious businesses alike, and then using the enormous profits to move into the world of banking and financial trading. They had successfully manipulated the trade unions to provide much of the means and the muscle which had enabled this expansion to take place, and consequently, political associations had formed. While Amy and Thomas looked after business, Manfred used these contacts to fashion a blossoming career in the security section of the Secret Service, the SD, under the direct command of Himmler's right-hand man, Reinhard Heydrich. Working and socializing with such prominent Nazis gave Manfred enormous power, and for the business: protection, and all the advantages of knowledge of evolving events. The SD was responsible for the security of the Nazi Party. After Hitler became Chancellor in January 1933, the SD was also responsible for seeking out and dealing with any who opposed and were a threat to the leading members of the Nazi Party.

Manfred had been promoted at the end of 1933 to SS-Standartenfuhrer, the equivalent of Colonel in the British army. Close was the moment Manfred had been working towards. He had become powerful enough to make his move, to confront those who had brought about the murders of his parents... to relish the look on the face of his murderous uncle, Johann Heinrich Huth, as he, SS-Standartenfuhrer Manfred Huth, the nephew who was supposed to have been executed, returned from the dead to exact his revenge.

The official reason for Manfred's visit to the massive head office complex of the Huth Empire was to investigate rumours that the organisation was opposed the rule of the Fuhrer. Manfred had wanted to have his arrival announced using his rank, not his name, and then, when he faced his uncle... he would announce his true identity; he had it all planned.

With his promotion, Manfred could get away with almost anything, and that was bad news for all the uncles who had ordered the killings of 1920. And it was also bad news for their wives, children, grand-children, in-laws and even close friends.

But the raid hadn't gone to plan! The uncles had found out about Manfred and his intentions, and had long gone. Manfred's inspection of the pool of typists was now nothing more than to give him time to think... and to quell the raging temper which threatened to erupt from his boiling veins. Nobody, above or below, knew the real reason for the raid, but still he had been outwitted.

The typist, Anna Semper, could feel him closing in on her. Fear had heightened her senses and she would swear that she could hear the thumping heart of the work colleague directly behind her as the man slowly made his way down her row. What did her document reveal? Was it important? Would he see her spelling mistake? She would be interrogated. She forgot to breathe.

There must be a traitor amongst his own men, his hand-chosen squad... under his command! Manfred could feel his hands shake with rage and he clasped them tighter behind his back. He pictured every SS member who had knowledge of today's raid; just a handful. In his mind he imagined how he would interrogate them, extract the truth. Fourteen years he had waited for this moment. He'd had them. He'd had them! Now they had gone! Somebody was going to pay dearly for this treachery. He had never felt like this before... on the very edge of losing control. The red headed girl was acting strangely, why had she stopped working?

Anna Semper couldn't take it anymore. She read her last sentence of type; it was gobbledygook; it didn't make sense! She would surely be arrested! For what? She hadn't done anything wrong. It's just a spelling mistake. She loved the Fuehrer. What did the Secret Police want with her... or with Franziska?

"Sit!"

Who was he talking to? She wanted to sit... fear overwhelmed her... she couldn't take anymore, confusion... she'd heard about the Secret Police, what they did to prisoners. She made a dash for the door.

"Sit," Manfred screamed. The rage engulfed him. The woman's action lit his short fuse... and he exploded. As he screamed the order again he didn't even realise the gun was in his hand.

The force of the bullet smashing into her spine threw her against the wall. The office erupted, screams ensued. Three more shots... orders shouted, demanding calm... then... there was quiet, and as a semblance of order returned around her, she felt a heat tear through her side... a bright light... then darkness.

* * *

Amy had been having a wonderful time. She no longer ran strings of girls, or sleazy cabaret bars... she ran people who ran them for her. She had just returned from her fruitful business trip to New York, her first time to America, and was looking forward to seeing the rest of her children. Little Franz, now ten years old, had accompanied her to the States. There were five other little ones; four girls and one boy, and she had decided that that was enough!

Thomas greeted them both as they stepped from the train.

"Thomas!" she hugged him. "We have so much to tell you. You must go to America, it really is the place to do business."

Thomas had a smile as wide as the Nile across his face. He hugged Amy back. Then he turned and took a long look at Franz, laughed, shook his hand vigorously, and then put his arms around the boy. Franz didn't like this. He shook Thomas off, pulled out his toy gun and shot him.

Thomas walked arm in arm with Amy and held Franz's hand. Franz pulled his away. Thomas held it again, Franz... behind them, a caravan of hired hands towed cases. All the time, Amy bringing Thomas up to date about meetings with American crime bosses, successful bankers and wealthy investors. "We'll soon be big enough to take on Johann Huth and his family." She didn't feel Thomas flinch at the remark.

* * *

"What!" Amy couldn't believe what Manfred was telling her. How could he and Thomas make such a move without discussing it with her? Because she wasn't here! She raged for days, her dream of revenge, all she lived and worked for, gone, forever. Even Manfred, with all his power, avoided her.

Eventually though, she decided that she would just have to hunt them all down, whichever corner of the world they had fled to. After all, she had her whole life to find them.

* * *

Her immediate concern was how easily the Maximilian Huth business empire had been confiscated and taken over by the Nazis. On this occasion, she, Manfred and Thomas had been the beneficiaries. Next time though, it could be their business that was being stolen. She worked with Thomas over the next few years, transferring everything they owned into an organisation virtually invisible, impossible to ascertain who the owners were. It became a ghost organisation; as far as anybody else was concerned, it didn't exist. They learned how to move money and valuable goods without leaving give-away trails or traces, and were able to siphon off all sorts of riches from the Nazis without much fear of detection.

Another bonus: As war approached, Jewish citizens were prepared to hand over vast quantities of wealth in order to escape Germany. Amy collected much of these riches, and with just a fraction of it paid out as bribes to Nazi officials, she arranged the escapes. Manfred oversaw it all. The ones who left it late had to hand over much, much more. And, by this time it didn't really matter whether or not they made it to safety! The family still took the money… then handed them over to the SS.

A fine haul of art-work, priceless treasures and a vast quantity of cash had just been moved into a Swiss bank vault. "We are going to become the wealthiest family in the world." Manfred toasted his prediction.

"Perhaps, perhaps not. It depends on who wins this war."

"We will of course." Manfred was indignant.

Amy gave him a hard long look. "You're changing into a Nazi. Since when have we been fighting for Germany?"

Manfred moved his shoulders about, flashing the SS insignia on the collar. "Haven't you noticed, I am a Nazi, a very fine Nazi."

Thomas smiled as Birgit and Heike poured more wine. Amy's two oldest daughters, now aged ten and twelve, loved waiting at the table for Papa, Mama, Uncle Thomas and their big brother Franz.

"You're probably right Manfred, Germany will conquer everyone who stands between her and world domination… probably. But let us consider the consequences if things don't work out that way. What if Germany is defeated? Where would that leave us?"

"We have an international business, having no borders."

"Correct, but we're all here. One of us needs to get to America and take care of business beyond these borders."

Manfred gave this some thought, while sipping white German wine. The topic had already been discussed at length by Amy, Thomas and Franz.

"You can't go, Manfred, for obvious reasons," continued Amy. "Thomas neither, we need somebody who actually speaks. I'm the only one."

Manfred poked his fork at his meal, moving peas around the plate as though planning a battle. "I must admit it makes sense. But not America, not yet. It would be too difficult to stay in contact. England! You would be able to control our American and British interests from London. What's more, if you went as an agent, as part of the German war effort, we could maintain contact quite easily, through spying networks."

Amy slowly nodded, knowing he was right.

Manfred continued. Dishing out instructions came easily. "Franz has been doing a good job helping to repatriate Jews, but, if you go, he'll have to assist Thomas, be his mouthpiece. Could he do that?"

Amy looked at her son, and declared confidently. "He could do that."

* * *

There was no hurry. While Germany was on top of the situation there were plenty of easy pickings to be had; the spoils of war! Amy used the time to perfect her English, and during this time the ghost business empire continued to expand, siphoning riches from the Axis countries and from wealthy Jews. They made their plans for the future, and a lot of discussion went on how they would do the same to the Allied powers.

Chapter 27

Tuesday 6th May 2008

Jack picked up his mobile and checked the caller ID. Jennifer, mm... He answered it. "Jen. Hi, nice to hear from you, I thought you had forgotten about me."

"Jack Painter, how could a girl forget about you? Sorry to phone you at work. The camera is really good, and nobody's found it yet, thanks for everything you've done."

"It was my pleasure. Rachel told me that you're almost ready to move in, anything else you might want, just ask."

"Well, I'm ready, but the house isn't. I'm going to give Rachel a call, I would very much like to see you both tonight; I'll buy you a *thank you* drink."

"That would be great, but your sister is being very difficult at the moment, she'll hardly leave the apartment, especially in the evening."

Jennifer was surprised. She knew about her sister's paranoia, but not how severe it seemed to have become. "Really, I didn't know. What about her work?"

Jack sounded a little depressed to Jennifer, even though they hardly knew each other. "She's off sick," he said, "She's become so obsessed about security. I wish I'd never said anything in the first place."

There was an uncomfortable silence before Jennifer continued. "Jack, I just wanted to thank you for the camera, you know, organising it and everything. We obviously can't mention it in front of Rachel. I also want to ask you if we can discuss some pretty serious extra stuff."

"What, me and you, or…"

"Well, I did mean Rachel as well, but now maybe I shouldn't include her. It's on the same subject, security. Look Jack, I wouldn't want to burden you with my troubles if you didn't want me to, and I know it would be difficult for you to turn me away, so maybe we should forget about it."

"No. I want to help, really, believe me, it's fine." He hesitated, then, "Why, has something new come up?"

Jennifer took his word that he was interested and she liked the thought of having his counsel. "No, everything's fine. It's just a few ideas I want to kick about and get some other opinions, so there's no need to worry. I know you are working so I won't keep you. I'll phone Rachel, but I won't tell her we've spoken, if that's alright with you. If she doesn't fancy the idea of leaving the apartment we could meet around there."

"Yeah, that'll be okay. I'm looking forward to seeing you."

"Brilliant, see you later, hopefully." Jennifer then added. "Before you hang up though, there may be more to things than what I say tonight, so don't push me too hard if I sound weird, we can meet up another day, just you and me, and I'll explain my thinking."

"Sounds intriguing."

"I suppose it does. I'll see you tonight then." Jennifer hung up. Then she phoned Rachel.

Chelsea.

By the time Jennifer arrived at the apartment Jack had organised a Chinese take-away and it had been delivered. Rachel had told her sister about her worries when they spoke on the phone earlier, so security became *the* topic soon after they sat down to eat.

They discussed Rachel's work situation, and then Jennifer said "I think the same way as you do, and I'm a little scared."

Jack didn't believe the bit about being scared, but said nothing.

"The farmhouse has a large cellar and I want to make it into a panic room."

"A panic room?"

"Yeah. I saw it on a film on the television. I forget what it was called."

"*The Panic Room.*" Quipped Jack, sarcastically.

"Yes, I've seen it," said Rachel "Jane Fonda I think."

"Jodie Foster," said Jack.

Jennifer was not sure who starred in it, and didn't care. "Do you mind if I go ahead and organise the work?" she said rather nonchalantly. She was going to do it anyway but having her sister's blessing would be better.

The thought of visiting Belfont made Rachel anxious, and extra security there sounded a good idea, but a panic room! "Isn't a panic room a little over the top."

"What are you frightened of, at the moment?" Jennifer asked her.

"Well," Rachel hesitated, "Um, you know."

"Yes I do know. Frightened that some weirdo will attack and murder you. How can anything that might stop that happening be *over the top*?"

"She has a point," said Jack.

All three were silent as they thought about the idea. Then Rachel gave the go ahead. "Yes. Okay. Tell us what you have planned."

"It's quite a big area. I thought of making a bedroom, a kitchen come storage room, a room with a toilet and shower and control room."

Jack had intentionally not said much, up until this point, but now he couldn't resist. "A control room?"

Jennifer was getting enthusiastic, this was the first time she had spoken to anybody about the idea. "Yes. A control room. I want to install closed circuit television and a good alarm system throughout the property, inside and out, so we'll need a room for the monitors and all the other stuff, you know, the control panel and things. There will also be contact with the outside world from there."

Rachel said, "Like the police?"

Jennifer didn't mean to, but she gave Jack a sly glance. "Yes, the police."

Jack wondered what Jennifer was really up to. Just to say something, he said, "It sounds as though it will cost a fortune."

"I think we'll be okay."

"Will you want any help, organising it all?" he asked.

"No, I want to know it all myself, inside out, so I want to be involved as much as possible." Jack looked a little disappointed. Jennifer smiled. "I think I can look after it, but if I do need any help, you'll be the first one I'll turn to, but what do you think?"

Rachel was beginning to lose interest, she constantly thought about her safety and she had been relying on Jack and Jennifer to help her forget the damn subject. She shrugged and pointed out, "It all sounds good, but the other alternative would be not to go there, at least until we know we are safe."

Jennifer replied, "We might be safe now... we could all be worrying about nothing. How long should we wait, Rachel?"

Rachel shrugged again, and sighed, "I don't know, until the police find this guy."

"The police are not looking for anybody, they're too stupid to understand the danger we are in. From their point of view, I'm the only killer around."

"She has a point," said Jack.

"Is that all you can say, Jack Painter?" jibed Rachel, in an attempt to lighten the mood.

"Sorry." He pulled a face and sipped some of his white wine. "What about planning permission?" he asked.

"I don't want anybody to know what I'm doing. Plus, me and Rachel would have died of old age by the time they gave us permission."

"You have a point."

Rachel thumped him on the shoulder and they all laughed.

Later in the evening, while Rachel was not around, Jack asked Jennifer more about her ideas, how he could help. Jennifer told him she was formulating a plan and would contact him sometime over the next few weeks. They would get together and she would explain what she was thinking, and why. When Jack objected about waiting too long she assured him that everything was cool, and that she was definitely going to need him… that he was going to play a big part in how her plan would come to fruition.

Truthfully though, she was having second thoughts about involving him behind her sister's back; she was buying some time.

Belfont-St-Mary

Martin Scott seemed genuine. Adam's father had recommended him, saying he was about as honest a builder as you could get. Another plus, he was based in Chelmsford and knew nobody from Belfont. Jennifer wanted to avoid using anybody local. He also didn't seem too bothered about the absence of planning permission, or of Jennifer's reluctance to involve the local building control office. Jennifer didn't want a price, "*Just let me know when you want some cash*," she told him. His two sons would start the work on Monday.

Jennifer toyed with her mobile. She was itching to tell somebody about the imminent start of work on her 'panic room'. She scrolled through her contacts. Adam was first; she invited him to the farmhouse. He would be with her in an hour. Holly; God, she was so tempted. Then, Jack. She sighed. No… not yet. And then back to Holly.

Holly Andrews; she missed her friend so much, and Jennifer knew that Holly would be over the moon to hear from her. She twisted the phone around in her hand. Should she? Shouldn't she? Her finger caressed the call button. Then she had a thought which froze her; why hadn't Holly phoned *her*? Of course, Jennifer knew. Holly wanted to sort out her own life; she wouldn't want the complications that could arise from hanging around old cell mates. Jennifer sadly pressed the back button and put the phone away.

Chapter 28

England 1942

In an unused room at the mansion house in Hertfordshire a petrified woman stood on a chair, hands and feet bound and a rope around her neck.

Hilda Von Seeckt had been a resident of England for the past eight years, she and her brothers having been brought here by their parents when they immigrated from Germany in 1934, fleeing Hitler's secret police. Or that's what she'd been told. Now this woman was telling her something different.

As a German national, she had just returned from a two year period of internment on the Isle of Mann, but this wasn't the reception she'd expected. Her parents had been released two weeks earlier and it was they who were supposed to be here to welcome her home.

Instead, a distant relative she barely remembered, and thought was dead anyway, sat at the edge of the room looking on. "You're about to die to quench my thirst for revenge. You're just another episode in our family feud."

"I know nothing of any feud."

"Well, that's your problem, had you known about it perhaps I wouldn't have been able to deceive you quite so easily." Who'd kept her in the dark, thought Amy, her parents, her grandparents… a stupid decision, trying to wipe out a past, pretending it didn't exist.

Hilda Von Seeckt's grandfather, Willie von Seeckt, was one of the four who had ordered the killings of Amy's family in 1920. Willie, his wife, their children and their families had all fled Germany after tip-offs that they were to be arrested by Hitler's secret police, thus avoiding the purges of Hitler's *night of the long knives*. This is the version of family history that Hilda had been fed.

* * *

Hilda was five years younger than Amy. They had similar looks, except when Amy smiled. "Officially, I'm in England to take your place in English society, to assist with our great German war effort," Amy was telling her. "Unofficially however, I'm here to take everything you own, including your life. It was a very bad day for you when your grandfather ordered the deaths of my family."

"I don't know what you are talking about. I know nothing about my grandparents, we lost touch with them… along with our uncles and cousins, when we left Germany. Hitler's SS were after us all. That's why we fled Germany. Have you murdered my brothers?"

"Not yet, but their time will come. I shall take everything they own… and then kill them, if they have children, they will die as well. I will not rest until every last individual who shares the blood of Isabel Huth is dead."

"Who the hell is Isabel Huth? You're a mad woman."

Amy ignored her and studied the woman. Manfred had been right; the Huth family was good stock. Hilda stood on the chair, hands bound and a rope around her neck; she must have known that her time was up. Yet she held herself so stoically – refusing to cry out. Amy wondered if the woman thinks she'll not go through with it. *Maybe she believes that her father and mother are about to come crashing through the door on a great charge and free her.* They will not be coming.

"You'll never get away with it…" Hilda said after a short period of silence, "…not on your own, anyway."

"What do you mean?" Amy found the '*not on your own*' a little intriguing. She pulled up a second chair, placed it in front of the woman and stood on it. Their eyes were level, just a foot apart.

Hilda continued. "I know that about thirty members of our family survived Hitler's purge in 1934, and fled to the far reaches of the world."

Amy corrected her, "It wasn't Hitler's purge, it was Manfred's."

"Well, anyway, you and Manfred are going to hunt all these people down, degrade and humiliate them, then kill them, and in the process, robbing them of all their wealth."

"The degrading part is just for my pleasure, it's not so important. But, yes, they will all die utterly penniless, although it's not *their* possessions I'll be acquiring; I'll be taking mine back."

"It will not be easy. It will take a long time."

Amy could almost taste the sweetness of her breath. She nodded, "True, but I have my whole life to do it."

"I could help."

Amy raised her eyebrows in surprise, "Except that you'll be dead."

The speed of the retort causes Hilda to take an involuntary gulp, however, she continued, "Only if you kill me. What about Manfred?"

"What do you mean?"

"He has ascended high in the German hierarchy, and from all you've told me he has such a cruel and dominating nature. He'll come to you after this war and he'll demand total control."

"*If* he survives this war... I'll kill him."

"I could help you."

Amy was full of admiration at the woman's attempt to stay alive. "I have eight children. They'll help."

"Can you trust any child to kill their father?"

"My first cousin, Manfred Huth, and I are man and wife, however, the father of all my children is Thomas."

"Thomas! You mean your brother, Thomas?"

"Yes. When I was fifteen and Manfred was seventeen, Manfred demanded, violently, that I bear his children. But he was not the man he thought he was; never has been. Thomas helped me. After being savagely beaten one night I cried to my brother and he touched me, comforted me. He was only thirteen himself but he helped me solve the problem of Manfred's infertility, and has helped me ever since. Manfred for ever believes that the blood that runs through our children's veins is pure. He just doesn't know how pure."

This scandal caused Hilda to momentarily forget her predicament, and she almost lost her balance. It was almost like confession over a nice English cup of tea. "What if he finds out?"

"He will not. He's too busy collecting priceless artefacts from all over Europe and diverting them to warehouses and banks in Switzerland, in accounts and businesses in the name of Hilda Von Seeckt. You thought you were wealthy... you have no idea how wealthy. Neither he, nor you, will ever get to see them though, to spend them. When he is unable to collect any more, he will die."

The sadness of missing out on all that wealth jolted Hilda and reminded her of exactly where she was.

Descendants of Maximilian Huth, irrespective of which womb they originated from, are a greedy bunch, Amy thought.

"You have it all planned. Amy, please spare me," Hilda pleaded. "Take my name, my identity, but let me live. I'll never cross you. Please."

"You and your parent's deaths are the first part of that plan, along with me taking your identity. The blood of the whore Isabel runs through your veins. The sons and daughters of Isabel killed my mother and father; their own step sister and her husband, and my dear twin, Frederick, in front of my very eyes. They killed Manfred's sister and his father and mother... and now you plead for mercy! I will not rest until the blood line of that whore ceases completely."

"Kill me when I'm sixty. Just not now! Please."

She was now becoming tiresome. Amy looked directly into her eyes as she gently pushed the chair with her foot. She held the hanging body steady so that they faced each other, Hilda watched Amy watching her die. To begin with Hilda refused to struggle; she began her short journey to death in control. But then the body's instincts took over, refusing to give up its precious grip of life so passively. It jerked and it kicked and it gasped. Amy felt a beautiful sensation rush through her body... her stomach... her groin, as the dying eyes fruitlessly pleaded for her life. Amy's body trembled and a magnificent ache engulfed her. The very last thing Hilda saw in the moment she exited this world was the look of uncontrolled ecstasy across Amy's evil and grotesque face; the face of the conqueror.

Chapter 29

Friday 13th June 2008

Edith could *always* rely on Peter's support, they were close.

Peter knew that were Edith to become head of the family, life would be bliss for both of them. So much wealth! So much power! Peter stood behind the seated woman, massaging her shoulders and neck. "Dieter has been to see me," he said. He felt her tense up very slightly.

"I know," she replied after a while.

"You know?" He was surprised. He stopped kneading her.

"Well, I didn't know for sure, but I guessed he would. He wants to be head of the family as much as I do."

"I'm aware of that, but I'm just about the last person he needs to see. And he would know that."

"Of course he knows that. Ooh… don't stop, you're so good at it. But if he is chosen, then he'll need your support."

He resumed massaging. "Perhaps. But he was digging. He mentioned Marylyn more than once. I'm sure he thinks you had something to do with her death. He also implied that Amy was suspicious. You know, I think her murder could sway her towards choosing Dieter."

"Look Peter, it's all under control. If Dieter is trying to start rumours, I can assure you, it'll backfire on him." She said it confidently enough to allay some of the killer's concerns.

"I hope you're right." He slipped the straps from her shoulders. "God… I hope she chooses you."

Edith sighed. "Well, you know that's what we both want. Dieter is a good book-keeper; the best in fact. But he has no mettle, he hates a mess, and he can't cope when things get a little out of hand."

"Maybe he would manage the business well enough so things never get messy."

"Things get messy sometimes, it can't be helped; it's the nature of our business. Amy knows that. She would say that you need to take whatever appropriate action is required, not run away from it. That's why I don't think she'll choose Dieter."

Peter teased. "Perhaps it will be neither of you."

Edith stood up, feigning indignation, pushed him back on the bed and jumped on top of him. "Who do you think then?" She pinned his arms down above his head.

Peter loved it when she mixed business with pleasure. "Franz has been spending a great deal of time with Amy lately. I've been keeping an eye on him."

"Franz is eighty four years old."

"He is next in line."

She started moving her groin in a circular motion. "We're not the fucking royal family."

He bit his bottom lip. Then he replied "No, but should Amy choose him then that would be the end of it."

She pressed herself down on him. "What if I refused to accept him as head of the family?"

He was breathing heavier. "You know the answer to that as well as I do. He controls the strong arm of the family. He's a powerful son of a bitch, cross him and you're in trouble. He's not known as the policeman for nothing."

She reluctantly agreed, "He could be head of the family anyway, whoever Amy chooses. He's that powerful."

He took a sharp intake of air as she undid his zip and felt her hand slide inside his trousers. "He'll always go along with Amy's choice." He wanted her. Breathing heavily, he managed to say, "What you need now is some mess, to remind Amy just *who* would be the best person to hand over to."

She could feel that he wanted her, badly, but she carried on talking. "That is actually what I've come to see you about." She slid down his legs and pulled his trousers after her. Wow, she loved to see a man in this state. "The situation with the Emmerichs," she caressed him gently, "while you're dealing with them, Peter, be as messy as you like – in fact the messier, the better." And she leaned forward.

* * *

Later the same day, scores of pairs of eyes watched enviously as a metallic black V8 supercharged Range Rover moved smoothly and quietly through Sampson's Farm Travellers camp near Basildon, carefully avoiding the dogs and small children as it did so. Eighty thousand pounds worth of gleaming high-tech engineering seemed alien amongst the junk and the trash, the rusty, broken-down and almost broken-down cars, vans and trucks. Slowly, the vehicle passed caravan after caravan... the residents of each one wondering what kind of person would enter their world in such a brazen manner. Each one was frantically working on a scheme which would remove some or all the wealth from this fool.

The driver, female, late thirties and alone, was Edith. She was dressed in keeping with the quality of the car she drove. Her jewellery was just as expensive. She drove slowly through the illegal campsite, aware of the eyes, neither afraid nor caring. She had been here before, although not in quite such an extravagant fashion. She knew he wouldn't like the flamboyant nature of her arrival, but she also knew he wouldn't say as much.

She remembered roughly where his caravan was situated. She passed low wooden fences that split the whole area into numerous sections or compounds, each containing at least one and some as much as a dozen shabby, mostly dirty white, mobile homes. Eventually she pulled into one of the smaller compounds which housed just one home. There was no litter and plenty of space to park and she stopped alongside a lone white van.

As soon as the huge four-by-four pulled up at this destination the eyes turned away in disappointment, to resume whatever they were doing prior to the vehicle entering the site. Nobody messed with the tenant who lived there, or with any guest of his. The travellers had long forgotten why he was always shown so much respect, but his reputation as a dangerous entity was embedded into the very fabric of the site, and was whispered to all newcomers as a matter of course.

Edith waited until the caravan door opened before stepping out of her vehicle. The welcome was warm but silent and it wasn't until they were both inside the mobile home that words were spoken.

Hans greeted her. "Dressed for the occasion I see."

"Don't be sarcastic. I thought it might be nice for you to see the real me."

"It's always nice to see you, real or otherwise." He didn't smile when he said it.

Edith walked over to the small table and sat herself down on a chair. "I've brought news from Dieter; the Madrid deal went off without a hitch. We're up and running properly in mainland Europe again, at long last."

"So, no trouble, from the police?"

"No trouble."

Hans scuttled around the small kitchen area preparing two mugs of tea. "You know it amazes me. While we've embraced the twenty-first century global economy, most police forces still think in national terms. It does make our business easier."

"I think they are changing their strategies though, because of the terrorist situation."

"Yeah, maybe, but fortunately, not very quickly… and anyway, terrorism is completely different; financially, the sums involved don't compare, so they're always looking at different criteria. By the way, how is Amy?"

Edith wanted to disagree, the last thing they needed was complacency, but she dropped it. "Still soldiering on. I think she's clinging on until the Emmerich situation has been resolved."

"And how is the Emmerich situation?"

"Peter's on it."

Hans always worried when Peter was taking care of business. He thought about it as he poured the tea.

"I'll be glad when it's all over," continued Edith. "Getting rid of all of them has been a distraction over the years."

"Revenge has galvanised the family," retorted Hans.

"Personally I don't think it has. Anyway, that's a different issue. Taking care of the Emmerichs is going to get messy – that's one of the reasons I'm here."

Damn! He knew there was something going down, coming here, all dressed up. "Explain. What exactly do you mean by messy?"

Edith shrugged, "My relationship with Amy has changed. I can't put my finger on it, but it's not the same. I'm worried that she's decided to choose somebody else as her successor."

"Dieter?"

"Maybe. Peter thinks it could be Franz."

"I don't think it will be Franz."

Edith was surprised. She thought he was a good choice. "Why not?"

"Running this family is a complicated affair. It's not just dealing with the criminal fraternity, it would mean getting into the ring with politicians, government officials and very successful businessmen. Not just mixing with them but being able to read them and outwit them. Even Amy knows that Franz would not be confident as leader."

"Amy doesn't mix with these people, why would Franz be expected to?"

"But she is a clever stick. Even now, at her age, she's intelligent enough to understand just what would be required, and delegate accordingly. Any one of us, you, me, Dieter. We could all go to Amy to discuss any part of the business and she would be quite capable enough to render advice. I know Franz, better than you do. I don't think Amy would choose him."

"So it's Dieter?"

"Not necessarily, there are a few who would be capable."

"You?"

Hans chuckled. "No. I kill people. I have no idea how the business side of the family is run. Look, we both know there is only one person for this position and that's you. You're the only one with the right mix of intellectual ability, social skills and ruthlessness to carry us forward."

"You know that, but I think that Amy needs reminding of it." She wasn't sure how Hans would take what was coming next, but he needed to know. "Between you and me, I've told Peter to create some headline news in his dealings with the Emmerichs. She'll see then who has the ability to deal with every aspect of our organisation."

Hans was poker faced. "I'm glad you didn't ask me to do that."

"Peter is dispensable, you're not."

"I can't believe you said that. Peter can be a maniac. If he's not careful, he'll end up dead."

"Don't be so negative. If I can, I'll take care of him."

"I hope you know what you're doing." He was quiet for a moment. Before continuing with the leadership topic, he asked, "What else brings you here?"

"Marylyn."

"Umm..." Hans sat back in his chair. They were still on the same subject. "Yes, I've been giving that some thought. There are rumours circulating."

"Started by Dieter?"

"No. I don't think so. I think somebody else is making a play to be Amy's successor. Some of the younger ones are blaming us for her death; some sort of revenge for her stance, re Terrence."

"I've already put the word out. We would never do anything like that."

"Then why was she murdered?"

Edith shrugged. "Coincidence. Lots of people get murdered."

"Crap. The way she was killed and the fact that there are no clues, nothing on CCTV... It has all the hallmarks of how we kill people. Somebody is trying to set us up."

Edith thought about that. "Right at the moment, I can only think of one person who might try something like this."

"Ben."

"Correct."

"But he's in Paris."

Hans didn't answer straight away. A sudden thought crossed his mind; maybe he was backing the wrong horse? Then, "Leave it with me, I'll look into it."

Chapter 30

Tuesday 24ᵗʰ June 2008.

The investigation team had grown to accommodate the murder of Patricia Fairport and the suspicious activities of the Defence Secretary, Sir Malcolm Henderson. MI5 had also been sucked into the affair. However, Theo had been granted a well earned break and had returned home to Northampton. He lived alone in a small studio flat, and after a visit to see his parents in Birmingham, he'd decided to spend a quiet night in.

He'd just eaten. The door to the flat opened directly onto a short driveway to the car park and, as he filled his small dishwasher, the doorbell rang. Outside, standing in the driveway, was Graham Morris. Confused, Theo stepped forward. That was all he could remember when he regained consciousness… with a thumping headache and feeling nauseous.

He pulled himself up, rubbing his eyes. "Where…" He broke off. He had a couch to himself. Opposite, sitting on an easy chair was Morris. Two other chairs were occupied by a man and a woman, and another woman sat at a table. They all looked at Theo as he came round. He registered all four but addressed only one. "What the hell are you doing? Where am I?" Theo was confused, this man was supposed to be in France, under the watchful eyes of the French authorities.

"Theo…" Morris started.

"How do you know my name, and how did you know where I lived?"

"We really haven't got time for this, all these questions. What I thought you might have wanted to know is, why are you here?"

Theo attempted to stare the man out, "Why am I here?"

"To meet some of my family. My name is Ben; my *real* name. The man who was on the iron lung, who died in hospital, his name was Terrence. He belonged to our family. A few years ago he decided that he no longer wanted to be involved in our family business, so he took about four hundred thousand pounds and tried to start a new life. They caught up with him in Barcelona and threw him down a well, to kill him."

"They?"

"The family, *our* family. The guy who did this to him goes by the name of Hans, but he was carrying out the orders of the family. That's what *they* wanted. The girl who you saw killed, you knew her as Patricia Fairport; her name was Marylyn. She was very close to Terrence, and she defied all of us. She saved the poor guy, looked after him and challenged anybody to harm him. In reality, the fact that he was paralysed from the neck down meant he was considered harmless and they left him alone."

"Why are you telling me this?"

"Terrence and Marylyn were what we call fourth generation, as I am." He turned to the others, "As we all are. Some of us feel trapped inside this organisation and have felt this way for a while. We didn't like what they did to Terrence, but we decided, at the time, because he had stolen money, perhaps it was justified.

But what they did to Marylyn… she was as loyal as anybody, but because she defied them, they punished her; killed her. Now some of us want out. We have brought you here to ask you to help us. We want new lives. If you do what we want, we'll help you break the family in return."

"How can I help? I need to talk to my superiors, I'm only a constable."

Ben ignored him. "What's going to happen now Theo… the four of us are going to have a conversation with you, to try to persuade you to help us."

Theo then acknowledged the other three. "And what if I refuse to help you?"

Ben shrugged.

The other male spoke. "We have everything we know about our family, its history, what crimes they've been involved in, names, dates, places; all of it here on this memory-stick." He held it up. "It's got a lot on it, I would think that you, the police I mean, will have to investigate this information and get more evidence, but, in exchange for this memory stick, we want new lives."

"I can't grant you that, I'm nobody."

"We understand that, but we want your word that you'll fight our case."

"Will you testify?"

The four looked at each other, a little uneasily it seemed to Theo, and then the woman sitting at the table spoke. "We're considering it. But you have to understand, these people are our family, and they're not all bad. But even the good ones won't forgive us for what we're planning, especially if we testify against them."

Theo thought about the offer. "What sort of crimes have your family committed? Is this memory stick going to be worth anything to us? And what if I think it's a waste of time?"

"You won't think we're wasting your time. But if you should, you can walk away," she said. "However, we're all confident that you'll want the stick."

"Why did you choose me?"

Ben shrugged, "I don't know, because we know about you, because you were easy to get to, you live alone… won't be missed. What more can I say?"

* * *

Theo felt in his pocket for his mobile. It wasn't there. Of course, why would it be? He wore his watch though, and that's all he actually wanted to know; the time. Close to midnight. His building excitement, as the four disclosed the activities of their family, had driven away the headache. "…And all this is definitely on the memory stick?" he asked for the umpteenth time. He could hardly suppress a grin.

Of the four, Ben did most of the talking, "It's all on there, and more… and in more detail. You're going to be pretty highly thought of when your people see this. We're doing you a big favour, not much longer a mere constable, hey." He laughed.

The other male brought out five mugs of coffee, already white, and a bowl of sugar. The sight of the drink reminded Theo that he had wanted to use the bathroom. "Do you mind if I take a leak?"

Ben shrugged as though it was a stupid question. One of the women wanted to escort him, "Ok, but I'll come with you."

"I'm not going to run off."

"I know you're not," she replied.

"She just wants to see your dick," it was the man who brought in the coffees. "She wants to see if it's true what they say about black men."

The woman didn't laugh. "Fuck off Robert. Come on," she said to Theo.

A few minutes later they were all back in their original positions. Ben nodded to the other male, who then held out the memory stick. "Here, it's yours. Don't lose it."

Theo tentatively took it, all the time expecting it to be snatched back and then to be ridiculed for falling for their little trick. It wasn't snatched back. Theo held it tightly in his hand. "What happens now?"

"You go," said Ben.

Theo looked at the others in turn, hardly believing that he was about to walk out of the place. "Thanks." He stood. "Actually, where am I?"

"London. The East End. You'll be okay," said Ben. "I'll see you out and point you in the right direction."

Ben led the way down the stairs and out into a dark disused car park. Theo realised he had spent the evening above a closed down pub.

"Out of that gate and turn right. There's a busy street about one hundred yards along the way. Then you're on your own."

Theo held out his hand. "Thanks Ben. You will not be sorry; I'll do everything I can to help you."

Ben's grip was strong. The grip of a genuine man!

The handshake lasted a little longer than Theo would have liked, but before he had time to react, Ben thrust his free hand into the policeman's stomach, just below the rib cage. The force of the blow caused every muscle in the man's body to become as rigid as steel, in shock, he stood completely upright, unaided, confused, and then dead. Before he collapsed to the ground, Ben slowly withdrew the long blade from Theo's heart.

The memory stick was still in the policeman's hand as he lay on the ground. The killer, using a tissue, gently removed it and placed it deep into Theo's jeans pocket; pushing it firmly and securely all the way, making sure it wouldn't fall out.

Ben wiped the knife clean and quickly returned upstairs. The woman who had escorted Theo to the toilet was alone. "Where are Tina and Robert?"

"Gone to find some sandwiches, or anyway, something to eat. That's strange; didn't you see them as they left?"

In a single movement, Ben leapt over to the woman, yanked her head back by her hair with one hand and slid his knife across her throat with the other.

In an instant he was back down in the car park, standing over Theo's body... But the others had gone. Shit! Two pairs of smudged, bloody footprints led across the old and scarred asphalt and onto the street. He bent down and checked for the memory stick; good, at least they didn't take that.

* * *

Tina returned to her flat and collected her emergency ID, debit cards and a wad of cash. She binned any perishable food and turned off the water and electricity. She didn't think she would be returning for a while. Robert had done likewise. After witnessing the killing of Theo Tester, realisation and panic had set in. Ben, for some reason, had set them up. They met up in the early hours of the morning to discuss their next move, how to keep out of the deadly clutches of the family… and how to keep out of the way of Ben.

Chapter 31

Suffolk Constabulary – Ipswich Divisional Headquarters.
Thursday 26th June 2008

It wasn't like the old days. In his day, when he was still wet behind the ears, problems were dealt with by your immediate superior... no way would he have dared trouble the Super.

As Detective Superintendent Frank Hollingsworth made his way through the investigations unit he saw that DS Andrew Fuller was alone. It would save valuable time if he spoke with him now. The Sergeant had requested a meeting.

"Sergeant Fuller. Hello, how are things?"

Andy looked up from his laptop, "Oh, hello sir. Things are quiet for a change. Did you get the message about me wanting to see you?"

"Yes I did, and seeing you alone in here reminded me. I have some spare time, would you prefer here, or in my office?"

"At the moment we can talk here, while it's quiet. Sir, I've been spending some time in Belfont-St-Mary, I'm in a relationship with somebody from there." Andy noticed his superintendent flinch a little. Was it the mention of Belfont-St-Mary or his relationship? It was common knowledge at the station that he was gay and found it damn annoying that the older officers struggled to accept it. Never mind, he continued. "Apparently Jennifer Emmerich is dating Adam Saunders, Billy's younger brother."

"I see, interesting. I wonder what her parole board thinks of that."

"Well, I know you're not particularly interested in Emmerich's love life, but, because we were on the subject an incident was mentioned that I think may have some bearing on the Emmerich-Saunders case."

Hollingsworth became serious. "That case is closed; for good," he said, and with some menace, it seemed to Andy.

* * *

In their hotel room, Tina and Robert had had their eyes glued to the television for the past two days. *They* couldn't understand why there had been no mention of the murder of Theo Tester.

* * *

Neither could Ben! He needed to find Tina and Robert. Fast. If he could take care of them, his plan would be back on track.

* * *

The original memory stick had been to forensics, then bagged and sent to the evidence room. What DCI Wentworth possessed was a copy, and studying it with him were the Metropolitan Police Commissioner, a representative of the Secret Services and the regional head of the Crown Prosecution Service. They had spent the last day and a half scrolling through page after page of serious allegations, some of which named persons holding very important positions.

"It contains plenty of information, lots of accusations," commented the head of the CPS, "but frankly, not much we're going to be able to use."

"There is an awful lot to look into. Investigating some of the names mentioned will cause a few waves," the Commissioner pointed out. "I think we should put a small trustworthy team on the stick, see if they can find anything which we could act on. Perhaps they'll dig up some information which will help us on the Theo Tester murder case."

The MI5 representative agreed regarding the team. "I doubt if there will be many prosecutions. Many of these so called crimes catalogued have not even occurred, as far as we can tell. And this name here… Dieter. He doesn't exist."

"No?"

"No, and if anybody would know, it would be us, at MI5."

Wentworth kept his thoughts to himself. This was his case, and he would investigate whoever and however he chose to. If there was any truth in these allegations, ministers or not, it was only right that justice was done.

* * *

A news blackout had been put in place. Theo's parents had listened to police reasoning as to why his death should not be made public, they didn't care either way… they just wanted the killer or killers apprehended.

* * *

A number of crimes had been purposely left off the memory-stick… the ones which had been carried out in order to satisfy Amy's revenge. That included the Emmerich project.

Chapter 32

**Duke of Wellington Place, Central London.
Sunday 6th July 2008**

The cleaners were working to rule, which meant rubbish which was normally collected on the Friday and Saturday night shifts littered the streets, loose and light stuff scurrying around in the light breeze and heavier bits and pieces pushed into corners or wedged under anything which rubbish could be wedged under.

Under a wooden bench a large piece of cardboard moved slightly and a tuft of scraggly hair popped into view. "Oh my God!" She couldn't believe it! How on earth did she end up here? This had to the most embarrassing situation she could ever, ever, have imagined herself ending up in. She promised her maker that she would never get drunk again if she managed to get out of this with any self respect left, in fact she decided there and then to give up alcohol altogether.

Trying to watch the world from beneath the park bench was a dazed and disorientated Stevie Gee. A thumping head didn't help as she tried to recollect how she managed to end last night by rolling herself in corrugated cardboard and sleeping here, like a homeless tramp. She remembered she was drunk, in fact, to be brutally honest, humiliatingly drunk. She remembered the mock speeches made at Speaker's Corner and she remembered coming on to a good looking guy young enough to be her son. She remembered laughing with him and his friends – of course, now, in the sober light of day, she realised they were in fact laughing *at* her. However, she cannot for the life of her remember moving on to Duke of Wellington Place, where she knew she was now because she could just see the monument beyond the rim of the cardboard tube which had been her bed for the night. Fuck! Why had she slept here for goodness sake? She didn't have to. She was booked into 'a three hundred pounds-a-night' hotel. Bloody hell, she thought, what a cretin!

She was in town to have some fun; that was the idea. She tried to tell herself that she would probably laugh about it one day, in fact, if it wasn't for the headache she would probably be laughing about it now... Who in hell was she trying to kid? Actually, no, it was not funny; and not under any circumstances would she ever be laughing! She sighed. She tried to examine the area, to see if she could crawl out without being seen. There was a guy walking past, and she would rather die than show herself now. At the very least she would wait until he disappeared. Just for the moment though, she was actually surprisingly comfortable. Or perhaps she had lost all feelings. She'd been using her forearms as a pillow so she could see her watch without moving much, ten past six. It was a beautiful morning, not a cloud in sight. She started thinking about making that move, to get back to the hotel, she just needed to wait until the two women standing about forty yards away, chatting, had moved on. She would not give them the satisfaction of looking down their noses at her predicament. They looked very much like cleaners and were deep in conversation, and as she waited she closed her eyes, shutting out the brightness eased the ache.

Stevie had come to London on Thursday, to chill out, to get away from a bad situation that had been developing for a few weeks. She was employed by a large plastic injection moulding company in Nottingham, a first-rate and steady firm to work for; good salary and interesting work. She'd been employed there since leaving school, starting in the purchasing department as a clerical assistant. She was now the facilities manager. It had been bloody hard work, lots of studying; two Open University degrees, one in business studies, the other in health and safety, but the endless evening after evening of study had been well worth the effort. Come September she would have been employed there for twenty-five years. Margaret had been the problem. She had been installed as Managing Director after the Management Buy-Out and had instantly embarked upon a vicious purge, *slash and burn* they had called it. She had sacked half the company management and reorganised the rest. The only safe positions were those who had moved into the board room with her; and Stevie was damn sure it was only a matter of time before some of those would fall by the wayside. It was the way industry was now, new broom and all that.

Stevie had come through unscathed but her older brother Mark, (tooling manager) and her long time boy friend Jonathon, (manager, human resources) had both gone. Jonathon, especially, had not let up since, questioning her family loyalty at every waking moment; *tell Margaret to shove the job where 'the sun doesn't shine'*. As much as she had felt sorry for her brother and for

Jonathon, Stevie loved her job. However, Margaret had been keeping a close eye on her. She was positive that her M.D. held her in high regard, but given that the woman had cut short the careers of Stevie's nearest and dearest, she was obviously suspicious as to where her facilities manager's allegiances lay.

Stevie's main project at the time was the automation of the production stores. Unfortunately the electrical contractor was struggling and consequently the whole job was running behind time. Margaret had misinterpreted this as a political manoeuvre; orchestrated by Stevie to undermine her, and had put her on garden leave to *'think about her future'*.

Stevie knew what an unforgiving bitch Margaret was, and that her career with the company was effectively over. She'd been able to put up with two days of Jonathon's barrage of hatred towards their old employer before she announced she was going to disappear for a while. She didn't tell anybody where she was going, just that she was going.

She hadn't anticipated being wrapped in cardboard under a park bench, waiting for the right moment to escape without the embarrassment of others' eyes - or their obvious comments. She had dozed off for a while and after waking for the second time she began to desire the luxuries of the hotel room enough not to care what two cleaners, or anybody else for that matter, might think when she emerged from this pile of rubbish. Then she sensed somebody sit on the bench! Damn. She was trapped, and had no choice other that to wait it out.

The two women had moved off and had been replaced by a steady but light stream of pedestrians and the much increased noise of mechanical traffic. She checked the time again; nine o'clock. Christ! She needed to make her move soon or she'd be arrested. Her new guest was so still and quiet that she began to think that he or she had moved on. Then she heard the musical tone of a mobile phone being switched on. Stevie's potential embarrassment increased dramatically as she now had to listen in on somebody else's phone conversation. She should make her presence known now, before this all went too far. She decided to count to three and... Then she heard the digital tones as a number was dialled.

It was a man's well spoken and very clear voice. "Hello, is this Michael? – Good – Michael how are you? Are you alone? – Good. Don't answer, just listen. Michael, I'm your old friend who delivered you the message; you remember that message, all those years ago. – Yes, but I'm disappointed, very disappointed. You have ignored it. If you had done as you were told all would be so different. You do know what you have to do Michael, to put a halt to this suffering. Michael, take your life. You have ten days or your two girls are next. Do you understand what I have just said? – Good, very good. Don't go to the police or everything will be many times worse, for all of you, do you understand? – Good. Thank you for your time Michael, just do what you know is right. Goodbye." And the mobile beeped.

What Stevie had just heard paralysed her. It wasn't until she felt the man move from his seat and then a good twenty yards away before she was able to resume normal breathing. She watched him walk through the open area in the direction of Knightsbridge. Just before disappearing from view he stopped and looked all around, including a long lingering look back towards where he'd been sitting. Could he see her? He didn't react as though he had. He stood in this position for about half a minute, as if he were deciding where to go next, all the time gently scratching his neck with his left hand; in contemplation. He then moved on, and as soon as he vanished from her view Stevie hauled herself from her bedding, no longer caring about the presence of others. She stood on the bench and was able to see him entering Knightsbridge. A woman appeared from his left, intersected him, and they talked for a few seconds. Then she crossed the road and disappeared through the gates into Hyde Park. Stevie switched her attention back to the man, just in time to see him discreetly drop the phone into the overflowing waste bin next to the bus stop. Stevie waited until he turned down a side street, and then again waited for a couple more minutes before making her next move.

She brushed herself down, wiped the sleep from her eyes and adjusted her shoes. With the sun behind her she nonchalantly strolled towards the bus stop, doing a good job of looking casual but remaining continuously alert for watching eyes, reconnoitring all ahead... the hundred or so yards taking just a couple of minutes. When she reached the bin she casually looked around before pushing her hand down to the very spot where she saw the phone drop. Nothing! She felt a little more, still nothing. In her frustration she frantically hunted through the whole bin, pulling rubbish out onto the street, quickly but carefully searching every handful before releasing it. How did he do it? She definitely saw the phone drop into the bin. She was standing, looking bemused, hands on hips and looking down into the virtually empty receptacle when she sensed something. She looked up.

He was standing against the wall, just thirty yards away, looking with dark penetrating eyes straight at Stevie. He did not look happy. He slowly began to walk forward and Stevie retreated at the same speed, taking backward steps… what happens now? Suddenly there was a loud whoop and she turned. A police patrol car had pulled up. The policeman in the passenger seat emerged from the car.

"What are you doing madam? We have just been observing you emptying the contents of the rubbish bin all over the street"

"I was looking for a phone."

"A phone?"

"That guy," she turned, but he'd disappeared, "Anyway there was a guy and he dropped the phone into the bin."

"Was it your phone?"

"No. I overheard a phone call, a threatening one, and I thought if I had the phone I could go to the police and hand it over."

The second policeman had joined them. "Was it the man who was watching you while you emptied the bin?"

"Yes, did you see him?"

"Yes. Can you remember the message?"

"Word for word, if I'm quick."

"Ok, sit in the car with PC Gentsome and write down what you heard him say. I'll check through the rubbish, to see if you've missed the phone, and I'll tidy the place up a bit."

Stevie and the policeman sat in the car and she wrote down the conversation before she had time to forget any of it. By the time she'd finished the other policeman had returned to the vehicle. "No mobile! Right. Both of us saw the man and we need to get back to the station while the image is fresh in our minds. We need you there as well, to make a statement."

Stevie flinched. "Look at the state of me. Can't I go back to the hotel and freshen up first?"

The two policemen looked at each other. One said "How long will you take?"

"Not long, I promise. Can you take me to my hotel and wait for me, it's in Charles Street?"

Again the two policemen seemed to converse with each other without uttering a word. A few minutes later she was walking through the hotel lobby. The policemen had reluctantly allowed her to do that unaccompanied; because of her attire and dishevelled look she said it would be even more embarrassing if one of them were with her. She showered and re-dressed in record time and not long after that the three of them arrived at the police station.

It was close to mid afternoon when she finally emerged. Everything that had happened had gone on record, and then the three of them, with the help of a police IT specialist and a new facial composite computer program, had managed to produce a very good likeness of the man. Other than the walnut colour of the woman's hair, that she was slim and perhaps youngish to middle age, they couldn't produce a good image of her. The CCTV in the area was checked but revealed nothing of either of them. The image of him and the information gleamed from the phone call were fed into a computer program to see if they matched up with any past or current investigation, but that also revealed nothing. Eventually, when offered one, she declined a lift back to the hotel; the walk would do her good.

Walking back, she started thinking about the stranger. She was so glad the police had turned up when they had, she was certain she'd escaped a lot of trouble. She couldn't help but look behind her. Of course he wasn't there. She looked again...

She raced across the road, then jogged at a fast pace along Piccadilly until she reached Half Moon Street where she turned left, up the full length, across Curzon into Queen Street and finally into Charles Street and her hotel. Only when she reached the reception area did she look back again. All was clear. She briskly walked through reception and made her way directly to her room. What the hell had she done? Why couldn't she just have looked the other way, pretended not to hear the conversation.

She put the 'do not disturb' sign on the door, stripped off and climbed straight into bed, too weary to wash. She was totally exhausted; her head was thumping and she felt nauseous. As her head sunk into the cool soft pillow she momentarily thought of food, which made her stomach churn violently, she thought she might throw up; then she slept.

Chapter 33

Stevie awoke and checked the time, nine-thirty; pm, unfortunately. She still had the stinking headache and her empty stomach gurgled. She didn't know if she wanted to eat or be sick. It was a real effort to rise from the bed. What about the phone call? Fuck the phone call. Almost blindly she made her way to the bathroom, stepping over scattered clothing on the way. She was appalled at what she saw in the mirror. No more alcohol for you sweetheart! She ran the shower until the water was as hot as she could bear it and then climbed in and stood until she was fed up… and then remained there for as long again. She washed herself as vigorously as any sick person could, trying to cleanse the previous night out of her system… but it didn't work. She looked better but felt just as bad. She lay back down on the bed and thought about the phone call. Maybe she could find this Michael by herself. But, Michael who? How on earth would she begin her search? She sighed. She felt a huge load bearing down on her and this really was not the time to decide. Her hands shook as she tried to make up, not through nerves, but through self abuse. She gave up. Before anything else, she should get food, and aspirin.

She left the 'do not disturb' sign on the door, passed through reception and out into the street. She made her way to a pub in Bruton Street, one that she had earlier noticed and promised herself a visit. They were still serving food and she went straight for the main course, steak and chips, no dressing, and black coffee. One of the barmen was kind enough to give her two aspirin. She picked at the food, forcing it down with copious amounts of coffee. As she felt herself recovering slightly she again thought about the phone call.

Did she do the right thing by involving the police? Would the guy now carry out his threat to harm Michael's daughters? But again, would *he* know that she told the police? The answer to that was probably yes; he would have hung around to see her disappear in the squad car, and she'd have only gone off with two policemen for one reason. Despite their resources, how enthusiastically would the police follow the call up, even they said that there was not a lot to go on. The facts, as they are, meant that Michael, whoever he was, has to kill himself. It really was not her business, she should forget it. But how could she? She couldn't just walk away from the problem. She knew that she wasn't thinking clearly and decided to put the issue on hold, just for a few hours, until she felt a little better.

Had it not been a Sunday evening she would have shopped, that was always good therapy. It was much too late to see a show; she could try the late cinema. After eating she made her way eastward, towards Leicester Square, walking rather than taking any form of transport. She stopped at almost every eatery she passed with vacant outside seating, and spent a good couple of hours walking, people watching and sipping black coffees.

Whilst watching some late night street artists perform at Covent Garden, she decided that she was not really in the mood for the cinema after all. The walking had made her feel better and her head was beginning to clear. Again she reasoned with herself about the phone call; any sane person would get on with their lives and forget it. Lives! That was just the point, lives were at stake and she had to do something. She decided that she would do her very best to find Michael, after all, she had plenty of time on her hands, and, if nothing else, it would be interesting to see how she got on. But - how to go about it? All she knew was that a guy called Michael had been ordered to take his own life within the next few days and that he had two daughters… and, what else? Yes, he had been contacted before this morning; the messenger was disappointed that Michael had previously ignored him. She must get in contact with the police again and point that out.

All this thinking had made her forget about her hangover. Suddenly she couldn't wait to get started. She flagged down a taxi and returned to the hotel. Her room stank! The state of it made her feel ill again and she lay down on the bed. Maybe the previous threat was witnessed or reported. She would check online. Was Michael in this country? She would have to assume the answer was yes, or, if not. Well, one step at a time. Should she return home and work from there? She would go back to the police station tomorrow morning and then make a decision. Michael obviously speaks English.

Her thoughts were mixed up and she wasn't feeling one hundred percent, so she opened the window slightly for fresh air, undressed and slipped into bed;

she would start working on the problem first thing in the morning.

Chapter 34

Monday 7ᵗʰ July 2008

She awoke with a start, she was sweating profusely; *he* was in the room; she could feel his presence. She reached for the bed-side lamp and knocked it flying. She screamed. "Get out. Leave me alone."

Within seconds her hotel phone beeped, it was reception. "Hello Miss Gee, are you okay?"

"There is somebody in my room" she shrieked. "Send somebody now."

There was scrabbling at her door. A click. The knob turned and the door inched open and the lights came on. "Miss Gee." It was hotel security.

She snatched at some bed clothes and covered herself up. "He's in here, check the bathroom."

"Who?" The security guard crept forward and, standing at the ready, gently pushed open the door. The room was empty.

"He's in here. Somewhere! Under the bed, try under the bed."

The guard rolled his eyes and bent down and checked. "There's nobody in the room Miss. Perhaps you were dreaming."

"Oh God." She buried her face in her hands. "I am so sorry."

"It happens," he said, trying to be sympathetic.

"I'm really sorry. There was an incident earlier today…" Stevie realised in mid-sentence that she was wasting her breath. "I'm sorry," she repeated.

Once she was alone she cried. The dream had really freaked her out. The only thing to be grateful for was that the window was slightly open and the room had smelled fresh when the guard came in. The window! She jumped out of bed and closed and locked it. What a mess.

After a fitful night's sleep she woke at six-thirty, her normal rising time for work. Thankfully the hangover had gone. The incident (or non incident) during the night was still fresh in her mind and the room made her nervous, she got out of bed with more than a little trepidation. Before anything else, she made herself a strong coffee and turned on the television. The news was mostly about the economy and she sat on the bed, drinking and not really listening at the same time. Her mobile rang.

She checked the number; not recognised. "Hello."

"Stevie." She instantly recognised the voice though. "Stevie, is that you?" he asked.

"Yes. How did you get this number?"

"I can do anything. That includes making your life very uncomfortable if you continue to poke your nose into my business."

"Your business is hurting other people."

"It's still my business, not yours. I have phoned you to warn you, forget everything you heard or things will get very unpleasant, do you understand."

"I understand what you are saying, but I know what you look like and you will not tell me what I can or cannot do. I will continue to help the police in any way I can, until you are behind bars you nasty little shit."

The phone went dead. She checked the number in the call received log. It was there! So, he's not that fucking clever!

She had a light breakfast brought up to her room, she didn't want to waste time but she did need to eat, and then she made her way to the police station.

The young detective constable who dealt with her the previous day was in, and she seemed very interested in the call. "Can I have the number, we'll get it checked. It shouldn't take long to get any information about our friend, that's if there is any, which I somehow doubt." The policewoman seemed too young to the forty-one year old Stevie. Probably not long out of university. Stevie wondered if this would be her first case.

The policewoman, her name was Amanda Barnard, added the information to the case file which was opened yesterday.

Stevie asked. "Did you notice the wording from yesterday's conversation, the call to Michael; this was not the first threat? He said he was disappointed that he'd been ignored."

DS Barnard said she had, and that they were making an attempt to see if there was a file somewhere on record with a similar threat. After giving Stevie some advice on keeping out of trouble, how to recognise danger and reassurance that the police force will always be there for her, another officer came in with news of the phone-number. "You won't believe this, we have some information already," he said. "The call made this morning was the first time the mobile has been used, or that number, anyway. It's a pay-as-you-go number, no surprise there, and it was purchased in Edinburgh in 2006 under the name of Arthur Scargill. Has a sense of humour, does our boy."

Stevie was astounded. "Arthur Scargill? I don't believe it."

"I don't suppose Arthur Scargill is the man we are looking for…"

Stevie stopped him. "No, I'm not stupid. But Arthur Scargill is the name of my cat!"

"Really!" said both police officers, in unison.

All three sat in silence until Stevie broke it. "What does this mean? And if he purchased the phone two years ago… none of this makes any sense."

Amanda Barnard was the first of the two officers to speak. "Colin, did the mobile information include where this morning's call was made from."

"Yes, Nottingham."

Stevie gasped.

"Nottingham, that's your home town isn't it, Stevie," stated DC Barnard.

"Do you think he's going to do something to my cat?"

"I definitely think we are dealing with a bit of a nut-case." Colin quipped. "With due respect to your cat though, surely he can't imagine we would halt an investigation with a threat like that."

"A threat like what? He hasn't threatened anything yet," said Barnard.

"I think he just wants to let me know how clever he is," said Stevie. "The cat, and the fact that the call was made from Nottingham."

Barnard gave her colleague a long hard look. He wasn't being much help. Without saying a word he got up and left. She sighed and then said, "I'm not sure what to do next." She tapped her pen on the desk. "I think I should get the help of somebody experienced, for advice."

Stevie's mobile rang. She looked to see who was calling; Jonathon. "It's my boyfriend. Do you mind?" she said, waving the phone in front of her.

Barnard just smiled.

"Hi."

"*Stevie, where are you?*"

"London."

"*Fuck Stevie, your house is on fire.*"

"What!" Stevie leant forward and grabbed Barnard's arm, stopping her from leaving the room. "My house is on fire!" She switched the mobile onto loud-speaker. "Jon, I'm at a police station, tell us what is happening."

"*A police station, what are you doing at a police station?*"

"Never mind that! My bloody house is on fire."

"*I had to drive past, on the way to the golf club, and, well, it's on fire. The fire brigade is here. It's going up like a real good'n.*"

"What about Arthur, is he alright?"

"*You're worried about the cat! Your house is on fire. God, I don't believe this.*"

Barnard held her hand up, "Can I have a word?" she whispered. "Jonathon, I am Detective Constable Amanda Barnard. Is there anybody in authority there who I can talk to?"

"There are police all over the place, they're saying it's arson, won't say why, just that it is. Here, this is one now." He obviously handed his phone to a passing policeman. *"Hello, Constable McWilliams speaking."*

"Constable, Detective Constable Amanda Barnard, Metropolitan Police, can you phone me back on…"

Chapter 35

About an hour later Barnard returned to the interview room with a senior officer. They informed Stevie that the burning was indeed arson, and that whoever did it went to great lengths to make sure that there was no mistaking that it *was* arson. They went through Stevie's immediate plans, which were to return to Nottingham. She was to check in at the main police station as soon as she arrived in the city, and by then arrangements will have been made for some protection.

Barnard escorted her back to the hotel. "Take this." She handed Stevie a card with her mobile phone number on. "Use it if you want to contact me directly."

Stevie thanked her. "I have another phone, a pay-as-you-go. I keep it, just in case. I'm going to use that for the time being. I'll text you from it so you know my number."

"What are your intentions, regarding this affair?" asked the policewoman.

"I think I've got the message. I'll hide up somewhere in Nottingham until either you get him or, hopefully, at least until he knows I'm not a threat."

"What about the man who has to kill himself? How do you feel about him and his two daughters?"

"What can I feel? You have all the resources, what am I supposed to do?"

"I'm not suggesting you do anything; just making conversation I suppose."

"But what can I do? Whoever this guy is, he's shown just how dangerous he can be. He's a clever bastard."

"I don't think he's been particularly clever," said the policewoman. "When you reported the original phone message, to be honest it would have been placed at the bottom of a bloody big pile. The stunt he's just pulled has moved it much closer to the top."

"Maybe he's done that on purpose."

Barnard shrugged. "Maybe, but why?"

When they arrived at the hotel they wished each other good luck and said their goodbyes. Stevie informed reception that she was going to check out and could they prepare her bill. She then went to her room to collect her things. What else could she do? Her earlier thinking had been rather fanciful; there really was nothing she could think of that would help the police. Barnard was right; the case had now become important enough to throw everything at it… and she'd had enough. Her house had gone; okay there was the insurance, but even so. Anyway, what it boiled down to was… she was no longer sure whether she wanted to help, even if she could.

She'd been travelling light and didn't have a lot to pack; one case, her laptop and a shoulder bag with the important stuff in. The bill came to one thousand and four hundred pounds. She produced a card and punched in her pin number. After a short wait she was informed that it had been declined. Damn. She tried another, the same result. She apologised and, knowing a branch of her bank was not far away, decided to wander along and see if she could find out what was happening. She left her case and car keys at reception, and they told her that they would load the case into the car, ready for her return.

At the bank she saw a junior manager. It transpired that her cards had been stopped because she had earlier informed her insurance company that her cards had been lost. They could not be reinstated, and after some security checks and pleading phone calls they allowed her to withdraw two thousand pounds.

The fact that this guy had been able to cancel her cards frightened her even more. Okay, I've been warned, now *please* let me be. He must have got all this information from her bureau... and from her computer. She had a new account with another bank, opened only a couple of weeks ago. She tried that card at one of the ATMs at the bank. It worked. Who's a clever dick now? She retracted that thought immediately... she was in no mood to tempt fate. The account had almost eleven thousand pounds in it, from a recently matured savings plan.

She made her way back to the hotel and settled the bill with cash. Loaded with her handbag and laptop, she made her way to the car park, which was situated beneath the hotel. She took the stairs. She was actually glad she was going home, even though she was about to lose her job and her house had been burned to the ground. Her job was stressful anyway, and her house; well it was just a house, a place to live. Her insurances were up to date. What was the worry? On reflection she decided that she'd already spent too much of her life kowtowing to self opinionated, jumped up nobodies. She was going to make a complete change of direction, nothing or nobody was going to stop her living a fuller and more rewarding life; except maybe a moron with a mobile. That thought made her shudder.

Whooosh!! The next thing she knew she was on her back on the stairs. An enormous flash and blast from the parking area had flung open the connecting double doors and violently smashed her backwards. The steps were covered with a thick deep pile carpet, as befitting the luxury status of the hotel, and probably prevented skull or bones from serious injury.

She watched the doors close again, and she was back in the bank, she was sitting on the soft floor and the manager was pleasantly telling her about the times of buses... then she was collecting wads of cash, spewing out from the ATM... all around people were laughing with her... it felt so good... And then she came around.

Breathing was difficult and her chest hurt. Her ears were ringing; she had been momentarily knocked unconscious. Her right arm and shoulder also hurt, it was this side which had taken most of the impact when she had been thrown against the steps. She coughed and spluttered and caught her breath as she pulled herself up to a sitting position, which was just about as much as she could manage. She sat on the step until her brain began to function again. Firstly she sensed smoke. Not much. The doors, heavy and fire rated, had re-closed. Then the sound of alarms, first quietly, and as her hearing recovered, louder... until the sound was deafening. It was not just the hotel fire alarm but alarms from a dozen or so cars as well. She managed to stand. The small windows in the doors were strengthened glass and were unbroken, and she could see hazy flickering light through the thick white-grey smoke; flames. Time to get out!

She dragged herself up to reception where hotel staff and a lone policeman were hurriedly ushering customers and visitors out through the main entrance, or through a smaller exit at the rear of the building. She chose the rear exit. This was manned by the duty security guard, who was instructing both staff and guests to make their way to the designated assembly point. She wondered if he was the same guard who came to her room during the night. Probably not, but she wouldn't have known. He did ask if she was alright as she passed.

There was a small boutique opposite and she made her way straight for it. Inside, she checked herself in a mirror, God, it was no wonder the guard asked after her, she looked as though she had been pulled through a hedge backward, and there was a smearing of blood on her face. There was a slight graze on the back of her hand. There were only two staff and they were both concerned for her well being. They allowed her to clean and straighten herself up in their washroom. Through all that had happened she still carried her bag and her computer.

By this time the first of the firemen and police were arriving. There was another explosion from below the hotel, and people automatically moved back. The two girls listened open-mouthed as Stevie told them how she'd been thrown against the stairs and had she been just a couple of seconds earlier she would have taken the full force of the blast. They both agreed with her that she'd been very lucky. They made her a cup of tea and they all stood in the shop watching as more emergency services arrived and swung into action. Two people, a man and a woman, stopped outside on the pavement, obscuring their view slightly. Stevie didn't think they were a couple, but they stood and commented to each other, obviously about all that was happening. He said something and the woman recoiled in shock... perhaps he had also just avoided the first explosion. As she spoke back to him, he scratched his neck gently with his left hand.

Stevie pulled back sharply. It was him! He looked completely different, but she instinctively knew it was him. She held her breath as the woman walked off. He slowly walked past the shop, looking all around as he did so. He stopped, waited, and then walked back towards the main street, and to the front of the hotel. He was looking for her, she knew it. She rooted around her bag, found the pay as you go mobile with Amanda Barnard's number saved on it and called her, but the police woman didn't answer. The call was directed to the voice mail, but, not wanting to alarm or involve the two shop assistants, Stevie hung up.

She thanked them both for their help and left the shop. She then cautiously made her way to the front of the hotel, looking out for him as she did so. Quite a large crowd had gathered and the police were pushing them back in an attempt to close off the street. Again she saw him. This time he was directly in front of the hotel building, and she could see that he was being asked to move along. For a moment he seemed to resist, but then did as he was instructed, taking a good look around as he did so. Unlike most of the other onlookers though, he didn't stop to take up a new position, but kept walking.

Stevie retreated back into the side street as he passed on the opposite pavement. She didn't take her eyes off him as he walked off at quite a brisk pace. Again she phoned Barnard and this time left a message. *I'm following him; get back to me as soon as you can.*

He crossed Piccadilly near the end of Half Moon Lane and entered Green Park; she kept a good distance. He skirted the front of the Palace, crossed the Mall and then made his way eastward along Birdcage Walk. The mobile bleeped. "Hi Amanda," she whispered. "I'm following him."

"How come?" asked the policewoman.

"I think he tried to kill me. Have you heard about the explosion?"

"Yes. I'm at the Mermaid Conference Centre."

"Where's that?"

"Blackfriars."

"God, he's coming your way. He's just turned along the Victoria Embankment."

"Can you keep him in sight?"

"I have so far, but he's choosing a very awkward route, I could loose him at any time."

"Ok, stay on the phone and I'll call for back-up. I'm on foot but I'll make my way in your direction. Tell me what happened."

Stevie quickly told the constable everything. "Shit, he's turning left, away from the river."

"Name the street."

"I can't see. There's a small pier on the river and the road is almost under Waterloo Bridge."

"Sounds like Savoy Street. I'll still make my way in your direction along the Embankment."

Stevie increased her speed, using the trees and shrubbery around Savoy Place for cover. It *was* Savoy Street, and he was about seventy five yards along the street by the time she reached the corner. There were quite a few pedestrians around, but not enough for her to lose herself amongst, so she waited at the corner for a while. She was just about to carry on after him when he suddenly did an about turn and began to walk back towards her. She turned back onto the Embankment and shrieked down the phone, "He knows I'm here. He's seen me."

"Run. Get away from there," ordered the policewoman.

Stevie ran into the clump of trees and bushes in Savoy Place. From amongst a bunch of small bushy trees she watched, and waited. He was back at the junction on the embankment. He looked both ways and then commenced eastward again beside the river. "It's okay," she reported into the phone with a sigh of relief. "I don't think he's seen me after all. He's coming your way again. Has help arrived yet?"

"No, don't worry. I'm beside Temple underground station. Where is he, what's he wearing?"

"Dark blue Fred Perry tee shirt with standard denim blue jeans."

"Light brown hair; I think I can see him. Has he got light brown trainers on?"

"Yes, and he's got his left hand in his pocket."

"Got him."

"Amanda, wait for help."

"I am. We'll both follow him independently, he doesn't know me."

Stevie could now see the police woman one hundred yards ahead, standing beside some wheeliebins, and she could see him walking towards her. Stevie heard his voice on the mobile. "Hello, you're a police officer aren't you, could you tell me where the Millennium Bridge is from here?"

Detective Constable Barnard's reply was not clear and Stevie watched as he suddenly pushed her in amongst the bins... they both disappeared and the call on Stevie's mobile ended.

Stevie waited, and after about twenty seconds he reappeared. A quick glance around and then he was back on his way to wherever he was going. Stevie went cold. She looked at the phone in her hand, and waited. It beeped. The display said the caller was Amanda Barnard. She was about to press the green button, but stopped herself. She looked after him but he'd disappeared, out of sight. The mobile needed answering. She did so in as deep a voice as she could manage. "Dixon," she said. The call ended abruptly.

Stevie stood, rooted to the spot. Trembling legs rendering it almost impossible to move, imagining what she would find in amongst those bins. Part of her was afraid for herself; she was getting to know this killer, for that's what he was, and part of her was afraid for the policewoman. She imagined the worst, but had to find out for certain.

Fearful of what she was going to find, it took a long time to cover the one hundred yards. She reached the spot and stepped in amongst the bins. She didn't see her straight away... her heart lifted... perhaps... then she saw two feet poking out between some bins. Using her shoulder she rolled one away from the prostrate body. It had a small wound to the left eye, but the pool of blood beneath her head was immense. Stevie had never seen a dead person before, but she knew Amanda Barnard was dead, even before she bent to feel for a pulse. Her legs went and she almost collapsed onto the body. She sat on the ground and tried to compose herself…

She had to get away. She rolled onto her knees, forced herself up, and managed to manoeuvre the bin back into its original position, hiding the girl's body from view. She needed to get to somewhere safe; away from here… and him.

Chapter 36

Tina and Robert seldom left their hotel room. They had gone through a number of theories as to why Ben had done what he'd done. In the end, they both agreed that the bastard had definitely set them up. There was nothing on the memory stick which implicated him… or them for that matter. But certainly nothing about *him*. There was also nothing to implicate Amy, in fact she was not even mentioned; he'd made sure of that. The production of the stick had been Ben's idea – he'd been the driving force of the whole escapade; from beginning to end.

Robert had come up with a theory which made sense; Ben wanted to be the head of the family. Had he killed Marylyn to stir up feelings against Edith and Hans? Her death had certainly been enough to galvanise Robert into being prepared to rebel against the family. And the memory-stick had enough poison on it to deal with Dieter and Franz. He was after the riches and the power that Amy's position would give him.

Robert had followed Ben back into the building and witnessed his killing of Emmeline. That was after they had both seen him knife the policeman and plant the stick. It's a pity they couldn't have retrieved it, but their priority at the time was to save themselves.

Without seeing it, they would never have believed it. The way he had so coldly killed Emmeline made them realise that Ben had it in him to kill Marylyn. Robert and Tina... and Emmeline, had fallen for his lies... hook, line and sinker.

They had considered a number of theories, and eventually reached the conclusion that Ben's plan had been to kill the three of them, and then to go to the family and tell them that he'd foiled a plot. The memory stick being in the hands of the police would certainly herald the end for the hierarchy of the family, especially Dieter, Edith, Franz and the small army of assassins. That would leave the way clear for Ben to take over from Amy!

The two of them understood perfectly well that staying alive spelt disaster for Ben; they had to remain on high alert as well as coming up with some kind of scheme which would get them out of the hole they found themselves in.

* * *

Stevie knew the police woman was dead... but there was nothing she could do about that. What she had to do now was make a few quick decisions. The first one was to get away from here; she went into Temple underground station, purchased a ticket at the machine using cash and rode the Circle Line while she mulled over her options. She removed the SIM cards from both the mobiles, she would crush them... for a while it might be a good idea to play dead and the mobiles would have obviously been destroyed with her, had she been blown up. She needed time. Did *he* know that she was still alive? Hopefully not, but she shouldn't take anything for granted.

She needed to take care, think about her every move. Don't make bad decisions, like entering London's Underground, with probably the highest population of CCTV cameras in the country. Damn. But who was she hiding from, *him* or the police? Whoever it was, it was now too late, and sooner or later the police would have video proof that she survived the blast. Somehow she also felt that as soon as they knew, he would know.

She left the underground at the next station, which was Notting Hill Gate, and plunged straight into Portobello Road market. This was perfect, masses of people and the chance to purchase anything required for a change of appearance. She bought shopping bags, sets of cheap clothes, a couple of wigs, hair colouring and makeup, and then dipped into a busy bar and into the ladies, unnoticed. In there she changed just about everything in order to look completely different, except she stayed in jeans, after all, just about everybody wore jeans. She thought the long black wig looked good.

She had purchased a new shoulder bag. The old one, along with the lap top, old clothes and new toot went into her new shopping bags. There! What next? She needed to find somewhere, a small hotel to allow a little breathing space, and to work from. She considered catching a taxi but quickly changed her mind. That wouldn't be clever, not from here anyway. She would have to walk for a while. She checked the time; five minutes past four. It was hours before it was dark, too long to hang around.

So she walked, heading north, using residential streets as much as possible. Every now and then she popped into a pub and did a changing act, even different styles of shoes, thus forcing herself to walk differently. By the time it was dark she had reached Barnet, where she found a small family run hotel who didn't ask to see her passport, and accepted Stevie's word that she did not possess a credit or debit card. Importantly though, she could get online. She chose a twin room with a small en-suite.

Her lap top turned out to be broken so there was nothing she could do other than watch television for any news bulletins. The hotel received just the main five channels and the usual radio stations, but the news on television had finished for the evening so she checked the CEEFAX service, and there it was; *Bomb Blast at London Hotel. A car bomb exploded in the underground car park of the Willem II hotel in London's West End early this afternoon. Police would not say if there were any casualties but witnesses believe at least one woman was in the car with the bomb. The police also believe that this was a gang related incident and not a terrorist attack. They are currently looking for a dark haired male, who they would like to question.* That was it. She set her alarm for an early start and went to bed.

In the morning the explosion was not quite top of the news. It was beaten by reports of the discovery of Detective Constable Barnard's body. The two incidents had not yet been linked, not publicly anyway. Crucially though, there was no mention of Stevie's involvement in either. Perhaps Amanda Barnard had not mentioned her when she called for back-up; assuming she *had* called for back-up. Both stories hogged the early morning news viewing time, but there were no further developments.

Chapter 37

Tuesday 8th July 2008

After a much needed fried breakfast she purchased a new plug and play lap top, a pay-as-you-go mobile using a false name and address, along with fifty pounds worth of credit, and a small radio. She picked up some snacks, cold drinks and some pens and writing materials. It also occurred to her that travelling so light could make people at the hotel suspicious, so she bought herself an overnight bag. The phone had a camera. She took a picture of herself and called it '*hotel arrival*', to remind her of how she should always look in front of the hotel staff. By mid-day the computer was up and running. The explosion and the dead policewoman dominated all the news and the police seemed to be issuing a steady stream of new information to keep it that way. There had been a body in the car, they said, but it would be a while before it could be identified. Was that true? Lots and lots of information about Constable Barnard: how she had only recently joined the Metropolitan Police Force after obtaining a degree in forensic science, where she had lived for most of her life, interviews with and tributes from friends, colleagues and not so close family. No mention of her involvement on the "Phone Call" case.

Stevie spent the rest of the day trawling through old news, visiting social networking sites, asking questions about threatening phone calls, and following names and quotations over the internet, all without success.

Wednesday 9th July 2008

On Wednesday morning it was being suggested that the explosion and the murder of Constable Barnard could be linked. The image of the character, which Stevie and the two policemen had produced on Sunday morning, was shown. The police wanted to talk to this person, urgently. There was no news of the body in the car, which Stevie thought very strange. Had they suspected that she was the victim, it would only take a short time, forensically, to prove those suspicions wrong. She was a vital witness, the police must know that, so why were they keeping her out of the news?

However, a police spokesman did ask if anybody recalled an incident from anytime in the past, even as much as twenty years ago, of a threatening message ordering a man to commit suicide or his family would suffer... the father had two daughters? This was a little vague, he added, but, nevertheless could be a very important lead, and the public were urged to contact the police if they had any information.

All Stevie could do, she concluded, was wait. She would keep her head down for the time being.

Chapter 38

Towards the end of the same morning Edith and Hans met at an Essex pub. They ordered two coffees and sat at a table in the garden. The topic was the news... and Hans was angry. He kept his voice low, even though there was nobody else around; it was a habit. "What the fuck's going on? Peter's face is everywhere... have you both gone fucking mad?"

Edith palmed away his anger and answered casually. "No Hans. Everything is perfect. Dieter is seething and running around like a scared rabbit." That pleased her hugely, and she laughed as she said it.

Through clenched teeth, Hans said, despairingly, "Why, why, why are you doing this? Peter will not survive this rampage, you must know that."

Edith replied in an indifferent manner, shrugging, "Why not? Give him some credit, you underrate him Hans." She lowered her voice to a whisper and continued, "But, what is important; if he doesn't survive, what does it matter? If he's arrested, you know the procedure, he'll admit to every murder we've ever committed, and then..." she left it hanging, "Even if he's caught *we* are safe."

This didn't do anything to dissolve the anger Hans felt. "Peter is a member of the family. I don't like the way you're prepared to drop him at a whim. Besides that, if certain people connect these incidents to us, we'll lose millions of pounds worth of business."

"Only the kind of business we would be better off without."

Hans sighed. "Oh no, not that old fucking pony. Look Edith, I totally disagree with you as far as that is concerned. You know Dieter has built up some fantastic business over the years. If Amy knew how you felt, you would definitely never be chosen."

Edith acknowledged that point, but replied, "We're moving money around the globe for corrupt businessmen, corrupt politicians, corrupt government agencies and corrupt civil servants. God Hans, if we fall foul of any one of these, especially the agencies, we're in really big trouble. I say, stick with the criminals, we know how they think. At least we equal them in power. We may be making big money but we are being used, and one day something will happen and we'll be dropped like a hot potato."

"But how does this rampage which you and Peter have embarked upon help you with this mission to ditch so much good business? Explain this to me."

"Peter is the one on the rampage, don't you forget that!" she replied indignantly. "Look Hans, you've already said it. The slightest hint of our involvement with this and these people will run a mile; they'll not touch us with a barge-pole."

Hans suddenly realised what she was up to, "You can't be serious. Please don't tell me that you would leak information that 'what Peter is up to' is connected to the family…"

"Look. The way Dieter is carrying on, Amy will never choose him. He stinks of fear. So, assuming I do get the nod, there will be no need to leak anything to anybody. I'm telling you now, if I ever get control of this family, I'll drop that part of the business, it's too dangerous. I say stick with the criminals and dump the politicians."

Hans shook his head. "Edith. Politicians are the pawns of international crime, they just don't know it. We have nothing to fear from them."

"They are also pawns of government agencies and civil servants."

"Yes… and they are all criminals. These people want us around. We make life easy for them. Dealing with these people is safe. Publicly they say dirty money distorts the world's economies, but they know that the destruction of international crime would herald the collapse of the capitalist world. They tolerate us and use our services because we are good at what we do; we help keep those wheels turning. We are too valuable to them, and contrary to what you say, these people are our protection."

"You don't believe that, surely."

"Absolutely."

"Look Hans, you have to see sense. We are a family, with the resources of a family. I know we are rich but I'm not talking about money. I'm talking about brains. Dieter is producing an extremely complicated business but we need skills and intelligence we probably don't possess to run it. We have to stay one step ahead of the people we are dealing with. We have to outwit and outthink them on every move; one mistake and… The politicians are bloody clever people. But they are not as clever as the businessmen, or the civil servants. *We deal with them all.* As soon as it's not in their interest to have us around they'll squash us, just like that," she clicked her fingers. "At the moment it's not too late to cut our ties and walk away from this."

"It's not too late because they don't know who we are, and we can continue to keep it that way. We can cut our ties, as you say, anytime we wish."

Edith paused, looked directly at Hans and said, "About a month ago I had a visit, at the office. Somebody approached me, asking for Monica Davies, saying that he represented an African President who wanted to purchase the war treasures."

Hans was silenced. He analysed what Edith had said. "That's not possible. Only a family member would know about those, and who outside the family would know you operate as Monica Davies... unless they had been put in the picture by one of our family," he was astonished. "Nobody knows the connection."

"I had him followed and he went to the Nigerian Embassy. Then we lost him."

"I still don't believe it."

"I'm not a liar."

"No, I don't mean it didn't happen. What I do mean is, I can't believe that somebody from outside this family knows that you operate as Monica Davies." He suddenly grinned. "How much did he offer?"

"Don't be stupid. I told him I had no idea what he was talking about." Edith was not fooled by the sudden lightening of his mood; he was trying to manipulate her.

Hans laughed. "How much would he have to offer?"

"Hans, this is not funny. Possibly a billion, at least."

He was slightly disappointed, "It must be worth more."

"It probably is, but it's all stolen, so it would have to be sold at a discount."

"It's probably worth more because it *is* stolen." They were both silent again before Hans continued. "I think we were right all along, there is somebody else in the family making a move for top position. I really can't see how an outsider would have knowledge of anything on that scale. Somebody from within the family is playing games, and I think that somebody is Ben, I'm sure of it."

"Did you check on him in France?"

"He's not in France. He's using his secret little doppelganger again, you know, the guy called Spider."

"Well I never. He really is an idiot if he's sending black businessmen to see me. He's in way over his head."

"He seems to have a little gang of followers as well. Emmeline, Tina and Robert are nowhere to be seen. You know they've always been close to him."

"Are you certain about all of this? I can't believe that all of them would be involved with Marylyn's death."

"I tend to agree about that, so, no, I'm not certain, not yet. Give me a little more time. Once I find them… then I'll find out… for certain."

"Well, don't hang around. We need to know where this Nigerian came from as well."

"Let's get back to the Emmerich thing. Put it on hold, let things cool down a bit."

"The Emmerich thing, as you put it, is for Amy. You know that."

"Amy will be dead soon. How much are they worth?"

"Twenty odd million."

"The art collection is worth fifty times that, and that's probably nothing compared to the cash reserves, why bother, for twenty million?"

"Well you've changed your tune. A little while ago you were all for it. It's still twenty million. Anyway, it's almost over. There's no point in stopping now."

"Peter is stirring up a hornets nest. That would be reason for stopping." Hans knew he was wasting his breath. He slipped into a rueful silence before continuing. "I do hope Ben's as stupid as you say he is."

"He is if he's making this move." She toyed with her empty cup, "If he's decided to make a stand against us it'll be the end for him, he must know that."

Hans rubbed his chin. He wasn't so sure. Perhaps he should listen to Ben's pitch, assuming he had one.

Suffolk Constabulary – Ipswich Divisional Headquarters.
Thursday 26th June 2008

Andy Fuller burst into DS Hollingsworth's office.

Hollingsworth almost fell off his chair. "Sergeant, what the hell do you think you are doing?"

Andy slammed the images down on his desk. "Now tell me that the case against Jennifer Emmerich is closed! Sir."

Chapter 39

Leytonstone.
Friday 11th July 2008

Ian Matheson, the builder, stood awkwardly, both hands stuffed into his trouser pockets and shuffling his feet on stony earth which should by now have been a patio, he would take the dressing down, which he was sure was on its way, like a man.

Jennifer Emmerich was standing on stony earth that should by now be a lawn. Ian had started work at the house in May, completely gutting the place, rewired, new central heating, moved walls, plastered, painted and decorated, you name it… And it was just around the corner in Leytonstone. The project had gone like a dream, but it was now coming to an end.

He'd had to keep an old customer, Freddie Cohen, happy by sending his man Mac off to do some maintenance, and then Ian had to help out a little as well. On top of all this, in an attempt to secure some other decent work for the both of them… and not be back in the same dire situation as they were before they began this work, Jennifer's project had inadvertently been relegated to a hospital job.

She attacked. "I moved in over a month ago Ian, and you haven't even started on the garden. Do you want the rest of the work, or not?"

"I'm really sorry Jennifer," and he told her of his predicament. "But of course I want the work," he added.

"I appreciate you need to take care of yourself, but I've kept out of your way and allowed you to get on with things, and I think now, because of that, you're taking advantage of me. Summer will have come and gone, and I've promised my father that the garden will be ready before winter arrives."

As she spoke Ian was furiously trying to work out how he could make amends and get on with the work. Mac was tied up all the time with Freddie Cohen, as he was half the time. One option he came up with was to lay Mac off and look after Freddie himself, and sod this work. But that really was a downward spiral, nobody would win.

Jennifer seemed to read his mind. "I like Mac, the work he's done in the house has been very good, so I can see why you don't want to lose him. What about if you employ another man to work with him at Mr. Cohen's and you can make a fresh start here?"

Is this woman stupid? "But the work will dry up even sooner. I've just pointed that out."

"But I need this work done, sooner rather than later. How do you feel about working in the country? I've been having a lot of alterations done on the farmhouse at Belfont-St-Mary, which has now been completed, but in the process some damage has been done to other parts of the property and there's quite a bit of repair and redecorating required. On top of that there is some other small building work that needs doing. I'm sure I can find quite a few weeks work for a couple of you and I'm sure Rachel would agree to you doing some of that."

Ian was all ears now. Work! "Well yes, I'd love to give it a look, but local builders would be cheaper."

"I don't care, providing you continue to do a good job here," she paused to let that statement register, "and I can't see why you shouldn't, the other work is yours. Get somebody to help Mac and find yourself somebody to help you here, and when this work is complete, I'll make sure that there will be enough work at Belfont for you and Mac for quite a while. You can do it all on a day rate and you can stay at the house during the week. You can then use that as your hospital job, I think that's what you call it, but I want this place finished."

Ian wanted to hug and kiss her. Jack had said that she was a good girl, and how bloody true that was turning out to be. "Thanks Jennifer. Thanks very much. Mac will be pleased as well. How far is Belfont?"

"About an hour or so, fifty miles maybe," she shrugged. "You'll enjoy it there, three pubs. I'll phone Rachel later, just to put her in the picture, but that will just be a formality. When are you going to start this?" She waved her right hand over the garden. "That's the important thing. If this isn't finished soon, there'll be no work in the country."

"I'll get somebody started with Mac and I'll be here, hopefully with some help, tomorrow morning. Thanks again," and he stepped forward to shake Jennifer's hand. "Thanks."

"Before you go, come and speak to my father. You can discuss with him what you intend to do here. You'll also see a lot of him at Belfont, so it'll be good to get more acquainted. Remember, he's not too well at the moment, so treat him gently."

Michael Emmerich looked up as the two entered the kitchen. Jennifer thought that her father was looking a little more depressed than usual this morning, maybe it *had* been a mistake for him to move in, even temporarily. But it couldn't be avoided while all the work was going on at the farmhouse. "Dad, Ian's going to get on with the garden." Michael offered a very feeble hand, which Ian accepted.

"Hello Mr. Emmerich, how's it going? Would you like to come into the garden and I'll run through what we're going to do."

It was really all a bit too much for Michael, but he felt he should show some interest. He'd hoped Jennifer was going out, then he could go back to making his plans. Never mind.

* * *

Just a few minutes after Ian left there was a knock at the front door; Jack. Jennifer laughed as he stuttered and stammered, making out that he wanted to meet up with Ian. "I thought he would still be here."

Jennifer hadn't contacted Jack since the Chinese meal at Rachel's and guessed that he was getting a little desperate for information. "No, you've just missed him. Still, now that you're here, you can have a coffee," and they headed for the kitchen. "Next time, don't knock. Just come around the back and let yourself in."

"I can never do that, you never know what I might find you up to."

"Don't be boring Jack. We're family, and if you catch me up to anything, well…" She laughed. "Anyway, you're safe today, Dad's here."

"Thank God for that!" said Jack, pretending. "Anyway, seeing that nothing untoward *is* going on, while I'm here you can show me around. I've not seen the place for ages. It's coming along nicely, it looks good from where I'm standing."

"Well, the work in the garden has not been started, but apart from that… shall we have coffee first, or look around?"

"Where's Mr. Emmerich?"

"Look, out there," she pointed to a wooden seat where her father was seated, lost in his own private world and studying an object on the ground. "Perhaps you would like to see my bedroom."

"Your bedroom will be a good place to start."

Jennifer detected the playful tone of his voice but, being wary of whom he was, she mustn't allow anything to go too far. But what was the harm of being a little flirtatious? Mindful of what she was wearing, short summer frock, naked legs, she led the way up the stairs.

Her bedroom was the first room they came to, he turned and whistled. "Wow, this is really nice. Rachel wasn't wrong when she said that you had good taste."

"I'll have to remember to tell her you said so," she teased.

Jack answered, a little slyly. "I think that she might have wanted to show me around herself, so it's probably better not to tell her that I've seen it."

"Do you want me to lie to my sister?"

"Just a little," he chuckled nervously.

She stood by the window and looked out at her father. He made a desperately sad and lonely figure, and she wanted to say as much to Jack, but it didn't fit with the moment.

Then she felt him standing beside her; very familiar, very close. "You needn't worry so much about him, you know. He's a bloody strong character." Jack looked warmly down at Jennifer, "He's damn lucky to have you back, caring and loving him, and he knows it."

Jennifer led him away from the window, stood on tip-toe and kissed him on the cheek. "You're all right Jack Painter, Rachel's a lucky so and so."

They returned to the kitchen. *Coffee with Jack and dad.*

After the coffee the two left Mr Emmerich in the kitchen and walked around the garden. Now that the other stuff was out of the way Jack could say what he came here to say. He said it quietly. "Jen, why haven't you contacted me, I've been going crazy waiting for the call."

"Is that why you've turned up here?"

"Of course it is. What's happening with Belfont? And what are you planning?"

Jennifer thought for a moment. "Okay Jack. Can you get to the farmhouse on Sunday morning, alone?"

"Without Rachel?"

Jennifer stared at him in silence.

Jack answered the question. "Yes. Okay. I take it that it has to be secret."

Again Jennifer didn't say anything.

"Alright. But only if you promise to tell me everything."

"That is exactly why I want you there."

"And there is nothing to tell me now, to think on?"

Jennifer laughed, "Think about *you know what*!" she did a twirl for him and she gave him a sweet lingering kiss on the lips. "No. Sunday morning… I'll be there early so get there whenever you can."

After Jack had left, Jennifer gave him a lot more consideration.

She had her plan. Granted, not much of one at the moment, but she had to start somewhere, and she needed people she could trust, to brain storm, to discuss it with and to develop it. If things went the way she thought they might, it could turn out to be dangerous, for her. However, she felt sure that Jack would support her. He'd shown an enormous amount of interest and had come up with some sound ideas regarding security. He'd also agreed with her that the Leytonstone house should be monitored in case somebody broke in. Her father's wellbeing, although important, was not her real reason for wanting the camera, and Jack knew that, and knowing that, he had still agreed it should be installed.

The big dilemma for Jennifer was that she was increasingly thinking that this assault against her family had something to do with money, and she was reluctant to go behind her sister's back and tell Jack just how wealthy they were. Rachel was turning out to be much too lightweight, afraid of her own shadow, and too law-abiding to be considered. Poor Adam was not a contender.

But, what about Jack? Why was he so interested? It could be he thought of it as a big adventure, or he could be using the situation to get inside her pants. The idea of that made her tingle inside… she had to take care. If that does happen she would have to make sure that she stayed focussed… this wasn't a game.

Anyway, she would find out more on Sunday. In the meantime she decided to have a Friday night out, back in Ongar. She would stay at the White Horse. She phoned and booked a room, under the name of Sandra Mannion.

Chapter 40

Jennifer's return to Ongar, particularly the White Horse, felt odd. When she lived in the town she did occasionally visit the inn, but only ever with Adam, and apart from friendly chit-chat with the locals, she had not got to know any of them. Now, strangely, she was greeted like a long lost friend and found herself automatically acting like one, even though she didn't know a single soul by name.

It was a group of youngsters who had pounced on her, the minute she arrived. "You're Sandra, from William Drive."

"Sandra, yes but I've moved now."

"Where to?"

"Leytonstone."

"We don't blame you, not a lot happens around here. So what are you doing back? Come and sit with us, tell us all about it, that's of course if you want to."

"Hey Sandra." It was the barmaid. "What are you drinking?"

"Dry cider please."

And so it went on. She was introduced to everybody and made an effort to remember everybody's names. To begin with there were six or seven new friends. As the evening wore on the number increased to about a dozen. She was having a great time… and getting mildly drunk on both the euphoria of the occasion and the cider. It seemed everybody talked to everybody else at the same time. This lot is a loud crowd, she was thinking. The little rhyme made her chuckle to herself.

"What's so funny Sandra?" one of them asked

"You lot are a loud crowd, that's what I was thinking, and it made me laugh."

A blond girl in a white outfit leant forward and asked. "What else do you think of us?" She said it in a friendly way.

"You're okay. In fact I really like you all. It's a shame I moved away before getting to know you. You're the best out of everybody in here."

A boy said, "Look around, we *are* the only ones in here."

She looked around, he was right. She checked the time. Half past ten. Not late, but she remembered that she'd wanted to check the web cam and decided she should do it, before getting too drunk. "I've just got to check something out in my car."

"You're not driving are you?"

"No, I'm staying here, I've booked a room." Relieved that nobody had offered to chaperone her, she climbed into the driver's seat, booted up the laptop and logged onto the internet, using her dongle she found a strong signal. She clicked on the icon she had labelled "night owl" and waited.

She narrowed her eyes, squinting, trying to make sense of what she was seeing. The drink had an affect and what she was looking at on the screen didn't sink in immediately. There was a man, she could see him clearly now, standing over her father, just looking at him as he slept in his bed. A shiver went down her spine and she instantly sobered up. MY FATHER IS IN DANGER!

She threw aside the laptop, jumped into the driver's seat, started the car and slammed it into first. Fortunately the car park was almost empty, otherwise she would never have made it out onto the road in one piece, but, unfortunately, the road was not so clear. The two police officers sitting in the patrol car couldn't believe their eyes as the woman in the Ford Focus slalomed past three oncoming vehicles.

It didn't take long to catch her. At least she had the sense to pull over as they drew up behind her, lights flashing and siren blaring.

As fast as the car stopped she climbed out onto the street. "My father!" She ran towards them. "There's a man in our house, quick, phone somebody, radio in, help me."

One of the constables stepped forward and reached out to steady her.

"Get off me! Please, my father's in danger!"

"Slow down Miss. Just slow down! You're not in any condition to be driving a car… the way you took off down the street you could have killed somebody. Have you been drinking?"

"Don't be fucking stupid, of course I've been drinking?" She was raging. "Get somebody to check on my father… please."

One of the policemen stepped forward. "Can you sit in the back of our car, we would like you to calm down."

"Fuck the car you stupid bastard. I told you… my dad!"

The officer looked at his partner and shrugged. "I'm very sorry Miss, but before we do anything about your father, you're going to have to accompany us to the station."

"Fuck you!" Jennifer made a dash for her car, opened the driver's door and tried to climb in, but the two policemen were much too quick for her. Before she knew it she was handcuffed and sitting in the back seat of the police car. She tried to kick and punch her way out of the vehicle, but was taken, screaming and blaspheming, to the local police station.

She refused to take a breathalyser test or give a blood sample, so was locked in a cell, where she shouted for attention for about an hour before she realised that nobody was going to talk or listen to her until she calmed down. It was past midnight before they took the sample of blood and eventually she was taken to an interview room.

The constable who had arrested her and the custody sergeant were present. She was informed that she had tested above the legal limit and had therefore been driving under the influence of alcohol. She was also told that she was to be charged for resisting arrest. She was informed that a request had been made to the Metropolitan Police to check on her father. Her car had been impounded until somebody could collect it for her.

The custody sergeant disappeared with Jennifer's details.

"When will I be able to leave?" Jennifer asked the arresting policeman.

"Have you got anywhere to stay?" Jennifer sensed that the reply didn't necessarily mean she would be able to leave.

"I'm staying at the White Horse. I'm booked in for the night."

"Ok. We need to get clearance from the custody desk, after that you'll probably be allowed to go, that's the normal procedure."

They both fell silent while they waited for the sergeant to return. After about fifteen minutes the constable decided to go and see what the situation was. "Will you be alright, left here alone for a while?"

"Of course I will," she answered tersely. It didn't matter how nice the guy was trying to be, he was an enemy.

Jennifer was exhausted. The drink and the histrionics began to take their toll and she now wanted nothing more than to sleep. She tried to stay awake, but when the constable returned he found her slumped forward across the table, head nesting on her arms.

He gently shook her and she stirred. "Come on Miss Mannion." She sat up. "Come on. I'm afraid you will have to stay in the cell for the night. The sergeant says you can't leave. I'm sorry." Jennifer didn't care anymore, and she allowed herself to be led back to the cell, where she collapsed onto the hard bench and instantly fell back to sleep.

Chapter 41

Saturday 12th July 2008

When she awoke the next morning it was past ten o'clock. At first she was confused, images of her trial and her time in detention momentarily flashed through her mind, until she remembered the previous night. She noticed that the door to the cell was open. Gingerly she poked her head out and looked along the short hallway. There was a smartly dressed middle-aged man, arms folded and leaning against the wall opposite the doorway of the adjacent cell. He was obviously listening to somebody from inside, nodding and using facial expressions; to agree, or otherwise.

He sensed Jennifer's presence and turned his head. "Hello there. So you've finally decided to wake up then?"

"Hello. What's going on?" she asked.

He pushed himself away from the wall using his backside and walked over to her. "You've had a nice lay in. It seemed a shame to wake you." He then introduced himself, "I'm D.I. Ray Littleton and I'm taking care of you for a while." He placed his hand gently on her shoulder and guided her back into the cell, where they both sat down on the bench that had been her bed. He called out. "Jane." It turned out that Jane was the cleaner he had been in conversation with in the next cell. She appeared at the door. "Would you fetch me a coffee please and what do you fancy miss?"

"Um, Yes, I'll have a coffee, white with one sugar."

Jane shot off. "Well," he said, "You're causing quite a stir upstairs." He seemed friendly enough. "So your name is Jennifer Emmerich, not Sandra Mannion. No need to explain though, I know all about it."

Jennifer was not quite sure how to respond. '*A stir, why?*' She was still a little groggy, and then she remembered. "My dad, I must…?

"Your father's alright. Don't worry. Your sister is with him."

Alarm bells rung. "Why. What's happening?"

"Don't worry. Everything will be explained in due course."

"But if my sister has ventured from her apartment then there must be a problem, something must have happened."

Littleton shrugged. "All I know is, it seems that everybody and his dog need to talk to you. There is a meeting arranged for later this morning. You're actually not under arrest, but we would like you to hang around for a while. How about you freshen up a little, and we'll go to the local café and have some breakfast. You never know, by the time we get back, something might be happening."

"But why? What's this all about?"

"I'm sorry, I really can't tell you, because I don't know anything myself." He seemed sincere.

Jane returned with two plastics cups of coffee from a vending machine and handed them both to Littleton. "They're both the same," she said. She looked at Jennifer, smiled, and disappeared back to her chores.

Littleton held one out for Jennifer. "Drink it down, you must be parched."

They both sipped their hot drinks, for a short while in silence, and then Jennifer spoke. "So, I can leave if I want to."

"Well, as I said, you're not under arrest, but I have been told to keep you here. If I found it necessary I would have to arrest you on some charge or another. People want to speak to you; I think they need your help. I *must* ask you to hang around."

"And you say you don't know why."

"I think it's about the person you saw on your webcam."

"And Rachel is with my father, who is okay."

"Yes."

"Alright." The coffee had cooled a bit and she gulped the rest down. "Where can I freshen up then?"

"Your car is parked at the back of the station. We can get a few things out if you like, and I'll take you to the ladies rest room."

"You don't trust me then."

He smiled.

"Okay, thanks," she said as she stood.

She followed her new friend out of the cell and up the stairs to the reception area, where they collected her car keys from the duty officer. Everything seemed relaxed enough. She didn't have to be anywhere else, and she needed something to eat, so she decided to go along with whatever was going on. She spent about fifteen minutes sorting herself out and slipped on a fresh top with the jeans she was already wearing. Then D.I. Ray Littleton took her to a busy little café about two hundred yards along the street.

"Hello Ray," sang the lady behind the counter, "I see you have company today."

"Hi Sal, yes, this is Inspector Mannion. She's a police officer from the Met."

"Err, hello Miss. My goodness, the bloody police are getting younger and younger. You look familiar though... you from around here?" She laughed as she said it, not really expecting an answer.

When they had seated Jennifer asked why he had lied.

"She's a nosey bugger. The way she sees it, if you're with me and not a police officer, then you're a criminal. You don't want her wondering whether you're a prostitute or something along those lines, so let's just leave her thinking you're one of us."

"It seems as though I've come a long way in the last few months; from prison to policewoman." Jennifer studied the man in front of her. Middle aged, about forty, stocky and with a slightly full belly. "I bet you come in here a lot."

He laughed. "Too much," and pulled in his stomach, but only briefly, before puffing out and relaxing. They both laughed.

"Do you know who I am? I know you know my name, but do you actually know about me," she asked.

"Yes. I remember the case. It was big news."

"I didn't do it. Do you know that?"

Littleton didn't answer her, he just looked at her, a kindly look, she thought. "Shall we order?" Sal had walked over from behind the counter, pad in hand.

"What are you having?" Jennifer asked Littleton.

"I thinks I'll be 'avin' a full English and a nice mug o' tea."

"Then I'll have the same please."

Sal busily scribbled on her pad. "It's a *big* fry-up," she pointed out as she wrote.

"I'll burn it off… you need all the energy you can get in this job." She looked at Littleton, who winked slyly back.

Sal scurried off and yelled the order into the kitchen.

"You didn't answer my question." She looked at him, waiting.

"I followed the case and I think I share the views of many police officers, which was that you didn't seem the type of kid who could do that, bludgeon somebody to death. But, evidence is evidence. What more can I say?"

"Fair enough. But I'll show you, when I do clear my name."

"Well good luck to you, I really hope you do."

"Do you mind me talking about it? It's good for me to get the ear of a detective, it doesn't happen too often."

"I haven't got a problem listening to you, but as far as having the ears of detectives, it looks as though there are a whole bunch of them about to form a queue at your door."

"Yeah. Are you sure you don't know why?"

"Apart from what or who you saw, on the webcam, no. Did you get a good view of him; it was a 'him' wasn't it?"

"Yes, it was a 'him' and yes, I did get a pretty good view. It was a full frontal, although he was looking down at my dad. He was standing over him, by his bed.

But not only did I get a good view, it should be recorded."

"Why have you got the web cam set up?" he asked.

Jennifer decided that it was probably not wise to confide too much. "Just for my piece of mind really. Dad has had a series of strokes. The first one, the worst, was just three days after I was arrested for killing Billy. He's been much better lately, but you never know. So I had the camera installed, discreetly, he doesn't know it's there, so that I can check up on him if he stays at my place and I'm out for the night. That's what happened last night. Half past ten. I booted up and saw this guy just standing there. I went berserk, I needed to get home. Of course it was stupid. I don't know how quickly I thought I was going to get from Ongar to Leytonstone."

"Well, it's a good job you passed the breathalyser test. I think they are going to drop the resisting arrest charge."

"Passed! I refused to take one. I was well pissed."

"Well you can't have been."

"What about the blood sample?"

He shrugged. "Don't look a gift horse in the mouth young lady, that's all I can say."

Jennifer deliberated on what she had just heard. What do they want? They both sat silently for a while, watching other customers. Then the breakfasts turned up. They were huge and Jennifer winced. Littleton smiled. They dug in.

"Do you know who's coming to this meeting?" she asked between mouthfuls.

"There's a detective from Suffolk and two from the Met. There's also somebody from the CPS… the

Crown Prosecution Service. Your probation officer and a lawyer are to be present as well."

"Wow, quite a line up. If my probation officer is going to be here then I must have done something wrong, especially as it's a Saturday. If that's the case then I suppose it makes sense that a lawyer is present."

"Look, I really don't think that you've done anything wrong. We wouldn't be sitting here if you had. Your probation officer was called because of the charges made against you last night, but now that they have been dropped…"

"Ah, so they *have* been dropped."

"Whoops. I didn't tell you that."

Jennifer was not sure if it was a slip. He seemed too clever for that, maybe he was priming her, but for what?

Nothing much more was said while they finished their breakfasts. Jennifer declined the offer of another mug of tea and asked to be excused, to visit the toilet.

"Can you wait until we get back to the station? I'm not supposed to let you out of my sight."

"Wow, this is serious. Yes, I suppose I can wait."

Littleton paid for the food and they returned to the station.

Chapter 42

The lawyer and one-time very close friend of her mother, Monica Davies, was waiting to greet Jennifer in the police station reception area. Littleton said his goodbyes and the two women made themselves comfortable in a small office.

The two had periodically come into contact during the past years and, despite Monica Davies making an effort towards cordiality, Jennifer didn't like her. She believed that the lawyer had failed her, big time, and wasn't prepared to forgive or to forget.

"How was your night?" asked the lawyer.

Jennifer shrugged. "Not too bad under the circumstances. I slept the biggest part of it."

"Good. You look well. It's been quite a while."

Jennifer then asked curtly, "Miss Davies... What are you doing here?"

The lawyer shuffled a little before answering. "Sorry Jennifer. Jack Painter was murdered last night."

Jennifer gasped "What! Jack... How?" The news sent a shockwave reverberating throughout her body and she suddenly found it difficult to breath. Placing her hands on the table, she just managed to remain on her feet. She thought she was about to cry. Jack!

"He was stabbed."

"Stabbed. What... in a fight?"

"No, they don't think so. The police said that there was no evidence of a fracas. They seem to think that he was taken by surprise. He was stabbed just once, fatally."

"Oh my God." Jack! She was reeling. "Does Rachel know, is she alright?"

"Yes, of course she knows. She is as well as can be expected. She's with your father and a work colleague. She's in good hands, don't worry." The lawyer pulled out a file from her briefcase, removed a notebook and placed it on the desk.

Jennifer fought to remain in a standing position but couldn't. As she sat a thought struck her. "How did you know I was here?"

"I was about to come to that. Spending the night in a police cell was the best thing that could have happened to you. The knife that was used to kill Jack was from your kitchen. It was covered with your fingerprints. As soon as the connection was made a warrant was requested and was about to be issued, then they found out you were here."

Jennifer's heart was pounding furiously and she was feeling nauseous. All colour had drained from her face.

"Are you going to be alright? I'll get some water." The lawyer called for a glass of water.

"Now, you are to be interviewed by two detectives from the Metropolitan Police Force. They knew exactly where you were because a request was made, from here, for a drive past your house in the early hours of this morning. The reason for it was also given and they want a description of the intruder in your father's bedroom, if you can give one."

"I can give them one, is he the killer?"

"They don't know, but it seems logical that this person stole the knife and then carried out the crime.

Coincidently though, the police have discovered evidence of an incident that might have a bearing on all of this, and I think this includes your case."

"What evidence?"

Monica Davies answered uneasily. "Well.... apparently, just a few months before Billy died, your father was handed a very threatening note... telling him to kill himself or his family will suffer."

There was a pause. Jennifer couldn't quite get her head around what her lawyer had just said. The content was clear, just the circumstances that surrounded it. "Explain this incident a little more clearly, and then explain to me what exactly you mean by '*the police have just discovered this.*' Please"

Monica Davies knew that she had just set a short fuse. She needed to tread carefully. She cleared her throat and took a deep breath. "In February 1999, your father was with friends in the Plough Inn in Belfont when he was handed the note. Before he had read it the messenger had disappeared. It read as I just said, kill yourself or your family will suffer. Your father took this seriously enough to contact the police, who visited the pub that same night and took statements from other customers. An identikit image was subsequently produced. The incident *was* filed. The problem seems that because the Plough is on the Essex side of the river, it was filed at Braintree. Billy's death was investigated by Suffolk constabulary. This is why the incident was missed."

"Fucking missed. I can't believe you can put it that simply. I have lost a third of my life. The most important third, my education - fucked, everything other than me - fucked. Everybody else has set themselves up with qualifications, careers, friendships. What have I got?" She slammed her fist on the table. "You're a load of incompetent bastards! You! Them! Every - fucking - body. And two police stations about thirty miles apart can't even produce this... And I suffer." Jennifer was shouting now. "I pay the fucking consequences because they are fucking idiots." She stood and her chair tipped over. The door flew open and an officer rushed in to restrain her. "Get out you fucking bastard!" He held back.

"Okay, okay Jennifer." Monica Davies tried to calm her. She instructed the policeman to leave the room. "Okay Jennifer." She picked up the chair and placed it behind her client. "Please Jennifer, sit down. Please."

But Jennifer had not finished. "You can get out. You're as useless as they are. Fuck off." Davies tried to reason with her, but to no avail, Jennifer continued. "You represented me at the trial and you should have investigated and found this. I can understand why Dad didn't bring this up... he was ill. But you! And what about Mum... what kind of hold did you have over her? You're fired. Go!" Eventually the lawyer gathered up her paperwork and left. After pacing angrily around the small room a few times Jennifer sat and buried her face in her hands.

After a while Ray Littleton entered the room and sat before her. He didn't say anything, he just sat.

"What do you want?"

"Just to see if you're okay."

"I'm not."

"I'm sorry about your friend, and I've been told about the note."

"So?"

Again there was a period of silence, and then Littleton stood and left the room. Jennifer guessed the room was under some sort of surveillance and was determined not to show anybody how she was feeling. She sat stony-faced, for about fifteen minutes, thinking about how everything was unfolding. The police were not her friends, not because they were evil, but because she considered them incompetent. She tried to recollect the threat made against her father, without success. S*he* would have remembered it for the trial, had she known.

She had been framed for the murder of Billy; she had worked that out a long time ago – but why? Had she gone to prison because her father didn't kill himself? If so, was it all to get to her father? No, that didn't make sense, it had to be something else. If it was about her father, why didn't this man just kill him? So... it pointed to something against the whole family; to make all of us suffer, and why did Jack have to die? Another why! Unless of course, he or they had tried to set Jennifer up again, to make her father suffer further by seeing his daughter convicted for a second time.

Okay. Let's say he, or whoever, *was* after her father. Again, why? What about his money? She thought about the newspaper article about the Huth family and decided that the money would be the first trail to follow.

She'd had the camera installed in her father's bedroom because she thought the killer might pay her a visit, in case he broke into the house, and it worked! It was her first success.

Had that success led to Jack's death? Now what? Poor Jack, she was going to have him as somebody to bounce ideas off. He'd turned out to be the one person she could trust. She had told him the real reason for the camera, and although he thought she was playing a dangerous game, under the circumstances he thought that he would have taken the same action.

She needed Holly Andrews at her side. They had worked well together inside, protected each other. Fuck the restrictions of her parole license.

Surely now they must believe that she was innocent. She decided to go ahead with this meeting. She would not trust the police but the intelligent thing to do was listen, and she wanted to see what her probation officer had to say. But first she had to formally sack Monica Davies. She went to the door and asked for Ray Littleton.

He asked Jennifer if it was a little premature to sack her lawyer, considering that she was about to face a whole bank of officials.

Jennifer reflected. "For a long time I felt extremely bitter towards my father, mother and sister for abandoning me at the trial. Davies should have told me that my father was ill and could not be there for me. I'm sure that she could also have influenced my mother much more, to support me. And my sister was young. Davies could have made a big difference, how I felt, even if I was still found guilty. Even now I still feel just as bitter for being abandoned as I do for being locked away for the whole of my teens." She shook her head, "No, she has to go."

The second decision, more of a solemn promise to herself, she kept to herself; she was going to kill the man who killed Jack! And if she could, she was going to make him suffer.

Chapter 43

There were four police officers present at the meeting. DI Baker and DI Roach from the Metropolitan Police Serious Crime Squad, DS Andrew Fuller from Suffolk Constabulary and DI Ray Littleton, whose presence Jennifer had requested. Also there was Bernie O'Rourke, Jennifer's probation officer. However, there was no Monica Davies; she had stormed off in a furious rage after Jennifer had formally sacked her. Apparently there should also have been Ms Caroline Clarke from the CPS, but she was held up in traffic. Baker and Roach were a team and DS Fuller was representing the force which had put her away. "I'm not sure that I want him in there," Jennifer had told Littleton before the meeting. The DI had explained that it had been Fuller who had dug up the file on the threat to her father. Jennifer relented.

She listened to what Detective Inspector Millie Baker had to say, and it was interesting stuff. Firstly, she said, we think your father has received a telephone call, telling him to kill himself.

"You think? I know," replied a sarcastic Jennifer.

"No, I don't think you know about this one. Last Sunday."

This time Jennifer didn't reply.

"The conversation was overheard by a female member of the public, who then reported it to the police. Since then, our man, we'll call him that to keep things simple, has burnt down the witness's house; a warning, he had said. Then, when the warning was not heeded, he attempted to murder her by blowing up her car... that was the hotel bomb blast in London which has been all over the news this week. We believe our man then murdered a police officer who, we think, was on his trail."

The new Jennifer listened to every word, but held back from asking questions. She had seen the news and she knew of the events, she wondered who the person was who had overheard the conversation. She was told that her father was under police protection and that he was being monitored. "Apparently he has refused to acknowledge that he received the phone call, but the police believe he *was* the person contacted, because of the content of the message, the fact that it had happened before, and especially now because of the murder of Jack Painter." The police were in the process of checking telephone records. "We have to ask your permission to keep a police presence at your premises, to protect your father and, also, if we can make a search of the house for evidence."

"I wouldn't have thought that you needed my permission to search the place, after all it's a murder enquiry."

"Well, we're asking."

"Then of course you can."

Millie Baker thanked her and then continued. "Would you also be able to give us a description of the man you observed on your web cam?"

"Yes. But it should have been recorded, as well."

"Excellent. And, have you any idea who might want to harm your family; your father especially."

Jennifer had endured hundreds of questions over the years, but this was the first time this particular one had been fired at her. "I've been trying to figure that one out for eight years."

"And, have you, any idea?"

Jennifer had the thread of an idea, which she intended to pursue, but she was not going to let on at the moment. "No, I've no idea," she said. Before Baker could continue Jennifer asked, "Does this mean that you're now looking for somebody else for the murder of Billy Saunders?"

Baker opened her mouth to speak but DS Fuller beat her to it. "Yes, we are."

There was a deadly silence all round. Jennifer sensed that Fuller had spoken out of turn, and that Baker and Roach were very annoyed at their colleague. Jennifer turned to Fuller and said, "Thanks for being so honest. Where does that leave me?"

"Well sergeant, please answer her question," snapped DI Baker.

"It doesn't really leave you anywhere other than where you are now. Of course, if we can prove it was not you…"

"Or if the conviction turned out to be unsound." Jennifer pointed out.

"But *that* would be a judicial decision, not a *police force* one."

Jennifer couldn't figure Fuller out, he seemed cagey. "What do you think, Bernie?" she asked her probation officer.

He replied in his soft Irish accent, "I'm your probation officer and I'll continue to supervise you as I have done so up till now."

Good old Bernie. She hadn't seen him for weeks.

She turned to Baker and asked, "The person who overheard the threat to my dad last Sunday, what has happened to her?"

"We're not at liberty to say," she spat, still annoyed with Fuller.

It was Jennifer's turn to be angry. "Look, I've just spent eight years of my life in prison because you lot have been fucking useless, so don't get shitty with me. I'm sitting here because I'm clever enough to understand that it wasn't you personally who put me away. Answer my fucking question or leave me alone!"

DI Roach spoke for the first time. "We don't know. At first we thought that she'd been killed, but it turned out that the victim had been male, probably breaking into her car. We've not broadcast this though; we decided that she deserved not to have this bastard on her back."

Jennifer stood. They all looked surprised. "Where are you going?" asked DI Baker.

"To help produce a photo fit, or whatever you call it. You never know, maybe the recording didn't work. Come on Inspector Littleton, lead the way."

* * *

In reception Littleton seemed a little edgy. "What's the matter?" Jennifer asked him.

"Nothing really, it's just that in there, it seemed to be you against them, and I'm on your side."

"Is that a problem?"

"Only that I am one of them, a policeman, and I feel a little disloyal, that's all."

Jennifer shrugged. "Sensitive or what?"

Baker and Roach exited the room and said a curt goodbye. Bernie O'Rourke was far friendlier. DS Fuller was last out and came over to talk. "Can you hang around for a while?" he asked Jennifer.

"Why?"

"Please. It won't be for long, Caroline Clarke will soon be here and she has some news for you."

"What is it with you lot, why can't you just tell me what I should know?"

Fuller didn't answer.

"Look, I have to sort out this photo fit thing with Inspector Littleton. If she arrives before I've finished then I'll see her." Fuller acknowledged this and wandered off. "Well," she turned to Littleton, "What are we waiting for partner?"

Littleton smiled. "Our IT expert… and Ms Clarke."

* * *

Ms Clarke turned up twenty minutes later. Jennifer had become quite morose, thinking about Jack, and was slumped heavily into a chair in the small interview room where she'd been told about his murder by Monica Davies. Also present were Clarke, Fuller and Ray Littleton, whom Jennifer had asked to hang around, again as a favour.

Caroline Clarke explained to Jennifer exactly who she was and the powers she enjoyed in her position. Jennifer thought she carried herself well and came across as a friendly and very competent individual. The way she brought the two policemen into the conversations was a clever way of softening the meeting up, but where was this leading? Then she found out. "DS Fuller has been looking into your conviction for the death of Billy Saunders and has discovered new evidence."

"Do you mean the death threat?" asked Jennifer, wondering if this was what she had been forced to hang around for.

Clarke didn't respond and signalled Fuller to answer. "No. Do you remember old mad Millie Monkhouse?"

Jennifer thought of the old Belfont woman, a nutty artist. Dad had said she was like Vincent Van Gough, brilliant, but completely mental. "Yeah I remember, a harmless old lady."

"I'm afraid she passed away in January, with no next of kin. Apparently her estate has been a nightmare to sort out. Well, anyway, to cut a long story short, two Belfont kids, university art students, have been organising an exhibition of her work. A few hundred paintings and more than fifteen thousand photos, printed and digital, have been scrutinised." He looked at Clarke.

She took the baton. She pulled out a picture of a man. "This is part of a photograph found on her computer. There were six altogether, photographs... showing this man murdering Billy Saunders."

Jennifer raised her hand to take the photo, but couldn't bring herself to touch it. She studied the top image... it clearly showed... she felt as though she was going to pass out. She tried to stand but her legs failed to support her and had it not been for the quick reaction of Ray Littleton she would have gone over. He jumped up, held her and placed her back on the chair.

Tears were streaming down her face as she cried uncontrollably, and she was finding it difficult to breathe; she gulped air as her head spun, and she thought she was going to be sick. Slowly it passed. Caroline Clarke stood back as the two policemen cared for the girl as she recovered a little, enough.

Jennifer had longed for this moment, when proof that she was innocent was found, but she never anticipated that the news would affect her quite this way. Her head ached and her heart thumped; her ribcage felt like somebody had been standing on her. She breathed as Littleton instructed her to breathe and accepted the water DS Fuller offered her. When she was able to, she spoke. "How long have you known?"

"Are you alright?" asked Clarke.

Jennifer nodded.

Fuller spoke. "The students came across them on Wednesday and called us straight away. They were digital images, on her computer. Miss Monkhouse was a real nutcase, she had more IT equipment than Computer World and her photographic equipment would put a professional photographer to shame. Although, to give the woman credit... she was a real expert. We had to carry out thorough tests on the images to make certain they had not been tampered with. However, as we suspected, they are genuine, that was finally established about an hour ago. Miss Clarke was already on her way, in the expectation that they were genuine, and got the go-ahead to inform you as soon as that news was confirmed."

Between sobs Jennifer managed, "I don't understand, why didn't she tell anybody about what she had seen?"

"Obviously we'll never know," said Fuller. "She seemed to have been overlooked during the investigation, I checked but there is neither record of her ever being interviewed nor of any intention to interview her. There will be an enquiry to look into why that was."

"You don't need an enquiry," said Jennifer, "I can tell you now, put it down to incompetence."

Caroline Clarke ignored the remark and carried on from where Fuller had got to. "Within the next few days a judge will officially exonerate you from the records as having committed this offence. You can attend the hearing if you want to, I'll let you have the details as soon as I can, there will be an official apology at the same time. After that your lawyers will want to start proceedings for damages. I don't think there will be much resistance to that. In the meantime I can only say how sorry I am that you have had to endure such a terrible experience, especially as the Crown Prosecution Service was the main instigator to making that experience happen."

Jennifer sighed. "What happens now?"

"What do you mean?"

"Well, can I go?"

"Of course you can. I don't understand why you might think that you cannot."

"I've wanted to leave since this morning, but dear old DI Littleton has persuaded me to stay."

Littleton stammered and stuttered.

"It's alright," continued Jennifer, "I understand, I was teasing you."

"I don't think you're fit to drive," said Littleton.

"Well I'm not staying here any longer."

"That's not what I meant. I can arrange transport to take you to Leytonstone, assuming that's where you're going next. We'll bring your car as well."

Jennifer considered the offer and accepted. Littleton was right, she wasn't fit to drive. She left the room without as much as a thank-you or goodbye to Fuller and Clarke. She didn't care about being rude, after what they'd put her through. Although, she understood, Fuller had done well; but it *was* about time.

Chapter 44

It was late that Saturday afternoon by the time Jennifer arrived at Leytonstone. Littleton had given her a lift and a police driver had followed in the Ford Focus. As soon as Jennifer's car had been parked in the small driveway which ran alongside the house, Littleton had wished her the best of luck and left for Ongar. There was a uniformed police constable waiting to greet her at the back door, who informed her that she could not enter the house until she obtained permission from the officer in charge of the crime scene, which happened to be DI Millie Baker. Slightly annoyed that she couldn't go into her own house, especially on the orders of Baker, of all people, Jennifer headed for the garden, where she found Rachel and their father. The sisters embraced and commiserated over Jack.

Rachel was not looking so good. She was ghostly white and the blue shadows under her eyes revealed how upset she had been, but for now she was obviously totally cried-out. "Jen. Oh Jen. I am so glad you're here. I'm so frightened. What's going on? Why is Jack dead?"

Jennifer suddenly felt disappointed with her sister. She was being pathetic, wasn't she supposed to be a lawyer; she was supposed to be able to handle situations like these. Yes, be upset, but get a hold of yourself, *please*. She replied in a slightly churlish manner. "I thought you had a work colleague with you, to look after you."

"She was here, but I sent her away. She really couldn't do much anyway, with the police all over the house... and... I do have Dad."

"Have they spoken with you, the police?"

"Yes, ages ago. But the one in charge wants to interview us again."

"Have they told you anything, about Jack?"

"They told me what had happened. Jack's parents had told them about our relationship, and that I could be told everything, that I should be treated like any member of the family. The police told me how he was killed," she sniffed, "With a knife stolen from the kitchen, here, and that it had your finger prints on it. But they also said that there was no way that you were implicated. They asked me questions, where was I last night? When was the last time I saw him? Did I know where he was going, etcetera, etcetera?"

Michael Emmerich coughed and they both looked in his direction. Jennifer suddenly felt guilty that she had ignored him. He said quietly, "I know I've not been well but I need some input in this affair."

Jennifer replied, "I'm sorry Dad."

"They also asked me a few questions, and they told me about the camera. I can tell you now young lady, I'm not too pleased about it. I'm not an invalid, yet."

"You might not be at the moment, but you have been. You are improving by the day. I am sorry about the camera but I needed to be able to keep a check on you when I'm out."

"If that's the case, why didn't you talk to me about it?"

"I don't want an argument Dad, I'll remove it. In future I'll tell you everything I'm planning."

Michael Emmerich accepted the apology in silence.

"But you must promise to tell us about anything that happens to you, like, for example, threatening phone calls."

He shifted uneasily, "I haven't received any message."

"Yes you have! And the police will confirm that you have, in time. Look Dad, something's going on which is putting us all in danger. You have to work with me to stop it."

Her father fidgeted again and then said, "I'm sorry, I just want to protect you, both of you."

Rachel covered her face with her hands and sighed. "Dad!"

Jennifer clenched her teeth and ignored her sister. "You were going to commit suicide, weren't you? Just because some creep told you to, you're fucking pathetic!"

"Jennifer!" Rachel screamed.

Jennifer turned on her sister. "Shut up you idiot. Dad, I'm sorry, but you cannot just curl up and die just because somebody tells you to."

"And, if I don't do as he says... look what's happened to Jack. His death is my fault, if I'd had the guts to kill myself he would still be alive."

"Who says so? If this guy wanted you dead so much, he could've just killed you, like he killed Jack, like he probably killed Mum. There's more to this than wanting you dead. We're being played with, like a cat plays with a mouse. If you kill yourself he'll still come after me and Rachel, I'm sure of it. We must fight back, all of us!"

At that moment DI Baker approached from the house. "Jennifer, I've just seen you from the house can…"

Jennifer cut her short. "Piss off, can't you see we are having a family conference?"

"But…"

"Go away, *please*."

Baker turned and stormed off. Rachel rebuked her sister. "You cannot talk to a police officer like that."

Jennifer snapped back at her. "Why not? And it's about time you pulled yourself together. There's a madman running around out there, fucking up our lives, and all you can do is whine and lock yourself away. We have to get him before he gets us."

"Why are you being so horrible to me? Jack's dead."

"I'm being horrible because you don't want to fight. All you want to do is hide away in your apartment."

"And what about you? What's the difference with being safe in Chelsea and you hiding away in your so-called *panic rooms* at Belfont?" responded Rachel.

"I have a plan. I'm going to trap this bastard and kill him, before he kills us!"

"Christ! You're mad. Dad, listen to her. Your precious little girl is going to kill again."

Jennifer lunged at Rachel and slapped her hard across the face, and Rachel surprised her younger sister by fighting back. Michael tried his hardest to intervene but Detective Inspector Baker, who'd been observing proceedings from a distance, managed to jump in and separated the pair. Jennifer was sulking and Rachel, who was trying very hard not to cry, sat sniffing. However, the one most upset was their father.

He felt totally inadequate, and that's when he made up his mind. He asked the policewoman, politely, to leave. "We cannot continue like this," he said to the girls. "Maybe Jennifer is right, we should formulate some sort of plan." He addressed Jennifer. "Jennifer, you said that you were off to Belfont early tomorrow. Carry on with that. Rachel and I will be there on Monday, and we'll have dinner at one of the pubs. We can run through your ideas." He then included Rachel. "We can all stay here tonight and keep each other safe. Tomorrow, when Jennifer has left, we'll go to Chelsea and stay at the apartment. I'm sure they'll even let us have a policeman to guard us, under the circumstances. Jennifer, I don't suppose you will want one?"

That surprised Jennifer. She didn't, but she was still surprised that her father had figured it out. She looked at her sister, who was wiping a tear from her eye. "I'm innocent."

"I know," said Rachel. "I'm sorry."

"No, you don't know. I was told today, they have proof that I didn't murder Billy."

There was a long silence as that news sunk in. Michael eventually asked, "What... explain, tell us all about it, what have they found?"

Jennifer told them both about mad Millie Monkhouse's photographs, and everything that had happened in Ongar.

"How do you feel?" asked Rachel.

"I don't know. Depressed, actually, and angry, which is weird. For years I've fantasised about the moment when I'm proved innocent, how wonderful it would feel. Now that moment has arrived I just feel bitter at what they've done to me, and jealous of everybody, every single person who has never had to endure what I've been through."

Now Rachel did cry. She sobbed so much she couldn't speak, and Michael soon joined in, then Jennifer also. They all stood and hugged tightly, the father kissing both girls on their foreheads... backwards and forwards, backwards and forwards. DI Baker, who'd not heard any of the conversation, looked on in amazement, and considered the three of them very, very strange.

Chapter 45

Belfont.
Sunday 13th July 2008

A subdued Jennifer arrived at the farmhouse before eight and was showing Adam around the basement, or the bunker, as Jack had previously christened it. All the work had been completed and the surveillance and security devices were up and running. Adam considered it all quite impressive, and Jennifer agreed. Over breakfast they talked about Jack, Ongar and mad Millie Monkhouse, and the pending exoneration.

Her wrongful incarceration was breaking news and was all over the airwaves. The front page of one of the Sunday newspapers ran an exclusive on the story, which meant that somebody in the police force or the Crown Prosecution Service was in the pocket of the press, and Jennifer figured that it was only a matter of time before reporters turned up at the farmhouse. She had left Leytonstone at six am, where they'd already gathered en-masse. She'd had to enlist the help of the police (it was still a crime scene) and managed to leave unrecognised, disguised as a policewoman. She told Adam this, and that yesterday at the cafe she masqueraded as a detective from the Metropolitan Police Force. It certainly made a change from being a criminal.

At just after nine o'clock they heard a vehicle crunching along the gravel driveway, and a battered old Ford Escort van pulled up at the house. The two made it to the front entrance in time to witness a shaven headed and tattooed overweight brute struggling to remove himself from the driver's seat. Loud heavy rock music blasted from the van's speakers. Eventually the monster managed to stand upright and approached them. "Is Miss Carter's friend here?"

"Don't you mean Miss Wilson's friend?"

He nodded, eyes looking towards the heavens, he thought the coded exchange over the top.

"That's me." Jennifer stepped forward.

Adam, baffled by the proceedings, and in an attempt to be protective, puffed up his chest. The brute, looking at Adam, said menacingly to Jennifer. "Get rid of the monkey."

Jennifer turned to Adam. "It's okay. Go and make coffee, for two." Jennifer could be rude as well.

Adam studied the sweaty Neanderthal as it stood, hands on hips and legs apart; reluctantly he did as he was asked.

The man spat. "I've got a package for ya." He walked to the back of the van, pulled out a long object wrapped in an oily rag and handed it to her. "And this," he passed a small but quite heavy bag. "There's a pistol, ammo and cartridges in this one." He didn't seem to care who heard. "Now, do I get a cuppa?"

"No. You can fuck off. If you cause any trouble I'll make another phone call. I don't ever want to see you again."

He bit his lip and made a thing of restraining himself from responding. Then he turned towards his van. "Fuck you, cunt," and kicked the front tyre before climbing in, then raced off as fast as the rusty old van could, which was not very fast.

Jennifer looked around to see if she could see any of the imminent press, or anybody else for that matter, fortunately nothing, as yet, and carried the packages up to her bedroom and placed them under the bed; she would find a more suitable place later. She hoped that Adam had not been nosey. She joined him in the kitchen.

"Who the hell was that?" he asked.

"He was nothing, just a delivery boy, trying to make out he's a tough gangster. I asked an old friend to check out a few things for me, and the ape delivered the results."

"You should have told your friend to email whatever the bloke delivered, it's a lot easier… and more sociable."

"Yeah, next time I'll remember that."

Jennifer's mobile rang. It was her sister. "Hello Rachel."

"Hi Jen. Dad's a bit upset, worrying about things. He says that the wine in the cellar must not be moved."

"Oh bloody hell, it's a bit late for that. Let me have a word with him… Hello Dad, what's the matter?"

"Hello Jennifer. Nothing is wrong. It is the just the wine collection, it should be moved by somebody who knows what they are doing. Do you mind if you wait until tomorrow before you move it, I'll get a local wine merchant to transfer it to the summer house."

"Dad, don't worry, the wine was moved weeks ago, don't you remember? You organised it. You'll be here tomorrow and you can check to make sure it's okay." Jennifer sensed that something was still not right. "Are you sure you're alright?"

"Yes. Yes of course I'm alright. I just had a fitful night. All those newspaper people outside and the police inside… I'll be alright when I've eaten."

"Okay Dad. Take care. Hand me back to Rachel… …he's not himself. What do you think?"

"I agree. Perhaps he did have a bad night, although I wasn't aware of it. We'll talk later."

"Ok, see you," and they hung up.

Jennifer looked a little pensive as she placed the phone back into her pocket.

"What's the problem, is your dad alright?"

"I don't know, he's having a bad day. I'll speak to Rachel again later." Jennifer thought about the delivery and how lucky it had been that the idiot turned up before the press had arrived. She must not take such unnecessary risks; the facilities were downstairs to avoid mistakes, and she should use them. "Are you staying?" she asked Adam.

"That was my plan, why?"

"That's good. Take the coffees downstairs and I'll be with you in a minute." She then methodically checked that all the doors and windows throughout the entire house were closed and locked, before joining him.

More than one hundred square yards of basement had been transformed into a fully contained apartment, a bedroom with three single beds and an en suite shower-room, a kitchen and a dining area. A working area accounted for half the space, and housed the monitors, alarms and other security equipment. There were two desks with personal computers with internet and phone access and a storage area with filing cabinets and metal cupboards. Every square inch of the grounds were monitored at any one time by at least two cameras and everywhere was covered by an array of movement, audio and pressure sensors. Invisible laser beams criss-crossed the area. Jennifer flicked a switch which alarmed the house for unlawful entry, flood and fire. There was also a small room with a generator and battery back-up.

Adam studied the monitors. "All this must have cost you a fortune."

"It did."

Both were silent long enough for Adam to realise he wasn't going to find out how much, and he knew not to ask her where the money had come from. "It's pretty cool though." They drank more coffee and played with the monitors, watching birds and animals, setting the sensors to pick up various sounds and movements, and watching journalists and cameramen arriving. The cheeky bastards set up shop on their lawn and Jennifer contacted Ipswich Police Station to get them removed from the property.

"You need to hire a security firm to keep them off," Adam commented.

"Yeah, but what if one of the guards turned out to be him?"

"Him?"

"Yes, you know, the killer. He could be marauding as anybody, a policeman even," she added.

"Who *do* you trust?" he asked.

Jennifer shrugged. "You. And I have a friend who was inside with me. I trust her as well. But that's it."

"That's sad. What about Rachel and your dad? You must trust them."

"I can't trust them totally because Dad's not well and Rachel is too much of a wimp. I trusted Jack."

"Poor old Jack, he was a really nice guy. This bloke is a real nutcase, aren't you afraid."

"No, not really… I'm going to kill him."

There was a pause in the conversation as Adam took a sharp breath. Then he quipped, "I suppose you're owed one."

"What do you mean?"

"A murder. If you think about it, you should be able to murder somebody and not do any time; seeing that you've already actually served it."

Jennifer playfully pushed him. "Maybe you'll be my next victim." Her mobile sounded, again it was Rachel. "Hi." She listened as her sister spoke, hung up, and then told Adam to turn on the TV. "Switch on the BBC News Channel."

Jennifer's innocence was top of the news and a reporter was relaying the story live from the front of the farmhouse. The camera zoomed to a close up of the building, and it then panned around the grounds.

"Do you think they know we're here?" asked Adam.

"I don't see why they should," she studied the screen, "I can't see any sign of life. My car is in the garage, where's yours?"

"I walked."

Jennifer raised her eyebrows in surprise. "Walked, why did you do that?"

"Terry, the guy who lives in the flat below me, had boxed my car in, and it was early, so…" He shrugged.

"That was lucky." Again, she thought about the delivery. "Adam. I want you to go away."

Adam didn't reply.

"Two reasons, I don't want you to end up like Jack, and the other is that I might need to get away to somewhere secret, and in a hurry. You can get somewhere prepared."

"I don't want to end up like Jack either, but what about you? I don't think I can just run off and leave you."

"This is my battle. I didn't kill Billy, but I still feel guilty about it. He was killed because he was with me, in the wrong place at the wrong time, and I don't want the same thing to happen to you. I really am going to get this guy, and, if you stay, you'll be in my way."

"I still don't feel right about leaving. What about my job?"

"You work in a shop!"

"I know, but I can't afford to just pack it up."

"Yes you can. Have you got your debit card with you?"

Adam pulled a wallet from his jeans and handed Jennifer his card. She brought up her bank account and transferred fifty thousand pounds into his account.

"Fuckin' hell! Where did you get that sort of money?"

"Adam, don't worry, I can afford it. Look, we'll book you a ferry, Dover to Calais, for later today, and you can drive to a place called Quillan, in France. It's right down on the edge of the Pyrenees, you'll like it." She found it on Google maps for him. "Mum and Dad used to have a house close to there, and I remember there's plenty to do, especially at this time of the year. You'll like it. Splash out and stay at a nice hotel, there are some opposite the station. Go to an immobilier, that's a French estate agent, and find a property to rent, a nice one. Rent it for a year if you can. Garage your car as soon as you can and buy a French one. Don't be tight, enjoy yourself, and if you run out of money I'll transfer some more into your account. Whatever you do, don't mention me to anybody. When this is over I'll join you, or maybe even before it's over."

"What if you don't?"

"I will!"

Adam looked a little worried. "I've never driven on the other side of the road."

Jennifer held his hand. "You'll be okay. It will be an adventure, but at the same time you'll be doing it for us. Seriously Adam, you need to get out of here as soon as possible. I know the timing isn't good; I'll be thinking of you on Thursday." Thursday was the ninth anniversary of Billy's death.

Adam was nervous. Nevertheless, he wanted to go. He certainly didn't want to stay around while this maniac was loose, but at the same time he still felt as though he was abandoning Jennifer. He knew that finding somewhere for her to run to was just a ploy on her part; to make it easier for him to leave. Eventually he accepted the offer, and he informed his sister that he was going away. After booking the ferry and organising the key to his apartment for Jennifer, Adam managed to sneak out unseen, using the rear of the house and then the wooded area to return to the village. Jennifer finally relaxed when she received a text from him that evening, telling her that he'd arrived in Calais.

Chapter 46

Tuesday 15th July 2008

Michael Emmerich and the two girls had spent most of Monday together as planned, and now Tuesday lunchtime had arrived and Jennifer was sitting in the bunker, alone, watching the world pass by on her monitors.

She worried about her father; one minute up, the next down, even tearful. She was thinking about the suicide message and telephoned DI Baker to pass on her concerns. Baker promised to make sure that the constable with the duty of protecting her father and sister would be extra vigilant.

Jennifer still worried though. Her father, unusually, had talked a great deal, about his youth, about their mother and how they had met, about Jennifer's and Rachel's younger days, and about the family history; even Jennifer's birth parents. Everything there was to know about them was filed away in a cabinet in his office.

Jennifer had asked him about their wealth, but had got no more answers than Rachel had. There was one thing she did learn, though; she once had an uncle and aunt and cousins, who had all died just before Jennifer was born. When the topic arose she vaguely recalled hearing about them in her younger days, but that was it. Without having her memory jogged of the fact that they had once existed, she would never have remembered them.

It was Dad's older brother, Anthony, and his wife Gwen. They had three children, Samantha, the oldest, and two younger boys, Paul and William. Apparently Samantha had been very ill for years, and eventually died. The other four were all killed in a road accident on holiday in the French Alps – no other vehicle involved... and they'd died with debts, even their property had been signed away, which Dad at the time had thought strange; it had always been assumed they'd had money. "Just like we *have* money." When Jennifer's parents had disappeared from the ferry, it was like history repeating itself, he had said.

She again read the newspaper article about the Huth family that Holly had sent her. Money, and the fact that they lost it, linked her birth parents, Uncle Anthony's family and the Huths.

Jennifer had pleaded with her father and sister to stay in Belfont; that's why she'd had the bunker built... somewhere where they could all stay in safety. But her father was adamant, he wished to return to London, and Rachel, who had seemed very subdued during the visit, wanted to be with him. She also had some affairs to deal with. Jennifer guessed that her sister didn't want to be with her.

Rachel had always believed that Jennifer was guilty of Billy's murder, even though she'd tried hard not to. Then, to actually blurt out what she believed, just moments before finding out the truth! It was all so unfair. Her life, what with this, and Jack... it was all falling apart. She felt uneasy being with her sister at the moment.

Jennifer had her suspicions about how Rachel felt, but she had enough to worry about without causing ructions now. Rachel would always be her sister, but never her friend.

She considered phoning Holly but changed her mind, again; she had sent Adam away, fearing for his safety, and it wouldn't be fair on Holly to get her involved. She didn't mind being alone, but it was inconvenient, she needed to move the contents of her father's office down here, but was reluctant to do so while she was on her own. She had to begin to show some healthy respect for this guy.

She studied the monitors, panning the grounds. Out on the road there were cameramen and photographers, and probably journalists. They now all knew that Jennifer was at the house, getting to the pub had proved to be impossible, and they ended up having Mrs Potts come in and cook a meal. Ah ha, she thought, Mrs Potts, the housekeeper. She had a couple of sons. She picked up the phone and asked if they could all come over and help her for two or three hours. Problem solved, they would be here later that day.

Suddenly, obviously activated by a sound, cameras zoomed in on a figure, crouched amongst the rhododendron bushes, on the left side of the drive. Jennifer studied it… her. She didn't look like a reporter… but you never know. She had a massive dark maroon bag which could have held a whole film set. She looked about forty, weird coloured curly hair, jeans, trainers and, strangely, considering it was quite warm, a large hooded jacket. Jennifer watched as the woman slowly stood, brushed herself down, pulled the hood up over her head and started walking towards the house.

Jennifer armed herself with the hand gun, opened the door of the bunker and made her way to the front door. The woman tapped on the door, and Jennifer slid open a small hatch. "Who are you?" Jennifer asked.

The woman whispered through the opening, keeping her back to the outside world, "My name is Stevie Gee. Are you one of the Emmerich sisters?"

Jennifer recalled the name from the week's news. "How do I know you are who you say you are?" she asked.

Stevie held a forefinger against her lips. "Shhh… I think *he* might be here, let me in and I'll explain." When Jennifer didn't react, Stevie continued, whispering but insistent. "Look, I need your help, and you need mine. The same bastard who told your dad to kill himself is out to get me. You owe it to me to let me in."

"I don't owe you anything." Jennifer whispered this time.

"That's unfair. I'm in this trouble because I warned the police about the call. I've seen him here, let me in."

Jennifer nodded. "Ok, point made. Lower your hood and let me get a good look at you."

"Don't be stupid. The whole world is probably watching the back of me on the television. Please let me in."

Jennifer decided to take a chance. She slid back the security bolts, unlatched the door and took a step back, gun raised. Stevie pushed it open and slipped in. The first thing Stevie noticed was the weapon, and she noticed how steady and firmly it was being held. She closed the door and relocked it without Jennifer saying a word, and then removed her jacket.

Jennifer realised that she'd not actually seen an image of Stevie Gee... she'd not watched the news that closely, and didn't recognise her. "I don't recognise you."

Stevie pulled a face. "Shush," and as she shushed she motioned her hands as though pressing something down. "He's in the house." Jennifer didn't take her eyes off the visitor. Stevie slowly and deliberately opened her bag and pulled out a pile of cards; and a passport. She held out the passport, open at her picture, and Jennifer took it with her free hand. She studied it and looked at Stevie, her eyes darting back and forth quickly. She had to make a decision.

Stevie was becoming impatient. "Come on," she whispered, "I've been sneaking around this village for nearly two days now. Take my word for it; I am who it says I am."

"You look different from your passport photo," said Jennifer.

"That's because I've had to disguise myself, I think my hair has been ten different colours during the past week. I don't want the police to recognise me, and that shit-bag..."

"Why don't you want the police to recognise you?"

"Because they think I'm dead, and I'd rather they continued thinking that, I haven't made up my mind whether or not to trust them."

"Well, that makes two of us, except they know you're alive, they told me so."

"Oh." Stevie seemed surprised, she shrugged. "Did they say why they haven't broadcast it?"

"They said that you deserved not to have that bastard on your back."

Jennifer thought that the woman looked a little disappointed on hearing that piece of news. Perhaps she didn't want to trust the police. She waved the pistol and shepherded Stevie towards the entrance to the bunker.

After locking the heavy door Jennifer told the woman to sit at the table in the work room. She laid the gun on the surface, out of Stevie's reach, and sat opposite.

"Are you Jennifer?" Stevie whispered.

"It's okay, all this is sound proof, you could scream and nobody would hear you."

"Not a good thing to hear, under the circumstances."

Jennifer lightened up a little. "Yes, I'm Jennifer," she held out her right hand, "Pleased to meet you, I think." They shook hands.

"Can I have a drink?" Stevie asked, "I'm parched."

Without thinking, Jennifer walked over to the fridge and pulled out a couple of cans of coke, leaving the pistol on the table. She realised what she had done as she sat down. "Sorry about this," she said as she pointed at the weapon, "I have to assume he's out there at all times." She rubbed her thumb across the top of her can, "You said he's in the house, why did you say that?"

"I had been laying low in London, until Sunday morning, trying to find out who this *Michael with the two daughters* was, and then I saw you in the Sunday newspaper. It mentioned the original threat from years ago, and I figured that your family must be the ones this guy made the threat to last Sunday. Anyway, I made my way down here as soon as I could and have been waiting for a chance to get to you without the press seeing me. The buggers have been parked out there since I arrived; I slept at the edge of the woods, over there." She made an attempt to point in that direction, but wasn't sure of what direction that was, "On the left of the front of the house. About two o'clock, this morning, I noticed somebody prowling around the house. I could hardly see him. He was dressed in dark clothes. In fact, what I actually saw was a series of movements. I couldn't make out any real shape, and at first I thought it was a reporter... but I don't think so, it was all too suspicious. I think it was him, and I never saw him leave. I waited all morning, and when the other two left, your sister and your dad I assume, I thought you might be here on your own, so I decided, whoever was watching, to come down and warn you."

"And you really think he's in the house."

"I'm just saying I didn't see him leave. But I didn't see him arrive either, so... But he is a clever so-and-so." Stevie told Jennifer about her ordeal, the house, the explosion, the policewoman, Amanda Barnard, her cat (Arthur Scargill) and the phone.

As Stevie was telling her story Jennifer watched the monitors, and noticed the press begin to move from the road and back onto her property. "Look at those... They've already been thrown off by the police."

"Why didn't the police stay?"

"I don't want them here."

"But you should. Surely you would be a lot safer with them present."

Jennifer didn't answer.

"Okay, why don't you bring in a security firm?"

Jennifer gave her the same answer she had given Adam.

"Fair enough. But don't you know a few tough guys who could do the job."

"No... However, thinking about it, I do know somebody who could organise some." There was another issue though, more immediate. "Why didn't the security devices pick him up?"

Stevie looked around at all the equipment and wondered the same question. "Perhaps he's supernatural, that's a scary thought. More likely though, you were all asleep, did you all sleep down here?"

"Yes, the rest of the house is virtually out of bounds. Alarms are supposed to go off, there are pressure sensors all over the place, and all of the gardens are covered by motion and audio detectors. It shouldn't matter if I had been asleep."

"I assume they're adjustable, to take account of different circumstances. Perhaps they're not set up properly; we need to test and adjust them."

"When you say *we*, what do you mean?" asked Jennifer.

"I'm up to my neck in this, and I want to help you, I haven't got a choice really."

"Maybe I don't need your help."

"Well, help me then. If I show myself, sooner or later he'll get me. If you let me stay I can make myself useful. I can pay my way if that's a problem."

"That's not a problem." Jennifer considered the proposal. "You can stay if you do things my way."

"What's your way?"

"This bloke set me up as a murderer and it cost me my youth, and has, frankly, ruined my life. It looks likely that he killed my friend Jack Painter, and I'm convinced he killed my mum. He's also pressuring my father to kill himself. I also think he wants to kill me and my sister. I don't know why he's doing this, but I'm trying to find out. More than anything else, I want him dead. I think that's the only way he'll stop."

"And you want to do this on your own, without the aid of the police?"

"I don't care if the police help, I'll even work with them, use them. But: one; I was convicted of murder mostly because of their incompetence, two; they still have no idea what's going on, even with all their resources, and three; if they do catch him, they will not kill him."

"Alright, now it's my turn. He's burnt down my house, blown up my car, wants me dead and killed a young policewoman, almost while I watched. I'm happy to do it your way, and I can see it would be good for both of us if he was dead, but I don't want to go to prison."

"If you really mean all of that, then we can work together. You can stay here with me." Jennifer smiled. "You must be hungry," and stood up. "Come on, I'll show you around, I've had it all set up so that we could survive here for weeks if necessary… and you'll need to know how everything works."

"Before I look around, do you know how to use that?" Stevie pointed at the pistol.

"Not really."

"I didn't think so, I can show you." She reached over, picked it up and inspected it. "I'm in the

Territorial Army and I've had training. Do you have anything else?"

Jennifer walked into the bedroom and returned with a double barrel shotgun, both barrels sawn down. She handed it to Stevie.

Stevie pulled a face. "Right, a twelve bore. This would make a mess of somebody. I've used these, at the clay pigeon club. Not a sawn off one though." She grinned as she cocked it and removed the cartridges.

"What are you; some kind of female Jean-Claude Van Damme?"

After they'd eaten, Mrs Potts and her two sons turned up. It took about half an hour to transfer everything from the office to the bunker. Stevie also wanted all the family photographs collected and brought down, and she recruited Mrs Potts to help her.

When they were alone again they told each other about their lives. They also talked about Jennifer's situation. Stevie asked, "Have you any ideas about why you are going through this? Someone must have it in for your family."

"My family, you mean all the family, each individual? I haven't thought about in that way. First I thought that it was something to do with Mum, but when it continued after her death I then thought it concerned my dad, maybe it does, but now I think it's to do with money."

"You have money?"

"The three of us are worth more than twenty million pounds."

"Umm…" Stevie nodded. "I see, yes, it could be money."

"It's not just because *we* have all that money." Jennifer pulled out the newspaper article about the Huths and the kidnap and murder of the sons. "Have a look at this. The article makes a big thing about a cursed family, unlucky in life, and how they made terrible investment decisions. Look how the mother died."

Stevie read the part that Jennifer pointed to, and shrugged. "She ran off the road in the Fens and drowned in a dyke. Her neck was broken as the car crashed, and then she drowned. Nobody else involved. That sort of thing happens in that part of the country."

"My mum ran off the road in the Fens and drowned. Nobody else involved. Read the rest of it."

Stevie read the whole article, "Ok."

"Summarise it."

"Two children of a wealthy family are kidnapped, one turns up murdered and the other stays missing until his remains are found, years later. The mother is killed in the accident, and then the father finally commits suicide. The estate is worthless because of reckless investment decisions made by the father."

"Now I'll summarise our situation, as it might be in a few weeks time; youngest child of a wealthy family falsely convicted of murder and spends seven years behind bars. While in prison the mother is killed in a road accident. The father commits suicide and then the two daughters are murdered. The estate is worthless."

"You are making it similar, anybody could do that."

"Alright, try this. The daughter of a wealthy family dies, after years of illness. The rest of the family are killed in a road accident in the Alps in France. No other vehicle involved. The family died penniless after reckless investment decisions made by the father."

"Who was *that* family?"

"My uncle, aunt and cousins. It all happened about eighteen years ago. And then... what about this? Two little sisters die, burned to death when a garden shed catches fire, the parents then disappear without trace from a ferry. They were supposed to be rich but their estate turns out to be worthless... My sisters and my parents."

Stevie gave Jennifer a questioning look.

"I'm adopted. Michael is really my uncle."

Stevie whistled. "But with all this happening, why aren't the police here in force... for protection."

"They haven't made the connections yet. I told you, they're useless, always two steps behind. But that suits me at the moment."

"Perhaps you're doing them an injustice, they're coming from a different angle. Let's write it all down in chronological order; we'll date what we can. That way we can see all of the things that link the three families... and yours."

"Apparently there is paperwork from my uncle's family and my birth parents amongst the stuff we've just fetched from the office, which might tell us a lot. We should be able to look up the Huth story on the internet."

Stevie nibbled the forefinger of her right hand and looked at her new friend. "The surnames, what was the surname of your uncle?"

"Emmerich; he was my dad's brother."

"And your birth name?"

"Emmerich."

"All the families have German surnames. Another thing, if your family is destined to go the same way as the Huths went, then it's taken years to carry out these crimes. If your uncle and his family, and your parents, all suffered for as long, then all of this has taken a long, long time to play out. If we *are* on the right track… then we're probably dealing with more than one man."

That possibility sent shivers down the spines of both women. After a while of silent contemplation Jennifer asked Stevie if she wanted to carry on.

"What choice do we have? I think, though, we should let the police in on what we find."

"Maybe, but not yet. Firstly, we're still guessing, you know how easy it can be to convince yourself of something, especially if you want to believe it, and secondly, if we are right, we have the advantage of them not knowing that we know."

"What, the police?"

"No… whoever *they* are."

Stevie was quiet for a while and then agreed to go along with her new friend.

Jennifer took a long deep breath. "For the time being I think we should assume we are working along the right lines. If we are dealing with an organisation rather than an individual, then I think we should get some help, you know, with security. I'll phone a friend and see if she can organise some guys, people she knows. Perhaps you can begin looking through this lot," she pointed at the pile of boxes containing the paperwork from the office, "And see what you can find regarding my uncle, aunt and birth parents. Look Stevie, we're in this together now, nothing in there is private; look at anything that takes your fancy."

"Good idea. But, while we're assuming we are on the right track, we must also bear in mind that we could be wrong. We need to be on our guard for anything."

Jennifer agreed with that. She felt good inside for the first time for a long time, and was glad that Stevie Gee had turned up. Together we can beat this bastard. These bastards. She phoned Holly Andrews.

Chapter 47

About three hours later Jennifer received the email she had been waiting for, from Holly, and attached were four portrait images. '*Hi Jen. Take a look at these. (Attached). I know them all well, although none are close (just as you advised). If I don't hear from you by 9 tonight they will be on their way to Belfont. It sounds as though things are getting serious, what are you planning? – I will be with you within the next couple of days. Holly.*' She showed it to Stevie. "What do you think?"

"Well," Stevie shrugged, "if you trust your friend then I should think these guys will do. It's a good idea for them to turn up tonight, though. I still feel uneasy about the possibility of *him* being in the house. Will they have a television to use, what have you left up there?"

Jennifer nodded. "Satellite, Sky sports, DVD player. They'll have everything up there, including food and booze."

"Do you think that having alcohol around is a good idea?"

Jennifer considered that. "I presume that they're solid guys, otherwise Holly wouldn't have recommended them. I'll contact her again later and ask her."

Stevie changed the subject back to her research of the families. "I know somebody who works on genealogy, he may be able to trace the family lines back;

to see if there is a connection between the Emmerichs and the Huths."

"That sounds like a good move, offer to pay him for his work, and tell him that it's urgent."

Stevie continued to slowly study pieces of paper which she had carefully removed from large envelopes. "We would have to pay him anyway," she said. "I don't know him that well. Leave it with me and I'll see if I can find his phone number."

Jennifer was at the computer looking for information on the Huth family. "Listen, while you're phoning around, why don't you let your family and your boyfriend know that you're still alive and well."

"They already know. I told my brother last week and asked him to pass on the message – but only to my parents and Jonathon. I explained how important it was that I was presumed dead, and the news that I wasn't mustn't get out to anybody else, even to other family members."

"That must be difficult for them – to lie about something like that."

Stevie let out a short laugh. "That's exactly what he said, so I told him to say that there was actually no proof that I was dead, but that I was just missing."

"Even that must be hard."

Stevie was carefully looking through a large pile of photographs of Jennifer's cousins and aunt and uncle. "Are there any pictures of the Huth family on the internet?"

"Yeah, lots, but only of individuals."

"No group photographs?"

"None, why?"

"I've seen it in films, where the sadistic killer likes to be close to the investigation. You never know; if the same man were to pop up in different sets of photos…"

Although Jennifer could see where her new friend was coming from, she was not convinced. "I suppose we have to try everything. We could pin them all up on the wall so that we can study them. Or I'll order one of those transparent notice boards, like you see on cops and robbers TV programmes."

"After the explosion at the hotel, he was there, watching. So don't take the pee… and the police might help. Do you know anyone you could get in touch with, regarding the Huth investigation?"

"I would think the best thing to do would be contact Ray Littleton, he's the detective from Ongar I told you about. He seems okay."

Stevie slipped the pictures back into the envelope. "I'm sorry but I'm knackered, I'll carry on looking at these tomorrow. I could do with something to eat and get some sleep."

"Yeah, I'm not really getting anywhere here either. We'll start again in the morning, have a full day of it. I'll tell you something though; I think we're making progress. I'm glad you turned up, it makes a difference. Can you cook?"

Stevie ignored the kind words. "Not really. I can throw stuff together, what about you?"

"The same. We'll have egg and chips then, is that okay?"

* * *

Around midnight Jennifer sat cross legged on the floor of the hallway, with her back to the door of the bunker. Grouped around her were four men; Sid Benson, Matt Stone, Reese Fenton and Pat Doyle. They were all in their thirties and all looked as though they could handle themselves if things got rough. They were Holly's little helpers, and were about to become Jennifer's little helpers.

Jennifer told them of her concerns regarding the press and about her fears of a stalker, but not about how dangerous that stalker was. She explained that all she expected from them was to occupy the house and gardens, to keep them clear of strangers, and to act as a barrier between herself and any visitor. She also told them that the *bunker* was out of bounds to any of them. They were a pleasant, outgoing bunch, and seemed happy with their duties, and Jennifer was pleased with them. She knew Holly would deliver, she had never let her down!

She left them to settle in, returned down stairs, and undressed for bed. Stevie was sleeping soundly and Jennifer studied her for a while, and thought, again, how much better she was feeling since her arrival. She thought about Jack, promised him that she would get the bastard who killed him… and said sorry. Before she slept she began thinking about Billy Saunders as well, and while she felt she had been harshly treated, at least she was still alive.

* * *

At just after three am her mobile sounded; it was a text message from Holly. *I'm outside x*. Jennifer rubbed her eyes. Outside? She checked the time.

She quietly slipped into the control room and checked the monitors. Sure enough, parked right outside of the front door was a huge red Ferrari. Trust Holly to be so flash. She slipped on a pair of jeans and a shirt and rushed out to greet her old friend, security procedures going to the wall. Sid Benson and Matt Stone, both dozy from sleep, followed her out.

The girls embraced. When they were back into the house they had a good long look at each other. They were both giggling with excitement, and sat in the comfort of the lounge; Sid and Matt outside in the entrance hall.

Over a glass of wine each they exchanged news and brought each other up to date. After about half an hour the mood became more sombre as Jennifer got to Jack.

"Any idea why he was killed?" asked Holly.

Jennifer shrugged. "That's what makes me feel even worse, it has something to do with our family, and if I hadn't involved him, he would still be alive." She went on to tell her about how Jack had supported her, even behind Rachel's back. "Somebody tried, but failed, to make it look as though I'd killed him."

"It's ironic that being in a police cell saved your bacon this time."

"Wait here." Jennifer left her friend alone for a few minutes, before returning with the newspaper article which she'd received in Leytonstone. "Thanks for sending this," she handed it to Holly.

Holly spread it out in front of her, rubbing her fingers along the creases, to flatten it. She hadn't sent it!

In fact she had never seen the piece until that moment. She studied it and at the same time tried to figure out if the writing scribbled along the top belonged to anybody she knew, if she recognised it; she had just a few seconds to decide... should she make out that she sent the item, or? She *did* know the Huth story, much better than most people did. That knowledge helped make up her mind, "It's the least I could do. It was something I saw, and thought that you might be interested."

"I was amazed," said Jennifer, "When it turned up... I couldn't understand how on earth you'd come across it, or saw the connection between their situation and ours. I had never seen you read a newspaper before."

"Well." Holly was thinking on her feet, "The *mums*, for a start."

"That's about it though. You must have really been on the ball to see it."

Holly began to panic, was Jennifer suspicious? So she added, for good measure, "And the fact that they started out wealthy, had all their money stolen, and then died penniless and in debt... I thought that perhaps the same could be happening to your family. I needed to warn you."

"Yeah. That must have been it. I've got a lot to thank you for, it's put me on the right track, I think." Jennifer quietly looked at Holly. A sad, long look. "Yeah... that must have been it."

Holly relaxed, relieved that Jennifer had failed to see through her deception. "Don't get all sentimental with me. Don't forget where we met." She laughed.

Jennifer's eyes were moist, she forced a grin.

"Hey, look at you. I'd do anything for you, Jennifer Emmerich, you know that."

Jennifer nodded slowly. "It's so good that you're here. I can't talk to anybody else about my plan... I don't know who to trust." She recovered her composure.

Holly smiled reassuringly. "Well I'm here now, and you can trust me. What's your plan?"

"I'm going to kill the bastard who killed Jack. I'm setting a trap for him."

Holly mocked, "Fucking hell, that's extreme."

"As soon as I can figure out how to lure him into the open, I'll kill him."

"Ok, how are you going to do that?"

"I don't know."

Holly sipped her wine as she perused the conversation so far. "Have you thought about what they want?"

They, thought Jennifer. "I've tried. Have you any ideas?"

"Umm... I think they're definitely after your money, and it's obvious that, at the moment, you have it safe. That's why they've not come after you yet. I think if you were to transfer it, out of your account... as soon as they were aware that you'd done that, they would come after you."

Jennifer was interested in Holly's 'theory'. "Where would I transfer it to, into another account?"

"That's a stupid question, how do I know?"

You seem to know an awful lot, thought Jennifer. "Okay, so let's say I figure out which account I should transfer my money into, how long do you think it would take for them to know it's in there?"

"I don't know that either, but probably not for a few days." Holly paused to mull over her advice. "No, definitely not for a few days, how would they know?"

"They seem to have their ways of finding things out." Jennifer folded the article, which had no mention of embezzlement in it, and placed it back inside the large envelope. Holly had never known about Jennifer's family fortune either. "Are you staying the night?"

"No," said Holly. She placed her hand over the top of her glass, "I can't stay and I'd better not drink too much, I'll end up killing myself... in that beast outside."

"God, I'd forgotten about the car. How can you afford that?"

"I can't. It belongs to a bloke I'm with."

"I knew you'd do alright on the outside." Jennifer laughed.

"Yeah, except if I don't get it back by the morning I won't be driving it any more. I really have got to go."

"Well, if you come up with any ideas, let me know." Jennifer then added, "I'll keep you totally up to date, you'll know every move I'm making... how I'm thinking... I'm so glad I have you at my side... at last."

Jennifer gave Holly a big kiss, fully on the lips, and she began to spin her web.

Jennifer thought about asking where she was going but then couldn't be bothered. She felt very, very sad, and at the same time incredibly angry that this friendship, her only *real* friendship, had turned out to be fake. Just who could she trust?

The fake friends parted, both displaying fake emotions, and both glad to see the back of each other.

Who were these people? How did they get to her ex-friend? Had Holly sold out, or had she always been with them? Holly never, ever, knew that the Emmerichs had money.

Jennifer was now convinced that there was more than one of them. She wondered about the four guards... and then about Stevie... especially about Stevie.

Chapter 48

Wednesday 16th July 2008

Nothing happened between Holly leaving and daylight, so the appearance of the police car in the morning created a reaction from the camped reporters, photographers and cameramen which was normally reserved for royalty. It was as though they had been waiting patiently for this very moment to arrive.

As the vehicle was driven through the main gate of the Belfont-St-Mary farmhouse the press men began clicking cameras and filming from the road and from amongst the trees and bushes on the verge; the border between the road and the lawn. But this respect for Britain's trespass laws didn't last long. As the front door of the house opened, a photographer stepped over the boundary. Almost immediately the others followed, then, en-mass, they couldn't help themselves. They rushed across the lawn, clicking, whirring and firing questions as they ran, and almost made it to the house – but three thick set thugs spewed out through the front door and advanced toward the invading horde, weighing heavily into whoever they reached first, not exactly violently, but certainly heavily.

Ray Littleton had almost completed the short distance between the police car and the door of the house but was shoved aside by the three. He turned to watch the ensuing battle with interest. Being a policeman brought with it moments of amusement and watching the press legitimately get a battering was one of them. His driver, a uniformed policewoman, had initially remained in the car. When the skirmish started she leapt out to intervene, but Littleton called out to stop her. The twenty or so newspaper and television men were no match for Jennifer's little helpers and soon retreated back to the road, waving fists and shouting obscenities. The three stood in defiance across the lawn, silent, and feeling very proud of themselves.

The fourth member of the team, Reece Fenton, had waited by the door. Perhaps as a second line of defence, *as if it was needed*. He greeted Littleton with as little politeness as he thought he could get away with.

"Nice show," said Littleton, "Can I see Jennifer Emmerich?"

"Is she here?" asked Reece, looking surprised at the request.

"Yes, she's here. In fact she's behind you."

Reece turned as Jennifer was just closing the bunker door. "It's okay Reece," she said, "let him in." She smiled warmly at the gorilla as she spoke, an indication of how pleased she was with the way all the team had performed. She also stood well back, out of view of those on the road.

The policeman nonchalantly brushed past Reece into the house and shook hands with the girl, they greeted each other using Christian names. "Quite a performance," he said.

"They deserved it," she replied, meaning the press. "They've no right to charge onto my property." She was a little surprised, but pleased to see the policeman again; there was a bond forming she thought, and she liked it.

Littleton nodded, "My thoughts as well. Jennifer, can we speak somewhere, in private?"

Jennifer led him into the drawing room. Reece strode across the hall and placed himself with his back to the door; sentry duty. He didn't flinch as Littleton closed the door.

Once alone in the drawing room Littleton suggested Jennifer should sit. Jennifer tentatively sat. "I have some very, very bad news, I'm afraid your father is dead."

Jennifer sat silent for a long time. Littleton waited patiently without saying any more. Finally she asked, "How?"

"It looks as though it was suicide, an overdose, sleeping tablets. Your sister found him in his bed this morning."

Jennifer sighed. "Stupid Dad!" She reflected about Monday; *that's why you talked so much, you had it all planned*. Then she thought out loud, "There was no need, it won't make any difference, *he'll* still come after us." Suddenly she stood and kicked the sofa. "Bastard!" She walked over to the bay window and looked out onto the gardens and she wondered how long this was all going to go on for. "How is my sister; Rachel?"

Littleton shrugged, "I'm sorry, I don't know. I came straight from Ongar to tell you about your father. DI Baker asked me to come and see you. Your sister is with her, in Chelsea."

"Would you mind trying to find out for me? Listen, do you also mind waiting here while I grab some stuff, I need to go to Chelsea."

"We'll take you. I don't think you should drive."

"I want to bring Rachel back here."

"That's okay; we'll bring the two of you back."

Jennifer raised her eyebrows. "So now you've become my taxi?"

"I'm afraid that you're going to have a policeman around you for the foreseeable future. I'm taking the first shift, that's all."

Jennifer left Littleton sitting in the drawing room and went down into the bunker where Stevie had begun to work her way through the piles of paperwork. "Stevie, my dad is dead."

Stevie looked down at the desk, "Oh fuck!" she said, almost to herself, then, "I'm so sorry," and asked how; as if she didn't already know.

Jennifer told her as much as she knew, and that she was off to Chelsea to fetch Rachel. "Do not leave this bunker… for any reason. You know you're probably next on his kill list."

"Thanks for letting me know that, but you take care as well, both you and your sister are in just as much danger as I am. More; at least I'm down here."

"I'll be back this afternoon and I'll introduce you to those four guys. Before I leave, I'll tell them that you're in charge."

"They look a pretty impressive bunch, I've been watching the three on the lawn," she pointed at the monitor. "I'll be okay with them around."

Jennifer grabbed her bag and a jacket and returned to the drawing room. Littleton was ready to go. Rachel was bearing up, he told her.

Jennifer walked to the police car shielding herself from the cameramen using her jacket. She also used it to make sure that nobody had sight of her as they drove off. *She'd been here before,* she reflected.

She couldn't remember anything about her trial; all that shenanigans as she was marched back and forth between Crown building and cell, but on a couple of occasions since, on other court visits, she'd had to use 'the blanket over the head' procedure in order to avoid being photographed. However, on those occasions the press had been just small opportunistic groups, nothing like this lot!

In case a photographer had been deployed away from the house she remained out of sight as they made their way through the village. As she was gently rocked from side to side by the momentum of the car being driven around the windy roads, memories seeped into her conscience, of herself as a small child, warmly snuggled under a cover in the back of the family car. *"Almost home..."* the soothing voice of her father would assure her. A tear trickled down a cheek and she wondered if she would ever be happy?

She spent most of the three hour journey sitting silently in the back of the squad car, tangled thoughts of her father and contemplating a plan for revenge. She was certain that the only safe place for her and Rachel was in the bunker, but, at the same time, if she was going to beat this guy, she needed to somehow lure *him*, Stevie's weirdo, out into the open.

Perhaps he would see the security the bunker offered as a special challenge; getting first past the police, then the guys and then into the underground rooms. She needed to create a controlled weakness.

She'd spent a lot of money and a lot of time thinking, but she still wasn't exactly sure of what he wanted, other than to kill. There *was* obviously another reason, otherwise she'd have been dead long ago… and that reason had to be financial. It *had* to be? *Holly had confirmed that*. When she collected Rachel she would also bring back any financial paperwork, and along with Stevie they would work out how to use their money as bait.

She had to assume Stevie was genuine but, at least until she was certain, Jennifer needed to tread carefully. The four heavies were to be used, but never trusted. While staying guarded with regard to Stevie, she must at the same time protect her.

Rachel would be a welcome addition to the team… she hoped.

If the three of them were able to produce evidence, even weak evidence, showing the offences carried out against all of the families were similar enough to be linked, then the police would surely be able to do something? If we could fight them with the backing of the state, that would be a bonus. But Jennifer wanted the weirdo dead! So her conclusion was, even with help… she was on her own!

Jennifer hadn't mentioned Holly's visit. She needed to phone the woman sometime, and now was as good a time as any, the false friend had become the conduit to pass on the information which would eventually help defeat the unknown enemy.

Wary that Littleton would be listening to any conversation she just told her *friend* what had happened to her father and that she was on her way to Chelsea in a squad car to collect Rachel.

She also asked her to see if she could find any genealogical links between the Huth family and the Emmerich family, after all, Holly was the one who took the credit for introducing the Huths into the equation. It would be interesting to see how the results compared with those of Stevie's contact. She noticed Ray Littleton's ears prick up when he heard her mention *Huth*.

* * *

There were two policemen on duty at the street entrance to the apartments above the shop and one in the top floor lobby immediately outside Rachel's door. DI Baker had recently left. Littleton had spoken to Baker on the journey and told her that Jennifer was planning to take her sister back to Belfont-St-Mary. After a brief consultation with Rachel's doctor, Baker had sanctioned the move.

Littleton accompanied Jennifer into the apartment and stood back as the two sisters embraced. Rachel looked and acted like a zombie; due to a combination of something the doctor had given her and the shock of finding her father dead. She stammered about finding *him* in that bedroom, she pointed. Jennifer told her to grab a few things and that they were going back to the farmhouse, where they would be safe.

While Rachel was in her bedroom Littleton made two mugs of tea… Rachel didn't want one. Jennifer had found a box of documents by the television and was looking through a couple from the top of the pile.

"What are all these papers Rachel, in the box by the TV?" she shouted.

"That's all the stuff to do with our finances; me and Dad were…" she trailed off for a moment. "We were looking through them yesterday, with Darius Felton."

"Who's Darius Felton?" Littleton asked Jennifer, quietly.

"I've never met him, but he's Rachel's, actually, I suppose, the family's, financial advisor." She raised her voice again, "Why were you doing that?"

There was no answer.

"Why do you think your father killed himself?" Littleton asked Jennifer.

"You know why, because of the phone call."

"He didn't have financial problems, then?"

"No, *he* didn't have financial problems. I suppose he just wanted to make sure everything was in order before… well, you know."

Littleton sipped his tea. "We should take the box back with us, to your farmhouse."

Jennifer agreed. She studied the papers she was holding. A huge money transfer! This could be her opportunity! She gave it some consideration, and then slumped back into the chair. "They're all way beyond me."

"At the moment they might be. But I would think you'd get your head around them, given more time."

"Yeah, you're probably right." She sighed. She needed to tell Littleton about her relatives, her Uncle Anthony and Aunt Gwen? Her real parents? She decided to wait, this place could be bugged. "When we get back to the farmhouse can you hang around for a while, to go over some stuff?"

"Of course I can, no problem."

Jennifer looked at the papers again as they finished off their tea. Then she asked Littleton, "Should we turn stuff off, like the water and electricity? We might not be back here for a while."

Littleton went out into the kitchen and checked in the freezer. It was full. "I would leave it on if I were you." Just at that moment the door to the apartment closed with a bang. He couldn't remember it being open so walked out into the hallway to investigate... nobody there. He stood for a moment to think things through and then decided to check on Rachel. He knocked on the bedroom door, and when there was no answer he looked past it.

He shouted. "Jennifer. Stay where you are, do not move!" Rachel's almost naked body was swinging in mid air, hanging by her neck on the end of a rope, secured to the hook in the ceiling. He shouted to the constable outside the door for assistance and then, using a chair to stand on, attempted to lift the girl and release the noose. But it was all too awkward, the ceiling being too high and Rachel being too high. Again he shouted for help as he supported the body... taking the weight. He heard Jennifer coming... he had to save her from seeing her sister like this. He jumped from the chair and rushed to the bedroom door in time to stop her entering and ushered the confused girl back into the lounge. He then stepped out into the lobby but the constable wasn't there... he screamed for assistance from the top of the stairway. He took a step down, and as he did so the apartment door closed behind him.

Jennifer sunk to her knees when she discovered Rachel. All the girl was wearing was her bra and panties and Jennifer strangely felt for her sister's embarrassment, as opposed to her dreadful situation. She instantly recovered and went through the same futile process that Littleton had. All the time Littleton was shouting through the door… "Let me in!" and Jennifer was shouting back, for help. She left her sister and tried to open the door but it was locked! The key? Where was it? She remembered the bunch which hung in the kitchen. She almost fell in her panic to get to them… they weren't there. She shouted to Littleton that she was trying to find a key and frantically hunted throughout the kitchen and then the lounge. Her head was spinning. Directions shouted through the front door. Panic set in with her manic search for the key… and Rachel… she must save Rachel!. She didn't want to go into the bedroom where her father had died but forced herself… nothing. She didn't want to go back to Rachel. She didn't know what to do! It was only Littleton shouting his encouragement and for more progress from the other side of the door which brought her back to her senses. Jennifer rushed across the bedroom without looking in the direction of her sister and made for the girl's hand-bag. She upended it and emptied the contents onto the bed; no keys. She turned to look for a jacket, or anywhere the keys might be. Getting nowhere and with frustration she stumbled back onto the bed and involuntary looked towards the hanging body – Rachel's panties had been pulled down around her ankles.

He was still in here!

Jennifer jumped from the bed and screamed. "YOU FUCKING BASTARD! WHERE ARE YOU?" She rushed from the bedroom into the kitchen and pulled a bread-knife from the cutlery drawer. She smashed into her father's room – Nothing! Into the bathroom – Nothing! Again into her sister's room and into the lounge and again her father's room and again into the kitchen. All were empty. "SHOW YOURSELF YOU FUCKING COWARD. I'M GOING TO FUCKING KILL YOU!! She tried to open the windows; they were all locked. All the time Littleton was screaming at the door. By this time assistance had arrived and they were trying to smash it open, without success. Littleton screamed for her to try a window. "They're all locked!" she shouted back. She picked up a chair and tried to break the glass but that didn't work either.

Amongst the commotion she heard other sounds, a rattle and some scrabbling. She stood still and waited, she was in the lounge. Controlling her breathing she crept slowly into the hall, the knife held high… ready to plunge… And then into her father's room, slowly passing through the doorway, listening... She took everything in, where everything was, before leaving it again. Then she slowly made her way to her sister's room.

She slowly crept through the doorway, ready in case he jumped out from behind the door. Her eyes darted back and forth; looking for any movement under the bed, movement of the wardrobe doors… She examined everywhere and everything, and at the same time waiting for any sudden lunge from behind. She knew that it was too late now to save Rachel, and Jennifer did her best to ignore the hanging body, she tried to listen for sounds other than those from outside the apartment, which were considerable. She carefully went back into the hall. Again she heard a scraping sound.

"QUIET!" she shouted, and the commotion from outside the door stopped. The noise was coming from the lounge. She crept forward, knife raised. As she entered the room suddenly a figure appeared at the window and she jumped back in fear. It was a fireman.

The glass window shattered with a loud pop, into a million pieces, when he held what looked like a short screwdriver against it. Then he quickly cleaned the one or two jagged edges around the frame and crawled in. Behind him another fireman appeared. Jennifer remained on guard, upright, knife at the ready... don't trust anybody! The first fireman asked her to relinquish her weapon... she wouldn't, but she lowered it. Once she had determined that they were friends, as apposed to foe, she asked them to help her with Rachel. "We shouldn't," said one.

"Help me!" Jennifer demanded. One stood on the chair and cut the rope while the second took the load. Together they laid the girl on the bed and Jennifer covered her with a sheet. A third member of the fire crew had entered through the broken window and had opened the door, allowing Littleton to re-enter the area.

The fireman was holding a large mortise key, which, he said, he'd found in the lock.

Chapter 49

With the help of one of the constables Littleton had cleared and sealed the apartment by the time the Met detectives turned up. An ambulance had also arrived and Jennifer sat in the back with a blanket wrapped around her, both hands wrapped around a mug of hot drink. A huge section of the King's Road had been cordoned off and everywhere blue lights flashed, the street was crowded with armed police in flack-jackets, dogs with their handlers and crime scene staff in white overalls.

DI Baker had arrived, and after speaking with Littleton, approached Jennifer. "Are you alright?"

Jennifer nodded.

"You're going to have to give a statement but first you'll need to go to hospital. You'll be in shock. We can interview you there."

"I'm okay."

"Perhaps you think you are. Please. Go to the hospital. After, you can return to your farmhouse."

"What about Rachel?"

Baker didn't answer immediately, as if she wasn't sure. Then, "We'll take care of your sister."

"There is a box of papers, financial stuff…"

"DI Littleton told me about them. They're gone."

"What do you mean?"

"Well, they're no longer there. The intruder must have taken them."

"No. That's impossible, they were there. I was looking at them when Ray..." Jennifer felt in her pockets, maybe she had stuffed the papers she had been looking at into her pocket. There was nothing there.

The detective asked the paramedics not to leave quite yet and went back into the building to double check. She returned, but still without the documents. However they weren't missing, forensics had removed them.

Jennifer asked for the top items, which had summarised the money transfer.

Baker shook her head, "They won't release them, it's a murder scene." She saw Jennifer's disappointment. "I'll tell them to send you copies by email. Will that be okay?"

"How soon?"

"As soon as they can."

Jennifer didn't feel like arguing but she was not going to leave it alone. "There was a transfer of a lot of money and there's often a cooling off period, you know, when you can change your mind, but I can't do that without the details. If I don't do anything soon, it might be too late. So I'm not going to give you a statement until I have copies."

Baker sneered, she couldn't help herself. "I would have thought you would want us to apprehend this guy."

Jennifer just looked at the woman, who shrugged, turned, and walked away.

"Take care," she muttered to Jennifer as an afterthought, and then continued towards the building. She was intercepted on the way by a tall man, smartly dressed in a suit, and after a brief discussion Baker pointed in Jennifer's direction.

He walked over and introduced himself as Detective Chief Inspector David Wentworth. Jennifer was now shaking; he called one of the medics over and asked him to wrap her in a warmer blanket. The medic wanted to give her an injection but Jennifer would have none of it. Wentworth understood that she would be in shock; *it must have been one hell of an experience*. After giving his commiserations and asking whether she was fit to talk, he said, as an extension of his introduction, "I'm heading the investigation team into of the murder of Detective Constable Amanda Barnard and I thought you may know the whereabouts of a lady we want to interview, Stephanie Gee." He showed Jennifer a picture.

"Who?" She pretended to study the picture and shook her head. "No... I'm sorry. Why do you think I might know her?"

Wentworth sighed. "Stephanie, generally known as Stevie, is a witness to a number of incidents leading up to the murder of DC Barnard. We're of the opinion that her murder and that of Jack Painter's are linked; and now your sister..." He paused. "Although it's early days I think we can fairly safely ascertain that the deaths of your father and sister will also turn out to be connected to the murders of DC Barnard and Mr Painter. I need to talk to Stephanie, urgently. We are also very concerned for her safety, as we are for yours."

Jennifer didn't want to be obstructive, but at the same time she decided it would have to be Stevie's decision as to where and when she would speak to the police. "I've never met *this* Stevie Gee, but if she does put in an appearance, I'll tell her to get in touch with you."

After further probing Wentworth realised he wasn't getting anywhere. "You should be taken to hospital," he said.

"I don't need to go to hospital."

"Ray Littleton has told me about your fortified farmhouse. It sounds secure enough. What about returning there with an armed police escort and a medic, I'll organise it."

"You're asking me to return to Suffolk with strangers!"

"Ray Littleton will be one and I'll vouch for the other two. One belongs to the armed response division of the Metropolitan Police Force and the other is a police medic. I've known them both for years."

"Knowing somebody for years doesn't mean a thing. And how do I know that *you're* not one of these people out to get me?"

Wentworth wasn't quite sure how to respond. He supposed he would be a little paranoid in her position.

"Okay," she said before he could come up with an answer, "I'll let your people take me back to my home. But I'm not feeling too well at the moment, so can we leave soon."

Wentworth called over the medic again. Then he spoke again to Jennifer, "You need to be extremely careful; we have good reason to believe that your life is in danger."

Jennifer's mind was wandering and she wasn't listening. The sight of Rachel hanging suddenly hit her and she began to weep.

Wentworth immediately regretted that he may have distressed her. He knelt down beside her and took her hand. "I'm really sorry if I've upset you or frightened you, but we're almost there with our investigation. Soon you won't have to worry, it will all be over. I can't tell you how sorry I am that we couldn't save your father or your sister, we just weren't fast enough, but I'm determined that nothing is going to happen to you. Now, please let us take care of you, go home and be safe."

"What do you mean *almost there?*"

"Look." He was tempted to tell the girl all he knew, she had a right to know, however… "At the moment things are moving at a fast pace, and I can't give you the time. But I promise I will personally come and see you, as soon as this is over. I'll let you look through all of the documentation we have, there is so much you should know and it explains a great deal. Please, trust me."

They looked at each other for a few moments, and then Jennifer nodded. He stood and wished her luck.

"And you too, good luck," she said. "By the way," she added, "Have you got a contact number? You never know."

"Yes, here's my card, with a direct number."

After a short while Littleton turned up. "Come on young lady, let's get you home."

* * *

Tina and Robert were still occupying their room at the hotel, only venturing out so that the staff wouldn't get suspicious. It had been over a week… a week and a bit of constant vigilance, of scanning television news channels, newspapers and the internet; looking for news or information about Ben's murders. There was nothing.

What they did see was the identikit photo of Peter. He was being linked with the London explosion, the murder of a policewoman and the murder of Jack Painter. Why? They asked themselves. What the hell was he doing?

"What the fuck are we involved in?" Tina felt her whole world caving in. "They'll lock us all up and throw away the key."

"Why would they lock us up? We've nothing to do with any of it."

"Yes we have. We know that it's happening. We could have picked up a phone or walked into any police station at any time during the last twenty years and put a stop to all their murders. None of these killings would have taken place."

Robert was silent. Hiding away from Ben had given him too much time to think… to think about the consequences of the meeting with Theo Tester and, more so, of his impending reunion with the family elite. He was very frightened. "Do you think we could just disappear?"

"We could, but it would mean spending the rest of our lives looking over our shoulders, waiting for them to catch up with us. They would find us, eventually, and I don't know if I could handle the fear, waiting…"

Robert was almost in tears. "God, Tina. Why did we ever listen to that bastard?" They both lay on the bed in each others arms…

After a long while Tina spoke. "What if we saved Jennifer Emmerich? Surely the police would be grateful. If they have the memory stick then the worst of the family would be locked up. We could testify against all of them, against Ben as well."

"Do the police know Jennifer is in danger?"

"They must do by now. But if they don't, we'll tell them, after we have her safe. We'll tell them about what they wanted to do to her, and why."

Robert wasn't convinced. "They'll still get us. Even the police can't stop them, even if they're all in prison, somehow they'll get us. You know that!"

"Ok, first we'll grab Jennifer. Then one of us can go and see Amy and tell her that unless she guarantees our safety the other one will go to the police and tell them everything."

Robert was thinking about it all. He doubted about it being a good idea; he was finding it difficult to see how they would be any better off than if they just disappeared.

Tina rolled onto her side and stroked his face. "Come on. Our lives are probably over anyway, so what have we got to lose? At least I'll feel better for trying to save the girl. She doesn't deserve to die."

"Nor do we," he replied.

There had always been somebody in the family who knew how everybody was related to each other and unless told to carry out the act, sex was forbidden between kindred; Robert and Tina could be brother and sister for all they knew. They had spent over a week lying beside each other without daring to broach the subject, lacking the courage to make any such move. Actually, they hadn't even considered it. Now Tina made that move.

Chapter 50

A few hours later Jennifer and her entourage arrived back at Belfont. There was already a squad car and a police van present, and four armed policemen patrolled the grounds. Two had dogs. The media were in a boiling frenzy, shouting from the roadside. "Jennifer Emmerich, tell us…" Idiots tried to run alongside the car, taking photographs of its occupants, and cameras flashed continuously when she stepped onto the drive.

Littleton instructed the policeman who had travelled with them from Chelsea to go and tell them to keep the noise down and explain that it is an offence to obstruct road traffic. One of the press shouted; *"Jennifer, now that you are the last of your family, how do you feel?"* Littleton was disgusted and flew into a rage. "Go and shut them up," he added to his instruction. The door of the farmhouse opened and Reece appeared. "You seem to have found *your* place," said the detective sarcastically.

"That's not fair," Jennifer objected.

Littleton ignored her and continued into the house and into the drawing room. Jennifer and the medic followed.

"What now?" she asked.

"Tell me about the Huth family," he demanded.

Jennifer wondered what had got into him, this sudden change of mood. She asked him.

Littleton sat quietly for a while and then apologised. "I'm sorry. It's the press. I hate them. There's a lot of bad history between us, and so far they've come out on top, so, they just wind me up. Sorry," he repeated.

On the return trip Jennifer had sat quietly in the back of the vehicle trying hard not to think of the last time she had seen her sister. She was on her own now, really on her own. She assumed both Rachel's and her father's wealth was lost – probably the farmhouse as well. She didn't need it, but what right did these bastards have; taking it.

Most likely Stevie was okay. However, just in case, Jennifer needed to use her for research and not involve her with any details of whatever plan she might come up with. The four guys supplied by Holly… Who knows? But in order to keep her fake friend from becoming suspicious she had to pretend that she trusted them. One advantage to having them around was an attempt to kill her would be more likely to take place than if it was police protecting her; especially if the four are on the payroll of the enemy. If she was going to trap this guy, something needs to happen fast if Wentworth was correct about the progress the police were making.

"Reece." Jennifer called. Reece opened the door and looked in. "Reece, where are the others?"

"Upstairs."

"Can you go and get them, bring them down here." A few minutes later they were gathered in the drawing room. The men were quiet. Firstly Jennifer spoke to the four. "This is DI Ray Littleton and he is the only policeman I trust. This is Brian, he's a police medic." And then she turned to Littleton. "Ray, you've met Reece. This is Sid," Sid nodded. "This is Matt and this is Pat." They both nodded. She then spoke to all of them. "I would like you all to get on, even if it's just until this is over. Wait here and chat, I'll be back soon." She left them sitting in silence and went down into the bunker.

Stevie was pleased to see her back at Belfont but listened in silent horror as Jennifer told her about all that had taken place at Chelsea. Jennifer told her everything, in minute detail, including her meeting with Wentworth, and even Littleton's mood change upstairs. They both cried, together. Then, "Come upstairs and meet them," said Jennifer, wiping her face with a wet flannel.

"Are you staying?" Stevie asked Littleton. Everybody had been introduced to each other and all were now lolling around on the ground floor of the house. Two of the lads had poured themselves a pint each. The rest were drinking tea or coffee.

"I'm not sure," he answered.

"You can if you want. There are spares of everything in the big guest bathroom," said Jennifer.

"It would pay you to," said Stevie, "We have lots to show you. You should stay overnight and run through it with us. You might be able to help us as well."

"You can have your own bedroom," added Jennifer.

"Alright. I'll make a couple of calls." He turned to Stevie, "I also need to inform DCI Wentworth that you're here."

Stevie thought about that and decided there was probably no alternative. "Are you married?" she asked him.

Jennifer smiled.

"No. I'm a bachelor."

"What's so funny?" Stevie asked Jennifer. "I'm not asking the bloke to marry me!"

"Who would marry a copper?" said Pat, light heartedly, listening in on the conversation. Then he added, a little more seriously, "But, more importantly Jennifer, what's with all the police presence? It all seems a bit over the top, for a stalker." The boys hadn't yet been told about Rachel.

Jennifer needed to tell them, not just about Rachel, but about the attempt on Stevie's life, the murder of the policewoman, and Jack… and her father. She gathered them all around. "…I don't know why this is happening but it seems somebody, or even some people, want to kill the whole of my family. Years ago I was framed for murder. Whilst in custody my mother was killed, I think murdered. Since I've been released, a close friend, Jack Painter, was stabbed with a bread-knife stolen from my house in Leytonstone. He died. A week last Sunday, Stevie overheard a man making a phone call to my father, telling him to kill himself. Because she reported the conversation to the police she has had her house burnt down, her car blown up while she was supposed to be inside it and a policewoman was murdered when she became involved." Jennifer steadied herself before continuing. "Last night my father committed suicide. As you know I went to Chelsea to collect my sister, to bring her back here. She was murdered while I was in the flat with her. DI

Littleton was with me; we never heard a thing." She shook her head. "The bastard did it right under our noses. He was there... just me and him, after..." She couldn't go on.

Shocked silence followed. While nobody wanted to embarrass Jennifer, none could take their eyes off her.

Littleton was first to speak and directed the conversation towards the four men. "You don't have to stay. I recommend that you return to London and let the police take over the security inside the house."

Matt asked Jennifer, "What do you want us to do?"

Good move, she thought. Make me feel as though it's my decision. "It's up to you. I don't want to put anybody in danger. But the reason for having you here is that you're not strangers. I feel much safer having you lot here rather than a load of unknowns, even if they are policemen."

Littleton butted in. "The policemen would be trained, surely that must be a factor."

"We can handle ourselves," quipped Pat. "Three of us are ex-army and the other an ex-copper"

"Which one is the ex-copper?" asked Littleton. When nobody answered he studied the four. "Sid." He said.

"How could you tell?" asked Sid.

"Because you stand like you have a truncheon up your arse," said Reece, and they all laughed at that.

Pat then said. "We're staying. Don't worry about us, we'll stay and take care of things in the house, and your lot," he waved a hand at Littleton, "can take care of things out there, look after the flowers and stuff." He jerked his head towards the gardens.

Jennifer looked at each of the four in turn. "Are you sure?"

They all confirmed they understood the situation and were prepared to stay on. Next, Jennifer and Stevie invited Littleton down into the bunker. Like all who went before him, he was impressed. Jennifer showed him around and gave him a demonstration of the security equipment while Stevie cooked something. It was edible and as they ate, Jennifer spoke to the detective. "There is more to this situation than we let on upstairs."

"How do you mean?" he asked.

"Stevie and I think that what is happening to us, the Emmerich family, and what happened to the Huth family in the early nineteen nineties is connected. Do you remember that case?"

"Everybody remembers the case. But what makes you think there's a connection?"

"They had money, as we have. Stevie and me think the reasons for their harassment and persecution was money. It was slowly stolen from the Huths, without them even realising it, and when it had all been taken, Mr Huth was finally killed. The way it was done to them is so similar to the way they are doing it to us. There were two other families you should take a look at. One... my uncle, aunt and cousins. They all died, again during the early nineties and again in suspicious circumstances. We also think that, going back a long time, I may have been somehow related to the Huths."

"And the other?"

"My real parents. They disappeared from a ferry in 1992."

Littleton nodded slowly, looking at Jennifer as he did so. "So that's why you want the genealogical investigation. We could find out if you were related to the Huths by carrying out a DNA comparison test." He wanted to ask more about Jennifer's childhood, but decided to leave it until later. "Good work, both of you. You should carry on with your investigation, in case it highlights anything else."

They both thought that he was being condescending and at the same time trying to take control. "Brilliant idea," said Stevie, a little sarcastically, and turned to the computer. "I have here as much as I know so far about the families; dates of deaths and other incidents. If you could email them to whoever led the investigations, they could add their bits and send back the findings."

"I don't think they would email them back to you," replied Littleton.

"You're right, but they would email them to you. They consider you part of the investigation, surely?"

"Okay. I'll talk to DCI Wentworth and put him in the picture. I'll also have to tell him that you're here. Is that okay?"

Stevie glanced at Jennifer. "Yeah, do that." She then said to Jennifer, "Can I have a private word?" They went into the bedroom. "Is he going to be helping us? Do we tell him everything?"

"Everything except the plan about killing the weirdo, and obviously not about the 'you know whats'."

"The what?"

"The guns," she whispered.

"And what's the plan?"

"I'll tell you about it later. There is something else. Dad liquidated his investments which he held with his broker and transferred all the cash into his current account. I have a feeling that that account is controlled by whoever is after us. There is now more than ten million pounds deposited in it… and I bet they've taken the lot."

"God!"

"That's not all. The Chelsea apartment and this farmhouse are not ours, according to the land registry. And, killing Rachel means they have her money as well, they must have."

This news made Stevie angry. "Are you sure about yours, is it safe?" she asked.

"I think so; I had the bank check my accounts last week… and the Leytonstone house; that's also cool. That's probably why I'm still alive."

"Are you going to tell him," she jerked her head towards Littleton.

"I'm not sure, so for the time being we'll keep it to ourselves."

"Why?"

"If I transferred my money into my dad's account…"

"You can't be serious."

"Why not? I bet if I did, he would come for me."

"Fuck. That would be scary."

"But it could work. If I'm right, they'll send him after me… and I'll kill him."

"Or…"

Jennifer stopped her. "Or nothing, stop there."

"Is there some way Ray and the police could help, or the guys upstairs, to sway the odds a little."

"No, this is my fight. Littleton must not find out. We'd better get back to him or he'll get fidgety. He's not going to sleep down here with us so we'll have plenty of time to talk, later." When Stevie didn't reply straight away, Jennifer exclaimed, "Stevie, he's too old. You're disgusting!"

"He's too old for you." She got serious again. "There is a picture of a woman standing with your mum. I'm pretty sure she was the woman who the pervert talked to when he dropped the phone into the bin."

"Really, show me."

"It's by the computer."

"Let's go then, show it to me."

"In front of *him*?"

"Yes."

They rejoined Littleton and Stevie pulled out the photograph. "Her." She pointed.

"Bloody hell, that's Monica Davies. She's been the family lawyer for years. She was one of my mum's closest friends."

"What about her?" asked Littleton. They told him. "I need to pass this on to Wentworth, with an image. I also have to send the driver back to Ongar, and my phone charger and lap top are in the car. Let me out and I'll sort things out."

"Make your phone calls from down here," said Jennifer. "This is the only place where it's guaranteed *they* will not to be able to hear us."

He pointed out, "No-one can overhear me while I'm in the squad car." When Jennifer just stared at him, he backed down, "Alright, I'll phone from down here."

"It would be ridiculous doing it from anywhere else. There are computers and email facilities here, totally at your disposal. We'll give you space if you want to be private." She turned to Stevie. "Isn't that right Stevie?" Stevie shrugged.

When Littleton had left, Stevie pointed out, "He's going to take up a lot of space."

Jennifer went upstairs and spoke with Reece. She wanted to make sure that if and when the police from the garden wanted to come in, for any reason, only one was to be allowed inside the building at any one time, and he should always be accompanied by one of the boys. She had organised for Mrs Potts to come and cook for everybody but the police would still have to eat and drink outside. Together they decided that the medic could stay in the house. Reece thought that the buggers should fend for themselves and that Jennifer was being too nice.

Downstairs again Littleton was making his phone calls and Stevie was checking her emails. Jennifer went into the bedroom, laid on a bed and thought about Rachel and her father; she started to sob uncontrollably and she buried her head in the pillow to muffle the sound. She felt cold and empty and crept further down under the bed covers, into her private, and safe, little world.

But she didn't sleep. Her mind worked nine to the dozen, how was she going to trap the killer? Guilt ridden thoughts of things she could have done to prevent the deaths of both her father and sister; was

Stevie friend or foe? Was she safe in her bunker while Stevie was with her? She came to the conclusion that she was safe until she transferred her money into the account which now held her father's and sister's money, but she would need Stevie out of here before she did so. There was no way she could relax enough to drift off and on the couple of occasions she did begin to slip into unconsciousness, images of her sister appeared. She heard Littleton leave and Stevie come to bed. She heard Stevie get up in the morning.

Chapter 51

Thursday 17th July 2008

She felt wretched. Stevie had fetched a cup of tea and a bowl of cereal, which was played with rather than eaten. "I need to go for a walk. I need to think."

Stevie looked at her in amazement. "There are about fifty reasons why you can't. Forty eight journalists, a police force… and worst of all, somebody who wants to kill you is lurking around out there somewhere, waiting for you to do something stupid, like going for a walk."

"He won't kill me, not until he's got my money, you know that."

"We don't know that. That's just what we've figured."

"*I* know he won't kill me yet. If he wanted me dead he'd have killed me yesterday." There was silence before Jennifer continued. "Look Stevie. I need to get out of here, just for a while."

"Maybe he'll kidnap you and force you to hand over your money. Going for a walk doesn't make sense. I'll go upstairs and leave you alone. If you need space I'll give you some, just ask."

"You need to be down here, all the time, or he'll kill *you*! You're probably next on his bloody list. And anyway, you've got things to do down here."

Stevie sighed and shook her head. "How will you get out?"

"I'll go out through the back of the gardens, you can get to the village that way."

"Okay, that takes care of the press, what about the police?"

Jennifer shrugged. "The boys can help me. Perhaps they'll keep them occupied at the front of the house somehow."

"And Littleton?"

"Tell him I'm in bed."

* * *

As well as its recreation ground, Belfont-St-Mary has an almost perfect equilateral triangular green situated at the heart of the village. The main through road runs along one side, a house and garden along the second and the river along the third. All sides are around one hundred yards long and three low benches are situated at various points on the riverbank, about twenty five yards between each.

Jennifer sat on the one closest to the angle where the garden and the river met; furthest from the road, and went over her plan. Could she kill him? Given the opportunity… yes. She would need to get rid of everybody from the farmhouse. How? That will require some thought. However, when alone, she would transfer most of her money into her father's account. She figured she would be able to do that because it wasn't really her father's account, therefore it would still be open for business. She also needed to leave some back for Adam… she needed to write a will when she returned to the house, just in case. That'll freak Stevie out, and managed a small chuckle at the thought. What about the four guys? Do they go or do they stay? She hoped they would go, to be safe, but she wouldn't be able to wait forever, and the chances were, they were not on her side anyway.

She would be safe as long as she stayed in the bunker. As soon as the money was transferred she would phone Holly Andrews; the bitch would pass on the news and the bastard would be sure to make his move soon after. She would watch the monitors, sooner or later he would make a mistake and show himself. How does she get to him? It's a pity she couldn't get some explosives and blow the fucker up, even if she ended up blowing herself up as well it would be worth it.

No, as long as she knows where he is, she must be able to take him unawares. She needed to hook up a laptop, or a tablet would be better, to the monitors somehow, that way she will still be able to keep sight of him when she left the bunker. That would work; tablet in one hand and gun in the other. Suddenly she didn't just want to kill him, she wanted to actually see him dead, to be able to stand over him and spit on the bastard.

Again she wondered why the killings had taken place. Maybe it was something to do with the Second World War. Perhaps a great uncle had worked in a concentration camp, stolen inmates' money before gassing them, and now descendants of the victim or victims are getting their revenge. That didn't run true with the knowledge that her ancestors had arrived here in 1934. But she bet it was something like that though.

A few ducks and swans had approached her when she first sat down; they probably expected a few bits to eat. Now they went on with their normal business of hunting for morsels amongst the weeds, the swans stretching their long necks under the water to get the better food, the ducks sticking their bottoms into the air to make up for their short reach. Their rummaging made her remember Birdie, the little caged bird at Ongar, and regretted how she had failed him because of fear. Inaction through fear was something she would never allow to happen again.

Jennifer hadn't noticed the arrival of a small child... she sat on the next bench staring towards her. "Hi," called Jennifer.

The little girl, about four or five years old, said a shy hello.

Jennifer was concerned that the youngster should be alone this close to the river, so she wandered over to her. The little girl had been crying. "Are you alright? Where is your mummy?" Jennifer sat down beside her.

"Over there." She pointed towards a clump of bushes and trees close to the road.

Jennifer couldn't see anybody.

"My mum knows you."

"Really. What's her name?

"Katy."

"Katy what?"

The girl didn't say anything so Jennifer asked what her name was.

"My name is Rebecca Butcher and I live at number three, the Rise, Belfont-St-Mary." She sniffed.

Jennifer smiled, "Well done. Now, why have you been crying?"

"Because Mummy is crying."

Jennifer wasn't sure whether she wanted to know any more.

"Mummy is crying because Daddy got drunk again, and now we haven't got any money to buy food and Mummy has to go and see Granddad Wellington to get some."

"Katy Wellington!" Jennifer's heart missed a beat. She stood, turned and held out her hand for the little one. "Let's go and find Mummy," and they made their way towards the bushes.

Jennifer hadn't seen her old best friend since before Billy Saunders was murdered, but she recognised her immediately. She was standing behind a pushchair which was occupied by a very small infant and holding the hand of a slightly bigger one who was standing beside her... another girl. Mum had an unsure look about her.

"Hello Katy."

"Hello Jennifer." It was almost a whisper.

"Wow, are all these yours?"

Katy nodded sheepishly.

Jennifer felt she should walk over and hug her old friend, that's how two people who had once been close should greet after eight years apart, but the pushchair acted as a barrier. Instead she bypassed it and held Katy's upper arms and stared into her face. "Katy, it really is good to see you. Why don't we walk over there, to a bench by the river, and you can tell me about your life."

There was a pause and then suddenly Katy wrapped her arms around Jennifer. "Oh Jennifer. I didn't know if you would remember me... or would want to talk to me. Yes, come on. I'll tell you about me and you can tell me about you." She was crying.

Jennifer hoped she was being emotional. She definitely didn't want to talk about herself.

Katy told how she left school before completing her education; she hated it, she said. She had to get married, to Greg Butcher, (didn't Jennifer remember him, he was a few years older) on account of her being pregnant with Rebecca. She didn't regret one minute of married life. Rebecca was followed by Samantha and then by Victoria, almost a yearly event. Her dad was against the marriage and so on… Jennifer didn't think it sounded like much of a life, but she kept that thought to herself.

"Tell me about Greg," she asked, "I'm afraid Rebecca mentioned him drinking all the house-keeping money."

Katy sighed. "He's a good guy really, so sweet. He's just a bit weak. He works locally mostly, you know, painting and decorating and gardening… that sort of thing, and sometimes he calls in the pub after work and gets carried away."

"Is he good to you? You know, he doesn't hit you or anything?"

"Oh no, you'll have to meet him. He's lovely."

"So you're going to see your dad, to see if he'll lend you some money?"

"He'll lend me some, he always does. But I'll have to sit through a tirade of 'we told you so' before he hands it over."

Jennifer checked the time; she'd been away from the farmhouse for almost two hours and was wary of the danger Katy and her children could be in, just by knowing her. "Look Katy, I have to go."

"Oh Jennifer, you haven't told me anything about yourself, I've been hogging all the talking... can't you stay a little longer? What's going on at the farmhouse, with all the police?"

"I really have to go... I'll tell you all about it later. It's been good to talk though. You don't know how good, but I must go. We'll swap numbers," they both got out their mobiles, "Call me before coming to see me at the farmhouse, that's very important, but I want to see you again and we can catch up properly."

Katy rounded up her children and was about to leave when Jennifer stopped her. "Katy, take this." She pulled some notes from her pocket, "There's about a hundred pounds."

Katy shook her head.

"It's okay, take it. Pay me back when you can, I really would like you to take it." She held out her hand.

Katy reluctantly accepted the money. "Thanks Jennifer. I appreciate it. I must admit I wasn't looking forward to Dad's ranting. I'll get it back to you as soon as I can."

"Don't worry. There really is no hurry. Look Katy, I must rush. Please come and see me soon." Jennifer left the little clan much happier than when she met them. They waved and waved until she was out of sight. That was nice, she thought.

She managed to return to the farmhouse without incident, much to the relief of Stevie, who was still trawling through paperwork and photographs. Jennifer couldn't settle. She produced a will, leaving everything to Adam, which Stevie and Littleton witnessed, and she called in one of the police IT experts from the operations van to link a tablet with the monitors. After this she tried watching television and reading magazines, anything to take her mind off recent events. It was nice bumping into Katy, but what a way to live. In lots of ways, even with everything that had happened, she was glad she was who she was. In the end she went and lay on the bed. In an instant she fell into a deep sleep.

Chapter 52

Sampson's Farm travellers' camp near Basildon.

Patrick O'Leary had taken on the responsibility of patrolling the travellers' compound every night because he was special. One day he would lead the whole community from disaster; he knew this because his mum had told him so. She told him he was the chosen one. Patrick was eleven.

He was the one person who could wander the site during the early hours and not be confronted with barking and snarling dogs. The animals were entirely familiar with everything about the boy. The distant rumble of the M25 and the night song of the birds were the two constant sounds at this time of the morning. The laughing and swearing from Mike Manner's caravan, where the all night card school took place, was always there as well, but tended to ebb and flow.

Patrick's hearing, as befitting the senses of a chosen one, was acute, and tonight there was an unfamiliar sound which none of the residents of the site were supposed to hear. The sound of vehicle engines and low talking from about half a mile away, probably at the second clearing, drifted up the lane. He'd crept down and seen them arriving, and within about fifteen minutes, four minibuses had spewed out at least fifty coppers, many with huge shields and black helmets. There were also two land rovers, each fitted with a huge floodlight on top of the cab, and three ambulances. To Patrick it was obvious what they were here for. *His* time was here already.

He'd been able to make it back to the site and rouse the entire community before the invaders had begun their move. They all waited silently for their moment to intersect the assailants, legs jiggling, dogs muzzled and weapons ready; nobody was going to evict them from their homes.

The card school had ended prematurely and most of the men had gone to help with the ambush. Just three remained; with an elevated view of the campsite from the porch of Mike's place. From here they could see the whole proceedings and were impressed at how silently the two land rovers moved across the fields and into position, each ending around seventy five yards from the perimeter and, once they were switched on, their powerful lights looked as though they would illuminate the front where the main gate was and the two adjacent sides. Only the back would be left in darkness.

In the light of the moon the three watched the column quietly worm its way up the lane. Containing their excitement wasn't easy. The shock the fucking police were about to get; half of them would probably have heart attacks.

They whispered to one another, "Come on, let's get down there and join in the fun."

"No, not yet, let's see what happens."

"I don't understand this. They don't evict using police, it's bailiffs and council workers what does fucking evictions."

"Well, why else would they be creeping up the lane? Maybe it's a training exercise." They all laughed and had to smother their mouths to avoid being heard. "They're in for one fucking training surprise alright."

The police column reached the main entrance, arriving in two's, and began to peel off right and left until around twenty had made it onto the site. Then all hell broke loose. The travellers, taking full advantage of surprise, and with shear numbers, overran the startled policemen. A shower of rocks and bricks accompanied a mighty roar and policemen were felled by missile and then by wooden club followed by canine attack and the ensuing charge of the travellers, all before the floodlights came on.

The three were nearly wetting themselves with excitement as they watched. They saw the standing coppers retreat to the gate and then the lads swung the barriers across, which were never enough of an obstacle to stop the bastards from coming back in, but, it was a token of victory.

"We should be filming this."

"But why are they here? You know, I think they're after somebody."

"Who?"

"Him!"

In the shadows of the vans, the fences, the vehicles and the rubbish, the stranger was lurking, trying very hard to stay out of sight. He wasn't one of them but the community tolerated him, they were even a little afraid of him. But they didn't socialise with him, or like him. Now it looked as though he had brought them trouble…

Hans had received a phone call, "Get out, quickly," just a minute before the lad had whispered the call to arms from outside his window. He'd thrown on some clothes and left the van, leaving behind what few possessions he had. While keeping out of sight he could not determine his best escape route, until the floodlights came on. Then... it had to be through the back, in the dark.

The commotion had died down considerably and a dialogue between the leaders of the community and the police was taking place. Then the barriers were drawn back and the police began to re-enter the site.

Hans noticed a number of policemen making their way around the perimeter towards his escape route; he needed to hurry if he was to have any chance of getting away. As he slipped past a van he was struck hard in the stomach by a pick axe handle, and went down winded.

"You fucking bastard – you won't bring any more coppers onto our home." And the three set about their victim, viciously kicking the hapless man as he lay on the ground.

Half an hour later the police had quarantined Hans's van and were carrying out a torchlight search of the Sampson's Farm travellers' camp. A shout! Just inside the back perimeter were the bloody bodies of three travellers... not dead... but not in a good shape, either.

Chapter 53

Friday 18th July 2008

Jennifer awoke to the smell of fried food. Stevie was sitting on one of the other beds, eating an enormous breakfast. "You should have some of this," she said.

"What time is it?"

"Almost eight."

Jennifer looked confused.

"Almost eight o'clock in the morning. You've been asleep half of yesterday and all the night."

Jennifer actually felt like she'd been asleep for ever. She pushed back the covers and smelt the warmth of her body. She felt heavy and was still fully clothed.

"Before you ask, I didn't cook it. Mrs Potts is in the kitchen, the boys are going crazy; you would have thought that none of them had eaten for weeks."

Jennifer grunted.

"It's okay, she's making you some. I came in here to wake you up, and I thought the smell would be a nice way to do it. However, you don't have to thank me; it's just the way I am."

"Where's Littleton?"

"He's outside, with the rest of them. By the way," between mouthfuls, "I think he's gay."

"Why, what happened?"

"Nothing. That's the point, we were out there, alone," she pointed over her shoulder with her fork,

"And all he did was work. I tried to be nice but he didn't notice."

"Perhaps he's a professional."

"So am I Jennifer, but all the same…"

Jennifer let it go. She did fancy some breakfast though. She quickly visited the bathroom and was about to go and collect it, but Stevie stopped her.

"Come and look at this." She led Jennifer into the work area. On the monitors they watched dozens of flack-jacketed, police armed response personnel, crawling all over the gardens. Dogs, men and vehicles were everywhere.

"What's going on?" Jennifer asked.

"We don't know yet. Littleton just told everybody to stay inside and then he joined his pals." Over the audio system they could even hear a helicopter. "You stay here and watch, I'll fetch your breakfast."

"Yours is getting cold."

"Don't worry, I love congealed eggs." She returned with the breakfast and two mugs of tea… and with Littleton at her heels. "Look at her, Ray, she looks a right mess."

"At least I can clean up and look good," Jennifer retorted.

"You both look beautiful," said Littleton.

The two girls slyly looked at each other without commenting.

"Have you told Jennifer what we found last night?" he was talking to Stevie.

"Not yet. She's only just woken up… she hasn't even washed yet." She wrinkled her nose.

Jennifer pulled a face. "What did you find?"

Littleton answered. "The Met have been working on this all night, and may by now have found out more, but by midnight last night they had discovered that the teams of investment advisors which your family use, your uncle's family used, and the Huth family used, all have connections. They may even be the same group."

This news halted Jennifer's chewing.

Littleton went on. "The Emmerichs and the Huths came from Germany to the UK in 1934."

"Together?"

"Who knows, but they did arrive in the same year. They're looking into every family who arrived here from Germany during that year, but that's going to be an enormous task, there were thousands. Also, you and the Huths were related, and the Monica Davies image has been matched by face recognition software and she was indeed around the West End last Sunday when Stevie said she saw her."

"Wow. Has she been arrested?" By this time Jennifer had pushed aside her uneaten breakfast and was listening intently. She was impressed at what had been discovered. "I'm beginning to understand why I was convicted, with that bitch pulling the strings, but why?"

"She should have been arrested during the night. In the early hours of this morning a massive international police operation has taken place. Over six hundred police officers raided a number of locations in this country and similar co-ordinated operations have taken place in Spain, Italy and the United States. We'll find out later how successful it's been. The arrests had been planned for a while and were imminent, but after the events of Wednesday, in Chelsea, it was decided to bring them forward."

Jennifer hadn't thought about Chelsea since waking and suddenly felt dejected, and guilty; the sense of excitement aroused by what was happening outside and by what she was hearing fled like a flock of startled birds. "This has all happened because of what they did to us?"

"No. This organisation has been in operation for sixty years or more and information has surfaced recently giving us the opportunity to react. It's a coincidence that this has come about now."

"And do you think you'll get them all?"

"There's no reason to think otherwise. Apparently the information the police have received has been first class."

Stevie asked "Did you know all this yesterday?"

"No. I knew something was going to happen, DCI Wentworth, you met him on Wednesday, told me as much. No, I found out most of this just a while ago."

Stevie again. "So do you think they have arrested *him*?"

Littleton didn't answer immediately but he knew who she meant. "Yeah, I should think so, as far as I know they had information of everybody in the organisation."

"Organisation?" said Jennifer.

"Family. Wentworth said it was a 'crime family'."

"And all the activity outside?" she asked.

"Protection, they said, just in case." Littleton began to look a little uneasy. "I'll go and make some calls. They have an 'operations van' outside," and he instructed Stevie to let him out.

"What do you think about what's going on?" Jennifer asked Stevie after the policeman had left.

"I think you should eat your breakfast and then have a wash."

Jennifer looked a little hurt by the remark, so Stevie walked over to her, bent forward, kissed her on the lips and then sat back down.

Jennifer thought how she could never recall anybody in her family doing that to her, kissing her. She had only met Stevie a couple of days ago but already she felt very close to her. "Stevie… would you adopt me and be my mum?"

"Fuck off you little tart!"

"I'll take that as a 'no' shall I?"

Stevie sat silently for a while, afraid to say the words… and what they implied. But it was time, she thought. "Are you going to transfer the money?"

"Not yet. I need time to think. Why don't you go off with Littleton and make that statement. When you come back we'll talk about it," replied Jennifer.

"Sure?"

About an hour later a very excited Littleton was preparing to leave with Stevie, they were off to London so that she could be interviewed and give a statement. "We have them all, every last bloody one of them. We'll leave a couple of uniforms here, but the rest are standing down." He stood in front of Jennifer and held her arms. "You, young lady, have been very, very brave, but now you can at least carry on without fear of being murdered. Well done! You're safe now." He smiled at her and then lowered his arms. The way Stevie looked at him made him feel slightly stupid and he retreated from the bunker without saying any more.

"When you leave," said Jennifer to Stevie, "Cover yourself so they think it's me leaving. With most of the police leaving as well, perhaps the press will bugger off with you."

Stevie nodded; good idea. She hugged Jennifer, squeezing hard. "Keep safe." She quickly did an about turn and left before she changed her mind. Before closing the door at the top of the stairs she shouted back down, "And, for goodness sake, have a shower."

As she was about to leave through the main door she glimpsed one of the guys in the drawing room. She shouted, "I'll be back later, this evening. You take care of her, do you promise?"

"I promise," he shouted back. He stood in the shadow and watched the police car leave, absent-mindedly scratching his neck with his left hand as he did so.

Chapter 54

Jennifer checked the door to the bunker, making sure it was locked and secure. Then she surveyed the grounds, scrutinising the monitors and all the sensors; everything was in order. There were three monitors, two computers and her tablet. That meant six screens to watch.

There were almost forty cameras placed around the grounds and the images scrolled automatically, each scanning for about twenty seconds at a time, it could be set faster or slower or Jennifer could control them manually. If a sensor; audio, pressure or laser, was activated, one of the three main monitors would automatically home in and scan that area. She left the system turned to automatic and it lazily went through the motions.

It felt good, being both alone and secure. She relaxed and thought about the events of the past few days: Her dad, Rachel and Jack; the acquittal; the arrival of Stevie, and the traitor, Holly. She tried to remember Billy and missed Adam. Again she wondered who these people were, these people who had taken away her youth, her family and her friends. Perhaps she would find out now these arrests had taken place.

She watched the monitors as the press began to drift away... and within an hour they'd all gone. There was no sign of the four guys. Two armed policemen remained to patrol the property and grounds.

She then opened up her bank account and transferred three million pounds into her father's current account.

Next, she phoned Holly Andrews and told her what she had done, and that over the weekend she was going to set a trap for the bastard. "If you don't hear from me by Sunday morning, call the police."

She waited. The hand gun was in her right hand, ready. That's how it was going to be from now on, or at least until he was dead. Everything was eerily quiet; suddenly she sensed something, *a twig snap*. This time she wouldn't ignore the feeling and switched herself to high alert. Still nothing happened. She turned one of the monitors to manual to look for the policemen. One of the other monitors homed on to an area when an audio sensor was activated and a silent alarm flashed on the panel. She scanned the area but saw nothing. Then it happened again in another area, then again. Still she saw nothing. The monitors were scrolling every few seconds, alerted by... nothing. She switched all of them to manual and checked every area in the gardens. She checked the garages, and the entrance hall of the house. She turned away from the screens in horror. The two policemen lay in enormous pools of their own blood. Their throats had been cut.

Jennifer's heart was thumping and she tried to calm herself down, telling herself that she was still safe. She forced herself to look at the policemen, her stomach churned... but she had to be strong. The front door was ajar. She left a camera on the hall, and also left one scanning the landing.

She set up the two computer screens so that she could see as much of the house as possible from the outside, and then manually operated the last monitor; switching from area to area. Then her heart sunk. Walking up the driveway was Katy Wellington, pushchair in front of her and two children by her side. Fuck!

Jennifer scrambled for her mobile… there was no signal. That wasn't right, how did he do that? She tried the land line; dead. Bastard. A quick check told her that the internet was also down. What could she do? She switched the other two monitors back to automatic… they scrolled normally.

He was no longer on the move; she bet he was watching the woman approach with her children. By this time they were halfway up the drive. The one thing she couldn't do was allow them to reach the house, even if they weren't in danger, the sight of the two dead policemen was… well, it just mustn't happen.

Ignoring her fear, she grabbed the gun and ran up the stairs, unlocked and unbolted the bunker door. She hesitated at the sight of the two policemen… be strong… and managed to vault the dead men without slipping in the blood. She made it outside just in time to intercept the three. "Katy, you can't be here. Please go away." She was waving the pistol around without realising the reaction it would have.

Katy retreated slightly. "I've come with your money."

"I don't want the money. Keep it. Now you need to go."

The woman just stood, confused and holding a small wad of notes in a stretched out hand. "I, I... I don't understand."

"Go!" and when she still didn't move Jennifer snatched the money from her hand, again ordering Katy to go, twice. The woman backed away until eventually she turned and stormed angrily down the driveway; she did not like being treated this way. Jennifer was frantic. She ran back into the house, vaulted the first dead policeman and slipped in the blood, slid across the floor and crashed into the second body. She shuddered as her hand brushed the man's face, but managed to contain a scream. As fast as she could, she picked herself up and tumbled through the bunker door. She locked and bolted it. Amazingly, all the time the loaded gun was in her hand and ready to fire.

She got back to the monitors in time to see Katy turn and stare at the house. The woman put a foot forward. No! Jennifer couldn't believe what she was seeing. Then she must have had second thoughts... she turned again and walked away.

Jennifer's clothes, hair and hands were covered in sticky blood and she retched violently. She realised she was crying. She sat rigid for about five minutes with the gun cocked and held in front of her face. Then she rose slowly, laid the gun down on the desk, removed all of her clothing and made her way to the shower.

* * *

Robert and Tina were surprised as they drove past the farmhouse; they had expected a plethora of press and the police swarming all over the grounds... but there was nobody. The place looked deserted.

They had worked out where Jennifer lived and had hired a car to make the journey. First thing... the plan was to save her from Peter. Doing that must be to their credit with regards as to how the police would consider them.

They had run through a number of scenarios about the memory stick. One; maybe it hadn't been discovered on the copper's body... but that, they both considered, was wishful thinking. Two; assuming it had been found, there was nothing on the stick to prove they had anything to do with the production of it... except their fingerprints... and also the police would probably be able to tell which computer the information had been downloaded from.

The fingerprints wouldn't necessarily prove that they had produced it, though; Ben could easily have stolen a blank stick from Robert's desk, with setting them up in mind. The computer, they decided, could be dumped.

Thinking *really* positively; maybe Ben had gone into hiding. That would give them the opportunity of convincing Amy that they had nothing to do with passing family information to the police. Even if Ben was around, it was his word against theirs, but it would be much easier if he wasn't there.

If it was just to keep in with the family, they could just kill Jennifer. But, no, neither of them could ever carry out anything like that. And importantly, that wouldn't help their situation where the police were concerned. So, they decided to try to save her from the deadly clutches of Peter and take her to Amy... and *she* could decide the girl's fate. At least that would placate the family.

They drove past again, before deciding... to hell with it... and pulled up at the front door. They had to watch out... Peter could already be here.

Jennifer scrubbed every part of herself in order to remove the sticky blood and its lingering stench. The soap had long since rinsed away and she tried to relax as jets of hot water, as hot as she could bear them, caressed and kneaded every inch of her. Dense steam filled the whole room and she didn't want to leave the cubicle. Nevertheless, she couldn't stay in here forever. She reluctantly turned the tap. The flow of water died. The shower cubical was enormous; it took up the whole of the back part of the room. With her back to the wall she took two steps to her left, picked up a large fluffy white towel from a small pile on one of the shelves and dabbed her face and hair. Using her right hand she reached across herself, and slid the shower door open...

He sat on the toilet seat, facing her, caressing the loose cord he held in his hands. He wore an evil, sadistic smile in anticipation of the fun he was about to have. The towel was the only thing hiding her modesty. "Drop the towel," he commanded. However, her modesty was not the only thing behind it. As the towel slid from her hand the smile was wiped from his face.
He didn't die instantly. He heard the blast as she simultaneously released both barrels. But that was about it.

Chapter 55

The children were drawn towards the sounds; they didn't go consciously, or think about resisting. The yells and the screams, and bizarrely, the laughter, acted like a human magnet.

That was almost ninety years ago and Amy was trying to remember the incident. The events occurred and reoccurred with vivid clarity in her nightmares, even now. But she was finding it difficult to recall everything clearly in the light of the day.

She always remembered the fear and recollected the two things she had wanted at the time. The first one; she had wanted them to stop their killing. She had prayed for them to stop… but they did not. And then she wanted to kill them… and that desire had dictated the rest of her long life.

The old woman sat at her antique oak desk; pen in hand, waiting for the right moment to continue writing. The furniture she occupied was solid and expensive and completely belonged amongst the sumptuous dark woods and deep reds of her library. The only thing which looked out of place was the old lady herself; her small and frail figure made the room and everything around her seem enormous.

She had forgotten exactly *why* she waited to write. Why, suddenly, had the need for any such timing become so important? Even at her age she felt sure this was something new, or maybe it wasn't new, perhaps it was because she *was* this age. She just remembered that she should wait for... She was suddenly struck by a peculiar thought; she imagined herself as a boy who rode the waltzer at the fairground; leaping, cat-like around the revolving platform, dexterously spinning the cup-like carriages, waiting for the moments, making the punters laugh and scream. She laughed to herself at the ridiculous thought. She had recently celebrated reaching the magnificent age of one hundred and two years old and could hardly write, let alone... But she could not shake off that image, seeing herself jumping and spinning and balancing. Imagine it! And just as quickly as she had laughed, tears welled in her eyes at the thought of how unlike that boy she really was. Old... and waiting to die. Whatever people said, when it came down to it, a long and full life was no compensation; she did not want to die.

She looked at her pen, her hand trembled. Sometimes it trembled so violently it would have actually been easier for her to ride that waltzer than lay words down on paper. Then, finally, she remembered why she waited; she'd been waiting for her hand to stop trembling. Each time it got this bad she had to take a deep breath, concentrate and compose herself, as well as she could anyway, and then force herself to keep going... but these days even concentration was becoming difficult. Nevertheless, she was still a very determined woman.

Now. Where did I get to...?

...The disagreements about the political funding reached a head in the autumn of 1920. All those years ago we lived very close to the centre of the city, on Friedenstrasse, and opposite the Volkspark Friedrichshain, which is the oldest park in Berlin. According to father our house was even older than the park, which was built to commemorate the one hundredth anniversary of Frederick the Great becoming king. I, along with my brothers; twin Frederick and little Thomas, spent lots of time playing there.

My parents had owned two houses, the other one was in Munich, but this was definitely the children's favourite, partly because of the park but mostly because of the basement, its cellars and the secret maze of tunnels, passages and stairways. Although mother had forbidden us to enter these we spent as much of our time as possible surreptitiously exploring the hidden rooms.

I remember there were three doors leading to the basement from inside the house, which were all kept locked, and one situated in an outbuilding, which was also kept locked… but we had a key. Cousin Manfred had found the door a while before with the key still in the lock, and we immediately hid it. Manfred was fifteen, two years older than me and Fredrick. Even then, all those years ago, he was very bossy. However, neither Manfred nor Frederick was with me in the cellar that day, just little Thomas. Although he was eleven, and small, he always acted very grown up, which meant I usually didn't mind him tagging along.

We knew our way around the dusty passages and rooms so well by this time we seldom had to use the bicycle lanterns. We were always keen to save battery life, just in case. The first place we generally made for was the scullery. Well, not actually the scullery but a room beside it. A two inch thick wooden wall separated the working room from the hidden room and had a long and narrow horizontal gap in it, where two boards should have, but didn't quite, butt together. It was through this gap that we watched the naughty antics of the staff, a few times very naughty.

The first time I saw them I would have told mother about it but that meant she would have known about our access to the secret area. The floor could not be seen through the gap and, if standing, neither could an adult's head. When two of them were together they sometimes ended up on the floor and we could only hear them. But when they chose to do it on the table or on the bench, or with one of them on a chair, we could see everything. When I went there with Manfred it gave him ideas and I had to do things with him.

That day though, it was just me and Thomas. As we were creeping towards the room we heard a commotion; shouting and arguing. By the time we reached the scullery there was a lot of scuffling from the other side of the wooden wall and I reached the gap just in time to see father and mother being set upon by others. To my horror a man squeezed his arm around father's neck, in a kind of head-lock. He couldn't breathe. He turned a bluish colour. The man held my father this way and squeezed tight for a long time, until he was dead, I think, and then threw him to the ground. Thomas also witnessed the whole thing and began to cry. I was so scared that we would be heard so I comforted him and buried his head in my woollen top. To my horror Mother was next. The horrible man did the same to her. I will never forget her eyes. That look;

as life left her. The sounds of men shouting and laughing filled the room... I am not certain that I did not cry out, I think I may have. But I was not heard...

Amy's head hurt and she wished she could dictate the work for her secretary. However, these words were not for outsiders... But the work was important; the girl had to understand who she really was, to embrace it; not fight it... And Amy knew that she was probably not long for this world. So the written word had become a necessity... except she had to rest; she laid down her pen and closed her eyes...

The old lady's purring and snorting puzzled Jennifer as she lay on the couch. She had roused from *her* sleep with a fuzziness of the mind. That was a little while ago, but she had not opened her eyes; she wanted to be fully alert before anybody knew that she'd woken. It was a trick learnt and mastered in detention.

She was trying to visualise her surroundings using every sense other than sight. Wherever she was smelt clean and fresh and was pleasantly warm. The snoring person didn't sound like somebody who was guarding her, she laid odds on it being a woman, an old woman; certainly not a heavily built male. She felt she was in a large room with lots of furnishing, the sounds of the outside world, birds, crunching footsteps, even those of aircraft flying overhead seemed to be sucked in through large windows and then instantly overpowered and muffled by deep pile carpets, cushions.

How did she get here? Wherever here was! She remembered the woman, standing over the two dead policemen in the entrance hall of the farmhouse, screaming that Jennifer was safe, that she would not be harmed. Jennifer remembered readying the spent shotgun, gripping it by the short barrel, ready to attack, to defend… And then, now.

Was that woman the snorer? Jennifer didn't think so. She thought about the events of the last few days, building up to the present, just to confirm to herself that she was mentally ready to open her eyes. Finally her mind scrolled down an imaginary check list, ticking little boxes representing sections of her body; without moving, all seemed in good order.

Her body stayed completely motionless as she raised the lids of her eyes and almost instantly heard a door open. The snorer snorted and then stirred. Jennifer then heard a man whispering but couldn't make out the words. A very old voice told him to go… the event ended with the door closing, followed by silence. Jennifer turned her head. An old lady sat upright looking at her.

Jennifer twisted, sat, and then stood, wrapping a duvet, her only covering, tightly around her body. She didn't say anything, just waited for the old lady to speak.

When Amy did speak, she said, "I don't know what to say."

Jennifer continued to stand silently and wait.

"I suppose I could introduce myself. Amy." She stood, waddled forward and held out a hand. "I am Amy."

Jennifer made her wait a moment before taking it.

"Come." Amy guided the girl towards two comfortable looking chairs and they both sat, Amy first. A low table serviced the two chairs, and on it was a large, leather bound book; an album. As Jennifer sat, a woman entered the room with a tray with tea and a jug of cold water, which she placed on the table, and poured two cups of Earl Grey. Suddenly Jennifer needed to drink and eagerly accepted a glass of the water.

The woman left and, still without speaking, the two shared the pot of tea. Then Amy said, "Look at this album," and slid the book across the low table until it was directly in front of Jennifer, and opened it. It was an old photo album. "Look at the photographs while I tell you about them." On the first page were old sepia photographs of groups of people. The first one was of a couple with three young children, two boys and a girl.

Jennifer rubbed her fingers gently across the figures.

"This album is the only thing I managed to save after my parents were murdered."

Jennifer studied the pictures and looked at the old lady.

"I have written some of the history down, and hopefully I'll write a lot more before it's time for me to go. But while we look through this book I'll briefly tell you my story. In the second half of the nineteenth century, in Germany, my grandfather built a large and successful business. He had four children with his first wife and two with his second. My mother was the first born of the second wife. In 1920, the four siblings of the first wife conspired to murder my mother and her brother, along with their spouses and all their children."

Jennifer stopped looking at the photos and studied the old woman as she continued.

"Altogether there were five children. The assassins were sloppy. They killed all four adults but only two of those children, and then lied to their paymasters, saying that we were all dead. I watched through a hole in the wall as my father and mother and twin brother were murdered. I swore then that I would kill the men that murdered my parents and my brother. I swore to kill my uncles, their spouses and every last one who descended from them."

She was silent for a while. Still Jennifer did not say anything.

"I wanted revenge. I have spent my whole life tracking down the descendants of those evil men, I have taken everything they owned... and then killed them. Every single one has died by my hands or by the hands of my family."

Except for one!

"All the time it was revenge that compelled me, but there was also something else. I never knew, until now, what that something else was, except that it was the real driving force behind everything I have done. Now I know."

On most of the photographs was a woman. Jennifer could not take her eyes off her. The woman was Amy's mother, but it could have been Jennifer. It was like looking at photographs of herself dressed in historical costume. Photographs of her longingly looking into the eyes of her handsome husband. Photographs of her holding babies, standing by groups of children... and portraits. Jennifer could hardly believe what she was looking at. What she was seeing.

Amy, who was clearly nervous, but glowing with happiness, continued. "Now I know... all the things I have done, I have done for you. And now you have returned to inherit all that rightfully belongs to you." Amy took her mother's hand and wept.

Made in the USA
Charleston, SC
24 November 2015